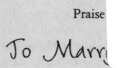

Praise

To Marry

"Ms. Hendrix has produced a mischievous and delightfully warm tale brimming with the charm of Ireland. The age-old never-ending romantic duel between the sexes has never been more fun." —*Romantic Times*

"*To Marry an Irish Rogue* will leave you in stitches. The plot is delightful. The characters make you feel like a member of the Midnight Court. This one you'll read again and again!" —*Rendezvous*

"A delightful and touching story of a contemporary Irish village filled with people I'd like to know." —*The Romance Reader*

"Lisa Hendrix displays her talent with [this] amusing and delicious romantic romp." —Harriet Klausner

continued on next page . . .

Runaway Bay

Lisa Hendrix

JOVE BOOKS, NEW YORK

This is a work of fiction. Names, characters, places, and incidents either are the product of the author's imagination or are used fictitiously, and any resemblance to actual persons, living or dead, business establishments, events, or locales is entirely coincidental.

RUNAWAY BAY

A Jove Book / published by arrangement with
the author

PRINTING HISTORY
Jove edition / March 2002

Visit our website at
www.penguinputnam.com

ISBN: 0-515-13264-0

A JOVE BOOK®
Jove Books are published by The Berkley Publishing Group,
a division of Penguin Putnam Inc.,
375 Hudson Street, New York, New York 10014.
JOVE and the "J" design
are trademarks belonging to Penguin Putnam Inc.

PRINTED IN THE UNITED STATES OF AMERICA

10 9 8 7 6 5 4 3 2 1

To good friends

Sheila
Angie
Tacy
Robin

And to my husband and children,
who put up with a lot

I am blessed.

acknowledgments

Many people contributed to the completion of this novel. I would particularly like to thank the following:

My literary agent, Helen Breitwieser, for her encouragement and business savvy.

My editor, Gail Fortune, for her patience and deft hand with a red pencil.

Leslie Gelbman, president, publisher, and editor in chief of Berkley Books and president of mass market paperbacks for Penguin Putnam Inc., and all those other wonderful people at PPI who shepherd my books from contract to store shelf.

Sheila Rabe, for her prodding, poking, nagging, and all-around friendship, as well as for her creative brainstorming on those days when ideas simply escape me.

Robin Breakey, Angie Butterworth, and Tacy Cleary for loaning me that most precious of commodities—a quiet room in which to write.

Captain Clyde McGowan of Captain Clyde's Charters,

Arnold, Maryland, for answering my questions on deep-sea fishing.

Robert McKee, Christopher Vogler, John Morgan, and all the other wonderful writing teachers who have enlightened and inspired me; and the faculty of the Department of Biology and Wildlife at the University of Alaska, Fairbanks, who did likewise.

And finally, my husband and children for their constant reminder of what's really important in life.

You've all made me better at what I do. Thank you.

one

He was huge, and he was trying to hide himself by crouching down beside the vanity in the bathroom. It didn't work. Jackie spotted him the instant she flipped the light switch on. A squeak escaped her, like the sound she made when she was ten and her brother popped out from behind a wall. But this wasn't her brother. This was an intruder. An ugly, menacing home invader who stared at her with dark, unblinking eyes. Her heart battered against her rib cage as she stared back at him.

"Go away," she said.

He didn't move.

"Go on. Just leave peacefully, and I won't do anything."

Still nothing. Just that flat, beady-eyed stare.

She reached down to remove her shoe, never once taking her eyes off her visitor. Gripping the shoe by the toe, she raised it heel first as a makeshift weapon.

"All right," she said, "last chance. If you don't get out

right now, I'll have to hurt you. I need to pee, and I'm not doing it with you in the room."

He wasn't going anywhere. He knew. They all knew. She was more afraid of them than they were of her.

She edged forward to within striking distance, then lifted the shoe high and took aim. He lunged forward.

She shrieked and skittered backward, bashing one shoulder against the door frame in her haste to get out.

Damn. Her record held. She'd never successfully smooshed a spider in her life.

Still carrying her shoe, she hustled down the hall to the telephone to dial for the cavalry. The dial tone beeped as she picked up, telling her she had voice mail. It'd have to wait. She punched in a number.

A moment later, the reassuring voice of the apartment manager answered. "Nordic Arms."

"Hi, Steve. It's Jackie Barnett. I have a little problem."

"Hey, Dr. B. Oh, man, I hope you're not going to tell me you've got a broken pipe, too. I tell you, this weather . . ."

"No. It's easier than that. There's this huge, hairy spider in the bathroom. Would you mind?"

He laughed. "Give me a couple minutes."

"Could you make it fast? I was stuck in traffic for almost two hours, and I'm, uh, getting a little desperate."

"Say no more. I'll be right there."

"Bless you."

She had the front door open when Steve bounded off the elevator, carrying a piece of yellow lined paper. She waved him past without a word. A moment later, the toilet flushed.

"Goodbye, cruel world," he said as he came out, saluting with the same piece of paper, which he'd undoubtedly used to scoop up the spider.

She shuddered at the thought of holding a live spider with just a piece of paper between her and it. "Brave man. Thank you so much."

"Not a problem. Some people do spiders, some people don't."

"I'm definitely a don't. Bugs of any kind give me the willies, but spiders . . ." She shuddered again.

"Well, call me any time you need me to flatten one. Say, you want me to collect your mail for you while you're gone?"

"Mrs. Cleary's taking care of it and the plants, thanks."

"Great. Great." He sighed. "Two whole weeks in St. Sebastian. Wow. You think I'd fit in your suitcase?"

"Not unless I buy a new one," said Jackie. She was about to bust a gusset. She maneuvered him toward the door. "I barely have room for my insect repellant."

"Leave it home. I'll stand around and shoo bugs, just for a chance to stay off the roads for a while." He shook his head. "Cripes, it's December. You'd think people would've remembered how to drive on ice by now."

"You'd think, but there sure wasn't any evidence of it tonight. Look, I'll bring you back a bottle of rum, but right now, I've really got to excuse myself."

"Oh, jeez, I'm sorry. Here I am standing around bending your ear and you need the john." He backed out the door. "If I don't see you before you go, have a good trip."

"Thanks. And thanks again for rescuing me. 'Bye."

"See you in a co—"

She shut the door in his face and dashed for the bathroom, unbuttoning as she went. Before she sat, she made a final survey of the toilet, just to be sure that her visitor hadn't survived the flush and crawled out with revenge on his mind.

A few minutes later, feeling much happier, she returned to the living room to grab her DayTimer out of her purse, stopping as she passed the stereo to put a Harry Belafonte CD in the player. It made her feel like she was already on the beach, and she did a salsa step across the floor. The DayTimer contained her master list of things she still had to do before Sunday morning, and she scanned it while she carried the bag with her new swimsuit cover-up into the spare room. She folded it and placed it in the smaller of the two bags that lay open on the bed, right on top of the perfect royal blue swimsuit it had taken her two months to find.

A check mark beside "cover-up" on the packing list she had taped to the mirror, and that was it. Except for the last-minute cosmetics, she was packed, with thirty-six hours to spare. No last-minute rushing around for her, and no forgetting anything, either, thanks to thorough lists. Those suitcases contained everything she could possibly need for two weeks in a strange country, from flip-flops to Kaopectate. She cross-checked the two lists, stuck the pen behind her ear, and moved on to other things.

A quick pass through the kitchen to put on the last of the leftover tortellini soup to warm up, and she was finally ready to deal with her phone messages.

There were four of them. Her mother's voice greeted her first.

"Hello, Pumpkin. I heard about your weather up there, and I just thought I'd check on you. Guess you're stuck in traffic. Make sure you give us a call before you leave."

Mom and Dad were on the list already. She hit "Play" again.

"Umm. Hi. It's Ben. I'll call back later."

Jackie smiled and retrieved the next message.

"Me again. I guess you're stuck in traffic. Call me when you get home. We need to talk."

He was so sweet. One more.

"Oh. You're still not there." Ben hesitated. "Aw, hell. I don't want to do this on voice mail, but it's almost seven and I'm headed out the door, and you really need to know this. I, uh, I'm going to cancel out on the trip, Jackie. I don't think we should go to St. Sebastian together. The truth is, I don't think we should see each other at all anymore. I've been trying to convince myself that we'll be okay, but we won't be. What it comes down to is, you're just not my type. You're way too . . . I mean . . ."

Jackie wanted to stop it but couldn't manage to lift her

hand, and all the while, Ben's voice rolled on like a boulder down a hill, heading straight toward her heart.

"Oh, to heck with it. Look, I need a little more excitement in my life, and frankly, I'm not getting it from you. You're a nice person, and all, but . . . well, you're kind of a stick-in-the-mud. Everything's so taped down with you. You never take any chances at all. You won't even try a new route home, for God's sake. And those damned lists. . . . I just can't live by lists like that. With this vacation coming, well, I thought I could do it, but I really don't want to spend the next two weeks wrapped in cotton gauze and protected from the real world at that resort you picked. It's just not my style. If I go to St. Sebastian, I want to see St. Sebastian, not a sterilized calypso show and the inside of a tour bus. I'm sorry. I should have had the guts to say something sooner. I hope I haven't screwed things up so you can't get your money back. 'Bye. I, uh . . . I'll see you around."

"Ben?" His name came out a hoarse whisper past the large, hard lump growing in her throat. *Not see each other?*

A neutral female voice came on. "That was your last unplayed message. Please press K to keep your messages or E to erase."

She found her hands again and hit K because it seemed like the right thing to do, and then she punched the speed dial for Ben—number 3, just behind Mom and the lab. *Not go to St. Sebastian?*

His phone rang until the recorded voice came on and told her he wasn't going to answer. She hit Redial twice before she gave up and put the receiver down. He'd been headed out the door, he'd said, but he must have left his answering machine off, probably to avoid her call. It was over, just like that. *I'll see you around?*

The lump sat there, choking her but not dissolving into the sob she expected. She should be crying, she thought numbly. She'd been dumped. Where were the tears? Ben

and she didn't have a grand passion or anything, but
surely eight months deserved some tears.

But then, she'd have thought that eight months deserved better than a voice mail blow-off and facile excuses
like "you're not my type."

"It's not fair," she said to her empty apartment. She sat
there, staring at her DayTimer and its incriminating lists
until the smell of garlic and chicken stock reminded her
of her dinner, boiling away on the stove. Operating on
automatic pilot, she went into the kitchen, turned off the
stove, then got out a bowl. She stared at it.

Screw tortellini soup. What she needed was chocolate.
She dumped the soup down the disposal, then raided the
freezer for that carton of triple fudge ice cream Ben had
inflicted on her last weekend even though he knew she
was trying to lose a couple more pounds before the trip.

The first bite hit her like a drug rush. She took a deep
breath and sighed. She didn't need to worry about those
extra pounds anymore. It didn't matter what the new
swimsuit looked like.

In the living room, Harry Belafonte began to sing "Jamaica Farewell."

More like farewell, St. Sebastian. She walked in, found
the stereo remote, and zapped good old Harry into silence.
Stupid song, anyway.

And then she sat down on the couch and finished the
best part of a half-gallon of ice cream.

*There were reasons your mother told you not to eat
when you were depressed*, Jackie realized the next
morning. Several, in fact, ranging from bloating and zits
to the fact that too much ice cream could leave you as
hung over as half a bottle of wine. Plus it didn't change
anything—Jackie confirmed that shortly after scraping the
fuzz off her teeth. Voice mail didn't lie. Ben really had
blown her off. She hit the E with a vengeance, erasing

him from her life the same way he'd erased her from his—electronically.

However, unlike last night, when the shock had left her numb, this morning she was just plain ticked.

Not his type? In whose universe did it take eight months to figure out someone wasn't your type?

And that bit about her being a stick-in-the-mud? That just wasn't true. She tried new things. She took risks. She ate grapes in the grocery store without washing them and went cross-country skiing in Canada every year. She'd moved clear to Tucson for graduate school, and then to Minneapolis for a job. She was the one who'd wanted to go to St. Sebastian, and—talk about taking risks—she'd paid for the darned trip on *her* credit card, hadn't she?

She got herself more worked up while she was in the shower.

So what if she made lists? At least she didn't run around forgetting things the way he did. Her life was tidy and organized, not boring.

Face it, it was all excuses. He'd used her. She'd been a convenient stopover on the erratic path of Ben Johannsen's love life, and now he'd probably met some bimbo who was willing to buy his hokey claim that having sex while wearing a condom was like taking a shower with a raincoat on. She should just be grateful that he'd moved on right before the trip instead of right after.

Hoped she got her money back, humph. She noticed he hadn't offered to pay back his share if she didn't.

After quickly toweling off, she slipped on a robe and got on the phone to ask her travel agent about a refund.

"Well, you bought the Trip Protection Option on the resort, so you can get all your money back there," said the agent. "But I'm afraid you're stuck on the airline tickets. You can change the dates, but you can't get a refund."

"But that's over nine hundred dollars!"

"Unless you can prove some medical reason you can't go."

"How about an injury? I can probably arrange something for my boyfriend."

Her agent chuckled. "It's hard to file the paperwork from jail. Do you mind a couple of alternative suggestions?"

"Fire away."

"You could go by yourself. You've already blown the wad, so just say to hell with boyfriends and wallow in the decadence. Fair Winds will take really good care of you."

The thought of spending two weeks alone in a strange country made Jackie noticeably queasy. What if something happened? "I don't think so. What else?"

"You could get a girlfriend to go with you. She'll pay for his half, you'll both have a ball, and it'll be good therapy to get far, far away from what's-his-name—"

"Ben."

"I know, I just didn't want to say it aloud. Anyway, you can get away and have some fun so you don't mope. Who knows, maybe you'll meet some hunky beach boy and have a great fling. You know, get your groove back."

"I don't want a fling," Jackie said sourly. She picked up a hairbrush and started raking at her wet hair. "And my name's not Stella."

"Then just get a good tan and go on a fourteen-day bender. That's the advantage of a super-inclusive resort— the drinks are free."

"No, they're not," countered Jackie. "They're just already paid for. With my so-called deposit."

"So you might as well drink them, right?"

"Mmm," said Jackie, not committing her liver either way.

"So. What do you say?"

"I don't know. I'm not sure any of my friends could even go."

"Okay, look, I have another client waiting, so I'll let you think about it. Call me before noon and let me know what you decide. Otherwise, I'll just cancel you out and get back what I can for you."

"Before noon," repeated Jackie. "Okay. Thanks, Billie."

She got dressed as she pondered the idea of recruiting a friend. It was worth a shot. She made herself a cup of instant cappuccino, then found her address book and flipped through the pages, looking for the most likely names.

Karen. Now she'd be fun. She reached for the phone.

It rang as she touched it, and she started, splashing coffee all over the H page in her address book. Blue-black ink spread like streamers through the milky brown wash.

"Shoot. Hang on," she said to the unknown caller. A couple of paper towels and a moment's blotting, and the names were at least legible, if no longer perfect. She grabbed the phone. "Sorry about that."

"A little excited about the trip, are we?"

"Not especially. Hi, Walt."

"You don't sound very cheerful for someone who's going on the vacation of a lifetime."

"It's a Caribbean holiday, not the Grand Tour of Europe."

"Ah, perhaps, but it just might be your dream come true." For the head of a major university research program, Walt Armstrong leaned toward the dramatic.

"Can I help you with something?" she said.

"No, but I can help you. I just found out that Farley Phelps is going to be in St. Sebastian for the next couple of weeks."

"Phelps. As in the Phelps Foundation for New Directions in Medicine?"

"None other. And it's even better. He's staying at the same resort you are."

"At Fair Winds?" Jackie groaned. She was a finalist for this year's Phelps Grant, one of the juiciest plums on the funding tree. A chance to meet Phelps, himself. . . . *Damn it, Ben. Your timing stinks.*

"You don't sound very happy to hear this. What's wrong?"

"Oh, nothing. It's just that Ben . . . had to back out."

"Son of a bitch." Walt always had been quick on the uptake. "I'm sorry, Jacqueline."

"It's probably better anyway. It would look bad if I turned up down there, as though I were trying to exert undue influence on Phelps."

"You sound like you're not going."

"I'm not."

"But you have to." Walt's voice went up a third. "You can't miss out on a chance like this."

"You mean the chance to suck up?" asked Jackie.

"Make contact. Network. Schmooze."

"Whatever you call it, it's going to look like I'm stalking him."

"You've had reservations down there for months."

"Mr. Phelps won't know that. All he'll know is, there he is in St. Sebastian for a long, wild party—"

"Or a nice, restful vacation."

"Yeah, right." She'd read the stories. Farley Phelps was an old hippie made good. Made outstanding, actually. But the money hadn't really changed his habits, just moved them upscale a notch. "Anyway, there he is, and lo and behold, one of the finalists turns up. By herself. And she's clearly looking for him. It's not a good professional image, Walt, at least not for the profession *I'm* in."

"For God's sake, I'm not saying you should sleep with the man."

"Of course you aren't. But I bet he has gold diggers after him all the time. I'll just look like one of the crowd."

"Then convince him otherwise. Impress him with your brain. You've got an outstanding one, you know."

"Thank you." She smiled slightly, the first smile since she'd checked her voice mail the night before. "But I'm really not the party type."

"Then catch him sitting by the pool the morning after. Come on, Jackie. The Fates mean for you to have this chance, or Phelps wouldn't have booked into the same resort."

"Speaking of which, people with his kind of money

usually rent private islands. Why is he staying with the common folk at Fair Winds?"

"I don't know. Maybe he likes having no bar tab. But never mind about why. I can't believe you'd pass up a chance like this. What's really going on here?"

"Nothing."

"Jacks?"

"I just don't want to go by myself, okay? It wouldn't be any fun."

"Scared, are we?"

"No. I just don't like the idea of being the object of pity in the hotel dining room."

"Order room service," said Walt.

"You're so understanding."

"I understand this much. Uncomfortable or not, you need to get down there."

"No, I don't."

"Yes, you do. You don't re—"

"Walt!" She cut him off. "Look, I know you have my best interests at heart, really. But I think I'll just rely on good science and my record to—"

"Hunter's going to be there."

Jackie stopped dead. "What?"

"That got your attention didn't it?" Walt chuckled. "Hunter is going to be at Fair Winds."

"*Reade* Hunter?" In a heartbeat, she was steaming like an old locomotive. "The same Reade Hunter who practically stole the Beauregard Young Scientist Award out from under me? The same Reade Hunter who tore apart my article when it came up for review? The same Reade Hunter who told the head of Northwestern's research department that I . . . never mind."

"Oh, come on. I haven't heard that one."

"I said, never mind," she snapped. "Where did you hear this?"

"I was on the phone with Craig Wilson in Pittsburgh last night, and Hunter came up."

"You'd better not tell me you're trying to recruit him."

"I'd love to, but I'd rather hang on to you. You're a lot less likely to get us sued. I was trying to find out what he's working on. Wilson mentioned Hunter was going to take some leave time to—get this—take his mother to St. Sebastian."

"His mother," Jackie sneered. "How sweet. I didn't think invertebrates had relationships with their mothers."

"He's probably packing right now."

"He wouldn't happen to be taking this so-called mother to Fair Winds, would he?"

"You know, I wondered the same thing," said Walt. "So I took the liberty of calling and, er, confirming his reservations for him. He's arriving tomorrow and staying for two weeks."

"The same time Farley Phelps is supposed to be there. How convenient."

"Isn't it. So are you going?"

"You bet I am," she said, without even weighing the relative risks. "That hotdogging weasel has worked me over once too often. It's my turn now."

"Atta girl."

"Have the champagne waiting when I get home. The Phelps grant *will* be mine."

two

"I'm sorry, miss. I had the men check again. Your bags were not on the plane."

This can't be happening.

"I checked them all the way through," Jackie said with a calm she didn't feel. She leaned over the counter, tapping a finger on the baggage claim stubs she had handed over a few minutes earlier. "See, right there."

"I know." He raised his palms and shrugged in the universal gesture of helplessness. "Sometimes they just don't make it, though. They get put on a wrong track and go whooshin' off on their own."

"Whooshing?"

"That would be an airline term," he said, flashing yet another charming smile in her direction. Between that smile and the soft Sebastiani lilt to his voice, Jackie was almost ready to forgive and forget. Almost.

"So where did mine 'whoosh' to?"

"Let's see if the computer can find out." He looked down at his terminal and started punching away at the keys. He suddenly stopped. "Now that's interesting. I didn't notice that before."

"What?"

He picked up one of the stubs and turned it around to her. He pointed at the airport code. "Do you see what that says?"

"MRE. Port Meredith, right?"

"Port Meredith is MER. Some fool got it backways when they checked you in." He wiped a creeping grin off his face with one hand. "According to my little machine here, your bags are on their way to Mara Lodge."

"Is that on one of the nearby islands?" she asked, trying to recall Caribbean geography. Then it hit her. "Mara Lodge. Kenya?"

"That would be correct."

"Great. Just great." Jackie squeezed her eyes shut in an attempt to keep her brain from exploding. She should never have gotten on the plane. She should have stayed home and told Walt to stick it up his . . . no, not Walt. It was all Hunter's fault. She wouldn't be here at all if Reade Hunter weren't trying to pull a fast one. She forced a smile to her lips and met the agent's sympathetic gaze. "What's it going to take to get my things back?"

He clicked his way through a couple of screens. "We might be able to catch them in London and turn them around. With any luck, they will be here sometime tomorrow."

"Great. But what do I do in the meantime? These clothes are all I have, and they're filthy. See?" She backed up a step or two and gestured to the pale, sticky stain that spread down her shirt and across the knees of her pants. "Ginger ale, courtesy of your flight attendant and clear air turbulence."

He tsked. "We heard your flight was a little rough."

"That's putting it mildly. So far this has not been my trip."

"You poor woman," he said, and sounded like he meant it. "Well, we'll see if we can fix things up for you. I can get you a few dollars so you can buy some clothes, and we have a kit with a toothbrush and shampoo and the like to tide you over."

"I have my own toothbrush," she said.

She had fresh undies, too, in a bag shoved down in the bottom of her purse, but she kicked herself that she didn't have more. That was the problem with carrying your laptop in one of those hard aluminum cases—your computer was safe, but there just wasn't room for an extra set of clothes. For years she had operated under the principle that splitting her possessions evenly between two suitcases was enough, that no airline could possibly lose both bags at once. Well, they could.

"Let's get the paperwork filled out and start the machinery grindin'. Your full name, please."

She answered all his questions, waited while he went off to gather authorizations, and then signed for what turned out to be £100 Sebastiani, or about $150 U.S.

"Well, we did wet you down pretty well while we were losing your clothes," he said when she expressed surprise at the generous amount. "I talked the boss into a little extra. With you being here on business and all, I knew you'd need some nicer clothes."

"I'm not here on business. Exactly."

"Oh. Excuse me." He looked confused. "I saw your computer and I assumed. . . . It doesn't matter. Use the extra to buy yourself a bathing suit. You probably need a swim after all this."

"Thank you"—she peered at the name tag on his blue uniform—"Mr. Montgomery. Thank you very much. Now, just point me toward the hotel shuttle and I'll be out of your hair."

He obliged, and fifteen minutes later, Jackie was on her way—and wishing fervently that she had picked a different seat in the van. She'd read warnings about the local drivers, but the reality of riding shotgun while weaving between vehicles and pedestrians at speeds approaching Mach 1—all on the wrong side of the road—made the warning seem inadequate by half. Behind her, the other Fair Winds guests chatted along, apparently oblivious to the impending disaster.

By the time the driver turned into the winding drive at Fair Winds some forty minutes later, sweat soaked her clothes and her fingernails were permanently imbedded in the door handle. As soon as he set the brake, Jackie pried herself loose and crawled out to collapse onto a bench at the base of an ancient fig tree that shaded the portico.

That was that. She was staying at the resort until she had to leave for the airport. Period.

And then a breeze, muggy but scented with sea salt and frangipani, wrapped around her, and in her imagination, Harry began to sing his folksy tunes. Her knees stopped shaking. Above her, through the branches of the old fig, the sky glowed a shade of sun-touched blue usually reserved for Renaissance paintings of Heaven. She inhaled deeply and sighed, the traffic forgotten.

"Which bags, miss?"

A bellman drew her attention toward the pile of luggage being unloaded next to the van.

"None, thank you. Mine are on safari." When the man looked confused, she laughed, grabbed her laptop, and stood up. "Don't ask. I'll check in now, if that will be all right."

"Of course. Right this way."

He led her into an open-air lobby that reeked of colonial-style elegance. Heavy bamboo furniture sat in groupings scattered among white columns and palms potted in big brass spittoons, while overhead, white latticework and filigree added to the atmosphere of age. The far side stood open to a wide veranda that looked over the gardens and pools. A swath of ocean glittered in the near distance, blending seamlessly into the cloud-dappled sky.

Jackie's lack of luggage let her beat her fellow travelers to the registration desk, where the staff welcomed her with open arms and expressions of sympathy over her state. There were both a sundries shop and a well-stocked ladies' boutique in the garden arcade, she was assured. And yes, Dr. Hunter had checked in, but no, Mr. Phelps had not arrived yet. He was expected sometime later.

Even though she had nothing for the bellman to carry, she let him lead her past the clots of ambitiously happy vacationers and between the various buildings and pools and vegetation to her cabana, so that she at least knew where it was.

The stream of cool, conditioned air that wafted over her as he opened the door was like a siren song, beckoning her to park her fanny inside and never go out again. Though it wasn't very hot by local standards, the switch from wintry Minneapolis to summery St. Sebastian in seven hours flat was throwing her system for a loop. The khakis and T-shirt and vest that had seemed so cold that morning had turned clammy hot, sticking to her skin like a full-body rubber suit. Even the turquoise water of the Caribbean, visible through the trees a few yards away, looked too warm, about as appealing as a hot bath. All she wanted to do was have a cool shower and get into some clean clothes, then find a shady spot and a glass of iced tea. She was suddenly very anxious to spend a little of that £100.

The bellman fussed about in the airy, peach and yellow room, throwing open curtains, checking towels, and plumping pillows on the wicker chairs. Thinking to hurry him along, Jackie stuck her hand in her purse for a five-dollar bill.

The man grinned at her, shook his head, and kept plumping. "No tipping here, miss, remember?"

"Oops. Sorry. It's habit."

Finally the man finished and left, and moments later, with her computer securely chained to the nightstand, she locked the door and headed back up to the ladies' boutique. A quick look at the racks left her frowning. It really did seem to be well stocked—just not with her kind of clothes.

The clerk finished with the only other customer and

came over. "Hello, I'm Vivianne. Welcome to Papagana. May I help you find something?"

"I hope so. Everything is so ... bright," said Jackie, glancing around for something that didn't scream sex and sand in size 6. "Do you have anything more conservative? And, uh, bigger."

"What is it you'd be needing?"

"Something I can wear this evening," said Jackie. She explained about her suitcases. "I'll be meeting a gentleman for dinner." *With any luck.*

"Where?"

"I'm not sure. We haven't connected yet." *No kidding.*

"A young gentleman, or an older one?"

The implication made Jackie cringe inside, but she kept her face neutral. "He's older."

"He may want to go to Saul's. That's the nicest restaurant. Plus it's Formal Night, anyway, so you'll want a nice dress."

"All right, a dress, then. Nothing too fancy, though."

Vivianne looked her up and down, the beads in her cornrows clinking slightly as she sized Jackie up. "You're about an American size 16, aren't you?"

"Um, more or less. An 18 is probably better." God, she hated to say that aloud, but it was better than it had been. "For the top, you know."

"I thought so. I'm right up there, too," said the woman, who struck Jackie as being statuesque, but hardly over-weight. "You go on into the stall and strip off. I know just the dress."

She came to the dressing room a moment later with a wrap-front dress in hazy shades of aqua, a paler version of the sea outside. Fine white lines traced out a jungle pattern, with faint smudges of orchid and creamy yellow tipping the flowers. The effect was subdued, but still wildly tropical.

"Try this," she said. "It's just cryin' for a real woman to wear it."

"It's beautiful," said Jackie, fingering the buttery material. "But I don't know. It looks a little low cut for me."

"Go on, give it a try," the woman insisted. "You'll see. Oh, excuse me. I have another customer. If you need me, just shout out." She hung the dress on a hook and disappeared.

Skeptical, Jackie tried the dress on—and discovered that Vivianne was right. It was, indeed, a dress for a real woman. One who didn't mind the whole world knowing she was a real woman. One, in fact, who liked to advertise her womanhood near and far. She checked the price tag under her armpit. A woman who didn't mind spending top dollar to advertise, at that.

"How is it?" called her fashion mentor.

"Um. It's, um. . . ."

"Come on out here, where we can have a good look."

Jackie peeked around the door to make sure the shop hadn't suddenly filled with men, then slipped out.

Vivianne beamed. "I told you it was perfect for you."

"I don't know." Jackie caught a glimpse of herself in the three-way mirror and quickly covered the deep vee with her palm. "My mother calls dresses like this open-toed."

"Mothers don't want their daughters to look sexy." Vivianne pulled Jackie's hand away. "I never would have guessed you had so much up top. How do you manage to hide it like that?"

"Years of practice," said Jackie.

"Well, you ought to be showin' those off, not tuckin' them away. Lots of women spend good money to fill their bikinis half so well."

"I gave up bikinis when I was thirteen, after I blew one out." Jackie surveyed herself in the mirror once more, then pulled the neckline together a couple of inches higher. "Maybe with a pin or something."

"Don't you dare pin it. Just put your shoulders back and stand up straight and proud. You must strut it a bit." Vivianne demonstrated, looking like a queen.

Jackie tried it and felt like Jessica Rabbit. She shook

her head and turned toward the racks. "Let's see if we can find something else."

Vivianne did try, hauling in an armload of dresses that, while not exactly like the tailored navy and white coordinates that were winging their way to Kenya, at least looked more modest than the aqua dress.

Unfortunately, none of them fit. Jackie was tugging at the last of them when Vivianne knocked on the dressing room door.

"How we doin'?"

"Okay, I guess." Jackie pushed the door open and showed her. "This is about the best."

"It's awful, girl."

"At least it covers me." Maybe a little too much. Jackie tugged at it some more, trying to rearrange the gathers so she didn't look so hippy. The dress really wasn't very flattering. It was the wrong shade of red, and the bodice bunched up to create one of those massive Victorian bosoms she'd seen in photos of Great-Grandma Stepp—not that Great-Grandma had anything on her in the chest department. "The others were way too tight across the front."

"I had the same problem when I tried them." Vivianne picked up one of the discarded dresses and slipped it onto a hanger. "I think they design them for scrawny little girls with no tits."

"That's definitely not me," said Jackie, laughing ruefully. She tugged at the dress a little more. "Okay. It's not great, but I can make do."

"That one?" Vivianne shook her head. "No, no, no, no, no. You look like a big red church bus. I can't let you walk out of here dressed like that. It wouldn't be good for trade."

"But it's just until tomorrow."

"That's one day too long to look that awful." Vivianne pulled the aqua dress out from behind the others and held it up in front of Jackie. "This is the right one, and you know it is."

Jackie molded the dress to her figure, recalling the fit. She'd never owned a dress so . . . blatant. "I can't. I'm just not the type."

"Bah," said Vivianne. "If you're not the type, girl, who is?"

Who, indeed? Jackie stared into the mirror and considered. It was certainly more flattering than the red one. And she had to take one of them, or she'd wind up sitting around naked while her clothes were at the laundry and Hunter was getting the jump on Farley Phelps.

She looked at the price tag again.

"Oh, all right. I'll take this one." She shoved the aqua dress into Vivianne's hands before she had a chance to change her mind.

"Good girl. Just remember to stand tall, and your gentleman friend will love it."

"Great," said Jackie. *Just great.* All she needed was for Farley Phelps to think she was out to seduce him. "I'll need some sandals or something, too. And a slip."

"I have everything you need. Just let Vivianne take care of you."

Reade Hunter sat at the poolside bar, his eyes sweeping methodically over his fellow vacationers.

She was here, someplace.

The front desk had confirmed that Dr. Barnett had checked in nearly an hour ago. Ever conscious of their guests' security, they had declined to give him her room number, although they had offered to put him through from a house phone. Reade had taken a pass. He really wanted to see Barnett's face when she realized she'd been found out.

So he had staked out a shady spot near the action where he could keep an eye out for her. Even allowing for time to unpack, which she would undoubtedly do before she so much as stuck her toe in the water, she should be starting to explore by now. And everyone came by the pool sooner or later.

He took another look at the black-and-white head shot of his nemesis that appeared on page 32 of last March's *Polypeptide Quarterly*. It wasn't much to go on, only the size of a large postage stamp, and grainy, to boot—*PPQ* wasn't known for its graphics—but it was the only picture he'd been able to find in the last-minute scramble to beat Barnett to St. Sebastian. It showed a stolid young woman with mousy, straight hair and enough extra pounds that she appeared bulky. She was neither pretty nor ugly, but sort of plain vanilla. There was absolutely nothing evident in the photo that set Jackie Barnett off from any other average-looking female, but Reade still had confidence he could pick her out in the crowd. She'd be the one wearing a lab coat over her swimsuit.

He'd never had the occasion to meet Jacqueline M. Barnett, Ph.D., face to face, but he knew her by reputation and correspondence. She was methodical, detail-oriented, and organized to the extreme, according to some assessments.

Plodding, picky, and anal, according to him.

Totally dedicated to her research, per her fans.

Utterly without a life, by his estimation.

But also, he admitted grudgingly, possessed of an uncanny ability to sort out the wheat of discovery from the chaff of raw data and to spot what others—he, in one unfortunate incident—had missed.

She had dogged him since grad school days, when they'd worked for cooperating researchers at different universities, and she'd lurked over his professional shoulder like his fourth grade teacher, trying to get a peek at his work before it was completed. What made it particularly annoying was that she was his polar opposite. He worked intuitively; she followed procedures and lists and precise methodology. He leaped from insight to insight; she moved forward by sheer, grinding effort. And yet, no matter what he set out to accomplish, she either bulldozed there just ahead of him or lumbered up right behind, somehow getting joint credit in people's minds, if not on paper.

In other words, she drove him crazy.

That's what made it such a delight to beat her out every now and again. That's what would make it especially sweet to undercut her this time, when, for once, he'd caught her trying to cheat. If he hadn't had to call John Neuhauser about those figures, she'd have gotten away with it, too. John had mentioned Barnett's trip because it was so unusual—her first real vacation since college— and then Harvey Deng happened to show Reade an article about Phelps in some in-flight magazine. The mention of Phelps and Fair Winds in the same sentence had set off bells. A couple of carefully worded phone calls had confirmed that Mr. Phelps would indeed be at Fair Winds for the next two weeks, and a travel agent and a credit card had taken care of the rest.

He was actually half grateful to Barnett for stepping out of her usual routine and forcing him into this trip. Her sudden, out-of-character impulse to take a shortcut had provided him with the perfect excuse to give his mother the Caribbean holiday she'd been nagging him about.

It also gave him an opportunity to find Mom a man.

Not that he liked thinking of it that way—it made him sound like a pimp. Plus, like most sons, he'd rather not link his mother and sex in the same neural impulse. But she clearly needed some sort of distraction, and a man seemed like the best bet.

His conclusion had been reinforced over lunch, when he'd listened to her recount her current medical status to some poor woman from Brooklyn who grew simultaneously more sympathetic and more desperate to escape. Reade understood the desperation, perhaps even more deeply than the lady from Brooklyn, for what he knew, that she didn't, was that his mother wasn't actually sick.

She wasn't faking it, either—not deliberately, anyway. On a certain level, his mother actually believed herself to be ill. The doctors said otherwise, however, and Reade had tired of being at her beck and call. Just because he was the only one of her three sons responsible enough to stick around didn't mean he actually enjoyed playing care-taker—especially when she didn't really need one. Which was why he intended to spend at least part of this trip searching for any man over the age of fifty that he might aim in his mother's direction. Maybe focusing on some-one outside herself, even just for a while, would make her forget her aches and pains and help her get her old vitality back.

Demographics were against him. St. Sebastian was for lovers, after all, and out of the few older men Reade spot-ted so far, most were with women who were clearly their wives. The remainder sported with young women who were clearly not wives—at least not first wives—or even daughters, the dirty old coots.

Reade tossed back the last of his iced tea, settled his sunglasses on his nose, and stuck the rolled journal under his arm, then wandered down to the beach. He doubted he'd find Barnett there, but whether he did or not, there was a certain charm in ambling along rows of female bod-ies clad for maximum UV absorption.

When he had his fill of sightseeing, he headed back to his room. His mother wanted him to escort her to dinner, and he needed to shower and change into something that passed as dressy in this summer camp for grown-ups.

With any luck, Farley Phelps would turn up and Reade could just happen to bump into him and start the basic male bonding thing over after-dinner drinks.

And Jackie Barnett could kiss the grant good-bye.

I'm an adult, I can eat alone if I feel like it. People are not staring at me, and if they are, it's their prob-lem, not mine. There's nothing wrong with eating alone. And this dress looks just fine.

Jackie sat at her table, feigning nonchalance and giving

herself a motivational lecture that wasn't working very well.

She'd read somewhere that eating alone at an upscale restaurant was high on the list of stress producers for women. Saul's was definitely upscale, even if it was all part of the super-inclusive package. It was by far the classiest restaurant in the otherwise casual resort, more of a dinner club in the Old Havana style, complete with white-jacketed waiters and tables arranged in a wide arc around a dance floor and bandstand. Couples occupied the majority of tables, with occasional larger groups scattered through the crowd. Jackie was the only person dining alone, and even though the maître d' had seated her off to one side so she wasn't quite so obvious, everyone in Saul's was aware of her, from the patrons to the busboys.

And she was acutely aware of them and their glances of pity, too, which was why her body was now efficiently ticking through the various physiologic reactions of fight or flight—increased heart rate, rapid respiration, increased muscle tone, heightened thought processes, flushed skin, sweating palms. She certainly offered a case study of the solo dining/stress connection. If called upon, she could give an undergraduate lecture, using her own reactions as demonstration.

Or an article for a popular magazine. In fact, that wasn't such a bad idea. She could have it ready to submit by the time she got back to Minneapolis. At the very least, she could distract herself while she waited for her soup. She made another quick scan of the restaurant to confirm that Farley Phelps had not turned up yet, then pulled a notepad and pen out of her purse and began scribbling away. She was soon lost in thought.

"Designing a new antibiotic?"

Jackie jerked and sent her knife flying across the table. The man grabbed it just before it sailed off the edge.

"I'm sorry, I didn't mean to startle you," he said, returning her knife to its place.

"That's all right, I'm like that when I'm—" She looked

up into the face of her visitor and stopped dead.

"—working?" he finished for her. "You're Dr. Jacqueline Barnett, aren't you?"

"Er, uh, yes." All the snappy opening lines Jackie had rehearsed dissolved in a squirt of adrenaline. She knew that hawkish face, yin-yang stud earring, and bald head with ponytail.

The man put his hand out. "I'm Farley Phelps."

"I know. I mean, I recognize you from CNN." She quickly laid down her pen and took his hand. "How very nice to meet you, Mr. Phelps. I'm surprised to see you here."

"It's quite a coincidence, isn't it? Both of us here at the same time."

Was that a note of sarcasm? Jackie smiled and tried to pretend there was no reason on earth why the man would be suspicious. "How did you know who I am?"

"I have your grant application sitting on my desk, complete with recent eight-by-ten, remember? Although I must say, you look entirely different this evening."

His eyes flickered down slightly, taking in exactly the view Jackie had hoped would go unnoticed. She felt herself pink up. Great. With him standing and her sitting, he probably thought he was looking at sunrise over the Grand Canyon.

Fortunately, the spectacle was interrupted by the waiter bringing her soup. He set the bowl in front of Jackie and turned to Phelps.

"Will you be joining the lady, sir?"

Farley looked to Jackie. "Aren't you waiting for someone?"

"No, unfortunately. My boyfriend . . . had to bail out at the last minute. I'm here alone."

"How wonderful. Not about your boyfriend. What I mean is, I'm alone this evening, too. We can have dinner together."

Without waiting for Jackie's invitation, he slid into the chair opposite her.

"I'll have the soup, too," he told the waiter. "And a daiquiri. What are you drinking this evening, Dr. Barnett?"

"Iced tea. But I'm fine."

"This is St. Sebastian, for God's sake. You've got to at least splash some rum in it." He looked back to the waiter. "Bring her a daiquiri, too, while you're at it. I'll let you know about the rest."

"Yes, sir." The waiter grinned, teeth bright white against walnut skin, then turned smartly and headed off before Jackie could object.

"Now, isn't this cozy?" said Mr. Phelps. "We can have a nice dinner and get to know each other."

"Yes. Um, thank you." That wasn't quite the right response, but Jackie didn't care. Her streak of bad luck had just ended in the grandest style. She had Farley Phelps to herself, and for the next couple of hours, her biggest problem was going to be resisting the urge to stand up on the table and crow like a rooster.

"She's sexy," said Lenore Hunter as she sat down across the table.

"Mmm-hmm. . . . Who?" asked Reade.

"That blonde in the turquoise dress you've been watching all evening."

"I'm not watching anyone."

"Don't lie to your mother."

Too late for that, thought Reade. And he wasn't about to explain that he really had his eye on the man who was with the blonde, either. Considering how long it had been since he'd had a date, she'd take that one completely wrong.

Reade had recognized Phelps right away, but the initial sense of victory had faded when he saw that his target was sharing his table with a woman.

Reade couldn't get a clear view of her face from this angle, but he was certain it wasn't Barnett—this woman had the zaftig figure of a Fifties pinup girl and Farley Phelps's undivided attention. They'd been deep in conversation for nearly ninety minutes now, barely slowing to eat.

Reade shook his head. An evening of chitchat would be the last thing on his mind if he were in St. Sebastian with a woman built like that. Sexy wasn't the half of it.

"You should ask her to dance or something," suggested his mother. "The band's about to come out. I saw them in the back hall. I took a wrong turn on the way to the powder room and nearly impaled myself on a trombone."

"I hope the spit valve held," said Reade.

Lenore grimaced. "I hadn't even thought about that—and don't start telling me about what horrible things you can culture from the inside of a trombone. Anyway, you really should ask her to dance."

"She already has a partner, in case you didn't notice. Besides, she'd probably like to be able to walk tomorrow."

"You're not that bad."

"That's one of the things I love about you, Mom. You forget my faults from year to year."

"You're trying to weasel out of dancing with me, aren't you? Well, it won't work. You promised, and I'm holding you to it. In fact, there's the orchestra now."

It was Reade's turn to grimace. A few dances with Mom hadn't seemed like such a big deal back in Pittsburgh, but now that the musicians were starting to trickle out and adjust their chairs and stands, the experience loomed like a romp through quicksand.

With no fewer than five restaurants on the grounds, he'd let her lure him into Saul's. Any dancing here was going to be the real thing, not the amorphous jerking around he might get away with in the disco.

The band settled in quickly, and after a brief introduction, started with a mambo or rumba or one of those dances with an island beat. Several couples got up right away and proved they knew which was which. Reade watched sets of feet dance by, hoping to pick up some hints.

"Don't look so pained," said Lenore. "You don't have to face it quite yet. I need to take my pills first."

She pulled a monogrammed brass pillbox out of her evening bag, flicked it open, and started popping tablets and sipping at her water. As much as he enjoyed the temporary reprieve, Reade personally thought it was a shame the doctors caved in to her so much. But then again, only a few of the pills contained actual medication. Sugar was a wonderful thing. He hoped she never developed diabetes.

"There," she said, slipping the pillbox back into her bag. As the band slid into another piece, she touched his hand. "I like this song. Let's give it a try."

"They're your toes."

They found an unoccupied section of the dance floor, and assumed the prescribed position. The rhythm was still exotic, but after a couple of false starts, Reade found a downbeat and led his mother into something resembling a dance step.

"What I don't understand," said Lenore, "is how a man as active and coordinated as you are everywhere else can be such a board on the dance floor."

He missed a beat. "Sorry. Hard work and talent."

"It's not that difficult, darling. You have a Ph.D. Apply all those brain cells."

"I'm not allowed to. When we take our orals, we have to promise never to dance again. I'm violating my oath just by being out here."

His mother rolled her eyes. "I might buy that, if I hadn't rumbaed with Richard Feynman in 1978. Your father and I should have made you take dancing lessons one summer, instead of letting you spend all your time outrunning your brothers."

"The world would be a better place if I had learned to cha-cha," agreed Reade solemnly. "May I suggest you discontinue this confidence-building exercise and simply enjoy what little skill I have to offer? This trip will be your last chance to torture me for a while."

"Why? Did Dr. Huddleston tell you something?"

"No, Mom, it's not about your health," he said, narrowly avoiding a patronizing tone. "But once I get the Phelps grant, I won't be available to trip the light fantastic with you for a couple of years. I'll be too busy to travel."

"Oh, well. This is probably my last big trip, anyway. I'll try to enjoy it as much as I can."

Reade gritted his teeth, but kept his mouth shut. They meandered through another couple of songs without further conversation until Phelps and his girlfriend danced past in a toss of wavy blonde hair.

His mother sighed. "Now that's a dancer. He even makes your friend look good."

She looked good all on her own, in Reade's opinion. Apparently Farley thought so, too. Unless he was mistaken, the old guy had just copped a quick peek at the lady's cleavage. *The dog.* Not that Reade could find too much fault. Every other healthy male in the joint had certainly noticed her figure—and a lot of the women had, too, if frowns and dagger looks were an indication.

"She doesn't really know what she's doing, you know," his mother said. "See how hard he has to work? He's practically manhandling her through those turns."

"Poor guy," said Reade dryly.

"They're doing the merengue." Her eyes were still glued to where Fred and Ginger had disappeared back into the crowd. "I haven't danced that since your dad died."

Under the wistfulness in her voice, Reade caught a hint of interest. Unless he was very mistaken, she wanted to dance the merengue. With Phelps.

It occurred to him that Farley Phelps was exactly the type of man to take his mother's mind off her symptoms and syndromes: fit, fifty-five, and filthy rich. And then there was the added perk that a fling between Mom and Farley could prove personally beneficial. He wouldn't actually ask his mother to seduce Farley on his behalf—that really would be too much like pimping—but perhaps while he was busy outmaneuvering Barnett, he could sort of nudge the two of them toward each other. If they happened to hit it off . . . well, it couldn't hurt.

Suddenly, Reade very much wanted to give her a shot at Farley, for her sake as much as his own. That would mean distracting the blonde without aggravating Phelps, but with a little thought, he might be able manage that. Taking a firmer lead, he started steering his mother across the floor after the pair, concentrating all his efforts on not crippling her.

When the music stopped, impeccable timing disguised as coincidence landed them within reach of their quarry. A compliment or two and a request for a lesson for Mom, and he'd—

"I think that's enough for me for this evening," said his mother.

"Oh, come on, Mom. I'm just getting the hang of this."

"I'm sorry, darling, but I'm exhausted. You know I don't have the stamina I used to." She tucked her arm into his, and smiled up at him mischievously. "Walk me to my room, and then you can come back and see if you can meet her."

"Very funny," said Reade.

But that was exactly what he did.

He found his quarry not on the dance floor or even back at the table, but at the long ebony bar that ran across the back of the room. She was alone, talking to the bartender as he poured her a tonic water and twisted a piece of lime into it. As she shifted on the tall stool to cross her legs, the skirt of her dress fell open in that annoying and delightful way wrap dresses have of doing. She reached down to flip it shut, but not before Reade caught a glimpse of powerhouse thighs. Maybe a vacation fling wasn't such a bad idea, after all.

Five minutes later, when Phelps still hadn't made an appearance, Reade decided the lady had been abandoned for the evening. His moment had come. He sidled in next to her.

A bartender in a spotless white jacket came by, polishing the counter. "Something for you, sir?"

"Myers Dark, straight up."

"Yes, sir."

He waited for his drink, took a fortifying sip, then turned and found himself face to face with the mystery lady.

And what a face: good, strong, Germanic jaw, set hard as a rock; dark gray eyes, narrowed in suspicion; and full, tempting lips, curved in an ironic smile. Her look practically dared him to try to pick her up.

There was something else, too, that Reade couldn't quite get his mind around, but it was too late to change course now. He put a lid on his libido and said casually, "I saw you earlier on the dance floor. You're very good."

She glanced around as if to see whether the comment was really addressed to her. "Thanks, but I'm a huge fake. I really only know three steps."

"That puts you two up on me."

"Well, then. No wonder I had you fooled." She spun her glass idly, and then her smile disappeared. "Look, Hunter, I'm not quite sure what game you're playing, but pretending you don't know who I am isn't going to get you anywhere."

"I beg your pardon, but—" Reade's jaw dropped as the Midwest twang and the unsmiling face came together with a clatter of test tubes and petri dishes. "Barnett?"

"Oh, give me a break. Like you haven't been staring at us all evening. It's not going to work. I know why you're here, and in about ten seconds, Mr. Phelps will, too."

She looked over his shoulder and smiled a greeting. Reade spun, only to see Farley Phelps less than a dozen paces away and coming straight toward them. With nowhere to run, Reade could only rely on bravado. He stepped forward, hand outstretched.

"Mr. Phelps. Dr. Barnett just told me you were here. I'm Reade Hunter."

Phelps shook the offered hand. "Dr. Hunter. Well, well, well."

"Dr. Hunter was just telling me about his last-minute decision to bring his dear old mother down here for a vacation."

How the hell did she know that? Reade hurried to explain. "She's been wanting to come to St. Sebastian for a long time. I happened to stumble onto a package deal I couldn't resist, and here we are."

"Isn't that just so sweet," cooed Jackie. "And what an amazing coincidence."

"Amazing," agreed Farley. "And how convenient to have both of you down here where I can get to know you. Maybe I should go check the guest register to see if any of the other finalists have checked in. We could hold a seminar."

Ouch. This was not going the way Reade had imagined, on any level. Time for some candor. Sort of.

"I have a confession to make. I really did recognize you earlier, during dinner, but I didn't come over because I knew how fishy it would look. Plus I figured you wouldn't want to be interrupted when you were with a lady of such outstanding . . . charms."

Barnett's eyes flashed, and the fingers of her right hand curled and uncurled, as though she wanted to smack him.

Reade smiled. "Of course, I would have been less reticent if I'd realized that the lady was Dr. Barnett. You may find this odd, but even though we've corresponded for years, we've never actually met before."

"Well, then, you should get acquainted," said Farley. "Which I'm sure you can manage without me around. I'm going back to my room to crash."

"That's not really necessary, Mr. Phelps," said Jackie quickly. "Dr. Hunter and I—"

Phelps held up his hand to stop her. "I was just coming back to tell you I was going to bail. I was up at four this morning, and I think I hit the wall during that last mambo. However, there's no reason for you two to give up on the evening. Stay, finish your drinks, maybe have a dance or three. I'm sure we'll all bump into each other tomorrow. It looks like it's . . . preordained."

He said good night, shook hands with each of them, and strolled off, bopping a little to the calypso tune the band was playing.

Reade watched until Phelps was well out of sight, then turned to Jackie and very deliberately let his gaze fall to her chest. "Gee, Barnett, can you be any more obvious?"

She stood up, and for just a second, Reade thought she was going to slap him after all. Then the bristles went down, and she smiled a knowing smile. "I'm not certain. But I can sure as heck try."

She straightened her spine and pulled her shoulders back to emphasize her assets even more, then strolled off as though she owned him and every other man in the joint. And for just a minute, she did.

At the door, she stopped and turned, one eyebrow raised to ask if she had succeeded.

Reade raised his hands and slowly clapped three times.

She blew him a kiss and disappeared.

It was, as far as Reade was concerned, a declaration of all-out war.

three

Safely *locked in her room, Jackie sagged back*
against the door and covered her blazing cheeks with
her hands.

What on earth had possessed her? She'd paraded
through that dining room like a North Side hooker. "Strut
it a bit," Vivianne had said. Well, she'd strutted it all
right.

Thank God Mr. Phelps hadn't been around to see her.

They'd had such a good, productive dinner, getting to
know one another, and generally enjoying a pleasant evening, even though she felt like such a fraud and Mr.
Phelps refused to discuss anything about the lab or phar-
maceuticals at all, saying he was on vacation. It had all
been very professional, exactly the impression Jackie had
wanted to leave. She shuddered to think what he'd have
made of her postprandial stroll.

Then again, she wouldn't have been so brash if he'd
been around.

"Really, I wouldn't have," she assured her reflection in

the mirror across the room. "No way, Hunter or not."

As if to contradict her delusions of good judgment, an unladylike belch escaped her.

Lovely. She pressed a hand to her midsection, where an uncomfortable burn told her that unfamiliar food and Hunter weren't a good mix. But then Hunter wasn't a good mix with anything.

She fished a roll of Tums out of her purse and chewed two tablets on the way to the bathroom sink, where a quick glass of water washed down the grit. Then she took a moment to strip out of her one and only wearable piece of clothing and hang it up before she collapsed on the bed in her underwear.

This is what she got for listening to Walt. And for letting Farley keep ordering daiquiris for two. And for letting Hunter's dirty-minded ogling get to her.

She should have stayed home, well away from aggravating men and alcohol.

And she never, ever should have bought that dress.

Right now, Hunter was probably wallowing in male self-righteousness, ranting about women who would do anything to get what they want.

Well, screw him. All she did was have dinner with Mr. Phelps. Hunter was the one jumping to conclusions. Granted, she'd just given him a healthy shove, but at least now he knew she wasn't going to take his innuendo lying down.

So to speak.

With a groan, she rolled over and buried her head in the pillow.

By the next morning, things didn't seem quite so mortifying. Maybe it was a good night's sleep and the prospect of having her clothes back within a couple of hours. Maybe it was the knowledge that she'd managed to beat Hunter off the starting line. Or maybe it was simply that she'd landed in paradise, a fact that she'd forgotten yesterday in the hassle of arriving without her luggage and hunting up Mr. Phelps.

She was reminded as soon as she opened the door. Framed by palm fronds and a riot of orange bougainvillea, the ocean stretched off into infinity in shades of ever deepening blue that finished with an indigo line against the sky. Early sunbathers turned the beach into a swath of pure white frosting sprinkled with candy-colored swimsuits. A pair of workers wearing Fair Winds' trademark lemon yellow shirts moved along the path, raking and tidying. Their banter provided a human counterpoint to the buzz and chatter of the birds overhead. Even the still, warm air seemed pleasant, less sticky than the previous evening.

Just like the travel brochure had promised. Well, Jackie was sold. She headed up to the Grand Terrace for the breakfast buffet. She wanted to eat early and be back in her room when her luggage was delivered. She intended to spend the rest of the day in her swimsuit.

She was fantasizing about her first ever dip in the Caribbean when a waiter came to her table.

"Miss Barnett?"

"Yes."

"There's a telephone call for you."

"Me? Um, thank you." She took the cordless phone he held out and hit the Talk button. "This is Jackie Barnett."

"Ah, Miss Barnett. I'm glad they found you. This is Gerald Montgomery at the airline."

"I remember. Hello," she said. "Is my luggage on the way?"

"It's on its way, all right. But I'm afraid it's on its way to Cairo."

Her stomach dropped. "That's not funny, Mr. Montgomery."

"I know. I know. I'm sorry."

"What happened?"

"I'm not certain, but apparently London didn't manage to pluck your bags off the track."

"Great." Jackie visualized her bags abandoned in a dark corner of a foreign airport, with God knew what pests crawling over them. "How long will it take to get them back now?"

"Just until tomorrow," said Gerald with great assurance. "By dinnertime."

"Two days?" she whined, then stopped herself and took a deep breath. "Okay. I can last that long. But tomorrow. You promise?"

"I'll do everything I can, Miss Barnett, but it's not all in my hands."

"I know. Thank you, Mr. Montgomery." She hit the button to hang up. The waiter swooped in from nowhere to collect the phone.

Okay. So her bags would take another day. It wasn't a disaster. Her khakis and T-shirt would be back from the laundry any minute, and she could wash out her undies tonight. She could manage.

She polished off the rest of her breakfast and headed for the front desk to check on her laundry. The clerk, the same East Indian man who had checked her in, knew the whole story. He got on the phone immediately, but as he talked, his smile faded and he turned away.

That did not look good. Not good at all. Jackie frowned and braced herself for the worst.

When the fellow turned back and hung up, he wore an expression of sincere apology.

"What did they do?" she asked glumly. "Shrink my shirt or scorch my pants?"

"Neither, neither. Your clothes are fine, Dr. Barnett."

"Oh, thank goodness. For a minute I—"

"But they have had a bit of a breakdown," the man continued with an apologetic smile. "One of the pipes burst, and they had to send the guest laundry to an outside service. It will be back at five o'clock, though, all pressed and ready to go."

"Oh. I guess that's not so bad. Thank you." She turned and started back toward her room, but the sea taunted her through the open wall across the lobby. Two more whole days before she could get in the water. That would make almost a quarter of her vacation stuck on the side of the pool.

She didn't want to wait two days. And she didn't want to spend all day in this dress, either, even if she'd already blown all of the money the airline had given her. She took her screaming budget firmly in hand and headed for Papagana.

"Let's see if we can find a swimsuit that looks as good as that dress," said Vivianne as soon as Jackie made her needs known.

"Let's not," said Jackie, following her toward the back of the store. "All I want is coverage. Last night proved conclusively that I'm not cut out to be Marilyn Monroe."

Vivianne stopped and leaned one elbow on a round rack of swimsuits. "Oh, now that sounds like somethin' happened."

"I just wasn't comfortable, that's all."

"But you look so beautiful. Wasn't your gentleman friend impressed?"

She meant Mr. Phelps, of course, but it was Reade Hunter's face that popped up in Jackie's mind—not when he'd been sneering, but before, when he claimed he hadn't realized who she was. Maybe he hadn't, because in retrospect, it seemed like he'd been trying to pick her up. "One gentleman was, at least."

"Now I know something happened. Tell all."

Jackie had no intention of rehashing the embarrassing scene, but Vivianne persisted, and under her good-natured prodding, Jackie found herself spilling the whole story: Farley, Reade, the walk, the whole thing.

"Ooh, girl, I can just see you sashaying out the door, and that Hunter man standing there with his tongue hanging out." Vivianne chuckled as she lifted a nice, conservative black maillot off the rack. It looked perfect to Jackie, but Vivianne shook her head and rejected it. "I told you all you had to do was flaunt it a bit."

"Well, I did that all right, and I'm still not sure why. He just made me so mad. Do you have any idea how tired I get of testosterone-loaded jerks talking to my chest like it has a higher IQ than I do?" She retrieved the black suit, glancing at a racy coral model Vivianne had picked out. "Which is why I don't care to flaunt it anymore. That one's way too bare."

"It's also got a proper bra in it," said Vivianne. She took the black suit away from Jackie and hung it up. "You'd be flapping like a bird in that thing."

"It's more my style." Jackie picked the suit up again. Time to get firm. "I want to be covered, and I will *not* try on that suit."

"All right," said Vivianne in a tone that said Jackie would see. She dutifully hung the coral suit back on the rack, let Jackie pick out a couple of others, and escorted her to the dressing room.

To Vivianne's credit, she refrained from saying "I told you so" when Jackie stuck her head out of the dressing room fifteen minutes later and handed her the black suit. And the blue one. And the red and white one.

"Maybe the coral, after all," muttered Jackie. Vivianne silently handed her the suit.

She nodded when Jackie invited her to view her handiwork.

"You're not going to get any more fabric by yanking on it," she said as Jackie tugged at the butt. "It's supposed to come up high like that. It makes your legs look longer."

"Only if you assume that legs include everything up to the waist." Jackie turned back and forth a few times, assessing. She might be on the big side, but at least she didn't have cellulite. "I guess it'll have to do."

" 'Do?' " repeated Vivianne. " 'Do?' It more than 'does,' girl. You look like you belong on the cover of that magazine."

Jackie turned sideways and frowned at her cantilevered bustline. "*Playboy*?"

Vivianne laughed. "No, that one with all the swimsuit models. *Sports Illustrated*."

"Oh, good. I'd hate to be confused with something sleazy," said Jackie dryly. She took a deep breath and frowned again at the inches that simple act added to her chest. But at least the seams held. "Okay, I'll take it."

"Good. Now, do you need anything else?"

"I might as well pick up a pair of shorts and a T-shirt while I'm spending money I don't have."

"I'll bring you a wrap, so you can come out and look around."

"Never mind about that," said Jackie, giving in to the inevitable. "Just pick out whatever you think is right. I put myself in your hands."

"Finally getting wise, are you? Don't worry, I'll take good care of you." Vivianne stepped back and eyed Jackie critically. "I think I'll have them send over a big bottle of sun lotion from next door. There are parts of you hangin' out that apparently have never seen the light before."

"And if I had my own suit, they never would. Where I come from, we call that shade fishbelly white, and work all winter to perfect it."

Vivianne's laugh filled the store. "Well I hate to tell you, but you won't be that color for very long."

It was the dress, Reade decided as he stood looking down at the *Polypeptide Quarterly* photo of Jackie Barnett. That dress she'd had on revealed everything the lab coat in the photo hid so thoroughly. And it did it in the most effective manner imaginable, short of total nudity.

He shook his head.

No way would he have guessed that the stodgy-looking female in the photo could have morphed into the siren that blew him off last night.

Damn it, it just wasn't fair.

Sex should not enter into the funding process. Surely

Farley could see past all that cleavage. Surely a man of his experience and business acumen wouldn't fall for such an obvious hook—though he'd certainly noticed it. A man would have to be blind not to notice.

Reade picked up the journal. He'd love to drop it in the trash, just so Barnett's unsmiling face wouldn't haunt his room for the next twelve days, but he really wanted to hang onto the article on the isolation of peptide anti-mycobacterials in traditional healing plants of Burkina Faso. Hell of an article, even if it was *hers*. He stuck the thin magazine under the folded jeans in his drawer, where it could remain buried until he headed back to Pittsburgh.

Five minutes later he was standing in front of his mother's door, waiting for her to find her room key.

"Oh, here it is," she said patting the pocket of her cover-up. "I knew I'd just had it in my hand. Now, let me get my book."

She grabbed a fat paperback and a straw hat off the end of the dresser, slipped a tube of sunscreen in her pocket, and came outside.

"How was breakfast?" she asked as they headed toward the pool.

"Terrific. I had fried plantain and rundown."

"Rundown? Isn't that some sort of fish?"

"Sort of a spiced mackerel stew."

"For breakfast?" His mother wrinkled her nose. "I knew there was a reason I didn't want to eat with you."

"Come on, Mom. I've seen you eat stuff that would curl most people's toes. Grasshoppers. Ants. Witchetty grubs."

"I know, I know. But that was a long time ago, when your father was around to egg me on and I still had a cast-iron stomach." She sighed dramatically. "I wonder if that isn't part of what's wrong with me now. Maybe I picked up some parasite or other."

" 'The worms crawl in, the worms crawl out . . .' " began Reade.

"Stop it." She pinched his arm, but she was smiling as she said, "You're not a nice boy at all."

"You're just figuring that out? Gee, Mom, where were you the last thirty-two years?"

"Looking the other way, so I could pretend I didn't notice what you and your brothers were up to."

"Good luck. Oh, by the way, I signed us up for that trip to Mystery Falls you wanted to take."

"Oh, how nice. Thank you."

"My pleasure, Mom." Only insofar as it would bring her pleasure. For himself, he couldn't think of anything more boring than following a bunch of tourists up some waterfall. "Here we are."

"God, I love this place." She eased down on the first available lounger. "If I had the money, I'd just stay here all year, baking. Now, you go swim, and I'll just sit here and relax."

Reade was more than happy to oblige. He really needed to loosen up before he tried to find Phelps. Between that dance with Mom and then finding out Barnett had gotten to Phelps first, his shoulders had locked up and stayed that way all night. He tossed his room key and his sunglasses onto a table next to his mother, stripped off his shirt, and hit the water.

He dove into the deep end and came up in a slow, powerful stroke that could have carried him a couple of miles if the pool hadn't started filling up. He kept going as long as he could dodge paddlers and floating lounge chairs, but he finally had to give up. As rewarding as it was to brush past a sun bunny in a skimpy suit, it wasn't getting him much exercise. And it wasn't getting him any closer to Farley Phelps.

According to that article in Harvey's magazine, Phelps enjoyed a hard game of beach volleyball, so Reade toweled off, checked to make sure his mother was okay, grabbed his shirt, and headed over toward the sand pit.

Phelps was nowhere to be found, but Reade lingered to watch the action and got pulled into a two-on-two game with a couple from France. His partner was a woman from Coeur d'Alene, Idaho, who had a killer serve, and he finished the game with a nice sweat and an invitation to sweat a little more that came complete with room number. He committed it to memory—just in case.

On the way back to the pool, he swung past the bar to pick up a couple of iced teas, then hung around a few minutes to listen to a steel drum band that had set up beside the pimento tree. Off in the distance, the roar of a high-powered motor boat competed for attention as it towed a parasail.

When he got back to the pool, his mother had disappeared, along with his shirt, sunglasses, and key. Even her lounger was gone. He stood there with condensation dripping between his fingers, looking around, until he finally spotted her in the deep shade of a nearby pergola.

"I thought you were going to bake," he said as he came up. He set the tea down on the table beside her.

"You were gone so long, I started to get crisp around the edges. What are you looking at?"

"Someone parasailing out over the bay." Someone with long dark hair and a red bikini, if his eyesight wasn't deceiving him. "I think I'll go up. I haven't dangled off anything in a while."

"You might as well, since it's free." She winced and put a hand to her temple. "I must have waited too long to get out of the sun, after all. I seem to be getting one of my headaches."

"You're probably just a little dehydrated. Have some tea."

"I don't think it's a matter of drinking iced tea, darling. But don't worry about me. I'll be fine. And I refuse to let my health problems ruin our trip."

Reade recognized the not-so-subtle note of martyrdom and didn't even bother to sit down.

She was true to form. "I think I should take something. Would you mind going to my room for my pills?"

"Sure, Mom. No problem."

She gave explicit directions on which bottle she wanted and where to find it, and handed over her room key. As she settled back on her chair with a pinched look on her face, Reade headed off, shaking his head and wondering what the hell it would take to cure what ailed his mother.

The coral suit might not be what she'd have chosen under other circumstances, but it fit. And more to the point, it was actually in her hands, and Jackie could hardly wait to get into it. She headed back to her room with her bag of clothes and her giant bottle of sunscreen, ready for some real vacation. She was going to park herself where she could hear that steel drum band and just vegetate.

R&R was postponed a few more minutes, however, when she spotted Farley Phelps under an arbor, his bald pate and ponytail silhouetted against the sky. He was behind a woman in a lounge chair, leaning over her slightly, and from where Jackie stood, it appeared he was squeezing her head.

Surely not. Jackie moved in for a better look.

He was. Squeezing it between his palms like an oversized orange. He had one hand on either side of the woman's skull, just above her ears, and his eyes were closed in concentration, as were those of the woman being juiced—who, Jackie realized once her eyes adjusted to the shade, just happened to be Reade Hunter's mother.

That rat. How low could the man go? Really, using his mother to try to get the grant went way beyond tacky. Jackie glanced around, fully expecting to see the rat himself, rooting her on.

"Now, reverse it," said Farley. "Make it go left to right."

Jackie turned her attention back to the odd couple and tried to figure out what they were reversing.

Whatever "it" was, it didn't show. Farley's hands stayed in exactly the same position, and he and Mrs. Hunter both remained perfectly still for several long moments.

Then Farley released his grip and straightened up. Mrs. Hunter's eyes fluttered open.

Jackie stepped forward slightly, a cheery good morning on the tip of her tongue.

"We're not quite done," said Farley without looking at her. He gently passed a hand before Mrs. Hunter's eyes to close them. "Shhh."

He shrugged his shoulders as though loosening them, then shifted around to the side of the lounger, this time placing one palm on the back of Mrs. Hunter's head and the other flat on her forehead. His forearms flexed slightly as he pressed on her skull, and his eyes drifted shut with concentration.

Jackie wasn't sure whether Farley had actually seen her or not, but she wasn't about to interrupt. So she watched, her toe tapping slightly to the rhythm of the music in the near distance.

"Now, do the same thing again," murmured Farley. "Picture the energy running from one palm to the other. "From the back of your head to the front. Do you feel it?"

"Mmm-hmm," said Mrs. Hunter.

"That's good. Keep it moving just like before. A big, smooth circle of energy."

Energy circles? As Jackie contemplated this new snippet of information, she spotted Hunter headed in their direction. He was tossing a brown prescription bottle up in the air and catching it.

"Here you go, Mom. You must've—" He stopped dead. "Mr. Phelps?"

Frowning slightly, Farley opened his eyes just long enough to make a silent appeal to Jackie.

So, he had been aware of her. And he wanted her to help out with Reade. Lovely. She should have minded her own business and just kept walking. She lifted a finger to her lips. "Shhh."

Hunter's expression darkened as he noticed who was shushing him. "What are you doing here?"

Jackie shook her head and touched her finger to her lips again. Reade glanced from her to his mother and back, then strode over, took Jackie by the elbow, and propelled her off to the side a dozen yards.

"What the hell is going on?" he demanded. "And what do you have to do with it?"

"Turn loose of me," she said, and waited until he did before she answered. "Mr. Phelps wants quiet, and I think we should oblige, that's all. They'll be done in a minute or two. I think."

"Done with what?" Reade stared back at the odd pair in the shadows.

"You don't know?"

"No. Why should I?"

"She *is* your mother."

Reade's lips thinned, and he gave Jackie a raking once-over that made her bristle. "Is that the only dress you own?"

"Why?" she asked. "Want to borrow it?"

"No. I was just trying to decide whether you under-packed or just hadn't made it back to your room last night."

Slimeball. She'd be damned if she was going to give him the pleasure of making her blush or explain. The same demon that had possessed her last evening made her draw a deep, bosom-heaving sigh.

"I can understand why you might be concerned," she said as his mouth fell open. She hoped he swallowed a fly. She gestured toward his mom and Farley. "It looks like they're done."

She turned and walked away, leaving him to recover and hustle after her.

"It's gone," exclaimed Mrs. Hunter as they approached. "My headache is completely gone, Reade. I can't believe it."

"You were getting rid of her headache?" asked Reade, looking to Farley.

Farley nodded. "Yep."

"By squeezing her head?" asked Jackie.

"I wasn't squeezing," said Farley. "Just pressing lightly. But what I was really doing was adjusting her energy flows. Or, rather, she was adjusting them. I was merely providing a conduit."

"Right," said Reade, in a tone that clearly said "Bull." Jackie was inclined to agree.

"I know, darling," said his mother. "I didn't think it would work, either, but this gentleman said it wouldn't matter whether I believed it or not. And it didn't. My headache is completely gone." She looked up at her bene-factor.

"You know, Farley—you did say your name is Farley, didn't you? My head was pounding so hard, I'm not sure I heard right."

"It's Farley," he affirmed. "Farley Phelps."

"And I'm Lenore, if I didn't say. Well, anyway, my son Reade, here, is a medical researcher, and I happen to know he's interested in pain control, among other things. He would probably love to hear about your technique."

No doubt. Jackie smiled brightly at Mr. Phelps and spoke up. "I want to apologize for interrupting you a few minutes ago. I just happened to spot you as I was on my way to my room, and wanted to say good morning. And to thank you for keeping me company last evening. I do hate eating alone."

"It was my pleasure."

"Phelps," said Lenore Hunter, talking to herself. "Farley Phelps. Now why does that name seem so familiar?"

Reade shifted uncomfortably and cleared his throat. "He's the head of the Phelps Foundation, Mom. The grant I was telling you about."

"Oh." Her eyes widened. "Oh. Well, no wonder my son was staring at you all through dinner last night."

Jackie swallowed back a snicker as Reade went scarlet to match the macaws printed on his shirt. Either his mom was the worst shill in the world or she really didn't know what her son was up to.

He cleared his throat. "Well, Mom, now that your head-ache's gone. . . ."

Lenore ignored him in favor of Jackie. "And you must be from the foundation, too."

"No, ma'am." Jackie shifted her bag to her left hand and put her right hand out. "Jacqueline Barnett. University of Minnesota."

"Dr. Barnett is a finalist for the same research grant as your son," said Farley as Lenore shook Jackie's hand. "We bumped into each other last evening, then discovered Dr. Hunter later."

"I can't believe he didn't mention this to me," said Lenore. "That's the disadvantage of being a mother. We're the last to know anything about our own children."

Reade rubbed his forehead, as though his mother's headache had migrated his way.

"Listen," said Mrs. Hunter, blithely ignoring her son's distress. "Since we're all here and the three of you have common interests, why don't you two join Reade and me for lunch?"

"Mom," Hunter said sharply. Lenore looked up at him and he shook his head slightly.

"I'd love to," said Farley. "But I already have plans."

"Me, too, I'm afraid," said Jackie, relieved that Mr. Phelps had given her an out. The last thing she wanted to do was ruin a perfectly good meal by eating it with Reade Hunter.

"What a shame," said Reade. "Nice seeing you again, Barnett. We'll touch base later, Mr. Phelps. I really would like to hear about that headache technique of yours. I'm investigating natural pain relief, and you never know where a piece of the puzzle might turn up."

He scooped up his mother's gear and held out his hand. "Come on, Mom. Let's grab something to eat and get changed for this afternoon. You don't want to miss the van."

"I asked Reade to sign us up for the trip to Mystery

Falls," explained Lenore. "Would you like to come along?"

"Mom, I'm sure Mr. Phelps has—"

"I'd love to," said Farley. "It's been years since I climbed the falls."

"Oh, good. What about you, dear?" she asked Jackie.

"She's busy," said Reade quickly. "She just told me she's booked for a facial or a massage or something this afternoon. Didn't you?"

His look challenged her to call him a liar in front of Farley. She couldn't, of course—not without looking like a bitch. Anyway, she'd had her shot at Farley, and it was Hunter's turn. She'd give 15-to-1 odds that Phelps wouldn't let him talk business, either.

"I'm afraid so," said Jackie. "In fact, I need to go drop these things off in my room and grab a quick sandwich before my appointment. You all have a good time."

As she left, they began discussing times and organizing the afternoon. Jackie was feeling all magnanimous and patting herself on the back for grace under fire when she glanced over her shoulder and caught Reade looking her way, smirking like he'd gotten away with something. Any inclination to give him a break vanished like a drop of water on hot concrete.

That jerk. She'd be damned if she was going to let Reade Hunter spend the afternoon cutting her legs out from under her with Phelps. She flagged down a passing bellman.

"Yes, ma'am?"

"Could you tell me where the activity desk is, please? I just got the urge to visit Mystery Falls."

four

Climbers should be sure to use plenty of waterproof sunscreen. Insect repellant is also suggested, especially in the late afternoon, when bugs tend to swarm.

Bugs?

Jackie's enthusiasm faded rapidly as she skimmed the brochure they had handed her at the activities desk when she'd signed up. She didn't recall that warning in her guidebook—but at the time she hadn't been planning to climb Mystery Falls, so maybe she'd just missed it. The pictures in the brochure revealed that this was not nice, civilized Niagara they were talking about, but a steep, wild river plunging several hundred feet through the jungle. Jungle with bugs. Probably spiders.

Something brushed her shoulder, and she shrieked and slapped at it before she realized it was just a vine trailing from one of the hanging baskets that lined the promenade. Everyone within hearing turned and stared at her like she was some sort of nutcase. She blushed and buried her nose in the brochure.

Maybe crashing Hunter's excursion wasn't such a good idea after all. Her image as a serious, responsible scientist would be shot if Phelps saw her hyperventilating over a spider. Especially if she happened to be in a wet swimsuit at the time. Shades of Raquel Welch.

She'd been stupid, letting Hunter get to her, and she'd reacted without thinking things through. Well, it wasn't too late. She could revert to her original plan and enjoy a pleasant afternoon on the beach by herself. There would be plenty of time in the next twelve days to buttonhole Mr. Phelps again and undo whatever damage Hunter did to her position.

Relieved, she turned around and headed back to the lobby to cancel her reservation. She'd just turned the corner off the promenade when she spotted Farley at the activities desk. She ducked out of sight behind a pillar.

Okay, so rich people had to sign up, too. She waited for him to finish, but when she peeked out a couple of minutes later, he was still hanging around, laughing with one of the staff.

"May I get something for you, miss?"

Jackie whirled to find a bellman wearing a helpful expression. "No, thanks. I'm waiting . . . for a friend."

He glanced toward Farley. "Yes, miss. Let us know if we can do anything at all for you."

"I will, thank you."

He left, and Jackie frowned. All she'd need would be for Farley to hear she was spying on him from behind pillars. She'd better come back a little later, when he was gone. In the meantime, she could go back to her room, pour herself into her new suit, and oil up.

That was exactly what she did, after which she spent a few minutes walking back and forth in front of the bathroom mirror, working up the courage to wear the thing out the door. Then, just to make sure Farley had plenty of time to clear the lobby, she decided to take a few minutes to check her E-mail.

She had preconfigured her laptop with the right phone

numbers before she left home and it was all charged up, so all she had to do was plug it into the phone jack and turn it on. A few clicks, and the miracle of modern electronics delivered and sorted 132 messages in under a minute, even in St. Sebastian.

Most of her mail, as usual, consisted of newsgroups and intercampus memos. She was really only interested in the personal messages, and of those, the one with Walt's address and an attachment labeled "inspiration.txt" grabbed her attention first. She pulled it up.

"Jacks. Figure you're getting cold feet by now," read the message, dated late the previous day. "Here's a reminder why you can't. Be bold. We're all depending on you. Walt."

She opened the attachment. Page 1 was the abstract of her grant proposal. Page 2 was an abridged version of next year's lab budget, complete with projected shortfalls and personnel cuts. Page 3 read simply, *$1,000,000.*

"Gee, thanks, Walt." No pressure there.

She slumped back on the bed.

One million dollars. The amount of the Phelps grant.

A million dollars would fund her projects for five years—seven, if she squeezed the numbers hard enough. It would keep several lab assistants employed. It would give her the freedom to pursue the new antiviral that just might be lurking in those samples from Guyana. Properly stewarded, it could let her discover something that would save lives.

She deserved that grant. She'd worked damned hard to earn the right to it.

Walt was absolutely correct. She couldn't get cold feet. There was no telling what dirty tricks Hunter would pull if she let him have time alone with Mr. Phelps. It might be Northwestern all over again.

Bugs or not, she had to climb Mystery Falls this afternoon. And then she had to do whatever it took to make sure Hunter was never alone with Farley. For twelve whole days.

She started to shut down her computer, then changed her mind and typed out a quick message:

"Walt. I hate you. Jackie."

"Canceled, my ass," muttered Reade to the back of Barnett's blonde head.

She didn't even bother to look over her shoulder. "You should know."

Of course he knew. She'd called his bluff, and now he had to live with it.

But at least she hadn't labeled him an outright liar. He'd been pretty sure he was sunk when she'd gotten on the bus and plunked her round butt down on the last empty seat, right in front of Mom and Farley. Instead of exposing him, though, she'd mumbled some story about the masseuse canceling because of a family emergency and then set about methodically insinuating herself into the middle of their outing. Unfortunately, Reade had been stuck a couple of rows back and hadn't been able to do much more than glare at her over Farley's shoulder. That's what he got for choosing a seat next to that redhead—and he hadn't even had a chance to chat her up, another thing for which he could thank Barnett.

Now they were off the bus and milling around the jumble of souvenir and snack stands that stood at the foot of the falls, and the redhead had given up on him and was gunning for some buff boy in surfer baggies. His romantic prospects vanishing, Reade trailed around after Barnett, making sure she didn't latch on to Farley and watching her fend off the hawkers who worked the crowd with their trays of cheap sunglasses and bags of peanuts.

She got more than her fair share of attention, too, especially after she stopped at the bank of lockers and stripped off her shorts and T-shirt to reveal an orangey-pink swimsuit. It had a lot more fabric than most of the suits he'd seen since he'd gotten to St. Sebastian, but it had a lot more acreage to cover, too—and it appeared to be stretched to its theoretical limits. At least it made her easy to keep track of in the crowd.

"All right, all right, you Fair Winds people. Gather 'round." The bus driver clapped his hands, calling together the resort group. He indicated a tall, skinny black man in a damp Peter Tosh T-shirt and a beat-up, white sailor hat. "This is your guide, Willy G. He'll be takin' you up. He knows the safe way to do it, so you nice people listen to him and enjoy yourselves. I'll be back for you at four o'clock. Meet me right where I left you off."

He waved and disappeared toward the parking area, and Willy G. stepped forward.

"Welcome to Mystery Falls, four hundred eighty-three feet of the most glorious water on any island, anywhere. I'll be telling you about the falls as we go, but before we start out, I want to talk to you about the route we're taking. I assume you know you signed up to get wet today?" Everyone nodded and murmured yes, and Willy G. grinned. "Good. No surprises, then. It's not a difficult climb, but we do cross the river itself several times, and we have to do some scramblin' in places. The rocks can be slippery, so unless you fancy spending part of your vacation in one of our fine local hospitals, you'll want to pay careful attention."

The Fair Winds group moved in closer, the better to hear Willy G.'s spiel. Reade noted with amusement that Barnett squeezed in right up front, where she watched raptly. Of course. It was about rules and procedures. Her forte.

Plus being up front made it impossible for Farley—or anyone else, for that matter—to miss that swimsuit. Most of the other women had T-shirts or cover-ups over their suits to keep the sun off. Some of them even wore their shorts. But not Barnett.

Christ, she has long legs. Reade didn't even realize he was staring at her until Farley, at the far side of the group, caught his eye and gave him a wink. He shook himself out of it and, keeping half an ear to the lecture, drifted off to take a look upriver.

The falls angled back and curved off into the jungle, so he couldn't see the top, but what he could see was pretty impressive. The river tumbled down terrace after terrace of buttery limestone, splitting into a multitude of stair-step falls that practically begged to be climbed. Plenty of people were willing to answer the call, too, wading through the streams and pools and standing under splashing rivulets for impromptu showers. A few folks climbed alone, but at every level as far as he could see, lines of tourists in swimsuits and bright vacation garb held hands and zigzagged back and forth across the stream like garlands on a Christmas tree. On either side, the lush jungle rushed right up to the banks and spilled into the riverbed in random tendrils of green.

As Willy G. reiterated his warning about the power of the water and the slipperiness of the rocks, Reade watched a pair of frat-boy types with an excess of bravado and a shortage of brainpower go bounding up the rocks. Suddenly one kid's feet went sideways and he took a major header, landing with an *oomph* and a splash that made everyone look up.

"There's some fool makin' my point for me," said Willy G. as the kid scrambled to his feet and tried to pretend he was still cool while he felt his ass for damage. "It's slippery, people, but I've never lost a customer yet, and I don't intend to ruin my record today. Now, are we ready to go? Everybody line up and hold hands."

Damn it. Reade moved quickly, but not quickly enough to keep Barnett from latching on to Farley's left hand. At least Mom got his right. Reade debated for a fraction of a second, then elected to step in next to Barnett, cutting out a guy with a GI burr who had been leering at the skin exposed by her swimsuit. For a minute, he thought the GI was going to argue, but the guy looked at the firm way Reade took Jackie's hand and shrugged.

"Sorry, man." He moved off.

Jackie shot Reade a drop-dead look and turned her attention to Farley as the motley group moved off, following Willy G. into the water.

"So, Dr. Barnett." Reade tugged on her hand until she gave in and looked back at him. "You never had a chance to tell me last night. What brings you to St. Sebastian?"

Her eyes narrowed. "The same thing as you, Dr. Hunter. Vacation."

He raised one eyebrow.

She raised one back.

"Are you two still on that 'Doctor' crap?" demanded Phelps from the far side of Barnett. "We're all going up a waterfall half dressed, for God's sake. Don't you think we should be on a first-name basis?"

"You're absolutely right," said Barnett. "You don't mind, do you, Reade?"

She made his name sound thin and nasty, like a plant that grew in a swamp, but he plastered a phony smile on his face for Farley's benefit. "Of course not . . . Jackie."

They started up the first short climb, and after a minute or two, he realized how easy it really was to keep right on smiling.

All he had to do was imagine strangling her.

One million dollars.

Jackie recited that number over and over as she slogged her way up the falls. The footing was every bit as treacherous as Willy G. had said it would be. Centuries of flowing water had rounded and polished the riverbed into layers of smooth stone pillows with no flat edges. The current pounded their feet at every step. Add a bit of algae and a slippery dead leaf here and there, and you had a slide an otter would love.

By the one-third mark, Jackie fervently wished she hadn't yanked Hunter's chain quite so hard. If she fell, it'd be nice to think he might actually catch her instead of giving her a helpful shove. Farley would try to save her, of course, but she didn't think he'd be able to hold her. He was just too scrawny. Not like Hunter.

Or, rather, not like *Reade*, she corrected herself. Had to keep good old Farley happy.

Whatever you called him, he was a good half a head taller than she was, which made him about six feet, two inches of nice solid muscle that could probably keep even an economy-size model like herself from falling over a cliff. She sneaked a peak at the strip of chest and belly showing in the gap of his unbuttoned luau shirt. The ripples of a good six-pack were evident, even if he wasn't bodybuilder buff. He had a fair amount of chest hair, not unexpected, considering how dark he was. She wondered if he was hiding hairy shoulders under that shirt. She didn't like hairy shoulders.

Not that it mattered. She was analyzing his potential as an anchor, not as a mate. But she had to admit he was a pretty nice specimen—for a lab rat. He was even good-looking, in an Eastern European kind of way, with black hair, a largish nose, and strong bone structure that made his dark brown eyes recede into caverns. It was a hunter's face, all right, and it didn't come from Lenore. She wondered what the family name had been before the clerks at Ellis Island had decided Hunter was easier to spell.

Their conga line started up another level, and she turned her attention back to keeping her feet under her.

They were knee-deep in the middle of a fast-flowing channel when Lenore bobbled a little. Farley dropped Jackie's hand and grabbed for her, leaving Jackie clinging to Reade as her only support against the knee-buckling current. If ever there was a time for him to knock her out of contention, no questions asked, this was it. Fortunately, however, he seemed more concerned about his mother than about doing in his competition.

"Mom? You okay?" he called.

"She's fine," said Farley. "I've got her. Come on. Let's get out of the water for a minute."

The whole line paused while Farley helped Lenore over

to the edge, where she sat down on the first available rock.

"I just need to rest a little," she said as Reade and Jackie waded over to join them. "I seem to be running out of juice for some reason."

"Maybe your blood sugar is low," said Jackie helpfully. "You probably need something to eat. Reade should take you back down."

"I have a better idea," said Farley. "I'll help your mom back down while you and Jackie go on up."

"Oh, that's okay," said Reade and Jackie simultaneously.

"I insist," said Farley.

"Is there a problem?" asked Willy G., who had picked his way back down the line to join them.

Reade summarized the situation and added, with a frown in Jackie's direction, "I guess they'll be heading down."

"Are you sure you don't mind?" asked Lenore.

"No, no, no. Of course not," said Farley. "I've been up the falls a half-dozen times, and these two haven't. It's a beautiful climb, and you and I will find a bench someplace and have a cold drink while we wait for them."

"Really, Mom, I don't—"

"Go on," she said. "Farley's absolutely right. I'll be fine, so long as I have an arm to lean on. You two have a good time, and Farley and I can get to know each other."

Jackie frowned. Had Reade put his mother up to this whole blood sugar thing? And here she'd played right into it.

"Come to think of it, I could stand a cold drink, too," she said.

"We'll have one waiting when you get back," said Farley.

How was she supposed to argue with the man with the checkbook? "I can last until then, I guess. Thanks."

"All right," said Willy G. "You two are coming, and you two are going back. It's all fine with me, so long as I know how many I should have at each end. There's a trail down right over there." He pointed out the route to Farley, who assured him that he knew it well. "Then let's start again, people. We're clogging up the river."

As Willy G. worked his way back up to the head of the daisy chain, a round-faced little man with a Southern accent held out his hand to Jackie. "You coming, sweet cheeks?"

Jackie had the uncomfortable feeling that "sweet cheeks" referred to the part of her anatomy hanging out the lower edge of her new swimsuit. She should have kept her T-shirt on. She'd considered it, but the way her luck had been running, her laundry wouldn't get back before Friday. She had to preserve what few pieces of clothing she actually had in her possession.

She took the guy's hand anyway, then held out the other to Reade. "Shall we?"

Reade hesitated, but Farley waved him on. "Have a good time. We'll see you down below."

"Be careful," said Lenore.

Reade grunted and took Jackie's hand just as she stepped back into the river.

Ignoring each other, at least as well as two people holding hands could ignore each other, they snaked their way up the falls with the others. The water was warm, but still cool and fresh compared to the air. Jackie could quite happily have sunk down into one of the pools and sat there, soaking, until the line came back down again.

A Southern accent interrupted her fantasy. "So, sweet cheeks, where're y'all from?"

"The name's Jackie," she said distinctly. "I'm from Minneapolis. How about you?"

"Atlanta. Have you ever been down our way?"

"Once. For a conference," she said.

"What line are you in?"

"Test tube juggling," Reade chimed in from behind her. "We do a lounge act in Vegas."

The man from Atlanta looked confused.

"I have to apologize for Dr. Hunter," said Jackie. "He

frequently gets carried away by his own perceived brilliance. We're research pharmacologists. At different institutions."

"Oh." His expression cleared. "So, are y'all here together discovering some new drug or something?"

"We're not together," said Jackie.

"Dr. Barnett came down to do some, uh, *hands-on* fund-raising," said Reade. "I'm just here to relax."

Okay, if he wanted to play nasty, she could, too. She hadn't grown up with all those snotty cheerleader cousins of hers without learning something about being a bitch.

"He came with his mother," she chirped in her most earnest voice. "They're very close. He's such a *sweet* man."

"Oh. *Oh.*" Atlanta's eyebrows went up and back down, as though they were jumping to a conclusion. His words confirmed the leap. "My cousin's real close to his mama, too. He lives up there in New York City. Greenwich Village."

"Ah," said Jackie, as though that explained everything.

If Reade squeezed her hand any harder, she was going to need medical attention, but she didn't let a little pain affect her enjoyment of the moment. She'd never realized climbing a waterfall could be so much fun.

"Let's stop here a minute," said Lenore, sinking onto a bench by the side of the trail. "My knees are still wobbly. It's a good thing we headed down instead of going on up. I obviously wouldn't have made it."

"Hold out your hand." Farley dropped down next to her. He rubbed his hands together briskly, then took her wrist as though checking her pulse. He closed his eyes. "Just lean back and relax for a minute."

Oh, my. That wasn't hard to do. The warmth of his hand radiated into her wrist and right up her arm in the most delightful way. Even the contrast of his tanned skin against her winter-pale arm gave her a lift. It looked so masculine.

When she realized what tangent her thoughts were taking, she laughed aloud. It had clearly been way too long since a man other than a son or a doctor had touched her.

"What?" asked Farley.

"Oh, nothing," she said. "I'm a little giddy, that's all. Just what is it I'm supposed to be doing?"

"Nothing." He gave her wrist a pat, then stood up and reached into his pocket, from which he pulled a zipped sandwich bag half full of pale yellow chunks. He shook off a few drops of water that clung to the plastic. "Here. Try some of this. It's dried pineapple."

Lenore stared. "You carry dried pineapple in your swimsuit?"

"I carry dried fruit almost everywhere. Never know when I might get hungry." He opened the bag and held it out. "Weird habit, huh? It's a carryover from my hitchhiking days. Have some."

Lenore helped herself. The pineapple was chewy and sweet, and she felt the boost almost immediately. "I wish you'd given me this earlier. We probably could have gone on up the falls."

"Possibly." He stood up and held out his hand. "But then I wouldn't get to talk to you without twenty other people kibitzing."

"Oh." Suddenly feeling like a young girl, she took his hand and they headed down the path.

At the bottom, Farley found her a spot on one of the blue wooden benches that were scattered among the trees at the edge of the beach, then sauntered off to retrieve the contents of their lockers. He came back strung with clothes and cameras, and carrying two bottles of something pale yellow.

"There you are, madam." He sat, and handed one icy-cold bottle to Lenore.

She looked at the bottle. "Ting. I've heard of this."

"It's from Jamaica. It's my all-time favorite soft drink. Go ahead. Try it."

She took a tentative sip and swirled it in her mouth.

"What's the verdict?" he asked.

"Delicious," she said. "Mostly grapefruity, but more exotic."

Farley nodded. He took a long draw from his own bottle, then wiped the corner of his mouth with the back of his hand. "So, are you mad at me for not letting you go up the falls?"

"Not especially. To be honest, it was getting a little nerve-racking. The water was faster than I expected, and I'm not what you'd call athletic anymore."

He gave her an assessing once-over. "You look like you're in pretty good shape to me."

Lenore looked away, slightly embarrassed. "Well, thank you, but you can't judge a book by its cover. Anyway, I saw enough to keep me happy, so, no, I'm not angry with you. Besides, it's not like I've never splashed around in a tropical waterfall before."

"Oh, yeah? Where?"

"Hawaii. Costa Rica. Bali. Among other places."

"Really? You don't strike me as the world traveler type."

"Well I am," she said defensively. "Or at least I was when my husband was alive. We went all over the world with the boys—Reade's the oldest of three, you know. My husband was a geologist, and if his company didn't send us somewhere, we found another excuse to go. I've visited thirty-four countries, and lived in five."

"Have you really?" Farley looked at her with new respect in his eyes. "What's your favorite?"

"Sri Lanka," she said without hesitation, and when Farley mentioned his own experiences there, the conversation took off.

When the bench grew too hard, they got up and wandered around the foot of the falls, still talking. Lenore used her new digital camera to snap a few photos. She even managed to get a close-up of Farley when he wasn't paying attention.

"You'll break your camera doing that," he warned as she checked the shot.

"I will not. You're actually very photogenic. See?" She held the camera out. He stepped in much closer than necessary to look.

"It's only because I have a hat on," he said. "Otherwise the reflection off the top of my head would burn out the lens."

Lenore laughed. "I happen to like bald men. Much better than all that." She pointed at a man in the near background of the photo who wore a scraggly, salt and pepper beard and long, thick dreadlocks that stretched well past mid-shoulder. He was squinting against the sun, which gave him a slightly feral look. "How odd. He seems to be looking straight at you."

"Just a trick of the camera," said Farley. He strolled off.

She followed him, still looking at the view screen. "You know, I think I noticed the same man watching us when we first sat down. Over there."

"Probably just someone who looks like him. There's no shortage of long hair around here. Even on us bald guys." He grabbed his own straggly ponytail and waggled it.

Lenore laughed. "It's hardly the same." She switched the camera off and slipped it back in its case. "You're probably right, though. Although I think you should keep track of your wallet, just in case he's a pickpocket sizing you up. They're in every crowd in every country."

"No kidding. Know where I got ripped off last year? Chicago. Right in the doorway of the downtown Sheraton." He reached out to take her hand. "Come on. Let's walk on down the beach a little ways. You can tell me all about your son. Er, sons."

*   *   *

"Wow," said Jackie as she scrambled up onto the last terrace. They had reached the mystery of Mystery Falls.

The pictures hadn't done it justice. An entire river's worth of water thundered out of a narrow slash in the hillside a few yards above them, appearing to arise from the earth itself. Because of the terraces and the low angle of the hill, they hadn't been able to see the source from below, and the surprise of it gushing out of the ferns and vines that crowded the opening made the sight that much more impressive.

"Wow," she repeated to no one in particular. She started getting her camera out.

"I'll second that," said Reade, coming up behind her. "That's a heck of a lot of water for a spring."

"It's not a spring," said Jackie. "It's an underground river, which you would know if you had read the brochure they handed out when you signed up."

"I'm not a big brochure person."

"Why doesn't that surprise me?" she muttered, earning herself a nasty glare.

"The young lady is right," said Willy G., stepping in between them. "The falls are indeed the place where the Howell River reemerges after disappearing into the ground about six miles thataway." He pointed inland. "Since the river is heading east when it goes under, and since the falls are west of that point, no one put the two together until some children up in Twelve Mile dumped their mama's dye pot into the river and the falls turned purple. But you folks are missin' the real treasure. Turn around. Turn around and see the most spectacular view on the island."

Everyone turned around and oohed, but rather than shuffle en masse to the edge with the others, Jackie decided to grab the chance to get a few pictures without a herd of people in them. By the time she got a good shot framed, however, another chain of tourists had piled onto the terrace and crowded in to admire the cascade. She

sidled to her left a little, trying to get another clear shot.
A heavyset man who really should have been wearing a
shirt stepped into the frame. She shifted again.

Reade wandered over. "You're passing up the best view
on the island to take pictures of tourists' backsides?"

"Buzz off, Hunter."

He was quiet for a moment while she stepped away
from him and lined up another shot. "Do you ever find
that trying to photograph everything gets in the way of
actually enjoying the experience?"

"No." Keeping her eye to the viewfinder, she stepped
left another foot or two. "I can only think of one thing
that might do that right now."

"Falling off a cliff?"

"Why? Are you planning to push me?"

"No. But you might want to check your footing."

"What are you—" She glanced down to her left, and
the world spun away. A wave of dizziness knocked her
knees out from under her. She started to buckle.

"Whoa!" Strong arms grabbed her and pulled her back,
gathering her against something sturdy and solid and safe.

The disorientation passed as quickly as it had come,
and her wits returned. It turned out the something sturdy
was Reade. Specifically, Reade's chest. And with his shirt
flapping open, there was nothing between her and him
except the insubstantial fabric of her damp swimsuit.

Face flaming, she pushed away, but her legs weren't
quite working right yet and he had to steady her.

"Give yourself a minute," he suggested. He shifted
slightly to slide one arm around her waist, then snugged
her close to his side. "I'm not going anywhere."

"Um, thanks."

"Not a problem. Look, I'm sorry. I should have handled
that differently, but I figured you were still far enough
from the edge to be safe. I didn't realize you had a problem with heights."

"I don't. I just happened to look down at the wrong
angle, and there was nothing there. It caught me off guard,

that's all. Plus I've had a little more sun than I'm used to."

He nodded. "That'll do it. You know, you really are missing the best view hanging around back here. If you want, you can lean on me for a few more minutes."

She checked to see if he was smirking, but he wasn't. She nodded. "That might be a good idea. Thanks."

They eased out toward the edge of the terrace, slipping into a gap between the fellow from Atlanta and a newlywed couple from England. Jackie made a point of looking out, not down, and with Reade's arm around her, she had no problem at all.

The view truly was spectacular. The river had carved a wedge in the trees that revealed the northwest end of the island. Along its margin, white sand beaches created a dashed line that separated land from sea, while in the interior, resorts, villages, and cultivated fields imposed their hard edges and paler greens onto the dark swirls of the natural growth. A multitude of boats crowded the water, skimming between the reefs of the nearer shore and clustering around a perfect circle of deepest indigo in the distance.

Jackie pointed at the blue hole. "That must be Jonah's Bathtub. I read about it in one of the guidebooks."

"I wouldn't know," said Reade. He looked at her. "Do you dive?"

"I've snorkeled a little. . . . What?"

He had the oddest look on his face. And his face was getting closer.

He kissed her. No prelude, no sweet nothings whispered in her ear, just a kiss. A long, sweet, expert kiss that first startled her and then seduced her into closing her eyes and kissing him back, even as one corner of her mind clicked over the possible reasons why he was doing this and, more important, why she was participating.

Curiosity, she decided. Nothing wrong with that. Know the enemy and all. Instinct made her lift against him, and she felt his body tense as he deepened the kiss. Very, very nice, lab rat or not. She might as well relax and enjoy.

When they finally pulled apart, she opened her eyes to see half the tour group wearing sappy smiles and pretending they hadn't been watching. Flustered to realize she'd forgotten about all those people, she stepped away from Hunter and nervously smoothed her hair.

"That was. . . ." Her voice came out a little husky, and she cleared her throat. "Interesting."

"Very," he agreed, with a little half-smile that sent a ripple of pleasure running down her spine. However, her brain hadn't stopped working just because she'd been kissed by a pro.

"I just have one question. Why?"

"Because you're beautiful. Because your eyes are the color of the sea at dawn. And because. . . ." The corners of his eyes crinkled in amusement, and he leaned over and put his mouth next to her ear. "Because now you and your friend from Atlanta both know I'm not gay."

five

Reade braced himself for the explosion.

"Thank you," she said.

"Huh?" He blinked, confused. She didn't appear to be all that mad, a fact which raised the hairs on the back of his neck. "You're welcome?"

"I'm serious. Thank you. For a couple of minutes there I thought I'd been wrong all these years, but you have set my mind at ease. You really are a horse's behind."

She turned around and marched off toward Willy G., various bits of her bobbling in an unrestrained way that contradicted her stiff posture. Several of their fellow travelers looked from Reade to her and back again, questioning. He shrugged, as mystified as they were.

"All right, people. Time to head down." Willy G. gathered his troops together and explained that they would be using the trail that switchbacked through the trees beside the river, instead of trying to maneuver back down the falls. Barnett found herself a different place in line, in between two couples right behind Willy G. The wives didn't appear to be too happy about the new arrangement, but from Reade's viewpoint it was just dandy. He clearly needed to get some distance, even if it was only the length of the Fair Winds tour line.

He hadn't intended to kiss her. In fact, it had been the furthest thing from his mind. But he'd had to grab her, and then she'd been so warm and soft against his side. Curvy. Womanly. Tempting. It had been strictly a spur-of-the-moment thing, pure male reaction to a very female presence.

And boy, had he reacted. Ahead of him, that hot coral swimsuit of hers stood out like a beacon against the jungle backdrop. He couldn't keep his eyes off it. Off her.

Whoa. This was Barnett the Bulldozer he was dealing with here. His professional rival. His chief competition for the Phelps. He couldn't afford to let her get to him this way, and even more important, he couldn't let her realize she'd gotten to him, or she'd take advantage of that to do Lord knows what. Thank God his brain had reengaged and presented them both with that "now you know I'm not gay" excuse.

He slowed, dropping back until Barnett was out of sight and he could clear his head.

Okay, so his body had momentarily mistaken her for an ordinary human female. He could ensure that didn't happen again simply by staying well away from her—primarily by seeing that she didn't keep tagging along where she wasn't wanted. That shouldn't be too hard. He'd spent years ditching two troublesome younger brothers; surely he could handle one lady scientist.

All he really wanted was two or three hours of solo face time with Phelps to tell him about the idea he'd had since he'd mailed off the grant application . . . and to make it crystal clear why he was the best candidate. He could run with the money and the state-of-the-art equipment it could buy, making leaps forward instead of plodding along in old lady shoes like Barnett, who would probably use it to fund more research assistants. She might get more data out of the money, but he'd get more real progress.

When he reached the bottom, he found his mother and Farley sitting under a tree. To his surprise, Barnett was nowhere in sight. Maybe he'd made her so mad she'd just go away on her own. That thought lightened his step a bit.

Farley waved him over. "We thought you must have gotten lost. Jackie showed up five minutes ago."

"I picked up a rock in my shoe," he fibbed.

"Well, she's getting her clothes. She'll be right back."

"Oh." So much for that theory.

"How was the climb?" his mother asked.

"Terrific. Too bad you two couldn't make it."

"Oh, we had a nice time. We walked down the beach a little way and found a reef that was just full of fish. One of the little monsters bit me." She held up a bandaged finger, but she was smiling.

And so was Farley. Maybe *this* was going right, at least.

"I think I'll pick up something to drink before we get on the bus," said Reade. "Can I get anything for you?"

"Not me," said his mother.

"Nothing here, either, thanks," said Farley. "But I forgot I promised Jackie a soda. Could you grab a bottle for her, too?"

"Sure." Reade caught the one-pound coin Farley flipped at him and tossed it back. "It's okay. I'll spring for it. What do you think she'll want?" *Arsenic? Cyanide, maybe?*

"I bet she'd like one of those Tings," said his mother.

"What kind of thing?" asked Reade.

Farley and his mom laughed.

"Ting," she said more clearly. "It's a brand of soda. Don't take too long, dear. It's almost four, and we don't want to miss the bus. Farley's going take us out for dinner."

"He is?"

"There's this little shack on the beach at Halfway," said

Farley. "Looks like a dive, but Mary Ann serves jerk pork that will make you weep."

"Sounds great. I, uh, suppose Jackie's going with us."

"Hadn't invited her yet, but since you mention it . . . ," said Farley. "However, there will be no business talk. I don't want to hear one word about laboratories or experimental protocols. She chewed my ear off last night, and I came down here to get away from all that."

Perfect. Just perfect. Reade dug deep for a smile. "No argument here. I'll be right back."

It was enough to make a grown man cry.

It turned out that Mary Ann's was, indeed, a shack on the beach, little more than a wide tin roof over a concrete block grill that saturated the air with the seductive aroma of pimento wood smoke and roasting pork. Makeshift tables and benches sat nearby on the sand, shaded by an odd assortment of old, faded café umbrellas. Entertainment was supplied by a huge boombox that pounded out a mix of Caribbean sounds and Beatles tunes, to which Mary Ann—who was nearly as large as the shack—sang along as she basted meat and shouted at patrons and employees alike. The place was packed.

"Told you it was good," shouted Farley over the genial roar of their hostess's rendition of "Hey, Jude."

Jackie nodded and made appropriate noises as she reached for her beer. Apparently, when Farley had boasted that Mary Ann's jerk pork could make you weep, he'd meant from the heat as much as the flavor. Her recipe was a concoction of tropical juices, assorted spices, and some kind of insanely hot pepper whose sole purpose was to relieve the consumer of any trace of mucous membrane. The meat came to the table on big squares of brown paper, with a slab of chewy bread and lots of beer. Once her taste buds stopped screaming for mercy, it was fabulous.

By the end of the meal, Jackie had gone through somewhere between three and six ice-cold Carib beers—she wasn't sure exactly how many, because Reade kept shoving his empties her way—and made a commensurate number of trips across the road to the Halfway Inn, which provided facilities for Mary Ann's well-watered customers. When she returned from yet another run, Farley and Lenore had disappeared.

She stood across the table from Reade, who was nursing the last of his beer and staring out at the ocean. "Let me guess. Sunset walk along the beach?"

"Knowing my mother, it's going to be more of a medical convention. I think she's out to learn the secret of his healing hands routine." He propped both elbows on the table and looked up at her. "How many suitcases did you bring?"

She eyed him suspiciously. "Two. Why?"

"Because that dress is starting to get old. I was going to offer to help you unpack."

"I'll be happy to let you," she said. "Why don't you just fly to Cairo and get them for me?"

"Cairo?"

"Yeah. Or maybe Nairobi, by now." She started to explain about the airport codes but was interrupted by Reade's snicker. "It's not funny, Hunter."

"Yes, it is," he insisted. "At least, if it's true it is. Look at it from my side: the impeccably careful Dr. Barnett, always prepared for any contingency, falls victim to the most pedestrian pitfall in travel. Ah, the irony. . . ."

His comment was a direct shot at her analysis of his lax style, made in a letter a couple of years back, but the echoes of Ben's voice mail accusations gave it a sharper sting than it deserved.

"Being careful," she said, enunciating clearly, "is the reason *I* only have to deal with things like lost luggage instead of government investigators."

He raised his bottle. "Touché. But it's also one of the reasons the Beauregard is hanging on my wall instead of yours. Besides, I was cleared of all malfeasance. Does it ever worry you, how boring you are?"

"Look, you paramecium. . . . Oh, never mind. You're not worth the strain on my vocal cords." She turned around and stomped off—hard to manage on sand.

At the water's edge, she kicked off her sandals and took advantage of the easier footing in the damp, hard sand to get up some speed. She didn't want to go far, just get away from Hunter and the ghost of boyfriends past.

Boring. Careful. Ben had said the same thing in different words. What was so darned wrong with being careful, anyway? Everybody didn't have to live on the thin edge of disaster. Being careful kept her safe and prevented all kinds of trouble, from unnecessary wear and tear on her car to errors in her lab. Careful didn't mean boring; it simply meant careful.

Unless you were *too* careful.

Which she wasn't, she assured herself.

But the thought, once in her brain, would not be dismissed so easily. It followed her down the beach, tugging at the hem of her dress like an insistent child.

What if she *was* too careful? What if, in the process of keeping her life safe and convenient, she was going a little overboard? What if she really *was* boring?

No. That was just Ben and Reade Hunter talking. She'd let their macho baloney get through to her just because they'd happened to dish it out back to back. Like they were such shining examples, with Ben's untidy life and the controversy that swirled around Hunter's lab.

But, asked the child, *was* she boring? Was she too careful? Even Walt had felt obliged to tell her to be bold.

The beach petered out at about the same time the sun did, and, being the tropics, the light faded rapidly. Suddenly uneasy—justifiably so, she noted, seeing as she was alone, after dark, on an unfamiliar beach, in a foreign country—she turned around to head for the safety of the crowd around Mary Ann's.

There was a figure coming toward her, a man. Her heart pounded for the seconds it took her to recognize Hunter, and then she let out the breath she'd been holding and waited for him to reach her.

"Are you following me?" she asked.

"It's pitch black. You shouldn't be out here by yourself."

"What?" She feigned shock. "You mean I should be *careful*? What a concept."

"Don't push it, Barnett. It wasn't my idea to come after you."

"Well, tell your mom or Farley or whoever, thank you, but I think I'd be safer by myself. Less likely to be molested."

"Trust me," he said flatly, shoving his hands into his pockets. "No one's going to touch you."

Count on Hunter to make a reassurance of safety sound like an insult.

"Farley decided he wants dessert after all," he said. "Are you coming or not?"

She brushed a strand of hair out of her mouth.

"Yeah. I guess so," she said, and they walked up the beach toward Mary Ann's and a slice of the coconut cake that Farley had promised was the best on St. Sebastian.

Okay, so Barnett was harder to ditch than a little brother.

Reade shifted away from her as far as possible and considered just what he could do to keep the next twenty-four hours from being a repeat of the last twenty-four. Dinner at Mary Ann's had been bad enough, but since then she'd turned up at breakfast, joined them on the driving range, eaten an early lunch with them on the terrace, and was now along for a cruise up the Dominion River— the last three invitations having been extended by his mother, who now clearly considered them a couple.

It was his own fault, of course. His innocent question about whether Jackie was coming along last evening had led Mom, and probably Farley, to the conclusion that he actually wanted the woman around. That shot to his own foot was now costing him an afternoon of being trapped on a narrow bamboo raft with Barnett.

A really narrow bamboo raft, where he was, to both his pleasure and his dismay, in nearly constant contact with those long legs. Considering they were both wearing shorts, it was very close contact, indeed. Worse yet, Farley was on a separate raft with Mom, where Reade couldn't possibly talk to him about his research or anything else. Of course, since the rafts were strictly two-person affairs, that would have been true whether Barnett was along or not, but Reade couldn't help feeling that he was rapidly becoming the poster boy for life's ironic injustices.

The Dominion River was a flat, lazy stream on the eastern end of St. Sebastian. Years ago, when there had been a banana plantation upriver, the owner had thought it charming and quaint to have visitors ferried up to the main house on the bamboo rafts his workers used to haul bananas down to the waiting cargo ships. Today, tourists apparently found it just as charming and quaint to ride the rafts up to the living museum that had replaced the plantation.

Their own trip had come about when Barnett had gotten a phone call during lunch—it seemed her cockamamie story about her luggage going to Kenya was true, after all. The news from the airline wasn't good, so Farley had suggested the market at the lower end of the raft ride as a great place to fill out her wardrobe on the cheap, and suddenly they were all on yet another outing. While Reade had purchased tickets for the rafts and scoped out cold drinks for everyone, Farley had happily escorted the womenfolk from stall to stall on a hunt for bargains. Now the rafts had launched, and Reade was contemplating the universe's bizarre sense of humor.

Up ahead, he could see his mother and Farley chatting away. Reade and Barnett, on the other hand, were absolutely silent. Much as he appreciated it, he knew full well that it would have to change. Two people couldn't possibly sit cheek to cheek for ninety minutes without talking. She was already giving signs of breaking, occasionally taking in a breath as though she was about to say something, then clamping her lips together and turning away. For his part, not talking was giving him way too much time to think about her legs: long, bare, and right there next to his.

What he needed was to direct the conversation toward a topic that would knock all thoughts of lewd and lascivious behavior right out of his mind.

"I guess the shopping wasn't as good as Farley said," he began.

She glanced at him out of the corner of her eye. "What makes you think so?"

"No bags," he pointed out. "Just that hat."

"They're keeping everything for me until we get back," she said. "Except the dress. Eunice is making that."

"Who's Eunice?"

"The lady who's making my dress."

"Do you have to teach as part of your position?"

"I don't have to. I do, occasionally."

"I pity your students. They must have to pry answers out of you with the Jaws of Life. *Who* is Eunice?"

"She's a woman with a little factory back there in the trees. You pick out a style. You pick out material. She measures you and her ladies sew it, and you pick it up on the way back from the museum. There. Is that a complete answer? Are you happy now?"

"Yes."

She flicked away a leaf that had drifted down to land on her leg. "You know, Hunter, you seem overly concerned with my clothes. Are you a cross-dresser or something?"

"I thought we settled that yesterday," he said. She pinked up nicely, and he let her stew for a minute before he mused aloud, "So, no more turquoise jungle dress. Just because of the cracks I made?"

"Your comments had nothing to do with it," she said. "However, if my clothes are going to travel the world, I need more to wear than one dress, two T-shirts, and a pair of shorts."

"I didn't bring much more than that."

"Fascinating," she said. "Excuse me if I don't model myself on you, though. A man can wear the same jeans and shirt for a week, and as long as he doesn't stink, no one notices. A woman wears the same dress two days in a row, and she gets commentary from fashion mavens like you."

"I've been promoted to maven?" Reade asked. "Gee. I'll have to update my CV."

"Why don't you fly home and do that right now? I'm sure the department secretary would be happy to type it up for you."

"Can't. Nonexchangeable tickets."

"You should have bought them sixty days ago, like I did. You know, if you *are* a transvestite, I bet Eunice would be willing to make a dress for you, too."

Enough was enough. He twisted to face her, rocking the raft. "Let's get this straight once and for all. I like women. I wear Jockey shorts, not French lace. And no matter how hard you try, you're *not* going to get me to kiss you again."

"You think I. . . ." She spluttered and huffed. "Like I would want you slobbering on me again, you egotistical ba—"

A loud whack of bamboo against bamboo startled them both. They looked up to see their boatman glaring back at them from his position at the front of the raft.

"You two are about as pleasant to listen to as a pair of cats mating," he said. "Make nice, or I'll put you both out on the bank and let you walk."

"Sorry, man." Reade met Jackie's eyes. She was blushing furiously. "He has a point, you know."

She grimaced. "Unfortunately."

"We don't want to use up all the good insults in the first forty-eight hours," said Reade.

A faint smile appeared, and she shook her head. "We'd get stale. So, what do we do instead of fight?" She looked up at the boatman. "We don't have a lot of experience with this."

"Some folks actually look at the birds and the trees," he suggested.

Jackie flexed an ankle, and a buzz ran through Reade's system.

"Nope," he said. "I don't think that's going to cut it."

"I could sing for you," said the boatman.

They both shrugged.

"Maybe we should reserve that one until later," said Jackie. "In case we run out of other options."

"We could talk about our research," said Reade.

"What, so you can find out what I'm doing and leapfrog me again?" demanded Jackie. "I don't think so, Hunter. You taught me that lesson already."

"Now wait a minute. I never—"

"Ah-ah-ah-ah-ah," said the boatman.

They subsided into a thick silence. The plant-cluttered bank slid past as the boatman poled along.

After a minute or two, Reade gave it another shot. "How about if we discuss someone else's research?"

"That might be acceptable," said Jackie. She reached up and gathered her hair into a ponytail that she held away from her neck for a moment before letting it fall back. "It's so much stickier on this part of the island. Okay, whom shall we dissect?"

Reade was too busy observing the way her breasts lifted as she raised her arms and almost missed the question.

"Er, uh. Hang on a second. Let me think. I know. How about Roy Hinkley's latest paper. Have you read it yet?"

"Of course." She gave him a look that said he was dumb for even asking. She'd apparently missed his little voyeuristic side trip, or she'd be wearing a different look altogether. "I read all of my journals as soon as they come in. What did you think about his fractionation technique?"

"Much bettah," said the boatman, smiling. "I might not understand what you're sayin', but at least you're not making me head pound like a gombe drum."

They analyzed Hinkley's work all the way up, and reached the museum landing with genuine smiles on their faces instead of the forced, phony ones of the past couple of days. The only problem was that Mom took the smiles as further evidence of couplehood. Reade could tell from the way she elbowed Farley in the ribs.

Terrific. He really was going to have to clue her in on what was going on.

The full tour of the museum took a couple of hours, and the trip back down to the park was accomplished by horse-drawn omnibus, which dropped them off almost directly in front of the stall where Jackie had bought her dress. She and Mom went off to pick up their purchases, leaving Reade alone with Farley for the first time since he'd gotten to St. Sebastian. Here was his chance. He took a deep breath and turned.

"How about if you wait here for the ladies while I go get the car?" asked Farley. "They're going to need a Sherpa."

"Uh, okay. Great."

"I'll pick you up down by the gate."

Gee. Twelve whole seconds, thought Reade as he watched Farley jog off through the crowd. At this rate, it'd take his entire vacation to work in a full minute alone with the man.

By midevening, even that timetable looked optimistic. Barnett showed up at the beach barbecue in her strappy new purple sundress looking like an ad for the St. Sebastian Tourist Board, then somehow managed to choreograph seating at the long picnic tables so that she was on Farley's right, Lenore was on his left, and a pair of French businessmen and their mistresses occupied the other side of the table. Reade was stuck trying to shout at Farley over Barnett's head.

She wasn't being overtly obnoxious, she was just being *there*. Nonetheless, Reade was about ready to tie a barbecue grill to her leg and heave her into deep water when Mother Nature blessed him. She had to pee. So did his mother, so off they went, in that female ritual of powdering their noses, like noses had anything to do with it.

Alone at last. So, naturally, Farley was talking to the Frenchmen about the cellular service in Lyon.

Reade waited impatiently for a chance to interrupt. There wasn't much time. The ladies' head was just down the beach.

Farley reached across the table and shook the man's hand, then turned to Reade. "I'm going fishing tomorrow. Want to come along?"

Finally. Reade beamed. "Sure. Sounds great. What did you have in mind? Surf casting?"

"Nah. *Real* fish. Wahoo. 'Cuda. Sailfish. Whatever we can find. I always charter a boat when I'm down here. You ever have a big marlin hit your line?"

At Reade's negative, Farley launched into a story about a three-hour fight he'd had off Nassau a few years ago. As he talked, Reade fantasized about the next day: hours alone with Farley on a boat—no Barnett, no Mom, just a couple of guys drinking beer, fishing, and talking shop.

"Good heavens, I can practically hear the testosterone running," said his mother when she and Jackie returned moments later. "I have never understood men and their attraction to fish."

Farley turned to Jackie. "What about you? Do you get it?"

No, shouted Reade inside his head. *You don't get it at all.*

"Sort of," she said. "My uncle has an ice shack up on White Fish Lake. My dad goes up every year, and he used to take me along."

"Did you like it?" asked Farley.

"Are you kidding? I was a kid, and he let me drink

coffee with a ton of sugar in it and eat as much beef jerky as I wanted. I loved it."

"Would you like to come with us tomorrow? I can't promise beef jerky, but there'll be plenty of cold beer."

With this opportunity slipping away like the others, Reade jumped in. He had to do something.

"We're talking about a whole different kind of fishing, here. Big game fish. Hard fights. Plus, we'll be up a tuna tower most of the day, right?"

"Sure," said Farley. "That's part of the fun."

"They're what, twenty or thirty feet in the air?" Reade was grasping at straws here, but you could turn straws into rope if you had enough of them. "All that tossing and rolling and tossing." He mimicked the motion with his hand.

A crease formed down the center of Jackie's forehead and deepened rapidly. *Score*. She did have a problem with heights. Or with seasickness, which might be just as good.

"It's not a good place if you've got vertigo," added Farley, inadvertently aiding the cause.

"Oh, that sounds awful," said Lenore. "Why don't you spend the day with me, Jackie? We'll hit the spa and make ourselves gorgeous, instead."

"Well . . . ," said Jackie.

"You wouldn't want to get dizzy again and—" Reade stopped himself, but it was too late. He knew it the instant that little muscle in her jaw twitched.

"Thanks for worrying about me," said Jackie in a too-sweet voice. "But I'll be fine with the tuna tower. Lenore, I hope you don't mind, but I think I will join the gentlemen. I haven't been fishing in a long time, and it really does sound like fun."

"Oh, I understand," said Lenore, giving Reade a wink. "I can manage the spa by myself."

"You sure?" asked Farley. "Reade was exaggerating a little. You can always just sit in the shade and read while we whack fish."

She shook her head. "I'd probably get seasick anyway."

"That's okay," said Reade. "You can chum for us."

"Don't be gross," said Lenore. She turned to Jackie. "Are you really sure you want to go off with these cavemen, dear? I have visions of fish guts and lots of belching."

"Sounds just like Uncle Vern's ice shack," said Jackie. "What time do we leave?"

six

Tossing and rolling and tossing.

Jackie frowned up at the chromed aluminum frame of the tuna tower and recalled Hunter's words. He'd been trying to scare her out of coming, of course, but he had also been speaking the truth. Even though the boat's motion was barely detectable at deck level, the top of the tower wagged slowly back and forth like the tip of a dog's tail. She'd hate to be up there in a major swell.

Fortunately, the sea was calm today and they were only going out for a few hours. She could handle this, no sweat.

That conviction was put to a test a couple of miles out when the skipper shouted down from the flybridge. "We have escorts. Off the starboard bow."

Farley leaned out for a quick look over the side, then shinnied up the tuna tower like a monkey. "Come on up."

Reade reached for the ladder, then stood aside and motioned Jackie past. "Ladies first."

"Nice imitation of a gentleman, Hunter. Thanks." She

grabbed a rung and climbed straight up, wishing she could bear to glance down, just to see if his mouth was hanging open.

Farley gave her a hand up onto the top deck grating as Reade scrambled up behind her. "Remember to keep one hand on the boat at all times."

Like she was going to turn loose.

He pointed slightly to the right of the bow. "Look. There."

A sleek, gray body arced out of the water just ahead of the boat. Then another and another.

"Oh, my gosh. Porpoises," she said. She suddenly understood why Farley had shot up the ladder instead of heading out onto the bow. From up here, the sea's surface turned to glass, revealing the many members of the pod that swam deep. "Look at all of them. There must be dozens."

"Do you know the difference between a dolphin and a porpoise?" asked Farley.

"No," she said. "But I can do ten minutes on northern pike and muskie."

Farley laughed. "I bet you can. A true dolphin is generally bigger, with a longer, flattened beak. Porpoises have a stubbier snout, plus they tend to swim in smaller groups."

"So, these are actually dolphins, then," she said.

"Right. Atlantic bottle-nose," said Farley.

"Like Flipper," said Reade. She and Farley both shot him you've-got-to-be-kidding looks, and he grinned and shrugged. "Hey, it's just a point of reference."

Jackie passed on the chance to razz him in order to watch the magic dance below. It continued for another ten minutes or so, and then the dolphins veered off and vanished as abruptly as they had appeared.

"Aw," whined Jackie. "Do you think they'll come back?"

"They might," said Farley. "But right now, we need to do what they're doing, which is find ourselves some fish.

You start looking, and I'll be back in a minute."

He pulled a pair of high-powered binoculars out of their holder on the handrail, handed them to Jackie, then headed down the ladder.

She looped the cord around her wrist a couple of times for security, then took her sunglasses off and hooked one temple into the neck of her T-shirt.

"What, exactly, am I looking for?" she asked.

"Birds circling one spot," said Reade. "A commotion in the water. Big fish jumping—especially if you see bills or sails."

"I take it you've done this before."

"Nope. But I read *The Old Man and the Sea* in high school."

"Ah. An expert." She brought the binoculars up and did a slow scan of the horizon. "I don't see anything except water and other boats."

"Give me a shot."

"Don't tempt me." She handed over the binoculars and put her sunglasses back on. "You look for marlin. I'll keep an eye out for my dolphins."

Reade took up the watch. A few minutes later, he asked, "Did you know there are pink dolphins in the Amazon?"

"Sure. They were on a *National Geographic* special or something, years ago."

"I actually saw one, once."

"You've been up the Amazon?" asked Jackie.

"Partway. Not nearly as far as I'd like to go. My dad had to go up to Santarem on a project, and he managed to convince his boss to let him take us all along."

"Your mother, too?"

"Sure."

"That kind of surprises me. She seems too . . . I don't know, delicate for a trip like that."

"She didn't use to be. Underneath that helpless hypochondriac lies one tough lady. She just kind of got lost after Dad died." He lowered the binoculars, and his eyes had a hollow look to them that gave Jackie a chill despite the heat.

Uncomfortable, she said the first thing that popped into mind. "Is it true what they said about pink dolphins?"

His expression cleared. "What?"

"That they come out of the river at night and take human lovers?"

"Mine didn't," he said. A faintly wicked grin curved his lips. "That would have been fun, though."

"I meant, is it true that the locals *believe* they come out of the river?"

"My, you're curious about dolphin sex. Maybe you should go to Brazil and find out for yourself."

"I'll pass, thanks."

"Why?"

She opened her mouth, then shut it again when she realized what mischief he could pull if she told him she'd never go because she was afraid of spiders.

"This is exotic enough for me," she said.

"St. Sebastian is about as exotic as . . . New Orleans," he said.

"Compared to Cedar Falls, New Orleans *is* exotic."

"Cedar Falls, Iowa? Is that where you grew up?"

She nodded.

"Farm kid?"

"Nope. My grandfather farmed, but Dad's an insurance agent. I'm a townie, through and through."

She waited for some smart comment about her dad's boring profession, but he just nodded and kept looking through the binoculars. "Do you realize what we're doing here, Barnett?"

"Fishing?" she ventured.

"Talking to each other," he said. "And not about work."

"Oh, that. Well, don't take it personally."

"Are you two going to yak all day, or are you going to find us some fish?" asked Farley as he came up the ladder with two more sets of binoculars around his neck. He took one off and passed it to Jackie. "How are you doing up here? Is it as bad as Reade made out?"

"Nah. Just like the top of my grandpa's silo."

That wasn't quite true. Grandpa's silo had been built from good, solid concrete block, and you got to the top from inside the adjacent barn, not by dangling out in space on some ladder. This flimsy contraption was more like a diving platform, a place where she'd never been particularly happy, no matter how many times her sadistic swim coach sent her up there to try to turn her into a diver.

Despite her denials up at the falls, she did have a touch of vertigo. It wasn't debilitating, but it could make life uncomfortable at times, and while she could climb the tuna tower to keep Hunter from showing her up, she probably wouldn't have come up on her own.

But then she would have missed seeing the dolphins from this angle. Maybe she should thank him. . . . Nah, it'd go to his head.

"You look hotter than hell in those long pants," said Farley.

Jackie looked down at her khakis. "I am."

"Take off a layer or two. You have a swimsuit under there, don't you?"

"Yes. But I got a little pink yesterday at the falls, so I figured long pants and a T-shirt were my best bet."

"A T-shirt alone isn't going to cut it out here on the water," said Reade. "You need a good coat of sunscreen underneath."

"Unfortunately, my very expensive, hi-SPF sunscreen is protecting the noses of lesser kudu about now. And I don't think the local version is very good. That's what I used yesterday."

"It's not," said Farley. "I've got some American stuff in my bag. Help yourself, and get out of those pants before you get heat stroke."

Going down the ladder was a little more nerve-racking than climbing up, but Jackie managed without looking too awkward. She peeled out of her T-shirt and khakis, found the sunscreen in Farley's ditty bag, and started smearing it on.

Farley called down a few minutes later. "How're you doing?"

She squinted up into the sun. "Fine. I'm going to need some help with my back, though."

"Sure. You want to get that for her, Reade?"

Oh, no. That was not what she'd intended. She couldn't hear Hunter's answer, but his feet appeared on the top rung of the ladder. *Just great.* She slapped one last handful of cream on her leg and rubbed it in quickly.

When she looked up, Reade was standing on the bottom rung of the ladder, just hanging there, watching her. His expression was unreadable behind his sunglasses.

She tossed him the tube of sunscreen, then braced herself against the door frame, her back to him.

"Can you get your hair up out of the way somehow?" he asked, his voice oddly husky.

She gathered up a loose ponytail, gave it a twist, and shoved it up under the crown of her hat. "How's that?"

"Fine."

The cream was warm from sitting in the sun. He spread a thick layer over the skin that her swimsuit exposed, from her shoulders to the small of her back, and then he began to rub it in.

Except he didn't just rub, he massaged. No. Caressed. Up and down, in slow, soothing strokes that made her relax against his hands. Down again, then back up to knead her shoulders and her neck until she turned to jelly. Down yet again, tracing the edges of her suit, slipping his fingertips just under the fabric so that she wondered if he was going to go further, make a move. If he did . . . if one of the others came down. . . . And yet she stood there, reveling in the pure sensuality of it.

"You're done," he said at last, but his hands lingered, hot against her equally hot skin. "You should let it soak in a few minutes."

"Thank you." She didn't move either, until the boat's

engine slowed and the sound of men moving around
drifted down from above. Reade jerked away and stepped
to the stern. Flustered, Jackie grabbed for her T-shirt and
had it back on by the time Farley set foot on the deck.

"All greased up?" he asked.

"Yes. Thanks for the sunscreen."

"Keep it. I have more."

"That's very kind of you. So, what's up? Did we find
fish?"

"Not yet, but we're over a good ledge here," the skipper
answered from the flybridge. "I think we'll throw out
some hooks and see what's hungry. Let's bait up, Ossie."

Ossie was the deckhand, a boy of about fifteen who
hadn't done much so far except hand them each a soft
drink as they came aboard and throw off the dock lines,
but now he scrambled down off the flybridge to obey. As
he and the skipper checked the rods and tackle, Jackie
stepped into the cabin and quietly kicked the bulkhead.

Jeez, what was with her, anyway? She knew full well
Hunter was just yanking her chain to amuse himself, yet
this was the second time her body had reacted like he was
not only human but a suitable bed partner. It was a good
thing she had a brain, because left on their own, her baser
instincts were as base as they got.

She needed to corral all that misguided horniness and
turn its wasted energy to her advantage. The question was,
how?

Farley stuck his head through the door. "You okay in
here?"

"Um, yeah. Fine. I just wanted to get out of the sun for
a couple of minutes while I still had a chance. I figure
once the fish start biting, we'll be busy."

"We can only hope. Ossie just tossed the lines in. Now
it's a matter of waiting."

Which apparently required beer, as he grabbed three
cold ones out of the reefer and popped them open. He set
one can on the table in front of her and carried the other
two out on deck. Jackie stared at the can a moment, then

picked it up, took a long draw, and walked out to join the others.

She'd been on deck only a few minutes when a loud snap made everyone jump. Ossie was the first to reach the chattering rod. He tapped the line to set the hook and then let the fish run.

"Fish on. Your line, Mr. Reade."

Reade reached for the rod. The forty-pound dorado he reeled in a few minutes later was only the first of many fish caught—so many that Jackie lost count. They moved around a couple of times, alternately trolling deep water and lying over shoals to pick up different species of fish. Per Farley's wishes, they released each one after the fight, including a sixty-five-pound barracuda that Jackie fought for twenty exhilarating, exhausting minutes.

Right behind it came a nice little blackfin tuna. When Farley brought it alongside, he checked it over, then signaled to Isaac. "Looks like one for the plate."

The skipper gaffed the struggling fish and flipped it into the ice-filled locker on deck. "Good, because your time's about up. We need to head back. Sorry we never found your marlin, gentlemen. And miss."

"There's never a guarantee, Isaac," said Farley. "About fish or anything else. Let's head for home."

Jackie sank into the fight chair. "My arms feel like Silly Putty in a hot car."

"You worked hard for that fish," said Farley. "I bet you're sore tomorrow. When we get back, you ought to make yourself an appointment for a massage."

"Maybe the masseuse will actually be there this time," said Reade, who was helping Ossie stow the tackle.

"Maybe so." *Smart-ass*. Jackie caught a glimpse of his face as he turned with one of the rods. He looked altogether too cocky, like he had something up his sleeve. He probably figured he could take advantage of her aches and pains to get rid of her.

Well, let him try. Sore or not, she had enough moxie to keep up with a lab rat and a fifty-five-year-old man.

Six months of Richard Simmons and all those hours on the StairMaster had to count for something.

As the skipper fired up the engines, Farley disappeared into the cabin. He came back out with a bottle of rum, a cut lime, and five paper cups, which he handed around, pouring and squeezing as he went.

When he finished, he lifted his cup high. "A toast to Drs. Barnett and Hunter, greenhorns no longer."

Jackie gasped as the liquor scorched its way down her throat. Spending time with Farley, she reflected through the tears, was going to be as hard on her liver as the self-pity bender her travel agent had suggested.

And from the way her arms felt, it was also going to be a lot more work.

"You're back."

"Hi, Mom." Reade eased down onto the low stone planter wall next to her lounger.

"You look tired and you stink," she said, laying her book aside. "It must have been a good trip."

"It was." He sipped at the Coke he'd picked up on the way past the bar. "There are a bunch of fish out there with sore mouths, and one with no head at all being carried to the kitchen."

"By Farley, I assume."

He nodded. "And Jackie. She reeled in the biggest catch of the day, so Farley said she should help him present our dinner to the chef."

"What are we having?"

"Blackfin. Tuna," he added when he saw the blank look. "Dinner's at eight, at Farley's cabana."

"Wonderful." She sipped at her iced tea. "You like Jackie, don't you?"

"It's not like that," he said firmly, although he couldn't chalk up all of her assumptions to maternal imagination. The recollection of Jackie's lotion-slick skin beneath his hands made him want to offer his services for a full body rubdown. Pushing his fantasies aside, he set his Coke down and wiped his palms on his thighs. "Mom, I need to talk to you."

"I always cringe inside when one of you boys says that." She sighed. "Okay. What is it?"

He started carefully. "You and Farley seem to have—"

"This isn't going to be a safe sex lecture, is it?"

"Hardly. I just—"

"Good, because I have no intention of discussing my sex life with my son."

"I assure you, that's not my. . . . Good grief, Mom, it's only been two days. You and Farley don't actually have a sex life already, do you?"

"Reade Emerson Hunter!"

He chuckled at her bristly tone. "I'm sorry, I couldn't resist. I don't want to know. Really, I don't."

"I wouldn't think so," she said primly. "So what is this about?"

"What I started to say—before I was interrupted—is that you and Farley seem to have the idea that Jackie and I are an item."

"The chemistry between you is pretty obvious," she said.

"That's not chemistry. That's antagonism."

"What on earth do you have to be antagonistic toward Jackie about? You have so much in common. Plus she's a very nice girl, not to mention smart and sexy and. . . ."

"She's my competition, Mom. For one million dollars in research money."

"A million dollars? Heavens. I didn't realize the grant was that large. Well, no wonder you. . . ." Her eyes narrowed into the universal Disapproving Mother expression. "Let me take a stab at something. Did you know Farley was going to be here at Fair Winds?"

"Nnn-yeah. How'd you guess?"

"Thirty-two years of experience as your mother. And I take it you knew Jackie was going to be here, too."

He nodded. "Yes. And I came down here to make sure she didn't get an unfair advantage."

"And brought me along to . . . ?" She started to take a sip, but the glass froze halfway to her lips. "Oh, no. Oh, Reade, you wouldn't. Please tell me you didn't bring me down here to seduce Farley Phelps for you."

"Mom! God, no. When I made the reservations, I had no idea you and Farley would meet, much less hit it off. I'll admit I was hoping you might meet someone, but the possibility that it would be Farley didn't even cross my mind until you said you wanted to dance with him."

"I never said that."

"Oh, no, you're right, excuse me. You only drooled all over my shoulder as he danced past us Sunday evening. Anyway, you were the one who managed to lure him in with that headache."

"I did no such thing. I assure you, my headache was not a lure."

"Nonetheless, I was not involved in you two meeting. I wasn't even present when it happened. And I certainly don't expect you to seduce him for me. Or even talk to him on my behalf."

"All right," she said, mollified. She stared at her knees, slowly shaking her head. "I must be getting slow in my old age. I actually bought that whole coincidence routine you and Jackie dished out. When did you find out about all this?"

"Wednesday."

"No wonder we had to pack so fast." She shook her head again. "So . . . if I'm not supposed to sleep your way to the top, why did you bring me along?"

"You've been telling me how much you wanted to come to St. Sebastian for years." He could tell from the look on her face that she wasn't buying it and quickly switched tack. "Cover. You're my excuse for being here, that's all."

She sat there, tapping her newly manicured fingernails on the arm of her lounge chair. A waiter walked by, and she motioned him over. "Another one of these things, please."

As she held up the glass, Reade caught a whiff of alcohol. "That's not iced tea."

"Yes, it is. Long Island Iced Tea," she told the waiter for Reade's benefit. "And I'd like one of those little paper umbrellas they put in the fruity drinks, too."

The waiter winked at her. "Right away, ma'am. Anything for you, sir?"

"I'm fine," said Reade. When the waiter departed, he chided his mother. "Long Island Iced Tea. I leave you alone for a few hours, and see what happens? You turn into a lush."

"I'm on vacation," she said. "And besides, I just found out my son—my pride and joy—is trying to steal a major grant out from under a colleague."

"I am not trying to steal it," he insisted. "I'm just trying to keep the competition on level ground. You heard Farley. Jackie talked his ear off that first night. And now she turns up for every single thing we do. I can't seem to catch up. You have no idea how the woman is. She's rigid and didactic and—"

"And determined and overly competitive. Like I said, you two have a lot in common."

"We do not."

She ignored him. "She's also apparently more successful in presenting her case to Farley. You might want to adopt some of her methods."

"I can't," he said. "I don't have the cleavage."

His mother scowled at him like he was a flyspeck on her glass. "That's not giving either her or Farley very much credit."

"I know, I know. But you've got to admit, those are major attention-getters she packs."

"She's got your attention, that's for certain," his mother said dryly.

"It's not mine she's after."

"Well, let me tell you from experience, having Farley's

attention won't do her a bit of good if she doesn't have anything to say once she has it."

"She has plenty to say. But so do I, and I take issue with her presentation."

"Okay. So let's say you're right. Let's say Jackie is throwing women's lib back forty years. Let's say she is trying to convince Farley that sex appeal counts more than brains and skill in the laboratory. Even assuming that *she* thinks he's that stupid—which I doubt—do you? Do you really think the man accumulated the kind of business empire he has by thinking with his shorts?"

"I don't know, Mom. I just know that she's had several hours alone with him and I can't get five minutes."

"Have you asked for five minutes?"

"I can't do that," he protested. "I'm supposed to be here by coincidence."

"The great lie," she muttered. "You have backed yourself into a bit of a corner, haven't you?"

"Looks like it." He recognized the line of her mouth and the set of her chin from a thousand arguments. She was not a happy woman. "Okay. Fine. I didn't really expect that you would jump up and down cheering when you found out. But will you, at least, *please* stop encouraging Jackie to come along every time we do something with Farley?"

"Excuse me?" She stared at him as though he were delusional. "If you'll recall, *I* asked her to come to the spa. Farley's the one who invited her to go fishing. And you're the one who asked if she could come to dinner with us the other night."

"That was a misunderstanding."

"Is that what they call it these days? Anyway, I happen to like Jackie, so if I feel like inviting her someplace, I'm going to do so. And I imagine Farley feels the same way. So deal with it."

"Mom!" He stood up, exasperated, just as the waiter returned with her drink, complete with bright yellow paper parasol. "This is obviously getting me nowhere. I'm going to go take a shower."

"Good. You need one," she said, taking her drink from the young man. "Meet me at my room at seven, and you can buy me a cocktail before dinner."

"It's all free, Mother," he muttered.

"I know that. It's a figure of speech. Go away, darling. You're getting positively anal."

seven

"I told Guillaume to let all the stops out," said Farley. "I have no idea what he's done for us."

"He can't possibly top what he's done so far," said Lenore.

Jackie had to agree. They'd already enjoyed course after amazing course, all served on the lower terrace of Farley's so-called cabana—a luxury villa in anyone else's book. The meal had been crowned by the tuna, barely touched by flame, arranged on avocado with a green pepper sauce and a fan of squashlike christophene on the side.

Fueled by wine, Farley's knack for playing devil's advocate, and way too many academic degrees among the four of them, the conversation was as savory as the food, wandering over a range of topics from cross-country motorcycle trips to ecopolitics. Even Hunter seemed to be behaving himself.

She was contemplating the possibility that he wasn't as bad as she thought when the waiter appeared with a tray.

What Guillaume had done, it turned out, was give

baked Alaska a Caribbean flare. The ice cream was piña colada—the real thing, made from fresh coconut cream, with flakes of the tender meat, chunks of sweet pineapple, and a kick of rum. A puree of mango swirled over the meringue like sunrise touching a cloud. Jackie took one bite and groaned.

"What's wrong?" asked Farley.

"Nothing." She shook her head. "Just the calorie count."

"Calories don't exist when you're on vacation," said Farley.

"Tell that to my thighs," she said, firmly laying down her spoon and pushing her plate away. "I've been over-doing, but this is overdoing the overdoing."

"I admire your willpower, dear," said Lenore. She took a second bite and rolled her eyes in ecstasy. "I'll just have to go back to Eunice and order a bigger dress."

"I'm sure Reade would be happy to take you," said Jackie. She couldn't resist. "He was fascinated with her factory—made me tell him all about it. I think he's sorry he didn't have a chance to check it out yesterday."

Hunter nearly choked on his meringue.

Lenore looked at her son with concern. "Are you all right, darling?"

"Fine," he said. He glared at Jackie. "Something just went down wrong."

"Do be more careful, dear, I don't want you to choke. Farley, I don't know how you eat and drink like this and stay as fit as you are."

"By not doing it all the time. Back in the real world, I live like a monk, in bed by ten and up at six. I eat mostly vegetables and rice with tofu, and I don't drink anything harder than guava juice."

"Really?"

"Absolutely. I've learned over the years that that's what it takes for me to keep up the pace. But St. Sebastian is a world apart, and when I'm here, anything goes. I eat what I want, I drink what I want, and I do what I want—

no schedules, no obligations, and no regrets." He swallowed a big spoonful of ice cream. "And then I go back and bust my butt for a few more months."

Lenore nodded in approval. "I know a lot of people who could stand to let go like that once in a while."

"I know a few, myself," said Reade, pointedly not looking in Jackie's direction. "The problem is, the ones who could benefit the most usually don't realize it until they're dried up like old prunes. Are there any good waves around here?"

Old prunes? Jackie steamed in silence.

"For surfing?" said Farley.

"Not board. Kayak. I checked out the boats the day we got here, and the surf runners look decent enough. I thought I might go out and play in the waves tomorrow, if there's someplace nearby."

"There's a great spot out on Devil's Hand," said Farley. "Long wave run, sweet curl, and hardly any board surfers because they have to hike in through about three miles of wicked saw grass. Whereas we can paddle in and keep our legs intact."

We? thought Jackie. *Our?* That sounded like Farley wanted to go, too. Shoot. She had paddled a canoe around a lake a few times, but riding a teeny little boat in pounding surf was not her idea of a good time.

"Sounds perfect," said Reade.

"You're not planning to go by yourself, I hope," said Lenore.

"Not if I can con Farley into showing me where these perfect waves are hiding," said Reade.

"That won't be tough," said Farley, confirming Jackie's fears. "I even know a place where we can put in that'll cut the run to the beach by half. I'd ask you ladies along, but I imagine Jackie's arms will be killing her by tomorrow."

No kidding. Muscles she hadn't known she had were already whining in three-part harmony, but she wasn't about to let Hunter go paddling off alone with Farley and his checkbook.

So she lied. "I recover pretty quickly. I should be up for a paddle."

"Are you sure?" Farley looked doubtful.

"Oh, yeah. In fact, it sounds like fun." A bigger lie, but it was for the cause. She grinned at Reade. *Gotcha*.

Her smile faded when she saw his knuckles go white around his spoon—undoubtedly a stand-in for her neck. To think that the same hands that had been so gentle and sexy when he'd been rubbing her back that morning. . . . Their eyes met, and a shiver danced its way up and down her spine, leaving random nerve endings sparking like so many short circuits before it settled in a confused knot below her belt line.

"Great," said Farley. "What about you, Lenore? Will you come along, too?"

"Oh, I don't know. I'm not sure I could paddle across the swimming pool, much less several miles of open ocean."

"You won't have to. I'll get a standard double kayak and you can ride with me," said Farley. "Jackie can paddle one of the surf runners, and then when we get to the beach, she and I can take turns while the other one keeps you company on the beach. What do you say?"

"It does sound like fun." Lenore hesitated, then nodded. "Oh, all right. If Jackie's game, I am."

"Great. We're set. Now eat up, everyone." He scooped up a big spoonful of ice cream. "You, too, Jackie. You don't want to insult Guillaume. He cries easily."

"Oh, what the heck." She reached for the plate and her spoon. "I'll probably need the extra calories tomorrow, anyway."

They finished dessert just about the time the ring of steel drums drifted over the tops of the palms to announce the start of Calypso Carnival night at the resort. Lenore excused herself, and Farley went inside to show her the way to the powder room and to speak to Guillaume and his staff. That left Jackie alone with Reade.

Trying not to look as nervous as she felt, Jackie slowly drained the last bit of wine from her glass, then blotted her mouth and laid her napkin aside. Reade watched every move, his dark eyes gleaming in the light of the torches that flickered at the edge of the terrace. The half-smile that curved his mouth lifted the hair on the back of her neck and made her heart pound. Every instinct told her to get up and move away from him, but she resisted. Instead, she settled back in her seat, feigning utter unconcern. A few yards away, the moonlight glittered on the water, shattering into diamond dust as a breeze riffled the surface.

She sighed. "It's amazing how private this little strip of beach is. You'd hardly know a whole resort is just a few yards away."

"You're really pushing it," he said softly.

"By commenting on the beach?" she asked, with an innocent flutter of her lashes.

"You know what I mean. What's it going to take to get you to back off?"

"You flying back to Pittsburgh."

"That's not going to happen," he said.

"I didn't think it would."

"All I want is an equal opportunity."

"That sounds reasonable," she said. "The thing is, past experience indicates that you borrow your concept of equal opportunity from Genghis Khan. I just can't seem to get past that little incident with Tom Grant."

"Try."

She grimaced as though thinking hard, then shook her head. "Nope. Can't do it. Sorry. 'Those who do not learn from history are doomed to repeat it.' "

"Damn it, Barnett." Reade stood up so abruptly that his chair fell over backward.

Jackie smothered a snicker with one hand as he reached down to yank the chair upright. He glowered at her, and when their eyes locked, she got that rush again, the one that said *danger* and *sex* at the same time. He took a step toward her.

"Everything okay down there?" called Farley from the deck above them.

They both started, as though guilty of some transgression. Reade backed away.

"We're fine," he said. "I just knocked my chair over. Sorry."

"No problem. We'll be down in a second." Farley went back inside.

Reade paced to the edge of the terrace to look out over the water. "I intend to get in a real workout tomorrow. Have you ever even paddled a kayak?"

"Don't worry, I'll keep up." And she would, too. Or she'd die trying—*thank you very much, Walt.*

What a chummy little quartet they'd been this evening, Reade thought as he watched Jackie jiggle off into the night. For a while there, he thought he'd fallen into a Twilight Zone inhabited by chirpy clones who had no idea what was going on—until he realized that all the cheeriness was just a cover for the fact that they were all observing each other like graduate students in some bizarre psychology experiment. Mom watching him and Jackie. Jackie watching him and Farley. Him watching Farley and Mom and Jackie. And all of them smiling and chatting like nothing was going on. It had almost been a relief when Barnett had started sniping at him.

It was more of a relief watching her head to bed, though. He was tired. She had hung on until the bitter end, waiting for Farley to escort Lenore to her room and then lurking on the edges of the party crowd until it was clear he wasn't coming back to carouse a little more.

Reade couldn't blame her—he'd been doing exactly the same thing, after all—but he also couldn't let her get away with it, which was why he'd spent the last hour watching her pretend to listen to calypso music and making sure she didn't go traipsing off after Farley. In the end, it had come down to who collapsed first, and he'd won. Last man standing.

Not for long, though. Bed and sleep beckoned like a lover, and he had no inclination to resist. He needed his rest, after all, because tomorrow he was going to run Barnett into the ground.

That was his new plan. Simply ditching her just wasn't working, what with Farley and Mom so enamored of her. Combine their invitations with her determination to stay in his face, and there was no way he was going to shake her loose. Either he had to make her turn loose on her own or he would have to resign himself to having her around and make the best of it.

He wasn't to that point yet, though, so for the next few days, he was going to see just what Barnett would go through to stay between him and Farley. If she wanted to play with the boys, she was going to have to keep up with the boys. He intended to put her through her paces. So far as Jackie Barnett was concerned, tomorrow was the world championship of surf kayaking.

And may the best man win.

Again.

*Lenore watched the unfolding scenery, kept an eye on Reade and Jackie up ahead, and chatted with Farley, all in an effort to distract herself from her discomfort. It wasn't working. Her life vest chafed under her arms, the spray skirt on the kayak felt like a python around her waistline, the darned plastic seat had her back in knots—her chiropractor would be having fits if he saw her right now—and to top it off, she was queasy and sweating like a steelworker.

"Why isn't this part of the island developed like the area around Runaway Bay?" she asked, trying yet again to get her mind on something else. "It's just as beautiful."

"A lot of it's locked up in a land trust," said Farley.

"Thank goodness. I mean, Fair Winds isn't bad, as resorts go, but sometimes I worry that every inch of oceanfront on the planet is going to be paved over with hotels and condos."

"I don't think you have to worry about that in St. Sebastian. The government's very conscious of the treasure they have, and so are the people. They've taken steps to protect key areas."

The shoreline really was spectacular, wild and intensely alive, with the jungle scrambling right down to the edge of the beaches. The aroma of ripe fruits, flowers, and decaying leaves washed out over the water, rich and fragrant over the tang of salt. Clouds of birds swarmed like so many huge butterflies. Lenore smiled at one big white pelican that sat on a boulder, halfheartedly clacking his beak at the gulls that rode the air currents a few feet over his head.

"It's getting a little rough," she said a few minutes later. "Maybe we should turn back."

"There's some crosscurrent here," said Farley. "It'll be smoother once we get around the corner."

Up ahead, Reade glanced over his shoulder, then said something to Jackie. They both stopped paddling, dipping their blades just enough to stay oriented in the waves.

"How are you two doing?" asked Reade as Lenore and Farley came up between the two smaller boats.

"Great," said Farley.

Lenore tugged at the shock cord around her waist. "I'm beginning to think I made a mistake coming along. I was foolish to think I could handle anything this active anymore. I should have known, after the falls."

"I told you, just sit back and take it easy," said Farley. "I'll do all the work."

"You already are, and it's not fair."

Reade took a half-stroke to stay even. "Let's pull out on the beach, Farley, and you and I can swap places. You can go ahead with Jackie, and I'll take Mom back."

"No, no." Lenore might not approve of her son's cause,

but she knew how much those words had cost him. "That's not necessary. I'll push on. I'll be fine."

"How about a compromise?" suggested Farley. "You two go on ahead. Lenore and I will stop here for a little while, and she can work out the kinks. When she feels better, we'll catch up with you."

"Now wait a minute," said Lenore. "I don't think we should split up. The whole reason we all came was to be together."

"Not to mention that Reade and I have no idea where we're going," said Jackie.

"Up around that little headland. It's only a couple of miles," said Farley. "You'll spot it—big dish bay, pink sand beach, waves marching in from the northeast. You can't miss it. Go on."

"What if Mom doesn't feel better?" asked Reade.

"Then we'll sit right here until you get back. I promise, I won't shanghai her."

"That's not—"

"Go on," urged Farley. "We'll be fine. We'll probably just be a few minutes behind you anyway, and in the meantime, you can give Jackie a run or two before she has to start sharing with me."

Lenore didn't like that idea at all, but Reade looked pleased, so she nodded. "Go on."

"Terrific. Come on, Jackie. Let's do it."

"Great," she said, a little faintly. Or that might have been Lenore's imagination. She paddled off after Reade, the two of them bobbing up and over the waves like corks.

"Watch the rocks on the near side of the bay," called Farley.

"Gotcha," hollered Reade.

"Rocks?" said Lenore. "There are rocks?"

"A few. Reade heard me. He'll check it out before they start playing." He turned their boat toward shore. "Come on. I have a couple of coconuts and some cookies in a bag back here. We'll have a snack."

Farley paddled toward the beach. At the last instant, he

took a couple of well-timed strokes and let a wave put them right up on the sand.

"Front door service." He scrambled out and helped Lenore out. While he dragged the kayak up past the wave line, she took off her life vest and wriggled out of the spray skirt. Then she stepped up on a nearby log to see if she could spot Jackie and Reade. "Are you sure it's wise, splitting up like this?"

"There are two of them, they'll be fine. And we're on dry land, so we're fine. No problem."

To her eye, the molded plastic surf runners looked awfully unstable, what with the way the paddler perched on top of the open deck. And they were so tiny—and getting tinier with every passing second. "They almost look like they're racing."

"They probably are, without us old folks to slow them down," Farley said. He stepped up beside her just as a bigger than average wave lifted Reade up high, then dropped him down into the trough, out of sight.

Lenore's heart skipped a beat, and a wave of dizziness made her sway.

Farley reached over and turned her face toward him. "You just went pale. Are you okay?"

She shook her head. "Not really. Maybe you should call Reade back."

"I don't think I can. Sit down." He tugged her down so she was sitting on the sand, then took off his life vest and slipped it behind her back as a cushion against the log. "What's going on?"

"Just one of my spells."

"What kind of spells? Have you seen a doctor?"

"Doctors and specialists and more doctors. They can't figure out what causes them."

"Bet that didn't stop them from giving them a fancy Latin name, though."

"Syncope of unexplained etiology, which, I take it, means I have spells."

"Syncope. That's fainting. Do you actually pass out?"

"I have a couple of times. Not recently."

"How long has this been going on?"

"Five, maybe six years." She pushed her hair off her forehead. "I could stand something to drink."

"I'll get the coconuts." He went to the kayak and unscrewed the rear deck hatch so he could pull a red coated-nylon bag out of the compartment. From it, he extracted a fresh coconut, a machete, a small package of Oreos, and two paper-wrapped straws, which he stuck in his shirt pocket. He held the coconut against one of the logs. A couple of whacks with the machete took the top off.

"The water of life," he said, handing her the coconut and a straw. He ripped the package of Oreos open and propped it on the sand next to her. "Not to mention the ultimate milk and cookies experience. This should cure what ails you."

She sipped at the coconut. "The last time I drank fresh coconut water on a quiet patch of beach, it was. . . ." The memory of Preston balled up in her chest so that she had to take a deep breath. "It was a long time ago. Thank you."

"My pleasure." He fetched the other coconut and decapitated it for himself before he plunked down next to her. "Pass me a couple of those cookies."

She did, glad for the excuse to shake off the mood. "Where do you get Oreos on St. Sebastian?"

"At the supermarket in Port M. But I smuggle them in for old time's sake."

"You mean I'm eating contraband?"

"Yeah." He put his arm around her and snuggled her into his shoulder. "Ain't it delicious?"

They sat there, mostly silent, watching the waves and the occasional passing powerboat, and destroying the evidence of Farley's criminal activities. When they got down to the last two cookies, he insisted she unscrew one and eat it the "right way," and then did the same. Watching a man his age lick the filling gave her the giggles.

"Do I look as silly as you do?" she asked.

"Sillier," he said. "You've got a big blob of frosting on the corner of your mouth."

She started to wipe it away, but he grabbed her wrist. "Allow me."

He cupped her chin in his hand, and she thought he was going to wipe it with his thumb. Instead he leaned over and caught it with his lips, brushing a gentle kiss over her lips in passing. He lifted his head a moment, and smiled, and when she smiled back, he kissed her again, more deeply. It wasn't the same as one of Preston's kisses, but it was very, very nice. Sexual awareness, a sensation she hadn't felt in years, spread through Lenore's body, and she was suddenly embarrassed. She pulled away.

"I'm feeling a lot better," she said. "We should probably see if we can catch up with the kids."

"Probably," agreed Farley. "Or we could stay here and make out for a while first."

She turned red clear to her toes, and Farley laughed.

"You're shocked," he said.

"Well . . . yes," she admitted. "It's not often a woman my age is invited to a make-out session."

"That's a goddamn shame," he said. "You kiss very well."

"I don't know how that's possible. I'm so out of practice."

"Are you? Well, then. . . ." He pulled her back into his arms. "I can hardly wait to see how you do when you're up to form."

Come to think of it, neither could she.

"Wow."

"I'll second that."

Jackie and Reade stood on a pile of lava rock at the western corner of what had to be the spot Farley had described: wide, shallow bay, pale pink sand, and waves that even she realized would make for good surfing. The waves weren't all that big, but they ran all the way across the bay at an angle and broke in a classic curl well out from the beach. A powerboat sat at anchor in a protected spot at the far end, but nobody seemed to be on board, and the bay was theirs to play in.

"I can't believe more people haven't found this," said Reade.

"Me, neither. It's like one of those secret beaches in *Endless Summer.*"

Reade snorted. "What do you know about *Endless Summer?*"

"We have cable in Minneapolis, you know. I just use it to watch old movies instead of *Flipper* reruns."

"You're funny, Barnett."

"One can only try one's best. Let's get off this rock. It's hot."

"Not so fast. You don't just throw yourself into strange water. You'll bash your brains out. Look." He pointed off to the left. "See that dark water? Those are the rocks Farley said to watch for. You'll want to stay well away from that area."

He walked her through the whole situation, pointing out spots to aim for and other areas to avoid. His knowledge and confidence set her mind at ease—right up until they headed back to the boats and he untied his helmet from the back of the boat.

It reminded her that she really could bash her brains out, and that everything he'd just told her could be so much BS, his way of arranging to get rid of her. If she wasn't trying to prove something, she'd just paddle home now. But she was, so she strapped on her helmet and snugged it down firmly, then double-checked the latches on her life vest. With any luck, Farley would show up with Lenore in a few minutes, and she could turn the boat over to him before she made either a fool or a corpse of herself.

Reade tapped the top of her helmet. "Time to pony up, Barnett."

He led her out to the center of the bay, taking a position

just outside the point where the waves broke. On the way out, he'd coached her on how to catch the wave; now he demonstrated a couple of times, bailing out to come back beside her. A couple of curious seagulls circled overhead, squawking.

"Okay, your turn," he said, backpaddling into the surge. "Just ride it a few yards, then cut out over the top like I did. Why are you looking at me that way?"

"I can't decide if you're being nice to me or just setting me up."

"Neither can I," he said. "Here comes your wave. Ready. Set. Go."

This was stupid. There were rocks in that water, and barracuda and sharks and God only knew what else, and Hunter was out to drown her. When she'd promised herself she'd die trying, she hadn't really meant it. The wave passed as she just sat there.

"Interesting technique," said Reade. "You do realize you have to paddle."

"I wasn't ready."

He shook his head. "You wussed out."

"I just wasn't ready," she repeated.

"Whatever. Let me know when you are." He dropped his feet over the side, set his paddle across his lap, and rested his chin on his chest like he was napping. Seconds later she heard the low rumble of a snore.

"Cute, Hunter."

"Just trying to occupy myself until the stars align or you see three white crows or whatever omen it is you're waiting for."

As he smirked, one of the gulls swooped in low and targeted the deck between his knees with a loud splat.

She grinned as he sat up. "That would be the right omen. I'm ready now."

"Figures." He splashed water over the stain. "You're sure, this time."

She licked her lips. "Yes."

"Okay." He sat up and twisted to look over his shoulder. "Here comes a nice one. Ready. . . . Now. Paddle."

She paddled. The wave lifted the back of her boat and passed beneath, letting her slide down the back side.

"Close," said Reade. "Put more power into it. The idea is to match the wave speed. Here comes the next one. Ready, set, go. Go!"

This time she paddled harder, digging in as he shouted encouragement. And then she was on the face of the wave, half-falling but somehow not. Riding. Scared spitless. She stuck her uphill blade in and turned, spinning the boat up and out, over the top.

"I did it. I did it!" Safely off the wave, her fear turned into a sense of victory. She hoisted her paddle high, Queen of the Waves.

"Fair. For a beginner," said Reade. "Now do it again. And this time put some muscle into it."

She did, again and again and again, until her arms burned. With each wave she managed to catch, she stayed on slightly longer and rode slightly better. Reade remained singularly unimpressed.

Eventually, the burn in her arms got to be too much to ignore. She was going to have to take a break, or she'd never make it home. It was getting dicey, anyway. Where the heck were Farley and Lenore?

"Next lesson," said Reade. He glanced over his shoulder and dug in. An instant later, she felt another wave lift them skyward.

As she slipped down the back, Reade caught the wave and shot forward, riding the crest. This time he didn't cut out, but stayed on, toying with the wave, dancing back and forth just in front of the breaking curl. Suddenly, he stuck his blade in and spun the boat in a three-sixty that sprayed foam in a wide arc.

Hotdogger. She hoped he fell off his silly boat. She certainly wasn't going to try any stunts. However, before she cried uncle, she did want to make one really good run, all the way in. So far, she'd just been dinking around. She paddled into position and waited for a wave.

Her timing was perfect. She felt the surge upward and forward, dug in and was on the wave.

"Easy as pie," she muttered to herself.

That was a lie. It took every bit of concentration and strength she had left to stay in the sweet spot just ahead of the curl. But she managed, and when she heard Reade whooping, she knew she'd finally impressed him.

The closer she got to shore, the steeper the wave got and the faster the curl crawled up behind her. Struggling, she decided to bail out, but in that millisecond, things got away from her. The little boat dove down the face of the wave, nosed into the water, and flipped end over, pitching her forward like a rock out of a catapult. Somewhere, Reade yelled again.

She hit the water with an *oomph*, and then the boat slammed down over her and she went under, tumbling through the surf, out of air.

eight

Reade knew the instant she lost control. It was a classic beginner error, leaning back instead of forward.

He shouted for her to correct, but he was too late. The boat rocketed down the wave, buried its nose, and pitchpoled, hammering Jackie into the water headfirst before it crashed down on top of her.

He held his breath, waiting for her to pop up. *Too long.*

Shit. He sliced across the waves diagonally, racing to get to the spot where she'd disappeared. Something pink and yellow tumbled past him. He leaned out, grabbed, and missed.

Before he could try again, she came up on her own, thrashing and spluttering, on the back side of the wave. The life vest did its job, letting her get her bearings, and by the time he got to her, she was treading water.

"You okay?"

"Yeah. I think so." She coughed again. "What's the deal? I figured you'd be cracking open a bottle of champagne, not coming after me."

"Crap. I want you out of the way, not dead. At least, not permanently."

"Thanks. I think." She paddled sideways, spinning in the water. "Where's my boat?"

"Never mind the boat. You're about thirty yards out. Do you want to swim in, or shall I give you a tow?"

"A tow. Please."

Taking her hand, he made sure she got a good grip on the edge of the boat. A few gentle paddle strokes were enough to bring them to the beach between waves. As soon as her feet touched bottom, she turned loose and slogged her way out of the water, unfastening her helmet and unzipping her life vest as she went. As she collapsed on the sand, Reade spun away to retrieve her paddle before the waves carried it out, then cut over to where her boat bumped along, upside down, in the foam at the edge of the beach. When he had all the gear hauled up on the beach, well out of harm's way, he grabbed his canteen and the waterproof bag with the first aid kit and went to check on Jackie.

She lay sprawled on her back, eyes closed and arms wide, breathing hard. A trickle of blood ran down one shin.

He dropped his helmet on the sand, yanked off his life vest, and sank down next to her. "How's your head?"

"Fine."

"Neck?"

Gingerly, she raised up on her elbows and tipped her head from side to side and back and forth. "Seems to be okay."

"Does anything else hurt?"

She shook her head.

"Great. Let's see that leg, then."

She bent her knee. "It stings."

"No doubt. You've got sand in it. Hang on." He cracked open the canteen and spilled a little fresh water over the cut, then ratted through the first aid kit for some gauze to blot it dry. "It's not deep. All you need is a Band-Aid."

He proceeded to find one and apply it, all the while trying to ignore the fact that he finally had his hands on one of the limbs he'd admired for the past several days. "What did you cut yourself on?"

"I'm not sure. Maybe the blade of my paddle."

"I can't believe that's all you hurt. That was some wipeout." He pressed down on the bandage to get a good seal and held his hand there, curved over her leg.

"For a second there, I thought I'd bit the big one."

"Good thing you didn't. I'd have a hard time explaining to Farley how I managed to drown you."

"Your concern is touching. Is that thing going to stick?" Pointing her toe, she lifted her leg so she could inspect it.

His mouth went dry. He must have made some noise—exhaled, perhaps—because she looked up at him, and suddenly Reade was drowning in blue-gray and desire. Without thinking, he leaned over and kissed her, quick and hard. Her lips tasted of salt and sunscreen, and when he lifted his head, her breath rose in a soft shudder that fanned his cheek. He kissed her again, more gently.

And then she was kissing him back, twining her fingers into his hair and pulling him closer. The need to possess her pounded through Reade. He shifted, pressing her down, bringing one leg up over her thighs to pin her, hold her to the land where the waves couldn't steal her away, as they drank each other in.

Sun, warm sand, and their own rising heat enveloped him. He slowly slipped the neck of her T-shirt out of the way as he kissed his way down the curve of her neck and across her shoulder. He wanted her and she wanted him and—

"Ow." Jackie jerked and swatted the ground beside her.

"Sorry, I didn't—"

"Ow. Get off me." She heaved him aside and scrambled

to her feet, a look of disgust on her face. "Oh, God. Crabs."

"I do *not* have crabs," he protested.

"Not that kind. That kind." She pointed to two little crabs scooting sideways across the sand and shuddered. "Ugh. One of them poked me. Get away." She danced backward as the bigger one, all of two inches across, scuttled a few steps her direction. "Nasty things. They're just big, hard spiders."

She was totally freaked. Panicked. He laughed. He knew he shouldn't, but he did.

"It's not funny," she snapped.

"Come on, Barnett. Jake Navarro's two-year-old puts crabs on her head," he said, referring to a colleague they both knew.

"Good for her. Fine. It *is* funny. It's an absolute hoot." She stood there, glaring at him but with one wary eye on the crabs. The big one popped down into his hole—right where she'd been lying, as it turned out. She flicked a little sand at the other with her toe, and it skittered off down the beach. Slowly, her face relaxed into an expression of chagrin.

"Got me right on the butt," she muttered, shrugging her shirt back into place.

"I can hardly blame him. It's a very nice butt." Still chuckling, Reade got to his feet and reached out to pull her back into his arms. "Jackie, I—"

"No," she said, quick-stepping away like he was one of the crabs. "I don't know what happened a minute ago, but it's not going to happen again."

"It's called a kiss."

"I know that, but you—"

"It was mutual this time," he pointed out.

"It was mutually dumb, is what it was," she said firmly. "We don't even like each other."

"Given. But we *are* consenting adults."

"I'm not consenting. And adult or not, I don't partic-

ularly want you pawing me in front of your mom and
Farley." She pointed out to sea.

He turned and groaned. There they were, paddling in,
so close that they had undoubtedly seen enough to keep
the myth of budding romance alive. He was never going
to live this one down.

There was nothing to do but raise a hand and wave
them on in.

Walt Armstrong checked his E-mail one last time be-
fore he headed home. The first one was from the dean
of the School of Medicine—he was having a cocktail
party next Thursday. Walt hit Reply and accepted, then
scrawled the date on his desk calendar. There were a couple of other messages from colleagues. And one from
Jackie Barnett. He double-clicked on that one.

Dear Walt. Being bold sucks. Jackie.

He laughed aloud.

He closed his E-mail, shut down his computer, and
spent the next five minutes getting dressed to go out in
forty-below weather. As he flipped off the lights, he
thought of Jackie, playing games with Farley Phelps on
the beach, and chuckled again.

Being bold sucks.

She didn't know the half of it.

Thirty minutes under the hottest water the pipes
would deliver and a large dose of ibuprofen took care
of the ache in Jackie's arms, but it didn't touch the
thousand-watt current running through the rest of her
body. She recognized it as the aftereffect of danger, but
whether it arose from the danger she'd survived at sea or
the more subtle one she faced on land, she wasn't sure.
Every time she thought of slamming into that wave and
popping out the other side, alive, she got another jolt. But
she got the same kind of jolt when she thought about

Reade's mouth descending over hers, or recalled his arms around her and his weight pressing her down into the sand.

She didn't much like either sensation. They both brought an unsettled stomach and shaky hands, along with the feeling of being out of control, a state she usually tried to avoid. But by far the worse of the two was the way she reacted to Hunter.

Like now.

Here they were, simply walking over to the casino that sat next door to Fair Winds, and every nerve in her body was buzzing with awareness of the man at her side. He wasn't even doing anything to warrant that kind of reaction, just talking to Farley about some bike trail up in the mountains, yet her body was busily gearing up for sex.

Like she would let that happen.

"I'm amazed you have the energy to come out tonight," said Lenore over her shoulder. "I'm tired, and I barely paddled at all."

"I'm a little tired, but I've never been to a casino," said Jackie. "I thought I should try it at least once." Not to mention that Reade's presence made hers a necessity, no matter how she felt.

"I think Jackie's in a little better shape than you are, Mom," said Reade, interrupting his conversation with Farley.

Maybe it was pheromones at work, she thought idly as he stepped ahead to hold aside one branch of a huge poinsettia bush that hung in their path. She'd done some undergrad research on human pheromones, and although the effects were usually subtle, they were also utterly undiscriminating. She could just be reacting to Hunter's sweat. Now there was an off-putting notion.

"It probably wouldn't hurt to get some kind of sports rub on those shoulders," he said as she brushed past him.

And he'd probably be all too happy to help her put it on, too. Another bolt of electricity danced through Jackie's belly. She pushed it aside. "Thanks. I actually

packed some Flexall, because I figured Ben would need
it. The only problem is that it's—"

"—in Kenya," he completed, falling in beside her.

She laughed. "Or maybe Togo, by now."

"I have some arnica gel back at my place," said Farley.
"I'll get it for you when we get back. Great stuff. You'll
be ready to go water-skiing in the morning."

"Water-skiing?" She stopped dead. The idea of hanging
onto a towrope brought her to the edge of tears. All those
poor little muscle fibers . . .

"You can't be serious," said Lenore.

Farley roared with laughter. "You two should see your
faces. It's a joke, ladies. No water-skiing. In fact, I have
to make a run into Port Meredith on business tomorrow,
so you're all on your own."

The space around Jackie's head suddenly got lighter,
as though the governor had phoned in a pardon. A whole
day of no Hunter. She could rest up and get her libido
back under control. She could even relax and enjoy herself
tonight. Maybe.

She wasn't really sure about this whole casino thing.
She'd never gambled in her life, unless you counted the
Fire Department's turkey bingo nights or matchstick
poker with her cousins. The whole idea of risking actual
money on some game that was in the house's favor before
you even started struck her as, well, stupid. Sort of like
throwing a bunch of bills in a toilet and flushing, then
convincing yourself you'd won if a few of them floated.
If Reade and Lenore hadn't jumped on Farley's suggestion to walk over here to check out the action, she never
would have come. She hated tapping into her emergency
money for something like this.

Inside the casino, it was a different world, totally artificial and cut off from the island outside. The windows in
the main room were curtained in thick velvet to block the
light, and the air-conditioning that washed over them was
devoid of the rich scents that pervaded the island breezes.
The patter of the dealers mingled with the whir and rattle

of roulette wheels and the electronic jangle of slot machines.

A blackjack game drew Reade in, while Farley and Lenore headed straight for the baccarat table. Jackie watched them for a few minutes, then wandered around the room, observing and trying to figure out the rules and odds. Most of the games were pretty straightforward, but the craps table mystified her.

Sometimes seven won. Sometimes it lost. Sometimes people were happy to see a three, sometimes they couldn't care less.

She was standing there, trying to decipher rules that made no apparent sense, when a ripple of awareness told her Reade had come up behind her.

"Are you planning to watch all evening?" he asked.

"Maybe."

"That's one way to hold on to your money."

"The only way, so far as I can see." In her current state, she should probably blow him off, but she couldn't resist asking, "Do you understand the rules for this game? I must be missing something."

"You've come to the right place." A couple left, and he grabbed their stools. "Here. There's fresh game starting. If you really want to learn, sit down with me and make a few bets. I'll explain as we go along."

"New shooter coming out," said the dealer as a different man stepped up to the end of the table.

Jackie hesitated. Sitting this close to Hunter was probably a lousy idea, but so was letting him get the idea she was nervous about either him or the game. When he patted the empty stool, she gave in and sat down.

"Okay. They probably use European names here, but I know the American ones, so you're stuck. You have a boxman with the money, a stickman who calls the rolls and handles the dice, and two dealers, each responsible for bets in his own end. Everyone else is a player."

The boxman swapped their money for chips. Reade

placed one on the table and caught the dealer's eye. "Five to Pass."

Five pounds seemed like a lot for one bet, but Jackie followed suit. "Okay. I know that Pass is betting that the shooter will win, and Don't Pass is betting that he'll lose. But that's about as far as I got."

"Okay." Reade scooted closer and spoke quickly, keeping his voice low. "The first roll is called the come out. The shooter has to establish his point, which is the number he has to match later on. Only four, five, six, eight, nine, and ten can be points. If he gets anything else, he keeps rolling until he gets one of those point numbers."

"But don't the other numbers mean something, too?"

"Yes, and what they mean depends on where you're at in the game, which is probably what's giving you trouble. On the come out, if the shooter gets a seven or eleven, our Pass Line bet wins. If he gets two, three, or twelve, we lose. A Don't Pass bet is the opposite, except that twelve is called a push, which is neutral—no win, no loss. Now watch."

The shooter made a show of blowing on the dice, then rolled.

"Six," said the stickman.

The dealer laid a white puck on the six on his end of the table. "The point is six, ladies and gentlemen."

"Now he has to roll another six before a seven comes up, right?" asked Jackie.

"Yep. That's called making his point. Since we bet Pass, if he does get his six, we win."

"And if he doesn't, we lose and he's out. But what about two, three, eleven, and twelve?"

"They don't matter now that the point's established," said Reade. "Don't worry about them again until the next come out."

"Geez. No wonder I couldn't sort it out."

"Eight," said the stickman.

"It seems like six would be a relatively easy point to make. There are . . . what?" She calculated quickly. "Five ways to roll a six out of thirty-six possible combinations of dice."

"But there are six combinations that add up to seven," said Reade. "And that tiny disparity is why, over the long haul, casino owners make money and gamblers don't."

"Six," said the stickman.

"Shooter makes his point," said the dealer. He flipped the puck to black, moved it to the Don't Come area, and started settling bets.

"We won," said Jackie.

"One pound. Beginner's luck," said Reade. "This shooter is still up. He starts all over again with a come out roll and keeps going until he either sevens out or retires."

She placed another bet, going against Reade's advice to try out the Don't Pass line. She won on the initial roll, which she shouldn't have because it was a harder bet than Pass, then turned around and lost on what should have been the easier point bet.

"That was entirely against the odds," she grumped as the dealer took her chips.

"That's why they call it gambling," said Reade. "Still think it's fun?"

To her surprise, she did. There was a certain excitement in trying to outguess the dice. She selected another five-pound chip. "Let's try that again."

"How about a more sophisticated bet?"

"I'm all ears, Professor."

He took her through taking odds, betting on hard ways, placing to win, and laying a number, coaching her on odds and strategy at the same time. It was like studying a foreign language and statistics at the same time, but the more she learned, the more fun it was, trying to get an edge on the house.

Several shooters came and went. With Reade guiding her bets, Jackie did well enough to stay nearly even. She was only ten pounds down when the game came around to Reade.

"I'll pass to the lady," he said.

"Me?" asked Jackie. "No."

"Yes. It's time. You can't call yourself a craps player until you've handled the dice."

"She's never played before?" asked a man in a cowboy hat who was passing by. He stepped in next to Jackie. "You've never played before?"

"No," said Jackie.

"Hot damn. A thousand with the lady."

"I'm sorry, sir," said the dealer. "The maximum initial bet at this table is one hundred pounds."

"Then put a hundred on Pass."

A buzz ran down the table. Three more people quickly put maximum bets on the Pass Line.

Jackie turned to Reade. "What's going on?"

"It's the Virgin Principle. Myth has it that a female virgin is always hot on her first roll."

"A man obviously dreamed up that one." She leaned closer and dropped her voice. "One problem, I'm not a—" She stopped herself. "I'm not."

"Thank you," said Reade with a twinkle in his eye. "I'll file that information away for future reference. However, in craps, a virgin is someone who has never thrown the dice before."

"Oh. Good." Heat flooded her cheeks, but she kept a straight face. The stickman, however, chuckled merrily, apparently having heard the whole exchange. She hoped no one else had. She didn't have the nerve to look around to see.

"Go on. People are waiting." Reade tugged her stool backward, and she stood up. "Aren't you glad you didn't have an audience the first time you lost your virginity?"

"What makes you think I didn't?"

Where'd that come from? Cheeks still glowing, she walked to the end of the table, tossed a single chip on the table, grabbed the dice, and quickly threw them, hoping to go out right away and get it over with, so she could retreat under a rock somewhere.

"Seven."

"Pass Line wins. The lady's still after her point."

She rolled again.

"Nine. The point is nine."

Jackie got her nine on her third roll. The cowboy gave her a thumbs-up and told the dealer to let his money ride.

This time, she established her point right away, a ten. Good. That would be tough to make—only three possible combinations. She'd be out of here any second.

She made her ten on the next roll.

"Thanks, gentlemen." She reached for her winnings. A massive hand shot out and grabbed her wrist before she could touch the chips.

"Whoa, darlin'. Where are you goin'?" asked the cowboy at the other end of the hand. Reade watched with interest.

"I figured I'd quit while I'm ahead," she said.

"You can't do that."

"Why not? Is there some rule I missed?"

"No, but you're right at the beginning of what looks to be a nice little streak," he said. "Come on, roll a few more. You only get to be a virgin once."

"Or twice," said Reade. The table erupted in laughter.

Okay, so everyone *had* heard the earlier exchange. Embarrassment jacked up the buzz she already had from her two little wins and turned it into recklessness. She patted the cowboy's mitt where it curved around her wrist. "Tell you what, Tex. Keep that fellow quiet, and I'll stand here and roll dice until you tell me to stop."

"That's a deal, darlin'." He released her and moved in behind Reade to rest one beefy hand on his shoulder.

"Does this mean we're going steady?" asked Reade. Tex didn't move.

"The lady still has the dice," said the dealer.

So she stood there and rolled, and whether it was the Virgin Principle, raw luck, or pure coincidence, she kept winning. And winning.

Her hands started shaking on her fifth straight pass. By

her tenth, so many people were pushing in around the table that the boxman had to ask them to step back. Excited by her streak, they did so reluctantly. Jackie was as jazzed as any of them. Jazzed and terrified, as if she had managed to walk halfway across a circus high wire and only now realized there was no net.

Technically speaking, the odds on her next roll were precisely the same as they had been on her very first one, but it felt entirely different. Thirty or forty people wanted her to make it. Tex, with his big pile of chips riding on her, building with each pass, wanted her to make it. Even the dealer and stickman seemed to want her to make it.

The only one who didn't want her to make it was Reade. Or maybe he did. She couldn't tell, because he refused to look at her, to signal what she should do. He just sat there, the tip of his index finger resting on his chips, looking at something very far away.

Fine. It wasn't his choice anyway.

"Tex, do you want me to stop?"

"You've done us both proud, darlin'. It's up to you, but I'm with you all the way."

He must have a couple of grand lying there in front of him. She looked down her own pile of chips, grown substantial through neglect. One more roll, and she'd have nearly enough to make up for Ben's share of this trip, and wouldn't have to worry about her credit card bill. Anxiety and greed vibrated through her system.

What if she lost?

She wouldn't. It'd be okay.

It was nuts. She should get out now.

No. She wanted that money.

And she wanted to know if she could do it. That's what it was all about, just knowing if she could.

She took a deep breath. "I'm in for one more. Let it ride."

Her come out roll gave her a six, the easiest point of all to make, and she smiled. Piece of cake.

Taking a deep breath, she reached for the dice, closed

her eyes, and let them rip. She heard the double thud as they ricocheted off the opposite end. She had it. She had it.

The group "oh" of disappointment told her before the stickman's announcement.

"Seven out."

Stunned, she stared down at the table as her chips were raked up along with a lot of other people's. When she looked up, her rooting section was scattering, moving on to other amusement. The dealer reached out and shook her hand, as did the stickman. Tex came around the table like a locomotive with no brakes.

"I haven't seen a run like that in my whole life," he hollered. He picked her up in a bear hug and set her down, then did it again for good measure. "I'm just sorry you wasted all that luck on this picayune game. You'd be hell on wheels at one of the high stakes tables."

She couldn't get her mind around what had happened. "But I lost. You lost. All that money."

"We only really lost our initial bets, sweetheart. The rest of it was never ours to start with. And think of how much fun we had. Win or lose, there's nothing that juices you up like goin' for the big roll."

He was right. Despite the loss, she was still floating on the leftover high. Twice today she'd been absolutely reckless, and she'd survived. Life was good.

"New player," said the dealer.

Tex tugged her aside. "Got to let the next poor sonuvabitch have his shot. Excuse me, but I hear my wife hollerin' over there by the roulette wheel, and it sounds like she's havin' way too much fun without me. It was sheer pleasure to bet with you, miss. See you around."

"See you, Tex."

He sliced into the crowd, and in a moment even the top of his Stetson vanished. Reade watched him go, then got up and slowly strolled over to her, his hands behind his back.

He stopped in front of her and rocked back on his heels

like a schoolboy. "May I please speak now?"

She winced. "I'm sorry. It was a joke. He took it a little seriously."

"A little? My shoulder has his handprint embedded in it. It may be permanent." He ducked his head a little, so that he could see into her eyes. "You look shell-shocked. How are you doing?"

"Starting to come down." Not fast enough, though, if her still-pounding pulse was any indication. Of course, there was the distinct possibility Reade was contributing to the racing pulse. She moved away from him, looking for some space and some time to get herself sorted out.

"Hang on a minute. I need to cash out, and then I'll buy you a drink."

He turned to the boxman and handed over a stack of chips in exchange for a handful of bills. When he came back to her, he quickly counted out half the money, stuck it in his pocket and pressed the rest into her hand. "Your cut, madam."

"What? I didn't win anything."

"No. But I did."

She looked down at the money. "This is over two hundred pounds. Did you bet against me?"

"No." He laughed. "But I pulled most of my money out before that last throw. I could tell you were thinking way too hard."

"I had to think. That was a lot of money."

"But you weren't listening to your gut." He touched her belly just below her rib cage. "Right there, Barnett. No thinking. What was it telling you?"

Every overactive nerve in her body zeroed in on the pressure of his fingertips through her dress. She could barely breathe, much less think. "Stop."

"That's right. And you stood there and argued with yourself and rationalized your way into one more shot." He took his hand away, and oxygen returned to her brain. "Let's get that drink."

Alcohol and Hunter, in the state she was in? Not a wise

idea, but she found herself ignoring her gut yet again and following him toward the bar.

He ordered Myers Dark, neat, for himself, and a daiquiri for her. She sipped the drink slowly, telling herself she was only going to drink half.

"Can we go see how your mom and Farley are doing at the baccarat table?"

"Sure. Just don't expect me to explain what they're doing," said Reade. "That's one game I've never played."

"That's okay. Baccarat, I understand. *I'll* explain it to *you*."

And then maybe she could get him to tell her what you should do when your gut gave you conflicting information.

nine

When they finally stepped out of the casino's artificial
atmosphere, Jackie was shocked to discover that the
sky was black and thick with stars. More time had passed
than she had realized. It was after midnight. The path back
to Fair Winds was well lit, however, and she and the
others strolled along slowly, enjoying the night breeze and
chatting about nothing in particular: some joke the bartender told, a wild-looking dress one of the other patrons
wore, why the moon looks bigger at the horizon than up
in the sky.

"I'm going to hit the sack," said Farley as they reached
the lobby. "But I want to get that arnica gel for Jackie
first."

"That's very nice, but it's not really necessary," she
said. "I'll be fine without it."

"You may think so, but I promise it'll make one hell
of difference in how you feel tomorrow. I'll zip down to
get it and be right back. Would you like to walk with me,
Lenore?"

"I'd love to."

"We'll meet you out on the terrace."

They took off, leaving Jackie standing there with Reade. She looked at him and shrugged. "I guess I'm going to the terrace."

"Apparently."

It was Cabaret Night at Fair Winds, but the show had just ended. Jackie meandered along the back of the audience, ostensibly looking for an empty table.

Reade followed. "You've had quite a day."

"Thanks to you." She stopped and turned to face him. "And I do mean that. Thank you. You made both the kayaking and the casino"—she hunted for a neutral word—"memorable. Although I'm still not sure why."

"I'll admit to a certain level of guilt over nearly drowning you this afternoon."

"You know, I almost believe that."

"Only almost?" He drifted around to the other side of her and leaned up against a post. "Who's Ben?"

"Where did you get that name from?" she asked, suddenly suspicious. It occurred to her that he had her wedged up against the shrubbery, where it would be impossible to escape without ducking under his arm.

"You said you packed Flexall for someone named Ben. Farley going for the arnica gel reminded me. Is he your boyfriend?"

She hesitated. Did she really want Reade Hunter to know this?

"Married lover?" he guessed.

"You have a dirty mind." When he kept looking at her with that totally unperturbed expression, she added, "He's my ex-boyfriend."

"Recently ex, I take it."

"If you consider Friday recent, then yes."

"Friday? I'm sorry."

"Don't be. Any relationship that can be ended by voice mail doesn't require sorrow from anyone."

"Voice mail?" His face wrinkled in disgust. "Maybe I

should be congratulating you on getting rid of him."

"That works for me," she said, fighting a smile.

"He sounds like a jerk."

"That works, too." The smile crept onto her lips, but she went for some damage control anyway. "I'd better not hear about this *anywhere* once we leave St. Sebastian."

He laughed, but he raised two fingers like a Boy Scout making a pledge. Before he could take any vows, however, the sound of raised voices made them both turn. Lenore and Farley were storming their way.

"I'm telling you, I saw him," she snapped. She spotted Reade and repeated herself. "I saw him."

"Saw who?"

"That man from the falls."

Farley shook his head. "There was no one there."

"What are you two talking about?" asked Reade.

"There was a man at Mystery Falls," said Lenore. "He kept turning up wherever we went."

"You saw him twice," said Farley. "Maybe. There were hundreds of people there."

"Not following you around, there weren't." She addressed Reade. "This man had very peculiar eyes and big, thick dreadlocks, and I saw him just now on the way back from Farley's cabana."

"Speaking of which. . . ." Farley pulled a green tube out of his shirt pocket and handed it to Jackie as he said, "I think she saw a shadow."

"Don't talk about me like I'm not here," said Lenore. "It was no shadow. I saw those dreadlocks."

Farley wasn't going to buy it. "Several of the resort workers wear dreads, you know."

"Why would one of the workers be sneaking around in the bushes outside your house at this hour?" argued Lenore.

"Maintenance?" suggested Reade.

"This was not a maintenance worker. It was him."

Farley swore, then took a deep breath. "Look, if it will make you feel better, I'll call security."

"Good. It's about time you took this seriously."

"Excuse me." He went off in search of a phone. Lenore stood there, hugging herself, a worried crease between her eyebrows.

"This concerns me," she insisted quietly to Reade. "That man could be a kidnapper or stalker or something."

"Assuming there is a man."

Lenore glared at her son. "It's bad enough Farley doesn't believe me. My own son should know better."

"All right, Mom. You saw someone. But let's not let our imaginations run away with us."

Farley came back. "Okay. Security is sending someone to check things out. Are you happy?"

"Happier, anyway," said Lenore. "Thank you."

"Good." Farley took her hand and kissed it. "Then let's get you back to your room, so I can go meet the security people. Reade, you'll make sure Jackie gets back safely, won't you?"

"It's really not necessary," said Jackie, but Farley and Lenore were already disappearing into the darkness. She turned to Reade and repeated herself. "I can find my way back on my own. I do it all the time."

"I know, you're an independent woman and all that. But I have my instructions, and just in case Mom's right and there really is some stalker out there. . . ."

A shiver ran up and down Jackie's spine, but only part of it had to do with some theoretical bad guy. "*If* there is, he's after Farley, not me. I'll go by myself, thank you."

"Don't tell me I make you nervous."

"Don't be ridic—"

"You are. Here I've been nice to you all evening, and you're more afraid of me than a possible stalker."

"You're delusional."

"Then prove it. Come on, Barnett, give me a cheap thrill. It's been years since I walked a girl home."

She hesitated. A whole day's worth of adrenaline, combined with her run at the craps table and now Lenore's flight of fancy, had her so charged up that if she stuck a light bulb in her mouth, she'd make a darned good reading lamp. She really didn't want to be alone with Reade just now. However, there wasn't much choice, unless she wanted to confess that the reason she didn't want to go with him was that she was worried about the effect he might have on her.

Reade stepped closer, as though her secret was already out. "You have my word. I won't do anything you don't want me to do."

That was just the problem. She was going to have to brazen this one out. "All right. Just to be rid of you."

They headed for her cabana, cutting through the gardens to avoid a group of drunken partyers who were on the main path. Exotic by day, at night the gardens took on a grotesque air, with their lush growth and unfamiliar shapes. The path lights painted wild outlines onto the walls and threw everything beyond their reach into inky blackness. As they passed one deeply shadowed grotto, they heard movement. Thinking it might be Lenore's stalker after all, Jackie slowed to listen. The rustle resolved into a woman's voice, moaning the name Charlie, followed by a man's answering murmur of need.

Feeling like she'd peeked into the wrong car at the drive-in, Jackie scurried on, head down, pretending she hadn't heard. Pretending couldn't undo the damage, though. Her body pulsed with the knowledge of what the couple in the dark was doing. What she and Reade could be doing in a few minutes, if. . . . She lost her train of thought as her nipples tightened in anticipation.

Adrenaline and hormones were *not* a good mix, she decided. As they neared her cabana, she floundered for something, anything, that would let her regain some sense of reality.

"So, what are you going to do tomorrow?" she asked.

"Why? Did you have some sudden inspiration back there?"

"No, but I'm *so* glad you asked. You hadn't made any smarmy comments all evening, and I was starting to worry. I thought you were going soft on me."

"No." They had reached her patio, and as she started for the door, he pulled her into his arms. "Definitely not soft."

He had the wickedest eyes—not evil, but naughty, flashing with the kind of mischief that could get a girl in serious trouble. And he smelled so good, an exotic mix of spices and woods that. . . .

Wait a minute. Pheromones.

What's-his-name in Hunter's lab—Navarro—had published a paper on artificial pheromones a few years back. What if Hunter had gotten his hands on a vial of leftovers? He'd said something this afternoon about Navarro's kid. They were probably friends. She wouldn't put it past him to douse himself in chemicals on the off chance he could jerk her around a little. There was definitely something unusual about the way he smelled—unusual and deliciously male.

She closed her eyes and inhaled, trying to analyze the mix of scents that enfolded her along with his arms—an exercise complicated by the fact that he was kissing her into a stupor. She momentarily lost herself in the sweep of his tongue into her mouth and the delicious dance of his hands over her body, possessive and seductive. He really did kiss well. She had a feeling he did a lot of things well.

However, it would hardly be wise to find out, no matter how many body parts he was making throb. This was Hunter, after all. When he started nibbling his way downward, she reined herself in hard.

"Whoa. Time out."

He groaned against the upper curve of her breast. "What? You're not going to convince me you're not enjoying this."

Enjoying it? If he got to her nipple, she'd show him enjoying.

No, she wouldn't. She put her hands in the middle of his chest and pressed firmly.

"Just because a person enjoys something, that doesn't mean she has to do it."

He released her and backed off a step, frowning as she readjusted her dress. "God. You sound like a nun who just caught a kid with a dirty magazine."

"Let's skip the rehash of your Catholic school experiences," she said. "Good night. It's been charming, but I'm safe and sound now. You can tell Farley you did your duty."

He didn't move, so she did, turning away and reaching into her purse for her key card. He stepped in close behind her and put his hands on her waist to pull her back against his body.

"You were enjoying it," he murmured.

Exactly the problem. His breath was hot against the nape of her neck, and it was everything she could do not to wiggle her hips against his crotch, just to see what would happen. She slipped the card into the lock.

"We would be good together," he whispered.

They would. And then they'd kill each other. "Good night, Hunter."

He stood there a moment longer, his hands still on her. Then they were gone, and he was gone, and she was standing there with her body soft and achy.

Jackie let herself into her room and flipped the switch. Her bed had been turned down, and for an instant after the light flared, she imagined Reade slipping in behind her, pushing her down on the cool, white sheets. She could call him back. . . .

Darn it if he hadn't managed to jumble up her emotions again. It was more disconcerting than tumbling around in that wave this afternoon. At least there, she'd had a helmet and a life preserver. On dry land, there was no protective equipment against Reade Hunter and his pheromones—at least nothing that was FDA-approved.

With a groan of frustration, she firmly turned the lock on Reade Hunter and her libido. *Never the twain shall meet.*

*   *   *

"*For God's sake, people, take it inside,*" muttered Reade as he passed the bower where "Oh-oh, Charlie" still caroused with "Mmm-Baby" in the dark. Ordinarily, male solidarity would lead him to be more sympathetic to Charlie's good fortune, but just now, Reade was pissed—at himself, at Barnett, at the situation, and most especially at Chuck for getting some when he wasn't going to. He headed for his room, grumbling about Barnett's inopportune moment of moral fortitude.

He had reason to be grateful for that burst of backbone the next morning, however, when he woke up alone, in his own bed, free of the complications that would have tangled around him along with Barnett's long legs.

God, what a mess that would be. What had he been thinking? He understood his reaction on the beach—he'd been stoked from the waves and relieved that she was unhurt, and that kiss had come as spontaneously as the one at the falls. But why he'd pursued her after dinner was a mystery known only to his gonads. He didn't even like the woman.

No. That wasn't quite true. He didn't like Barnett, the reserved and tightly wound scientist he knew from E-mails and journal reviews and patronizing, equation-loaded letters.

Jackie was an entirely different matter. The quick-witted, razor-tongued, sexy competitor he'd dealt with in the last few days was proving to be a lot more attractive than he would have predicted, even as she sabotaged his efforts to get to Farley. Jackie made his pulse pound, tempted him to steal kisses, and filled his mind with fantasies of long, sleepless nights buried deep inside her. Jackie would be an exciting diversion while they were on St. Sebastian—if only she and Barnett didn't share the same body.

But oh, lordy, what a body. Just the thought of her in that swimsuit. . . . If he was just slightly insane, he might go ahead and make a real pass at her, see if he could initiate that fling Farley and Mom already thought they were having.

A surge of pure lust pounded through his groin, even as he laughed aloud at the idea. A fling with Barnett.

Reade threw off the covers and went to splash some water on his face and brush his teeth. For whatever reason, he had awakened early, so he had plenty of time for the long ocean swim that had eluded him so far. He grabbed his suit off the towel rack where it had been hanging and stepped into the bathroom.

When he hit the beach a few minutes later, a dozen or so early birds were in the water but there was plenty of room for him to work the kinks out. He put in a good mile and a half, maybe a mile and three-quarters, and he might have worked Jackie out of his system, too, if the taste of salt hadn't kept reminding him of her lips when he'd kissed her on the beach.

A fling with Barnett. He shook his head. No way was that on his list of things to do on winter vacation. Not to mention that she'd made it abundantly clear she'd never let him past first base.

She might not look like the tight-assed, repressed, ball-buster he'd always imagined, but when push came to shove, she was. Dr. Barnett was nervous about sex, or at least about the kind of sex she couldn't schedule in her DayTimer. He could tell from the way she reacted when he kissed her, the way she threw on the brakes as soon as she started to get into it at all. Hell, a serious pass, one that threatened to make her lose control, would probably send her screaming into the hills.

Which would leave him a clear field.

Which was exactly what he wanted.

Oh, man, this was too good. And so obvious, he should be demoted to amateur for not thinking of it earlier.

All he had to do was rattle Barnett's cage a little, which shouldn't be all that hard, because despite her obvious distress about her reactions, she *did* start to get into it.

That fact would make it incredibly easy to keep her off balance, just by reminding her that her desires lay right beneath the surface and that he knew it. Keep her on edge until she couldn't stand it anymore, and he'd be rid of her.

He'd have to give this a little more thought today while he was off biking, but from here, he couldn't see any downside. If for some reason he was wrong and she didn't panic and run, he'd at least have had some fun. And if she actually ran toward his bed instead of away—a possibility roughly equal to the odds of contracting malaria in downtown Detroit—he'd figure out something to do with her.

No matter what happened, though, it seemed to him he won.

Which was, after all, the whole point.

A night's sleep and the prospect of a few Hunter-free hours put Jackie back on an even keel emotionally, and Farley's arnica gel and another dose of ibuprofen took care of most of her aches and pains. She hit the breakfast buffet with a light step and a hearty appetite that was only slightly diminished by the sight of Farley and Lenore with their heads together.

Wherever Farley was, Reade was sure to be nearby, so she wasn't at all surprised to spot him over the top of a huge pile of fresh fruit at the next buffet station. He was talking to someone hidden behind a pineapple; Jackie shifted to the right until she could see that the object of his attentions was a hyper-tan blonde who looked like she'd never eaten anything with more than twenty percent of calories from fat in her life. After a moment, she turned on her heel and walked away, leaving Reade standing there gaping after her. Chuckling, Jackie added a slice of bacon to her plate, smug in the knowledge that her skin would still be soft and smooth long after the blonde looked like a piece of low-fat turkey jerky.

She finished filling her plate and was pouring a glass of juice when Reade sidled up next to her. She caught a whiff of his cologne, or whatever it was, and a wisp of smoke curled up through her center. Great. The day had barely started, and she was already in trouble.

"Good morning," he said.

"It was."

His shoulders sagged. "Ah, come on, Barnett. I thought we'd gotten past the sniping."

"What made you think that?" She started to set the pitcher back into its designated hollow in the ice, but Reade reached across to lift it out of her hands.

"Thanks." He held it up and read the label. "Orange-*passion*fruit. Interesting choice."

She was not going to let him get through to her. "Do you actually want some, or are you just doing commentary?"

"Is that an offer?" he asked, his eyes flashing with amusement.

It took her a second to realize what she'd said. *Do you want some?* Oh, God. Someone should just shoot her now. Blushing in eight shades of pink, she picked up her tray and made a break for Lenore and Farley's table, where she'd at least be insulated from Hunter's more blatant comments. He followed at a much more leisurely pace.

They'd barely gotten settled in when Farley laid down his fork. "Now that everyone's here, I have an apology to make. You were right, Lenore. Someone tried to break into my cabana last night."

"Farley!"

"Oh, my gosh."

"Did he, er, they get in?" asked Reade.

"He. And no, fortunately, security was there before he could cause much mischief—thanks to a certain lovely lady who was looking out for me." He turned to Lenore and put his hand over hers. "I am sorry for the way I dismissed your concerns. I behaved like an ass."

"Never mind about that," said Lenore. "Did they catch him?"

"Unfortunately, no."

"I hope you called the police. We can print out a copy of the picture I took to give them. I bet they'll know exactly who he is."

"Mom, you don't know for certain it was the same man."

"In fact, we're pretty sure it wasn't," said Farley. "One of the watchmen caught a glimpse of the fellow. He said it was a young kid—small, skinny, and very fast on his feet. He apparently had dreadlocks, though, so you were right about that, Lenore. Chances are it was just some local kid out to rip off a rich American. It wouldn't be the first time, and it won't be the last."

"You're going to have to be careful. If he comes back, he might—"

"I doubt he will, but if he does, security will be on their toes from now on, and so will I." Farley curled his fingers around Lenore's. "And you can watch my back today."

Reade looked up from his fried plantain, surprised. "I didn't know you were going into Port Meredith."

"Farley just invited me a few minutes ago," said Lenore. Coloring slightly, she tugged her hand free. "What are you two planning for the day?"

Hunter stabbed a piece of plantain and dangled it from his fork. "Minnow Bridge Trail."

"I convinced you, huh?" said Farley.

"You made it sound pretty good last night."

"You're going hiking?" asked Lenore. Her voice sounded so tight that Jackie looked up.

Reade's eyes flickered in that same odd way she'd seen on the boat when he'd mentioned his father. He shook his head. "Mountain biking."

"Oh." Lenore toyed with the handle of her butter knife. "Where is this trail?"

"It runs through the cloud forest up on the east side of Mount Redoubt," said Farley. "It's a spectacular ride."

"It sounds like it, although, frankly, I'm surprised either of you two can even move today."

"Oh, I'm not going," said Jackie.

"You're not?"

"Nope. I'm doing the spa thing—facial, massage, sea-weed wrap, the whole works. And then I'm going to park myself in one of those hammocks down by the beach with a great big glass of limeade and just lie there, swinging in the breeze."

"A sybarite's holiday," said Farley, chuckling. "Very good for the soul. If you can't find an empty hammock, there's one over by my lagoon. Feel free to use it."

"Thanks. I just may do that."

"So you're going by yourself?" said Lenore to Reade.

"Unless Jackie changes her mind in the next thirty seconds. What do you say, Barnett? Interested in a bike ride?"

His tone was light, and Jackie was 99.999 percent sure he didn't really want her to go, but she was tempted to say yes, just to screw with him. However, this was a jungle-swathed volcano he intended to ride down, not a paved bike trail in a city park.

"Gee, thanks. I think I'll pass."

Reade shrugged. "Guess I'm going solo, then."

"Maybe you could ask your blonde friend," suggested Jackie.

"Blonde friend?" asked Farley.

"Blonde friend?" echoed Reade. "Oh, Kathy. The woman I played volleyball with the first day. I bumped into her this morning in the buffet line." He looked straight into Jackie's eyes as he took a slow and very deliberate sip of his juice.

Passionfruit. This time, heat flooded through her like a burning oil spill. Good grief, the man must be the only person in the world who could turn OJ into a come-on. And she must be the only nitwit who would respond.

"At least the ride is a resort activity," murmured Lenore to herself. She pulled her purse into her lap and started poking around. Her hand came out curled around a bottle of Motrin, which she set next to her plate. "Are you going to drink the rest of your water?"

"Help yourself." Reade passed her his glass. "Are you getting a headache?"

"Just a little one. Don't worry about it."

Farley checked his watch—the first time Jackie recalled him wearing a one. "If I'm going to get to my business agent's office on time, we need to hit the road."

"Let me take this and my other medicine first. I don't want to get sick and ruin your day." Lenore dug through her purse some more. "Shoot. I must have left my pill case sitting by the bathroom sink."

Farley rose and pulled Lenore's chair out. "Not a problem. Go get what you need, then meet me at the front desk. I'm going to stop off and tell security not to hassle Jackie if she uses my hammock." He pulled his cap down on his forehead. "See you two later. Don't get worried if we're late. We may have dinner in town."

Lenore's face was pinched as she leaned over to kiss Reade on the top of the head. "Please be careful."

"You, too. Have fun." He gave her a quick squeeze around the waist. As she and Farley walked away, he turned to Jackie. "So you're really going to vegetate all day."

"You bet."

"If you're sore, you should move around."

"Good idea." She took a last bite of melon and stood up. "I'll take a nice little walk, right over to the spa. It's time for my facial. 'Bye."

He shot to his feet, snatching at his napkin as it fell off his lap. "Come with me, Jackie."

"Yeah, right." She stepped around him, but he shifted to block her. His eyes said he wasn't teasing this time. "Why on earth would you want me along?"

"Because it would be more fun to share the ride with somebody."

"Even me?"

The corners of his mouth danced as he fought down a smile. "Even you."

"A ringing endorsement," she said. "Thanks, but I'm sore, and I'm tired. And I'm not sure I can survive another one of your little adventures."

"It's just a bike ride," he said. "And it's mostly downhill. And they have helmets and first aid kits and maps and compasses and all that nice equipment you're going to say we need to be safe."

She looked at him through narrowed eyes. "You think you have me pegged, don't you?"

He nodded. "Pretty much."

"So if you believe I'm such an overcautious bore, why do you want me along?"

He started to say something, stopped, then started again. "Everyone should see a cloud forest once in their life."

"*Pphht*. Tell me, what's the extra, added attraction today? Riding off a cliff?"

He threw up his hands and stepped aside, but his smile lingered. "I'm not going to stand here and beg you to come along while you insult me. You have a nice, *safe* day at the spa, Jackie. I'll see you later and tell you all about the fun I had."

He walked off, tossing his napkin on the table as he passed.

Jackie watched him until he disappeared around a corner, and then turned in the opposite direction and headed for the spa.

ten

"*I hope I didn't take too long,*" said Lenore as she hurried up to the front desk.

Farley thanked a man in a natty, white uniform, then turned to her, smiling. "Not at all. I was just finishing up. Did you get everything you need for our day in the big city?"

"I hope so. I double-checked this time."

"Then let us away, madam. Our chariot awaits."

Outside, the young man standing by a white Jeep jumped to open the passenger door for her. As she waited for Farley to walk around to the driver's side, she spotted Reade walking his bike toward the road.

"I wonder where he's going," she said as Farley got in.

"Looks like he's headed for the bus stop."

"A public bus? I thought this was a resort trip."

"It is, usually. He must have missed the van." He switched on the ignition, then fiddled with air conditioner controls. A blast of hot, humid air hit Lenore in the face.

"He'll be up there on the mountain by himself."

"Oh, I doubt that. There will be other people on the trail. Plus he'll probably run into the resort group."

"But what if he doesn't? What if something happens and he's alone?"

"Nothing's going to happen."

"You can't be sure of that." She fanned herself with her hand. "I wish the air conditioner would kick in. It's so hot, I can hardly breathe."

"We'll get going. That will help." He put the car into gear and started up the drive.

As Farley turned right onto the road, Lenore twisted to see Reade at the bus stop. He was checking something on the bike and didn't see her wave.

The air got thicker. Sudden dizziness made her stomach roll. "Farley, I don't feel very well."

"What's going on?"

"I think I'm having one of my spells. We should go back. Reade knows what to do."

"So do I now, remember? I'll take care of you." He reached over and took her wrist. "Just sit back and relax a minute."

She sucked at the air. "This is worse than usual."

"There's a clinic in the next village. If you're sick, I'll take you there."

"I want you to get Reade," she insisted.

"Tell me exactly what you're feeling," he said, but he kept driving.

She listed her symptoms—racing pulse, shortness of breath, dizziness. "Please go back, Farley, before that bus comes."

"If it turns out that you really need Reade, I promise I can get word to him, no matter where he is. However, right now you're stuck with me. So I want you to sit back, close your eyes, and take a few deep breaths. In."

He was so calm, so sure of himself, that she obeyed: a long breath in through the nose, hold for a count of four, breathe out through the mouth. The slow, controlled pace was difficult at first, but once she mastered it, she seemed to have more air. The dizziness gradually faded.

"That's it," murmured Farley. "Just relax and breathe."

She leaned back against the headrest, eyes closed, while she got herself back together. After a time, she raised her head and looked around. "How much farther to the clinic?"

"We passed it five minutes ago," said Farley.

"We what? You said you were taking me to the clinic."

"No, I said I would take you if you were sick. You're not sick."

"Yes, I am."

"How do you feel right now?"

She mentally cruised through her body, searching for some symptom outside her usual aches and pains. "Fine, I guess. For now."

"That's what I thought." He released her wrist, and she realized he'd been taking her pulse all along. "If you hadn't had these spells before and been checked out by your doctors, I would have taken you straight to a doctor. But since you have, and since you seemed fine by the time we got to the clinic, I decided to keep driving."

"You mean you decided to gamble with my life," she said angrily.

He glanced at her briefly and turned his eyes back to the road. "Do you honestly think that your life was in danger?"

She started to snap "Yes," but her anger fizzled out. "No."

"Neither did I. And now we can enjoy our day in Port Meredith instead of spending it sitting in a busy clinic waiting for yet another doctor to poke and prod at you and tell you he doesn't know what's wrong."

Lenore folded her arms across her chest. "I don't know whether to be furious with you or not."

"You can decide later," he said mildly. "There's a lot of day left, and since I'm driving, it'll be much more convenient to be pissed at me once we're back at the resort."

She had to smile at his warped logic.

"I'll take that as agreement," he said. "So, what would you rather do while I'm in my meeting—Gallery Row, the history museum, or the public market?"

All day alone.
        No Farley. No Lenore. No Reade.

Jackie smiled down at the floor through the face rest on a massage table. No Reade, and a masseuse named Cora with the hands of a saint.

She sighed in deep contentment as Cora worked her way down her right arm. "Can I take you home with me?"

Cora's laugh caressed as deeply as her touch. "That depends. Do you have room for my five children and my husband?"

"Five? Uh, no. Can't do it. Pits."

Chuckling, Cora milked each finger separately, drawing the tension out of the tips. When she finished, she shifted to the other side of the table and started on the left arm.

"You don't really want me anyway," she said. "What you need is a man who knows how to give a proper massage that includes all your sex parts. Now that will cure most any ache you have."

Oh, yeah. Jackie groaned as Reade invaded her mind in all his aggravating glory. He'd give a proper massage, all right.

"Am I hurting you?" asked Cora.

"No. No, I'm fine."

"You're thinking of one man in particular, then."

"No. No one."

"You lie, woman." Cora shifted again, this time to her shoulders, and Jackie's imagination immediately substituted Reade's hands, as warm as they'd been on the boat, slick with lotion and moving downward. He'd include her "sex parts," all right.

Enough, already.

"You know, Cora, I could really use a lot of work on

my neck. I took a bad spill in a kayak yesterday, and I'm kind of sore."

"Don't worry about your neck, I'll give it plenty of attention. You just relax yourself. By the end of the day, you'll feel like a new woman."

Hopefully, one who didn't like Reade Hunter.

The bells of Governor's Tower were chiming noon when Lenore spotted Farley heading her way.

"You're very cheery for someone who just spent two hours on a conference call during his vacation," she said.

He kissed her on the cheek. "That's because it ended on time, and we got everything settled so they won't have to call me again. How are you feeling?"

"Still fine. I'm glad you didn't let me mess up your day."

"That was never the issue," he said. "Are you hungry?"

"Starving."

"Do I have the place for you. Come on."

He took her down by the waterfront, where they stuffed themselves on deep-fried conch and dumplings at a huge warehouse of a restaurant that was filled with locals and tourists and workers off the cruise ship that was tied up at the wharf.

Afterward, they wandered through old Port Meredith, exploring the shops that occupied buildings that had once been the taverns and brothels at the heart of the original pirate refuge. Lenore found a pair of earrings she liked and bought a handful of postcards, and Farley picked up a shirt. When the shops petered out, Lenore and Farley just kept strolling, out the cobblestone road to the tip of the jetty, where a defunct battery had once protected pirates from the Royal Navy, and then the Royal Governor from the pirates.

When the sun got to be too much, they came back and bought shaved ice with soursop syrup in paper cups, and found a bench in the shade where they could watch people and boats come and go.

"Listen, you can hear the buoy bell," said Lenore. "I love harbor towns. If I had my choice of all the places I could live, it would be within hearing of a foghorn."

"So why are you in Pittsburgh?" asked Farley.

"Because Reade lives there."

"What about your other sons?"

"Ash and Kit? They travel too much with their work. Ash is a charter jet pilot, and Kit's a professional skier."

"So Reade stays home to take care of you."

"Not exactly," she said. "He just happens to be the one with a job that keeps in him one place."

"Mmm."

"What was that?" she asked.

"What?"

"That 'Mmm.' Like you didn't quite believe me. What was that?"

"The sound of my brain working. It groans sometimes when I'm trying to stretch it around an idea." He finished off his shaved ice and set the empty paper cup on the bench beside him. "This is a tough one."

"Maybe I can help."

"I hope so." He hesitated. "I've seen a pattern in the last few days that concerns me."

"What kind of pattern?"

"I have a big fat file about Reade sitting on my desk. I practically have it memorized, and that puts me in an extraordinary position—an outsider with a lot of detailed information. It gives me a unique perspective. And I'm just starting to understand something." He paused again, taking another deep breath before he started again. "Reade used to be way out there, always on the edge. Serious rock climbing. Skydiving. Backpacking the Brooks Range by himself. And not just for fun, either. He had a spot as the number two man on an expedition to Venezuela."

"He was going to look for new drugs," said Lenore.

"He always said he would find the cure for cancer in some witch doctor's pot."

"And then about six years ago, he turned into Mr. Homebody. Why?"

"My husband died. Reade decided that as eldest, he should be the one to take care of me. I told him I didn't need taking care of, but he insisted. It's not something I'm happy about."

"Then why do you keep insisting he does?"

"I beg your pardon. What is it you think I'm doing to Reade?"

"It's not what I think. It's what I've seen. Every time the kid starts to step away from you, starts to go off and do something for himself, for fun, you have one of those spells of yours to keep him safe or close or whatever it is you need. And because he loves you, he lets you get away with it."

The center of her turned cold. "I would never do anything like that to my son."

"I don't think you would consciously," said Farley. "But don't try to kid yourself that you're not doing it, Lenore. I've watched you."

"When?" she challenged.

"Yesterday, when he started to paddle off with Jackie, you had your spell and wanted me to call them back. And this morning, when you first thought he was going alone, you suddenly developed a headache."

"For which I took something."

"Yes, and then when you realized he wasn't going to be on an organized trip with others, you had another full-fledged attack and demanded that I keep Reade from going off."

"So twice makes me a scheming manipulator?"

"Of course not. But I would give you odds that when you look back, you'll see the same pattern repeating. For instance, that first day we met, when you had your headache—what did Reade say right before that?"

"I have no idea."

His expression was doubtful, but he didn't press. "Look before that, too—this didn't just start in St. Sebastian. You told me yourself that you had the first spell about six years ago—which would coincide with Reade withdrawing from the Venezuela expedition."

"So would my husband's death," she snapped. Indignation propelled her to her feet.

"Lenore, I didn't bring this up to make you mad."

"Strange. I *am* mad. I'm furious."

"For that I'm sorry. But you really need to take a closer look at what you're doing."

"Well, what I'm doing right now is going back to the hotel. Where's the nearest bus stop?"

"Don't be ridiculous. You can't—"

"Now I'm ridiculous as well as manipulative. What a wonderful opinion you have of me. Excuse me. I'll remove myself before I get any more offensive to you." She marched away with stiff back and even stride and went in search of that bus stop.

A street vendor pointed her in the direction of the central bus circle, not far away. When she found it, she was disappointed to read the posted schedule—it would be at least an hour before the right bus would come by.

She looked around to see if Farley had followed her. When she saw he hadn't, she sagged in relief and defeat.

How could he think she'd cripple Reade that way? She and Pres had done everything in their power to see that all the boys had grown up bold and self-directed. As the oldest, Reade had always been the most independent of all, the one who had led his younger brothers into, and safely out of, impromptu raft rides and guy wire death slides and midnight visits to cemeteries on the far side of town. Just because he'd also grown up to be the most responsible of the three didn't mean something was wrong. The very idea that she would deliberately stifle him by pretending to be sick. . . .

The concrete pavement of the bus circle reflected and intensified the afternoon sun like a solar oven. Standing there with no shade, she quickly began to wilt.

She had just pulled a postcard out of her purse to fan herself when a familiar SUV pulled up in the bus lane.

"Get out of here, you fool," shouted one of the waiting locals. "This is for buses only."

Farley leaned across and opened the passenger door. "Get in."

Lenore fanned herself vigorously. "No, thank you."

"It's going to take you nearly three hours to get back by bus. You'll be miserable."

"Three hours?" Lenore sagged a little more.

"I brought you here. At least let me get you home. Please, Lenore."

Three hours on a swaying, hot, stinky bus or forty minutes in an air-conditioned car with a man who thought she was the world's worst mother. Comfort won over dignity.

"Oh, all right. You can take me back to assuage your guilt. But don't talk to me. I don't think I can stand any more amateur psychology today."

"Agreed."

She got into the car, and they drove toward Fair Winds in complete silence.

"Let's go with this one," said Jackie, *tapping the top* of a bottle of medium pink nail polish.

The technician picked up the bottle and started shaking it. "Passionfruit."

Jackie looked up sharply. "What?"

"Passionfruit Pink. That's the name of this color."

It figured.

"I think it looks more like guava," the woman continued. "But I suppose no one wants to paint their fingers with something called guava."

"You'd be surprised," said Jackie sourly. Twenty-eight colors of nail polish, and she picks the Hunter special. Why not? The whole day had gone that way. She'd never been quite able to shake him, even at lunch, when the man at the next table had ordered rum and Coke and she'd remembered how Reade had tasted of rum when he'd kissed her.

The brush was millimeters from her fingertip when she pulled her hand away. "You know what? I think I'll pass on the polish."

"But you're—"

"I never wear the stuff anyway," Jackie reassured the manicurist. "And right now, I just want to get outside and enjoy the rest of the day."

She escaped with natural nail color and self-respect intact and headed for the sundry shop to pick up a magazine to read while she lazed in the hammock. As she crossed the Grand Terrace en route to the promenade, the sight of a graying head caught her attention.

"Lenore?"

"Oh, Jackie. Hello. I though you might still be at the spa."

"I just finished. What are you doing here? Aren't you and Farley supposed to have dinner in Port Meredith?"

"We had to cut the day short." Lenore smoothed her dress across her knees. "Would you like to sit down for a minute?"

"Of course. I'm sorry your day didn't turn out the way you planned. Did you at least have a nice time?"

"I saw some wonderful galleries," she said, leaving it at that. *Interesting*.

Jackie signaled a passing waiter and ordered drinks—a limeade for herself and an iced tea for Lenore. While they waiting for their order, they watched the scene around the pool below, where clusters of lounge chairs displayed several dozen half-naked people in various states of physical fitness.

"A cultural anthropologist could have a field day with the dynamics around this place," said Jackie. "Take the sunbathers down there. Look at the way they've each managed to carve out a private little space with their sunscreen, a towel, and a drink. Single. Couple. Couple. Single. Family. Couple. And a ring of clear ground around each one. They look like bacteria colonies."

"Hmm? Oh, yes." Lenore blinked. "I'm sorry. What did you say?"

"Nothing important."

The waiter came back with their drinks. When he left, Jackie asked, "What's wrong, Lenore? You're a million miles away."

"I'm just tired. It was a long hike out the jetty." She pulled a paperback out of a side pocket in her purse and set it aside, then started rummaging around in the main compartment. Suddenly, she stopped. "Do you think I use my health problems to manipulate Reade?"

The question caught Jackie off guard. "I don't know. I'm not even sure I know what you mean."

"I'm not sure I do either. I suppose what I really want to know is whether you've noticed me getting sick whenever Reade is going off somewhere."

"Gee, Lenore. I'm not the person to ask. I barely know either one of you."

"But you've been watching us for several days now. You must have some sense of it." She crumpled her purse in her lap. "Do I do that to my son?"

Jackie sipped her drink, delaying. She hated being put on the spot like this.

"I don't think so," she said, finally. "I mean, you haven't really gotten sick, from what I've seen. Just that headache, and Reade wasn't going anywhere then. And then you didn't feel well at the falls . . . but you sent him on up." *Unfortunately.*

"I did, didn't I?" Lenore straightened up. "So I have spells other times, too, not just when he's going off alone somewhere. It's simply coincidence."

"I think so," said Jackie. "But I've been told I'm much better with petri dishes than with people, so you may not want to go by what I say."

"You're just fine with people. In fact, you've made me

feel a lot better." She did look better, even though she stifled a yawn.

"Where did this come from, anyway?" asked Jackie.

"Hmm? Oh, that doesn't matter. You know how things get in a person's head sometimes. And then I couldn't turn loose of it. I think it's something parents do their whole lives, obsess about whether they're doing well by their children or not. It doesn't matter whether the children are four or thirty-four."

"My folks tell me the same thing," said Jackie, relieved that that topic had shifted to general child rearing.

"Being a parent is the most impossible job in the universe, and you can never, ever do it right. You'll have children one day. You'll see."

"Not anytime soon."

"Tick-tock," said Lenore.

"You're as bad as my mom," said Jackie, rolling her eyes. "I'm only twenty-nine."

"You are? I thought you must be Reade's age."

"Nope. I graduated from high school early, with lots of Advance Placement English and math credits. Plus I always knew what I was going to do, so I buzzed through my undergrad and master's degrees in under four years and went straight to work on my doctorate."

"You must be a very dedicated young woman." Lenore yawned for a second time. "I'm so sorry. I'm not bored, really."

"As late as we've all been staying up, I'm surprised we don't all fall over in our drinks."

"I think I need a nap." Lenore stood up. "And I can actually sleep now, with the reassurance you've given me. Thank you. I'll see you later?"

"Undoubtedly. Sleep well."

Lenore toddled off and Jackie breathed a sigh of relief. Finally, she'd get to her hammock. That *had* to be a Reade-free zone.

Oh, no. Think of the devil and here he came.

And he looked like he'd been to hell and back, too. He

was dirty and bloody from shoulder to ankle on the right side. Scuff marks covered his arm and thigh, and there were scrapes on both knees. A bandage covered his swollen chin.

"My God. What happened to you? Sit down."

He pulled out his mom's empty chair and eased down. "It's not as bad as it looks."

"I hope not," said Jackie. It made her wince, just to look at him. "That's major road rash."

"You should have seen me before I rinsed off at Minnow Bridge. I was wearing half the mountain."

"So, tell me all about your fun day. What did you do, decide to ride off the cliff without me?" asked Jackie.

"No. I did the loose gravel death slide." He touched his chin. "Into a stump."

"Ow. It's a good thing your mom's not still here to see you. You just missed her."

"What's she doing back? I thought she and Farley were putting in a full day."

"I don't know. Maybe he found out his business was going to be more complicated than he thought. Anyway, she went to lie down for a little while. I should probably warn you, she's in an odd mood. Some kind of maternal guilt thing. You'll want to talk to her."

"After I get cleaned up. It may take a while to pick the gravel out."

"I'd offer to help," said Jackie. "But I'm afraid I'd be laughing too hard to have steady hands."

"Like I'd let you near me with sharp instruments. The activities desk arranged for a physician's assistant to come in, to see if I need stitches to retain my boyish good looks. In fact, I'd better go meet him now." He pushed to his feet. "Don't gloat too much. It's not good for you."

She watched him walk off, admiring the way he just walked, rather than hobbling like an old lady, the way she would. That had to hurt.

But it wasn't her worry. The hammock was her only concern.

She picked up her limeade, but as she started around the table, she kicked something. Lenore's book. It must have fallen when she got up. Jackie scooped it up. Maybe she'd just borrow this instead of buying a magazine. Lenore was napping anyway, so she could return it later.

She looked it over and almost changed her mind. A romance novel? She'd figured Lenore for cozy mysteries or literary fiction, not heaving bosoms and steely glances.

But what the heck? It was a beach read, and she was at the beach. She tucked it under her arm—making sure no one could read the title—and headed toward the nirvana of late afternoon in a hammock.

She took the time to check the hammocks along the beach, but they were all full, so she followed the path through the gardens toward Farley's place.

She stopped first at the house, to let him know she had arrived to mooch some swing time, but a houseboy answered.

Mr. Phelps wasn't there, he informed her. Yes, he had returned from Port Meredith, but he had left right away to visit a friend. And yes, he had mentioned that she would be using the beach and hammock. Please let him know if she needed anything.

She thanked him and wandered down the various terraces to the beach. By daylight, the lagoon retained its postcard image of paradise: a pool of clear water flashing with multicolored fish, a fringe of palms edging a semicircle of pale ivory beach, and near total isolation. A small gap in the reef let the ocean waves through just enough to make music on the sand.

The hammock, a double canvas model, swung between two young palms, their interlaced fronds providing a wide oval of shade. A spotless pillow lay at the head of the hammock and a neatly folded blanket at the foot, both undoubtedly placed there fresh every morning and collected every evening by the houseboy. A small teak table stood nearby, with a cork coaster lying in the perfect position to hold a glass of something cold where the occupant of the hammock could simply put out a hand to reach it. Someone had arranged two flawless scallop shells and a small conch on one corner of the table. Jackie smiled at the idea of burdening this perfect scene with her booze-free limeade—Farley would not approve.

Getting into a hammock was always awkward, but once aboard, she found herself sagging into that state of exquisite relaxation that she remembered from summers under the oak in the backyard when she was twelve. She closed her eyes and just lay there for a few minutes, listening to the sounds of birds and the water lapping a few feet away. The noise of boats, so noticeable on the resort beach, was reduced to a barely audible buzz by distance and the ring of vegetation that almost surrounded the lagoon. The air stirred just enough to keep her comfortable. Bliss.

But she'd never been the kind to just sit and do nothing for long, so after a bit, she opened Lenore's book and started reading, a little reluctantly. Soon, however, she was engrossed in what turned out to be a fun, light story, with nary a throbbing bosom or icy glint in sight. Okay, so a boycott of all the bachelors in an Irish village was a bit far-fetched. But the characters reminded her of some of her neighbors back in Cedar Falls, and she was having fun. She read on, delighted, as the hero and heroine tangled and sparred with each other.

And then came the first love scene, a fiery and unexpected encounter in a parked van at midnight, and suddenly she was the heroine and Reade was the hero and her body responded as though it was her pressed down on the floor of the van.

This was not good. She slipped one of the scallop shells into the paperback as a page marker and abandoned the hammock to wade into the bathtub-warm water of the lagoon.

She should have changed into her suit after the spa, so she could go swimming, but she hadn't, so she just waded in up to mid-thigh and splashed a little water over her arms.

The fish that had scattered as she entered the water quickly overcame their fear and swam back to investigate this strange new visitor. A little yellow one, bolder than the rest, darted past her knees. Standing perfectly still, she slowly lowered her fingers into the water, letting them dangle like seaweed. Soon she had a school of tiny fish swirling around her as if she were nothing more than a convenient dock piling. She concentrated, trying to tickle one on the belly, but she was too fidgety and kept startling them at the last instant.

Giving up, she scooped a handful of water and splashed her neck and throat again. A thin, warm stream ran down between her breasts, and she blotted it away with her T-shirt.

"You'll never cool off reading stuff like this."

She whirled. Reade stood by the hammock, the paperback in one hand, her makeshift bookmark in the other. He wore fresh clothes and a different bandage on his chin.

"That was fast," she said.

"It turned out I didn't need stitches, and most of the gravel got washed out in the river. He gave me a big old shot of penicillin just to make sure I didn't get any bugs and told me to go enjoy the rest of my vacation."

"Good. Now go away, please. I'm trying to have a nice, quiet afternoon, and I don't recall inviting you to join me."

"I don't blame you. I wouldn't want people around if I were reading this stuff, either. Let's see. We have Brian and. . . ." He flipped back a page. "And Tara. And they're in a van."

"Knock it off, Hunter."

" 'He found the pulse racing at the base of her throat,' " he read, ignoring her, " 'lingered over her breasts just long enough to draw another moan from her, then traveled lower still, to her belly just above her waistband. She touched what she could reach of him as he moved down—

back, shoulders, then only his hair, and finally nothing at all as he raised up to strip off the last of her clothes. Skirt, tights, underwear: they all vanished into the darkness, along with any sense of decency as he caressed and explored her with mouth and hands.' "

He read it straight, like he meant it. Like he'd lived it, or at least imagined it, and wanted her to experience it the way he had. Unable to stop him or to escape, she stood there, trying not to react as his voice poured into her, touching places that so far she'd kept him from touching with his hands, but which now craved exactly that. Touch. His touch.

" 'Somewhere above her, he moved, shedding his own clothes. She wished she could see him, but at the same time savored the darkness. In the dark it didn't matter that she was lying there before him naked, her legs apart, her body liquid with need.' "

He closed the book and tossed it into the hammock.

She found her voice. "Did you just come down here to harass me?"

He tilted his head, thinking. "As a matter of fact, yes."

And without saying another word, he started walking toward her, unbuttoning his shirt.

eleven

Jackie took a step back, instinctively moving away from Reade. The water slapped at her bottom, soaking her shorts. *So much for staying dry.*

Without taking his eyes off her, he dropped his shirt on the sand and waded into the lagoon. A flicker of pain crossed his face as the salt water covered the abrasions on his calf, but he shook it off and kept coming.

"What are you doing?" She took another step back and went in up to her waist.

"Same thing you are. Cooling off." He stopped a few feet from her, the water surging against his belly at the line where his trunks rode on his hips. "It was your fault I got hurt, you know."

"You can't possibly blame me for that. I was right here getting a massage."

"And I was thinking about you getting a massage. Imagining I was giving it."

They stood there while spangles of light danced around their bodies. A long moment passed in which the only sounds were their breathing and the waves slapping softly against their skin, and then, slowly, they drew together like magnets, irresistible force, opposites attracting. Pure physics.

They just stood there kissing, forever, making out like schoolkids out behind the gym, finding new ways to drive each other wild with only their mouths and tongues. Reade's injuries made Jackie hesitant, but he didn't seem to notice. Beneath the water, he guided her hands to his waist, and as she explored the ripples of muscle, he slowly untucked her shirttail, fingers trailing over newly exposed skin.

"You made me get my clothes wet."

"Take them off. We'll skinny-dip," he murmured, swirling a hot circle just below her earlobe. He hooked his thumbs into the waist of her shorts and slipped them down a fraction of an inch over one hip, then the other.

Yes.

"No. We'll get caught." She'd get caught. By him. She still had enough mental capacity to know that much, even though most of her brain cells seemed to be shouting that what counted was how much she would enjoy the catching.

With supreme effort, she grabbed his wrists and moved his hands away. "We have got to stop this."

"We will." He kissed her again. "When we're finished."

"We're finished now." She wrestled herself free and bolted for the shore, the water slowing her to a parody of flight.

"Damn it, Jackie." He could easily have grabbed her as she went by, but he didn't.

"Is everything all right, miss?" A Fair Winds security guard stepped to the edge of the lower terrace, his dark face set in a frown and his hands on his hips.

"It's fine. I'm fine," she said, cheeks hot with embarrassment as she realized what he might have seen.

"Mr. Phelps said we weren't to let anyone disturb you. Shall I remove the gentleman?"

"I'm sure he didn't mean—"

"The gentleman will remove himself," interrupted Reade. He walked out of the water behind her, hooking his shirt with his toe to kick it up into his hand. As he passed her, his voice was low, but very, very certain. "I'll see you later."

He put his shirt on and crossed to the terrace and the security guard, who stood a half a head taller than Reade. "Speaking of Mr. Phelps, is he in?"

"No, sir. And he won't be back until late."

"Thanks." Reade ambled away as if it didn't make much difference one way or the other. The security guard stood there, squinting after him until he was well gone.

Despite her humiliation, Jackie felt obliged to thank her would-be rescuer.

"No trouble, miss. If you need me, shout out. I'll be within hearing." As he strolled off toward the house, he said over his shoulder, "You enjoy the beach as long as you like."

That's exactly what she intended to do, because she knew that as soon as she left, Reade would be lurking around somewhere, waiting to pounce on her and finish what he'd started. What *they* had started. She wasn't going to blame it all on him. She was every bit as responsible.

Which was why she was going to actually *be* responsible and stay away from him for the rest of the evening. Thank goodness Farley was gone, so she didn't have to worry about running interference.

She settled back into the hammock. After a while, when she'd calmed down enough to be a rational human being again, she picked up Lenore's book and lay there, reading, until her clothes were dry and it was too dark to read. And then she lay there some more, swinging back and forth in the warm night air, trying not to think about Reade.

*   *   *

"Where do you suppose Jackie is?" asked Lenore over dinner that evening. "She hasn't missed a meal since we got here."

"She probably found someone else to bug, since Farley's not around," said Reade, trying to pretend he didn't care. "Are you going to tell me what happened between you two?"

"Nothing happened. He wanted to visit friends and I didn't want to go, that's all."

That was her story, and she was sticking to it—almost word for word since the first time he'd asked. Reade contemplated his mother over the hibiscus that decorated her drink. Jackie had been right, she was in an odd mood, distracted; so much so that it had taken him only a few minutes before dinner to convince her that his injuries were inconsequential and not worth a major breakdown. He wondered if Farley had made a pass that got out of hand. It'd be a hell of a thing if he had to deck the guy. That would certainly blow the grant.

After dinner, his mother decided the Staff and Guest Talent Show would make an interesting diversion, but an hour or so of mugging and uneven performances—some of the staff showed real talent, but it was a lousy week among the guests—disabused her of that notion. He walked her back to her room, then returned to the bar for a nightcap.

He was headed back to his room with the refill when he saw Jackie ahead of him, and for the first time that evening, found himself smiling.

The woman knew how to walk. He'd heard someone say that about some old movie star, but he'd never really known what it meant until that instant. It wasn't the vampy strut that she'd put on the first night, nor the self-conscious way she usually held herself around him, but a relaxed stroll that let the appropriate body parts roll and sway in a way that made him happy he was a man. He trod a little more lightly, so she wouldn't hear him and tense up and ruin it.

She turned down the path toward his room, and for a moment his heart pounded a *soca* beat of anticipation and celebration. Then she stepped up to his mother's door and raised her hand to knock.

"Oh, damn," he said aloud. "You're not here to kiss me good night."

Jackie sighed. "Go away, Hunter."

"I can't go too far." He continued past her, swinging in three doors down at what had to be his patio, where he kicked back at the table with his feet up. "Mom's asleep by now."

"Oh." Okay, she was going to have to deal with him sooner or later anyway. She closed her eyes for a moment, organizing her thoughts, then turned. "Mind if I drop this off with you?"

He took a sip of his drink and waved her over.

She walked down to his patio and tossed the book on his table, facedown. "Your mom doesn't actually know I borrowed it, but tell her thanks anyway."

She tried to escape before he realized what it was, but he was too quick.

"Hey, *Brian Does Tara.* My favorite. You finished it, I assume . . . which would explain why you weren't at dinner."

"I wasn't at dinner because there was no reason to be."

He stabbed his heart with an invisible dagger. "You wound me. *I* was there."

"Like I said. Just give it to your mom, okay?"

"I'm afraid I can't do that," he said. "I could never look her in the eye again if I put that book in her hand. You'll have do it yourself."

"Hunter."

"Sorry," he deadpanned. "It would just be too embarrassing. However, you're welcome to sit here until I finish my drink, at which point I will open her door—I have a key card, just in case—and you can quietly put it on the table just inside the door."

It was the spider and the fly routine, starring herself as the fly—she shuddered at the image—but if she refused, he'd pull some other stunt. At least this way they were out in the open. She pulled the chair out from under his feet and dragged it to the far side of the table, where she could make a quick escape.

"Want a sip?" he asked, holding out his drink.

"No, thank you."

A few minutes later, he tried again. "There are a couple of bottles of juice in the minibar."

"No, thanks." She folded her arms across her chest and waited. "Go ahead. It's killing you."

"No passionfruit, though," he added with a grin.

"Surprise. Nothing, thank you."

"At least have some water." He disappeared inside, leaving the door open, and returned with a glass of tepid water. "Sorry, no ice."

"It's fine, thank you." She didn't need a drink. In fact, she should have stopped at one of the public rest rooms on the way back from Farley's. Her room suddenly seemed a long way off. "Come on, Hunter. Just let me leave the book. You can put it in her room."

"Nope."

"Then you're going to have to let me use your bathroom."

"Go right ahead."

She ducked inside and used the facilities with a great sense of relief. Afterward she was washing her hands at the vanity sink when she spotted an odd, brown plastic bottle in his shaving kit. It had a funky, old-fashioned label that read Porter's Lotion—maybe this was Navarro's home brew. Curious, she left the water running as cover, reached for the bottle, and unscrewed the cap.

The brisk scent of camphor washed over her, laced with spices and subtle undertones. She sniffed cautiously, unsure if this was really the scent Reade wore. She didn't recall quite so much camphor, but perhaps it faded after a few minutes. She dribbled a little of the liquid into her palm and rubbed it on her wrist as an experiment, then closed her eyes and inhaled deeply.

"Aha," said Reade, poking his head around the corner. "A bathroom snoop. I knew it."

She dropped the bottle. It hit the sink with a plastic thud. She trapped it before more than a few drops squirted out, and quickly screwed the lid back on.

He reached past her to shut the water off. "I bet you're one of those people who go through other people's medicine cabinets during parties."

"I do not. I just saw it and was curious, that's all. Is this some kind of custom scent?"

"Nope, I buy it in Montana when I get out that way." He turned the bottle over in her hand and pointed to the maker: Gallatin River Products, Bozeman, Montana. "Do you like it?"

"It's okay." So it wasn't Navarro's brew, but that didn't mean it wasn't spiked.

She set the bottle down and started past him, but he blocked the way. He laced the fingers of one hand into hers and raised it to his nose, turning it to sniff her wrist.

"It's so 'okay,' you put some on," he said. His mouth hovered millimeters from the spot where her pulse pounded so hard. He bared his teeth; her breath caught in her throat as she waited for them to close on the tender skin. Instead, he lowered her hand and slowly levered her up against his chest, so that her nose was next to his jaw, where the scent, mellowed and changed by his chemistry in some indefinable way, lay on his beard-shadowed skin. "If you want to get a good whiff, all you have to do is ask."

He held her there, pinned more by her own weakness than by his strength.

"Kiss me," he said. "I'm not going to be the one this time, so kiss me."

"Reade, we. . . . This. . . ."

Her shirt was still untucked from earlier, and his free hand, warm and restless, found the bare skin just above her shorts. *I'll see you later*, he'd said. It was later. Something shifted inside Jackie.

"This is crazy," she said.

"Probably." He slipped his fingers under her waistband in back, massaging a slow circle that slipped lower and lower.

"It's all hormones," she said.

"Your point being?" He found that spot by her collarbone that was so sensitive and traced its outline with the tip of his tongue.

"We don't even like each other." But she wanted him. She'd been wanting him all day, and now he was right here and all she had to do was let herself go.

"Stop thinking, Jackie, and kiss me."

"I'm not thinking, that's the problem." But she lifted, searching for his mouth.

He made her come all the way to him, not moving an inch until her lips touched his. Even then he waited, making her do the work, forcing her to be the one to urge more, to woo him to kiss her back with parted lips and searching tongue until, finally, when she was about to give up in embarrassment, he took back the kiss.

With a groan, he carried her back against the wall. His tongue swept into her mouth as he took possession of her body with his hands. She fought to retain one last little bit of will, but when he pushed a knee between her legs so that he could buck against her in that most primitive rhythm, her mind shut down so that the only fact in the known universe was the incredible need that arched her toward him.

This time when he left her mouth and began to work his way downward, she had no inclination to stop him. He kissed a line straight down her body, from throat to navel, then back up to find first one nipple, then the other, not bothering to remove her clothes or even shift them aside. The heat of his mouth penetrated her T-shirt and bra, leaving damp circles as he nipped and sucked. She clutched at his head and cried out.

His moan of satisfaction buzzed through her, and he started down again until he knelt before her, wincing as his skinned knees hit the floor but never stopping. He spent a long moment nuzzling her belly, and then slid lower as his hands toyed with the waist of her shorts. Trembling, she held her breath, waiting for him to strip them away, but instead his mouth closed over her, clothes and all. He exhaled, forcing hot air through the thin nylon of her shorts and panties until she squirmed away. With a warning growl, he pulled her back, hands splayed over her buttocks, holding her while he worked at her until her clothes, soaked from his mouth and from her own juices, molded around her and into her, revealing her as clearly as if she were naked.

She writhed there, needing him to continue, to finish her off, but he stopped and slowly, so slowly, slid his hands down her legs. Sitting back, he watched as he traced a line down the outside, curving over thigh and knee and calf and ankle, then back up the inside, up, so slowly up her thighs. Delicately, he grazed one finger over the dampness between her legs, then touched her more surely, finding her most sensitive spot. A slow circle made her jaws clench.

"Reade."

"What?" He drew another circle, watching what he was doing as though mesmerized.

"Ah, God. Don't leave me like this."

"I won't." Another circle, another gasp of frustration, and then his hands on her legs again, stroking down and then the long, teasing journey up. He found her again, but this time when she groaned and pressed toward him, he slipped his finger inside her shorts and the elastic of her panties and tugged them aside to expose her. The touch of the air and his eyes was almost painful and she trembled, waiting again for his mouth, not sure she could bear it. His fingers danced over her, playing with her like a new toy.

"Jackie, look at yourself. The mirror."

She didn't want to, knowing how out of control she'd look, but she did, and as she did, he slipped his fingers inside her and pressed his mouth against her, and she came, standing there, fully clothed, watching herself.

But he didn't stop, didn't even pause to let her be embarrassed at how she looked with her head thrown back, her mouth bruised, arching and shaking and at his mercy; he just touched her more gently, swirled his tongue a little slower, allowing time for her body to recover, barely, before he made her climb again. When he had her moaning, just shy of another orgasm, he stood up and kissed her, and she tasted how ready she was.

"What do you want, Jackie?"

"Aaah," she said incoherently. How could he seem so in control, so untouched by what he was doing to her?

"Tell me," he urged.

"To undress," she said. "I don't want these clothes. I want the bed. I want you."

"So undress. Let me watch you."

She did, stepping away from him to strip her shirt over her head and release the hooks on her bra, and he watched, his eyes narrow and full of heat. He skimmed his hands over her bare breasts, gently tugging at the tips until they pearled and she begged for his mouth on her.

He obliged, cupping her breasts, bringing them together so he could lave both peaks at once, driving her almost insane. And then he picked his favorite and sucked it into his mouth and she almost came again, just from that. He chuckled and did it again, stopping only when she jerked and trembled so hard she could barely stand up.

"The rest," he said, and that's when she finally noticed the tightness around his mouth. The strain as he held himself back. He wasn't as cool as she'd thought, and that made her want to see what he was like out of control, the way she was.

She put her hands to her waistband and with one motion, pushed her shorts and panties down together. They cleared her hips and slid down. She stepped out of them, balancing herself with a hand on the counter, then reached for him. He let her strip him, then groaned and gritted his teeth as she knelt and did to him what he had done to her with mouth and hands. His fingers curled into her hair.

"Whoa." He stopped her and tugged her gently to her feet. His erection lay hard and warm between their bellies as he cupped her bottom and pulled her close. "If you want me in you, you can't do that anymore. Do you want me in you?"

She nodded.

"All right. I'm going to take you to bed, but first I need to do something. Stay here." He grabbed a towel off the rack and wrapped it around his waist. His erection made an awkward bulge, so that he had to readjust the towel to get coverage. He walked out into the main room, and a moment later she heard the door close and lock, and then the slide of the draperies.

"Oh, my God," she said as he came back. "We were . . . with the door open?"

He nodded and dropped the towel, then kissed her into not caring about the door or anything else. He reached down and slipped his hand between her legs, curving his palm to fit to her.

"Now," she urged against his mouth.

Hand still pressed into her, he reached for something on the counter, then pressed a condom into her hand. "Show me you want me to."

She ripped the packet and rolled the condom down over him as slowly as she could, teasing. Taunting. Enjoying the ever deepening lines of tension at the corner of his mouth and around his eyes. When she was done, she slowly curled her hand around him. "I want you in me, Reade. Now."

Growling, he turned her around, bent her over the counter, and took her from behind, one, two strokes, and then pulled out. She gasped in surprise, then pleasure, then frustration.

He whipped her back around to face him and kissed her again. "Like that? Do you want it fast or slow, Jackie? Here or in bed?"

He didn't wait for her answer, covering her mouth with a blazing kiss before he scooped her up and carried her to the bed. He fell with her, and as they landed, he took her head between his hands and spread her legs wide with his knee.

"You can stop me now," he ground between clenched teeth. "It's your last chance."

Through the fog of arousal, she didn't know what he meant. Those few quick strokes by the sink had already taken them past stopping, past last chances. "Too late."

He entered her, not with the swift plunge she expected, but with a slow, erotic slide that stopped and started and swirled within her until she was thrashing beneath him. He lifted off her and started over. Again. Again. She heard a long, animal wail and in the instant before the world shattered, she realized it was her.

"Oh, God. Jackie." He controlled himself long enough for her contractions to peak, and then, when she began to relax, he took her hard and fast. Her name was a cry of desperation on his lips, and as he captured her mouth and drove into her, she tasted herself on him and she knew. She knew.

She had run too late.

Reade lay in the center of a tangle of bedding, alone, staring at the ceiling.

He wasn't quite sure what had happened. It had started as a tease, a game, a way to drive her off. He'd given her every chance to run away, even after she'd kissed him like that, even after she'd undressed. Right up to the point when she rolled the condom onto him, and even after, he'd tried to scare her off before it was too late, but in-

stead of running, she'd kept coming toward him, coming
for him oh God she came hard. Even when he'd made her
watch herself and taken her like an animal, she hadn't
run. She'd stayed until he'd had to have her, had to pour
himself into her, over and over; and then long, heat-filled
hours later, when he had finally slept, she'd slipped out
of his bed and run, and all he could think now as he
watched the light brightening around the edges of the curtains was how badly he'd miscalculated and how much
he wanted her beneath him again.

But she *had* run, and lying there, wrapped in sheets that
smelled of sex and of her was not going to make him feel
better about anything, so he dragged himself out of bed
and headed for the shower. The sight of himself in the
vanity mirror stopped him cold. He was a mass of scabs
and bruises. The bandage had fallen off his chin—it was
probably stuck to the sheets somewhere. His hair stood
up at every possible angle, and his beard and bleary eyes
made him look like a refugee from Margaritaville. No
wonder she'd left. He ran a glass full of water and drank
it in one long gulp, then downed another one.

A shower, a shave, and some basic personal hygiene
made him look and smell more presentable, and his favorite Parrothead shirt and a pair of baggies covered some
of the road rash and most of the bruises. He made sure
all the condoms and wrappers were properly disposed of
and located the missing chin bandage near the foot of the
bed. Oh, yeah. He'd dragged her down there, almost off
the bed, that last time. The memory hit him in the gut
like a fist, and he had to stand there and fight himself
back under control. When he did, he ignored the no-
tipping rule to leave a five-pound note on the pillow to
cover the extra mess, found his flip-flops in the corner,
and opened the door on the day.

The remains of his rum and Coke still sat on the patio
table, along with Jackie's untouched glass of water. He
left the bar glass there for one of the resort people to deal
with, but he dumped the water on a nearby bird of para-

dise plant and set the vanity glass inside. The book that had started the whole thing was gone; apparently Jackie had grabbed it on her way out.

Reluctant to face his mother at this hour and in this state, he locked his door and went in search of a cup of strong coffee and some protein.

What he found was Jackie, face scrubbed and shiny, hair pulled back in a ponytail, looking like nothing had happened—which was irritating enough, considering how much he wished she'd stayed so he could have taken her again, one last time, half asleep, waking her as he pushed into her. But the real pisser was that she was sitting right across from Farley. Nothing had changed. Not a goddamned thing.

He filled a plate with scrambled eggs and ackee and headed toward their table. Jackie stiffened as soon as she saw him coming.

There were a couple of ways to deal with this; he'd have to see how the spirits moved him.

Farley was the first to greet him. After they exchanged good mornings, he gestured toward Reade's chin. "Did I miss a good fight, or was your bike ride more exciting than you planned?"

Reade set his plate down and slid into his seat before he explained about the gravel and the stump. After the guy stuff was over, he turned to the silent woman to his left.

"And good morning to you, too, Jackie."

She blotted the corners of her mouth with a napkin. "Good morning, Hunter."

Hunter? They were back to Hunter and that prissy, wary look, too? The spirits got ornery, but not quite ornery enough to make him lean over and kiss that look off her face right there in front of Farley.

"Did you get a good night's sleep?" he asked solicitously.

Color climbed up her neck like red in a thermometer,

but she managed to keep her voice bland. "I've had better."

Zing. Reade reached for the saltshaker. "Really? That's a shame. I never slept better, myself. I do enjoy a hot tropical night. The hotter, the better."

If eyes were razors, he'd be singing soprano. Farley took one look at her and suddenly got very interested in a piece of ham. Grinning, Reade flagged down a passing waiter. "Could you bring me some coffee, please. Cream, no sugar."

The man was impossible. It was mortifying enough having to sit there next to him, her body still swollen and tender from the things he'd done to her, reminding her how out of control she'd been, how easy. But to have to play these silly games, too . . .

She stood up abruptly. "Excuse me. I'm going to get some more cantaloupe."

She took her time picking over the fruit, even though it meant leaving Hunter alone with Farley. She needed to get a grip. It shouldn't be this hard. She'd had a couple of relationships with classmates and colleagues before, but even in the throes of a new affair, she had always been able to step back and go through a day with some sense of self-control—even if the object of her affections sat next to her in a meeting. She'd never found herself so discombobulated by a man. But then, none of them had ever been quite so . . . Hunter.

She got her melon and a glass of milk—no juice, thank you very much—and was waiting for a slice of toast to pop when he sneaked up behind her.

"Carbo loading for tonight?" he asked.

Tonight, again. No. Be cool.

"You wish," she said flippantly.

"I do wish," he said. He ran a knuckle down her arm. "I wish you'd stayed."

Stayed for even more, he meant, and the center of her

softened and throbbed at the idea of what else they could have thought of to do to each other's bodies. She stared at the glowing wires inside the toaster, thinking how his hands had been just that hot on her skin. "I couldn't. It was . . . I don't even know who those people were."

"They were Reade and Jackie, that's all. No Hunter. No Barnett. Just Reade and Jackie."

She looked up at him, and when she saw the warmth in his eyes, she almost bought into it. But it wasn't that easy.

"Well, Reade had better get over it," she said firmly. "Because Jackie has decided it's not going to happen again."

"Yes, it is," he said with the same aggravating sureness that he'd used the day before when he'd said he'd see her later. Her toast popped, and he reached in front of her to pull it out and drop it on her plate. "You want to know if all those flames were a fluke, just as much as I do."

Damn him, she did. What a slut she was. "Stop it, before someone hears you. Farley's right over there."

"Not anymore. He took off while you were perusing the papayas. He had to go pick up a fax or something."

Jackie stood on tiptoe to see over the buffet. Sure enough, Phelps was gone. "I still don't want to talk about it."

"So you're going to pretend nothing happened."

"Yes."

"No. I won't let you do that. It did happen, and it was amazing." He reached past her for a beignet, a move which put his mouth next to her ear. "You taste good, and I want more."

His mouth on her. She gripped the edges of her plate until she thought it would break. Okay, so that proved the flames weren't a fluke. Now she didn't have to undress to find out. Of course, she hadn't had to undress last night, either. A rip current of pure lust swept her out to sea.

When she swam back, Reade was saying something about Farley.

"I'm sorry. What?"

"I've been having the same problem," he said, making her blush again. "Boiled down, what I said was, Farley suggested we go up to Redoubt Colony today."

"Redoubt." It took her another minute to get her mind out of her crotch. "That art community?"

"Yep. Mom's been wanting to see it for years—it's the main reason she wanted to come to St. Sebastian, in fact—so I'm assuming she'll be up for it. And since I need to rest up anyway—" *for tonight.* He didn't say that; her brain just tacked the words on all by itself. "—I figured this was an opportune moment. You'll be coming, of course."

Coming. No, not that coming.

"Like I would let you go alone," she said. "The war's not over, Hunter, and don't try to pretend it is. If you think my brain turned to mush overnight and now I'm going to step out of your way because of some misguided romantic impulse, you're fooling yourself. It's just not going to happen, no matter how good—"

She stopped herself a fraction of a second too late.

He grinned. "So, you admit it was good."

"No matter how good you *think* you were," she finished, improvising. "What time do we leave?"

"Ten. Wear good walking shoes." He started away, then came back. "And one more suggestion. If you're going to pretend nothing happened, you've got to get that blushing thing under control. Dead giveaway."

twelve

Jackie arrived at the front entrance five minutes early, just to be sure Reade didn't pull some stunt like telling Farley she'd decided not to go. Farley was already there, laughing with a couple of the bellmen—apparently telling dirty jokes, because they clammed up as she drew near and one of them stared at his feet.

"Ready for an adventure in art and gravity?" asked Farley.

"I know about the art part, but what's this about gravity?"

"Didn't Reade tell you?"

"No."

"Then I'll just leave it as a surprise."

There were other surprises, she discovered when Reade and Lenore showed up a couple of minutes later. First off, Lenore and Farley seemed very uncomfortable with each other, Farley acting very deferential and Lenore pretending nothing was wrong while she mostly avoided speaking to him. Jackie gave Reade a *What's going on?* look and got a shrug in response.

The next surprise arrived when the car was brought around: the vehicle of the day wasn't Farley's white Jeep but a green Mercedes. Farley let Lenore in the front while Jackie was left to deal with Reade and his cologne in the backseat. Not a good thing.

With the three of them loaded and buckled up, she got her third surprise: the man who had brought the car proceeded to get back in and drive them away, leaving Farley standing on the sidewalk.

"Isn't he going?" Jackie twisted to watch Farley wave them off. "He's not going."

"Didn't anyone tell you?" asked Lenore, who had relaxed significantly in the last five seconds. "Farley has other plans today. It's just the three of us."

"That seems to be something your son left out when he passed on the invitation," said Jackie.

"Did I?" The louse sat there playing innocent, but he was looking way too smug. "I could have sworn I mentioned it."

So she had been suckered into spending all day with Hunter, and for no reason. She wracked her brain for a way out, but couldn't come up with one. She couldn't exactly whine, "If Farley's not going, I don't wanna go either." It might be true, but it wasn't pretty. Plus the driver was already turning onto the main road and picking up speed. Short of flinging herself out the door at fifty miles an hour, she was stuck.

They were well away from Runaway Bay when Reade cleared his throat. "You know, Mom, there's something I may have forgotten to tell you, too."

"What's that, dear?"

"Farley's actually coming up to Redoubt later, after he finishes down here."

"Oh." Lenore's face froze somewhere between a smile and a frown. "How nice."

Jackie immediately felt more benevolent toward

Reade—she hadn't come for no reason after all—but sympathized with Lenore. The poor woman looked like she'd sucked a lime. Jackie was tempted to ask her if she'd like to switch places. That way Lenore could glare at her son without straining her neck, and Jackie wouldn't have to spend the entire drive with Reade ogling her and smiling that sappy smile.

At least he was staring at her legs instead of her breasts. Most men never got past her bustline, or even cared to, but Reade was definitely a leg man. Not that he didn't appreciate her breasts and give them due attention—oh, boy, did he give them attention—but they weren't the be-all and end-all of his interest or his lovemaking technique.

And just what was she doing thinking about his technique when she emphatically was *not* going to sleep with him again? She dug her fingernail into her thumb until the pain shut down all other sensations—real, recalled, or imagined—then turned her attention to being a good tourist.

Redoubt Colony had started as a coffee plantation during the Twenties, the driver explained as they drove the curving road up the flanks of Mount Redoubt. When the coffee trees failed, the owner, a retired British stage actress, had decided to cultivate artists instead, and at that she'd been much more successful. The workers' cottages and coffee sheds that she'd converted into bungalows and studios had burgeoned into a village, the center of the island arts and crafts scene, with a growing international reputation.

Today, the driver informed them, they would get a double treat. Redoubt was hosting the All-Island Pushcart Championships, and they could watch the races between gallery stops. That explained Farley's reference to gravity, and was, Jackie hoped, the last surprise.

Along the curving road into town, the brightly painted buildings sported flags and posters touting the race. Strings of pennants hung overhead, and policemen in spanking white shirts and shorts patrolled the crowd that milled along the sides of the road. A succession of officers directed them to a parking area on the upper edge of the village.

After arranging a rendezvous time with their driver, the three of them walked down into town, passing temporary bleachers and a cluster of plywood and canvas stalls from which vendors hawked foods ranging from oil-pan jerk to curries to coconut balls. Each stall smelled better than the last, and at Lenore's suggestion, they bought savory samosas before they continued. Reade snagged an acid green flier from a stack on the counter and read it while he ate.

"Farley said the start is the most fun when you don't know the racers," he said, raising his voice to be heard over the music blaring from a monstrous speaker hung on a pole. "That's where the most crashes are."

"We came to watch people crash?" asked Lenore.

"No one is seriously hurt," said Reade, but she still looked dubious. He shrugged. "We'll see. In the meantime, let's hit a gallery or two."

"There's one called Cho-Cho I've read about," said Lenore.

They asked around and found it, a pale yellow clapboard building with eggplant purple trim and a zucchini green door. As they entered, a slender black woman wearing a white gauze dress called out a greeting.

"Welcome to Cho-Cho. We just opened the debut show of a talented new wood-carver. His character pieces are absolutely wonderful. Come, let me show you, and then you can enjoy all our other lovely artwork."

Lenore was totally enamored of the new carver. Jackie might have been, except she couldn't focus because Reade kept drifting up next to her, giving her a fresh whiff of his cologne and throwing her right back into the middle of the previous night. And then there were the other things . . .

"Look at that curve. Like the inside of woman's thigh," he said, running his hand over an abstract figure sculpted in the native limestone, and in her mind she felt his hand, high on her leg.

A little later, he pointed to a painting of a voluptuous nude and whispered, "Her ear's shaped just like yours."

Her ear, for God's sake—most men would go for a boob comparison. But then she remembered how his tongue felt in her ear, and she shivered.

He continued in the same vein at the next gallery, commenting on the resemblance of the satiny finish of a hand-carved chair to a woman's cheek, his tone making it clear he wasn't talking about faces, and discussing the artistic merits of an erotic watercolor of two lovers. She tried to tune him out, to disconnect herself from the images he conjured up, but when he merrily showed her the way the pieces of a cedar puzzle box slid together, just so, over and over in *that* rhythm, she lost it.

"Hunter!"

Everyone in the gallery, including Lenore, looked at them, faces full of curiosity.

"Hmm?" He calmly slid the box together and set it back on the shelf.

She crooked a finger at him, then turned around and walked out the nearest door. It led to a veranda that ran along the back of the old house, and she walked to the far end. A moment later, he joined her.

"I know what you're trying to do," she said, her voice low so it wouldn't carry back inside.

"Seduce you," he said, completely matter-of-fact about it. "It's working, too."

"It's ticking me off, is what it's doing."

He shrugged. "They say anger and passion are very closely related."

" 'They' are wrong. Let it go, Hunter."

"No."

"Why not? You said yourself it was a fluke."

"No, I said I wanted to find out if it was a fluke."

"It was. A total fluke. An accident. Something that just

happened and will never, *ever* happen again. We don't even like each other."

"You keep saying that, but I have a theory. Hunter and Barnett don't like each other. Reade and Jackie, on the other hand—"

"There are *not* four people here!" she snapped. "It's just us. You and me. And a whole lot of trouble and past history and money stand between us."

"I know, I know. And the war's still on. You told me."

"That's right."

"So let's call a truce. They manage that even in real wars." He drifted closer to her. "Didn't you ever see movies about World War I? At Christmas, the Germans and the Allies would lay down their guns and meet in the middle of no-man's-land. They'd share whiskey and schnapps, show each other photographs of the wife or girlfriend, sing a few carols, and generally enjoy each other's company."

"They didn't have sex," hissed Jackie. "Plus the next day they were back in the trenches, shooting at each other—and don't even think about telling me you wouldn't still be trying to get to Farley while we. . . ."

"Of course I would," he said. "That's why we're here, and we both know it, so let's not try to fake each other out anymore. But that's a daylight occupation. At night, he's asleep, and we're two adults on a beautiful, tropical island." He lowered his voice to continue. "Two consenting adults who have already shared some incredible, mind-blowing sex. There's no reason we can't continue to do so. Nights can be our Christmas truce. And the bed can be our neutral ground."

He made it sound so reasonable. A vacation fling, just enjoying each other's bodies for the next week or so, then going their separate ways. Like that would be the end of it.

"I've got news for you, Hunter. Christmas only comes once a year. And it's already the day after."

"All right. Then I guess I'll just have to keep wearing

you down the old-fashioned way. We've got to find out, Jackie."

"This conversation is over."

"Fine. But when you finally realize I'm right, please try not to jump me in front of my mother. Now that I know what kind of books she reads, the idea of her kibitzing on my love life is even more appalling than usual." He winked at her, then sauntered back inside the gallery, leaving Jackie standing there, ready to scream.

She sagged back against the railing, pressing her fingers into her eyes. It'd be so much easier to deal with him if he wasn't right about the sex—mind-blowing was precisely the word for it. Mind-blowing, body-slamming, and totally nasty in the best possible, can't-get-enough-of-each-other sense of the word. Not that she'd admit it to Hunter. She couldn't afford to, not if she was going to keep things at all under control.

Speaking of control, what had happened to her nice, tidy, controlled life? Somewhere along the line, it had all gone wild and blowsy, like the jungle on this stupid island. She should never have left home. It was so much easier to stay inside the lines in Minnesota.

"Jackie? Are you all right?"

She peeked out from behind her hands. Lenore stood in the doorway, looking concerned.

"Fine. My eyes are just tired." *Because I stayed up most of the night screwing your son every which way from Sunday.* She stood up and raked her hair back into place and smoothed her sundress so she might at least look less disheveled than she felt. "Come on. Let's go find out what a pushcart race looks like."

The crowd that had been milling around earlier had now overfilled the grandstands and jelled into masses along each side of the race route. With Reade acting as point man, they plowed into the crowd, looking for a good spot from which to watch. They found an empty-ish space to stake out, but the gaps around them quickly filled with people jostling for places. Everyone was quite cheery about it, and Reade soon struck up a conversation with the couple next to him, who had three young children.

The crowd roared as the first racers took their places at the starting line. A pushcart, Jackie discovered, looked like a hybrid between a Soap Box Derby car and a scooter: a low, squarish car shape with a platform in the back where the drivers, typically young men of about twenty, steered from an upright position. Most were painted with wild graphics in the intense primary colors that seemed to be popular all over the island. Speed-increasing ballast and a certain amount of directional control were provided by a younger boy in a helmet—often an old football helmet—who perched facedown and head-first on the nose of the cart like a human battering ram and shifted his weight to help the driver steer.

"How could a mother possibly let her child do something so dangerous?" fretted Lenore under her breath as she watched the children mount up.

"How could you let your children sneak into the Great Pyramid after dark so they could sleep in the King's Chamber?" asked Reade.

"I didn't let you," said Lenore. "You just did it."

"Exactly."

"You do have a point," Lenore conceded.

"You snuck into the Great Pyramid?" asked Jackie. "Don't they have guards?"

"With machine guns," said Reade. "They weren't very happy when they found us."

"Don't let him snow you," said Lenore. "The truth is, the guards let the boys in because Reade charmed them into it. Although I suspect a little money changed hands, too. He's not beyond cheating a bit to get something he wants."

"That doesn't surprise me," said Jackie. That's pretty much what he'd done to her, after all. Charmed and cheated his way in. Talked and kissed and touched until her defenses fell like Jericho's walls.

Fortunately, her straying thoughts were redirected by

the start of the first heat, a chaotic display of bobsled-style pushing, erratic steering, and numerous minor crashes and tangles, all accompanied by much hooting and catcalling and rooting for favorites. The teams who survived the start straightened out as they picked up speed, and a wave of cheers followed them down the straightaway and into the first turn. Suddenly, one of the middle carts swerved into another, sending it and a third contender into the big round bales of straw that lined the road. Onlookers dove out of the way, but the wreck did little damage other than to pride. Seconds later the announcer on the big sound system truck parked down the mountain, near the finish, went crazy as the surviving carts came into his sight, calling the race as if it were the Indy 500. Number 4 won by two lengths.

The next heat featured a pair of drivers who slapped at each other as they passed. Jackie watched, shaking her head in amazement. "Are there any rules at all for these races?"

The men around them laughed.

"Just a few. Mostly, point downhill and stay on the road," said the man Reade had been talking to. He grinned at her, revealing no front teeth on top.

"And try not to hit face first, like Newton there, did," called out one of the other men, setting off gales of laughter in the surrounding crowd.

Joining in, Jackie caught Hunter's attention and tapped her chin. "This sounds like a sport you should avoid."

"Either that or I've prequalified." He casually put his hand on Jackie's waist; she lifted it off and dropped it so it fell to his side.

Another heat of ten carts careened down the hill. This time, only one cart was lost—in a truly spectacular crash that sent the driver flying through the air. He landed on the far side of the bales, sending up a cloud of dust and straw, but he got to his feet immediately and saw to his little copilot, who had managed to cling to his handholds on the cart. Moments later, they were pushing their vehicle back uphill along with the others.

Between heats, the children next to them got into a fight over who was going to ultimately win the trophy. The boy preferred someone called Buggy John, while the girl, all of eight, favored Eddie Moon, and continued to defend his reputation at the top of her lungs even when her brother called her a "lyin' rass" and slugged her in the arm. She hit him back.

The baby, about two, started screaming. The father scooped him onto his shoulders, out of reach of the older two, while the mother tried without success to separate them.

"EddieJohnEddieJohnEddieJohn."

Looking completely unperturbed, Reade flagged down a passing vendor. "I'll take three of whatever you have in that cooler."

"Frozen pops," said the man.

"Perfect," said Reade.

"Thanks," said Jackie, "But I really didn't want anything."

"Good." Reade handed over money and took the three big, bomb-shaped pops.

"Any earplugs?" asked Jackie. The man rolled his eyes and shook his head, then moved off, anxious to get away.

Reade quickly stripped the wrappers off the treats, then turned and held two of them out to the girl and boy. "If you want these, you have to promise to mind your mother and stop fighting."

"Yes, sir!" they both said. "We promise." The pops went in their mouths like plugs.

Reade held out the third to the baby. "You, too, munchkin."

"Dat," he said succinctly, then grabbed the bar out of Reade's hand and latched on like it was a frozen teat.

The noise level instantly dropped to the more tolerable roar of several thousand adults. The parents thanked Reade as if he had presented them with a winning lottery ticket, and several people in the immediate vicinity reached over to thump him on the back.

"Not bad, Hunter," Jackie allowed.

"I knew there was some reason we brought you along," said his mother.

"And here I thought it was my scintillating personality," he said. When Lenore turned back to the street with a relieved smile, he put his mouth next to Jackie's ear and ran his fingers up her spine. "Scintillate. To emit sparks."

She stood there, scintillating like one of those birthday candles that can't be blown out while the next heat ran. Too bad there wasn't a tub of water to dunk herself in.

Thanks to Reade's Popsicle heroics, they were now included in the jokes and banter that flowed around them as the afternoon blazed on, so eventually she managed to focus on something other than him. As the races progressed into the semifinals, several more pushcarts crashed with great clatter and much *ooh*ing from the crowd. The day ended with the big final race, followed by a parade of the day's winner up the hill. The little girl beamed as Eddie Moon passed by, but her brother was so morose that he just sat down without hitting her again.

"Where do you suppose Farley is?" asked Jackie.

Reade shrugged. "He must have decided not to come after all. Let's hang out for a while and let the traffic clear before we leave."

"But you must stay for the party," said their neighbor, Newton. The baby had fallen asleep on his shoulders, glued to his father's hair with sticky red juice.

"I thought this was it for the day," said Reade.

"Oh, no," said Ginger, the wife. "The real fun starts after we're rid of the tourists."

"But we're tourists," Jackie felt obliged to point out.

"Not really," said Ginger. She swiped at her daughter's dirty mouth with the edge of the girl's sleeve. "You know the ones I mean, in their expensive clothes that look cheap and their big buses so they don't have to get too close, like they think they might catch something. They want it all to be just like home, except with native people who look nice in their photos and good gift shops where they can buy trash to prove they were here."

Jackie winced internally. The woman had described exactly the kind of tourist she had started out to be, the kind she would have been if she hadn't fallen in with Farley and the Hunters—safely locked inside a climate-controlled bus with her camera and her coordinated vacation wardrobe and her budget for souvenirs. Oh, lord. No wonder Ben had wanted out—not that understanding his motives changed the fact that he was an inconsiderate ass.

"But you're not like them," said Newton, not knowing how wrong he was. "Nobody will complain if you people stay."

Reade put one arm around his mother and the other around Jackie. "Are you ladies up for a party?"

"For a little while," said Lenore. "But I want to go back to Cho-Cho and look a little more. I'm so tempted to buy that one carving."

"Things won't get started for an hour or two. Take your time," said Ginger. "Just don't tell any of the other foreigners about the party, or some fool will put us on the tour schedule next year and ruin it all."

"We wouldn't think of it," said Reade.

They walked back to Cho-Cho, moving against the flow of tourists headed for the parking areas. While Lenore consulted with Reade, Jackie loitered on the wooden stoop outside, where a slight breeze made things a little cooler—and where Reade couldn't start with his art commentary again.

She was watching the parade of people and buses and cars as the village slowly cleared when she spotted a familiar ponytail on the other side of the road.

"Farley." She called out and waved before she realized that he was talking to someone—a pair of men who were standing in a doorway. One was Latin-looking, and the other was a black man with thick, long dreadlocks and a scruffy beard.

Farley turned at the sound of his name. He spotted Jackie and raised a hand to wave. The two men immediately faded back into the doorway, but in the instant before they disappeared, Jackie saw the black man's eyes, oddly bright against his dark skin.

Farley dashed across the road between cars.

"Finally." He pulled off his cap and wiped his head. "I must have hiked through town half a dozen times looking for you. I was beginning to think you'd left already."

She shook her head. "Farley, who were those two men?"

"Hmm?" He glanced over his shoulder toward the now empty doorway. "Oh, just a couple of guys trying to bum cigarettes. Are Lenore and Reade inside?" He stepped around her without waiting for an answer. "Come on, let's pry them loose and go have a good time. I've got a secret—it's party night, and you've never partied 'til you've partied St. Sebastian style."

thirteen

Shortly after the last tour bus pulled out of Redoubt, and just as the surrounding jungle absorbed the last of the sunlight, the locals started trailing up to the school yard. While teenage boys strung lights from the trees, gangs of men set up makeshift tables and benches and hauled barbecue drums, still hot, up from the vendors' stalls on poles. The women produced food by the platter-ful: greens and fruits of every description, plates full of meat and fish to throw on the grill, and piles of breads and sweets.

The sound system truck blared reggae and rock and roll while everyone worked, but the party didn't really start until the band rolled up in an ancient Datsun pickup truck. Once the musicians piled out and plugged in, the thump of the bass guitar and the drums quickly drew in every straggler that the savory smells hadn't. People lined up to be served from paper-covered tables, then settled on board-and-block benches or upended buckets to eat. Chattering kids ducked in to grab tidbits and then run off to play, while dogs, chickens, and the occasional pig threaded between legs, looking for scraps.

Jackie was just finishing off a plate of grilled fish and stewed greens when Reade motioned toward the band. "They're playing our song."

"We don't have a song," said Jackie. She listened for a second, then amended her statement with a smile. "However, if we did, something called 'Animosity' just might be it."

"And you doubted me." He stood up. "Come on, let's dance."

"Aren't you the same man who told me he only knows one step?"

"That would be him, all right," said Lenore from her seat on the other end of the board bench. "And he barely manages that one with me—complaining all the while, I might add. I have never seen him volunteer before."

"What can I say? I'm inspired." Reade put his hand out, palm up, then stood there looking down at Jackie like an imperious dance master until she realized she was either going to have to go along or kick him in the shins. She glanced at Lenore, then at Farley, who was standing a few yards away, talking with a group of local men. She set her plate down and stood up.

"Thank you," he said as he led her out to the middle of the play court that served as dance floor. "I wanted to give Farley a chance to talk to Mom. She's been using us to avoid him all evening."

"I know. And that's the only reason I'm out here," she said.

"Damn. Here I thought it was because you were dying to rub up against me in public."

"I swear, Hunter, if you start in again, I'll. . . ."

"You'll what? Spank me?" he asked. "I'm not really into that kind of kinky stuff, but if it winds your crank, I suppose we could work something out."

She jerked her hand away. "If I could figure out where to buy saltpeter locally, I'd dose your beer in a heartbeat."

"That would make for a dull evening . . . although not necessarily for you," he mused, and the knowledge of what he was capable of doing to make her evening interesting, saltpeter or no, made her light-headed.

The band downshifted from the driving beat of dancehall into a more relaxed, tropical rhythm. Reade wrapped his arm around her waist and tugged her into dance position, fitting their bodies together as if they'd done this before. Their subsequent efforts, however, proved they hadn't.

"This is a samba," said Jackie after a moment. "You can't do a box step to a samba."

"I can do a box step to anything," he said.

"This is your one step? And you say *I'm* boring."

"Work with me here, woman." He tried to put on a gruff voice, but his laugh ruined the effect.

They did a little better when she stopped fighting the inevitable and did the darn box step—she simply wasn't a strong enough dancer to fake her way around him the way his mother apparently had the other night. It was amazing what a decent partner could do for a poor dancer, she reflected. Farley had made her look way better than she was, too.

She had to give Reade credit, though—he stayed on the beat, mostly, and he was at least trying where most men in his position wouldn't. It took guts to get out on the dance floor when you were that bad and knew it. But then guts didn't seem to be an issue with Hunter, in the lab, in a kayak, or on a mountain bike. Or in bed, for that matter. God, it was so tempting to just go crazy with him for a few days . . .

"A penny for your thoughts," he murmured, his lips brushing her temple.

"I, uh. . . ." She tilted her face away, so he couldn't see the color she knew spotted her cheeks, and desperately cast about for something to cover her mental lapse. "I was just wondering what's going on over there."

He glanced toward the road, where a crowd was starting

to collect under the banner that marked the race start. "I don't know. Let's go see."

"Anything to get out of dancing, huh?"

"You've got it."

They joined a growing stream of people headed in the same direction. It turned out that the local boys were getting ready to race; kids of junior high and high school age crowded around makeshift pushcarts that were cobbled together out of junkyard parts and packing crates. A group of adult men jogged down the hill to block off the road again and shift the straw bales to make the route shorter and the turns wider. Another group saw to the lighting along the road, hanging work lights and bare bulbs from trees and houses where needed.

The first pack of boys clattered down the hill, bouncing off each other and the straw bales, but all staying on the road to the finish. Jubilant cries could be heard all the way up at the finish, and a long-legged young man in running clothes sprinted up the road with the results, then turned and ran back.

"My God," said Reade. "That's Daedalus Shaw. He's a world record holder in the ten thousand meter."

"He does this to train," said one of the locals with pride, and the next thing Jackie knew, Reade was deep in conversation about track and field.

She was standing there by herself when Farley drifted over.

She looked around. "Where's Lenore?"

"I have no idea," he said. "We're 'not obliged to entertain each other.' Her words."

"I'm sorry. I don't mean to be nosy, but you two were getting along so well until yesterday. What happened?"

"I said something she didn't want to hear." He left it at that, stuffing his hands into his pockets. "Are you two going to drive?"

"Drive where?" asked Jackie, confused by the sudden change of topic.

"Here." He pointed at the carts. "The pushcarts. The

kids will let pretty much anyone take a run . . . although they might hit you up for a couple of pounds, since you're not local. And they definitely won't let one of the little kids ride the front. Frankly, I'm kind of surprised Reade isn't on one already."

"He must not know yet."

"Well, now *you* know," said Farley, as though she should do something with that knowledge. He rocked back and forth on his heels a couple of times, then added, "They do let women drive, by the way."

Jackie blinked. Farley was hinting for her to race Reade, and with all the subtlety of a Mack truck. However, before she had a chance to ask why, he raised a hand and called out a greeting. "Hey, Terron. Terron Lamping."

Jackie twisted to see a gray-haired man waving to him.

"Excuse me. I just spotted a friend," said Farley. "And you have more exciting things to do than put up with a cranky old fart like me, anyway. Have fun." He gave her a pointed look that shifted from her to Hunter and then to the pushcarts, then took off toward his friend.

Fun? Stunned, Jackie stared after him. Farley's blatant hint had just turned into an even more blatant challenge. Maybe even an order.

The question was, Why? What possible reason could he have for wanting the two of them to race?

It must be some kind of test. He probably wanted to see if they had the guts to try it. Reade did, of course. That wasn't even a question, but Farley probably wasn't sure about her.

For that matter, neither was she. She'd driven her neighbor's go-cart down Baker Farm Hill once, but that had been ages ago, when she was nine or ten and too stupid to realize she could get hurt. She knew now, though, and if she didn't know it, all she had to do was look at Newton, across the way. Her front teeth throbbed in sympathy, and she curled her tongue over them, wincing.

A more relevant question might be, What would happen if she didn't? As reasonable as Farley had seemed to be the past week, he did have the reputation of being eccentric, both in his personal life and in his decision-making processes. What if he had chosen tonight to get flaky and decided to make a decision about the grant based on a pushcart race?

Surely not.

But then again, without knowing for sure, she couldn't very well risk all that funding.

Okay. If Hunter suggested a race, she'd go. And if he didn't, she'd . . . what? Oh, the heck with it. She'd suggest it herself. She might as well reexert a modicum of control in her life, even if most of it had gone squirrelly. And it'd be nice to take the lead away from Reade in at least one activity.

Okay. She was going to do it—but she wasn't going to do it alone. She cut across the road to where Newton was hanging with his little boy.

"Hello," he said. "Are you all enjoyin' yourselves?"

"Very much. But I'd love to try out the pushcarts"— *What a liar.* —"and I'm hoping you can help me out." She quickly explained her needs. "Not too fast, though. I want to have fun, not kill myself."

"Not a problem." Newton reassured her. He waved over a couple of his friends, and within moments Jackie had access to two carts—evenly matched, according to Newton—and a pair of scratched-up football helmets, with face guards, thank God. The three men then gave her the short course on pushcart driving and tactics.

"Thank you, gentlemen. I owe you. I'll be right back." She turned and started back toward Reade, only to see him headed in her direction. Her heart speeded up for a second, and it suddenly dawned on her that the brew of emotions this stunt was stirring up was going to make it even harder to stick to her guns tonight. Shoot, she hadn't been able to resist him last night when she'd been com-

pletely relaxed. Tonight, all riled up and knowing how
terrific he was in bed . . .

She should call this off right now, before she got herself
into even more trouble. She had about two seconds to
make up her mind. She glanced toward where Farley
stood talking to his buddy and caught him looking back
at her. He raised an eyebrow speculatively.

"There you are," said Reade, coming over to her. "I
was worried you'd gone off to hunt for that saltpeter after
all."

"Nope." She paced up the road a few yards, away from
the crowd clustered around the carts. "I found something
more interesting to do." *Decision made.*

"What's that?"

"I arranged for a couple of pushcarts. We can race." As
casually as she could, she added, "If you're up to it."

He laughed. "Like you are."

"What's that supposed to mean?"

"For one thing, you're in a dress."

"It covers as much of me as that T-shirt and shorts does
you."

"Yeah, but my shorts won't fly up over my head."

"If you're looking for an excuse not to race, you're
going to have to come up with something better than another clothing critique." She waited for an answer, but he
was grinning off into space. "Hunter!"

"Hmm?" His eyes refocused. "Sorry, I got stuck on the
image of you with your dress around your ears. What did
you say?"

"That it's amazing you ever made it out of junior high,"
she snapped. "Do you want to do this or not?"

"Wow. You're serious. You really do have carts for
us?"

"I really do. Right over there." She pointed.

He pursed his lips and blew a low whistle. "You keep
finding ways to surprise me, lady. Okay, what are we
racing for?"

She didn't dare tell him that the grant just might be on

the line—his killer instincts would pop out and he'd run her right off the road. Shoot, even his own mother said he'd cheat to get what he wanted.

"Just for fun."

"Nope. Even the little kids get candy if they win. How about a small bet?"

"Okay. Five pounds."

"Well, we could bet money. Or we could bet something else."

"What kind of something else?" she asked suspiciously.

"If I win, you come to my room tonight . . . for a nightcap. If you win, I'll go to your room."

"Nice try," she said. "If I win, I go to my room alone."

"Deal." He held out his hand.

Jackie started to shake, then realized what she done and pulled her hand back. "Wait a minute."

Grinning, he grabbed her right hand with his, shaking firmly. "I hope they restocked the minibar."

She snatched her hand away. "We do not have a bet."

"Oh, but we do. I offered, you countered, I agreed, and we shook. Those are the basic steps of a binding contract. We have a bet, and when I win, you will pay off, because you're not the kind of woman who welshes." His manner and expression softened, and he took her gently by the shoulders. "It's just a drink, Jackie. Anything else that happens is entirely up to you, just like it was last night."

He stopped any argument cold with a brief, amazingly tender kiss that stirred up all sorts of delicious sensations before he turned and walked away. She stood there, body thrumming, knowing how out of control she'd been last night, but also knowing that he was telling the truth. Despite all his teasing and sexual innuendo, she was absolutely certain he would have stopped last night, any time she said the word.

And he'd stop tonight, too, except if she got as far as his room, chances were that the word she needed would take a detour someplace between her brain and her mouth, lost in the morass of conflicting feelings he stirred up.

Which was why she needed to win. *Had* to win.

Besides, it would really impress Farley. That had to count for something.

She pulled herself together and followed Reade over to where he was already checking out his cart with its owner. She motioned Newton and the fellow who owned her cart off to one side.

"Gentlemen, there's been a slight change of plans." Borrowing a page from Hunter's own book, she pulled a pair of nice, crisp U.S. twenty-dollar bills out of her purse. "I need the fastest cart you can get me. And I need it now."

Lenore stood in the doorway of the hallway that led to the school rest room that had been opened for the ladies and checked around for Farley. She was being petty, she knew, but she just wasn't ready to forgive him yet. She wished she could—for one thing, the band was very good and she'd like to have her dance partner back— but it was hard to forgive a man who didn't think he needed to be forgiven.

When she didn't see him, she slipped back outside and returned to her bench. While she'd been hiding out in the bathroom, she'd taken advantage of the good light to sort out her evening medications. But she hadn't quite trusted the water, so now she washed them down one at a time with the last of her ginger beer. After that, she wandered over to the serving tables to offer to help clean up. The ladies welcomed her and put her to work.

She and Ginger, the woman with the three screaming children, were scraping plates in preparation for washing up when a man jogged across the school yard.

"Leave those pots and pans, ladies," he called. "The visitors are startin' in." ·

Several women dropped what they were doing and ran toward the road, shouting and laughing.

"There's a few ready to kill themselves every year,"

said Ginger. "They don't realize how hard the carts are to drive."

"This time we got a brave woman, too. Some blonde lady tourist." He carved out a voluptuous figure in midair.

"Jackie? Oh, my God." Lenore dropped the plate and scraper on the table and scrambled up onto a nearby bench for a better view. Sure enough, there was Jackie's blonde head, right in the middle of everything. She couldn't pick out Reade, but if Jackie was racing, it was probably her son's idea. Jackie was much too sensible to come up with something like this on her own.

"Is that your daughter?" asked Ginger.

"No. A friend. But my son must be racing with her."

"A black-haired man who looks like he's been dragged across a railroad track?" asked the man.

"That's him." *Oh, my God!* Lenore's chest tightened.

"Then you should be there to watch him." The man held up a hand to help her down, and the three of them hustled toward the road.

They were halfway across the school yard when Lenore started having trouble getting enough oxygen. She stopped to catch her breath.

"Are you all right?" her friends asked.

"The air's . . . a little thin," she gasped. Her pulse pounded, faster and faster. "I can't quite . . . seem to . . . get a breath."

"Take it easy, there." There was no seat nearby, so the man helped her over to one of the basketball hoops where she could lean against the upright.

"You look pale," said Ginger. "Shall we get your son?"

"I think . . . maybe. . . ."

"Everett, go stop that bwoy right now, before he goes off. Tell him his mama's having some sort of spell."

Every time the kid starts to go off, you have one of your spells. Oh, dear Lord. Farley was right.

"No! Don't," Lenore said quickly.

The man stopped.

"Are you certain?" asked Ginger, her face a mask of concern.

Lenore nodded. "Let him race. I'm fine. . . ." Air was still hard to come by, but she was determined. "I'm a worrywart and I . . . panicked a minute. . . . That's all."

"And here I said all those things about visitors killing themselves," said Ginger, shaking her head. "I didn't mean it. The worst that ever happened was a broken leg, but that fool was so drunk, he would have found a way to break it walking to the toilet. And there were Newton's teeth, of course, but that was years ago."

Lenore touched her hand. "Thank you. But it wasn't your fault." *It was mine. It has been all along.* She shuddered as she drew in air. "Really. I'm better already. . . . Go watch the race." She had to reassure them several more times, but they finally believed her and walked off to join the others.

Alone, Lenore sagged back against the pole, Farley's accusation ringing in her ears. He was exactly right. She hadn't even seen it. That first day suddenly came back to her: Reade had mentioned going parasailing, and she'd put him off by getting a headache and asking him to go for medicine.

She clamped her hand over her mouth to smother the cry of guilt that welled up as other memories flooded back: times he had canceled trips because she was sick, times he'd passed on activities with friends, times she'd kept him from being who he really was. She hadn't even realized.

"Three, two, one. Go!" The crowd counted down the start. She squeezed her eyes shut against the pressure that gripped her ribs and stood there, silent and in an agony of self-recrimination, holding herself up with the pole until she could tell from the sound of the cheering that the race was over and they were both unhurt. Then, without even waiting to see who had won, she turned to walk away.

Farley stood there, just a few yards away, where he must have been for some time.

He smiled at her gently. Unaccusing. "Are you all right, Lenore?"

"No." She clenched her teeth to hold back a sob and summoned the effort to draw herself upright. "You were right, Farley. I have done terrible things to my son."

"Not intentionally," he said.

"No. But I'm sure I've done just as much damage as if I'd planned every step." Tears streamed down her face. "And I have no idea how to fix things. To give him back his life."

"Do you want to?"

"Of course I do. I've got to make it right."

"All right," he said. "We'll leave a message for Reade and Jackie, and I'll give you a ride home. We'll see what we can figure out."

Damn, if she hadn't beaten him.

Reade watched Jackie sail past the finish a good ten yards ahead of him, her cart rolling smoothly while his jittered along on misaligned wheels. Not that the outcome had been in much doubt. At the last minute, Newton had discovered some sort of "mechanical defect" with her original cart and rolled out a substitute—one with perfect, new wheels and which looked remarkably like one of the carts that had been in the championship finals earlier in the day.

Dr. Barnett had cheated.

She'd bought herself a faster cart, and now she was paying the price, because that greater speed made it harder to stop. She finally had to turn loose of the steering wheel and yank on the brake lever with both hands. The cart skidded and veered off the road. She tumbled off in the grass, and the cart came to a sliding halt in some bushes.

Reade steered his cart to a softer landing and jumped off to run down to her. "Jackie?"

She stared up at him, half in shock, then looked back at the finish as she took her helmet off. "I won. I actually won."

He helped her up, then wrapped his arms around her waist and spun her around. "You did, you little cheat. And you managed to do it with your dress down, mostly. Are your panties pink, or was it just the light?"

Her comeback was drowned by high-pitched screaming as a flock of young women and girls charged down the hill and surrounded them. They pried Jackie out of his arms and swept her away to parade her up the hill.

She was a local heroine, but Reade found himself facing a less enthusiastic pack of boys. They hung back, glaring at him sourly and muttering about the shame of losing to a woman.

Reade shrugged. "Come on, men. Let's get the carts."

It took him a few minutes to convince some helpers that pushing Jackie's winning machine back up to its owner wouldn't diminish their manhood in any way, so by the time they reached the school yard, the celebration was in full swing. Every woman in town was dancing, gyrating to a celebratory beat that conjured up images of ancient goddesses and warrior queens. In the center of the loose circle, Jackie stomped and swayed, her hips swinging to the rhythm of the music. She spotted him watching and flipped her skirt a little.

The glimpse of thigh was like a warm hand to his groin. God, he wanted this woman. Every time she surprised him like that, whether with an unexpected gesture or a push-cart race, he wanted her more.

He grabbed a couple of cold beers out of a tub of ice and twisted off the tops. When the victory dance wound down, he carried them out to Jackie. The women surrounding her backed off, giggling and nudging each other as he held one out.

Flushed, Jackie accepted his tribute. "Thank you."

Reade held his bottle up to her and spoke loudly

enough for everyone to hear. "To a woman who knows what it takes to win."

They touched bottles and each took a long draw, their eyes never leaving each other. As the crowd laughed and applauded, Reade leaned forward. "Apparently it takes cheating."

"Or just plain driving better."

"Let's trade carts and have a rematch. We'll see who drives better."

Laughing, she shook her head and hoisted her bottle high. "To gracious losers who follow through on their bets."

Another clink of glass. More applause. The music started again, and Reade backed away.

"Aren't you going to dance with me?" she asked.

He shook his head. If he danced with her, if he put his hands on her, he would never have the willpower to honor that stupid bet.

"I'll just watch the winner," he said. "It's your night."

So he watched, and he nursed his beer, and eventually he got around to wondering just how far it was between Pittsburgh and Minneapolis, because he had a feeling that a vacation fling wasn't going to be nearly enough.

"I can't believe you gave it away like that, mon," complained some fellow Reade had never seen. "To a woman."

"I didn't give it away," said Reade, talking about more than the race. "She stole it."

"You get to go home," the man continued, as though he hadn't heard. "We have to live with these women. We'll never hear the end of it."

"Neither will I," Reade assured him and drained the last of his beer. "Neither will I."

fourteen

*Lenore's riding back with me. See you tomorrow.
Party hardy. F.*

Jackie read the note, then folded it in half and passed
it back to Reade. "Well, that explains why we haven't
seen either of them for the last couple of hours. I just
figured they were off somewhere, making up. Where did
you get this?"

"Your friend Newton brought it to me."

"*My* friend?"

"He didn't give *me* the good cart," Reade pointed out.
"Apparently Farley handed it to Newton's kids to give to
us, and they got distracted and forgot. It fell out of a
pocket when Ginger was putting them to bed, so he ran
it back up here."

"Thank goodness," said Jackie. "We could have spent
hours trying to find them. And I might even have convinced myself those two guys had waylaid them."

"What two guys?"

"Oh, just a couple of fellows who were trying to bum cigarettes off Farley earlier. But one of them looked kind of like that guy your mom described, so. . . ."

Reade rolled his eyes. "Don't tell me her paranoia is rubbing off on you."

"All I said was that if we hadn't gotten that note, I might have wondered."

"Okay. I'm sorry. You're not paranoid," conceded Reade. "So, are you ready to head back? I think I spotted our driver raiding the tag ends of the barbecue."

"Let's just make sure he hasn't been in the rum punch."

They hunted up the driver, confirmed his sobriety, and headed for the parking area, where their car now sat pretty much by itself. Jackie climbed into the backseat with a sense of trepidation.

Since the race, there had been something in Reade's eyes she couldn't quite identify. Intensity, perhaps, or resolve, but different from the cockiness he'd displayed all day. If he had decided to go back on their wager, he would have plenty of time to work on her on the way back to the resort. In that hour, alone in the backseat, he could play his suggestive word games, find subtle ways to touch her, or just sit there and smell good, and she would probably react just the way she didn't want to. All that dancing had knocked the top off her adrenaline high, but she was still buzzing. Still susceptible. As Reade got in, she steeled herself.

However, to her surprise, he behaved, carrying on innuendo-free conversation the whole way back and bidding her good night at a respectable distance from her door.

It was such a change, it was almost creepy. Where was the guy who had been hell-bent on getting her back into his bed? She paused with her hand on the doorknob and looked back up the path. There he stood, watching her, so much heat in his eyes that he should be setting off every smoke alarm in the vicinity.

Her lips formed his name. Quickly, before she could say it aloud, she jammed the key card in the door, yanked it open, and stepped inside.

She stood there in the dark, her body throbbing, half afraid he might knock after all, and half wishing he would. Insane, that's what she was. Absolutely insane.

The knock didn't come, and after a few minutes, she flipped on the light. Two black shapes sat at the foot of her bed.

"Ohmigod. My luggage!"

She reached for the doorknob, ready to shout for Reade to come back and share in her good fortune. She pulled up short.

Bad idea, Barnett.

Deflating slightly, she walked over to the twin black bags, and touched them to be sure they were real, then boosted both of them onto the end of the bed and opened them. The last of her excitement faded as the navy blue boringness of their contents overwhelmed her.

The coordinated wardrobe that had looked so practical when she'd been buying and packing now looked dull and matronly, like something her mother would wear to a church picnic back in Cedar Falls and get compliments on. *What a cute outfit, Mary Ann. Where did you get that?* Not island clothes at all. Even her swimsuit. Especially her swimsuit. What had she been thinking?

Expensive clothes that looked cheap, Ginger had called them. But it wasn't that they looked cheap. They just looked *wrong*.

Jackie sank down on the bed between the open suitcases, utterly disheartened. Here she'd been waiting for her clothes, and now that they'd arrived, they were awful. She didn't even want to touch them.

No, that wasn't true. She definitely wanted her underwear—washing things out every night was a pain. She lifted the satin lingerie bags out of each suitcase and set them aside. Toiletries and cosmetics bags followed. And a nightgown and robe would be nice.

She picked through the rest, pulling out the few pieces of clothing that she thought might work: a couple of T-shirts, a pair of shorts, a long-sleeved gauze shirt for a cover-up, some white cotton drawstring pants that had slipped in there somehow, and one skirt. She found a pair of flip-flops in a shoe bag, and her beach book stuck in the outside pocket—too bad she hadn't had that a couple of days ago. It might have saved some aggravation. She stacked them on top of the other items.

That was it.

She put her few salvaged clothes in the bureau with her other things and carried her toiletries bag around the corner to the vanity to start laying things out: deodorant, hair gel, static spray—now there was a dumb one, even dumber than the condoms she'd packed with Ben in mind—and hallelujah, her sunscreen. Leaning forward to check out her poor, scorched nose for new freckles, she caught a glimpse in the mirror of her pink nylon shorts hanging over the rod in the bathroom. In a flash, she was back in Reade's room, watching herself in his mirror, and the torrent of erotic body memory almost knocked her off her feet. She had to brace herself against the counter.

Damn him! He'd made it worse by backing off so completely, by not giving her anything to resist against. His lack of pursuit made it clearer how much of this craziness came straight from the center of her. She wanted him, and she couldn't blame him for that anymore.

When the rush subsided, she went back into the bedroom, zipped both suitcases shut, and shoved them into the closet. The clothes inside were useless here, but they'd be just fine next summer in Minneapolis, when everything was back to normal.

Normal. As in no Hunter. All she had to do was make it through the next week without falling back into bed with him.

* * *

After a short and rather stiff run on the beach and a hearty breakfast, Reade found a comfortable chair off in a quiet corner of the terrace and settled in with a copy of the *Port Meredith Daily Journal.* Catching up with world events made a poor substitute for a lazy morning in bed with Jackie, but that's what he got for being such a Boy Scout last night and honoring that bet.

She was probably waking up about now. He wondered what she looked like first thing in the morning: whether she was one of those women who wake up tousled and gorgeous, or the wrinkly, puffy kind. He intended to find out. Tomorrow.

He steered his attention back to the paper and was deep in the middle of a story on European politics when his mother poked her head around the potted fig that Reade had thought would provide some privacy.

"What did you do to Jackie that you have to hide out?" she asked.

Not nearly enough. "Hello, Mother. I'm fine, thank you. How are you?"

"Thirsty. I've already been for a walk this morning. Has anything happened in the world since we left?"

"The usual, politics and scandal. They've got a new government in Italy."

"Another one? I never have understood how a country can operate with a new prime minister every fifteen minutes." She dropped her purse on the chair. "I'm going to get something to drink. I'll be right back." Her smile dimmed a watt or two. "You and I need to talk."

That sounded ominous, and Reade suddenly understood why his mother had reacted so strongly when he'd said the same words in preparation to telling her about Jackie and Farley and the grant. He refolded his paper and spent a couple of minutes psyching himself up before she returned with a large glass of what appeared to be iced tea.

She set it down on the cocktail table. While she dragged a chair closer to his, Reade picked up the glass and took a sip. "Amazing. It really is tea."

"Of course it's tea," she said snippily as she settled in. "It's not even noon yet."

"The umbrella threw me off," he said. "Plus I wanted an idea of how serious this discussion is going to be."

Her eyes pinched at the corners and she looked down at her lap as though embarrassed. "Very."

"Is this about you and Farley?" asked Reade, wondering if he was going to have to do that safe sex talk after all.

"Only peripherally," she said. "You know we've been on the outs the past couple of days."

"I . . . picked up on that, yeah," he said. "I thought you must have patched things up last night."

"More or less. But you need to know why I was mad at him to start with." She twisted at her wedding band, a nervous habit she'd had as long as he could remember. "When we were in Port Meredith, Farley made some observations that I didn't particularly appreciate. I thought he was way off base, and I told him so. However, last night I realized he was right, so I apologized to him. And now I need to apologize to you."

His theory that they were sleeping together shot down, Reade was lost. "You haven't done anything to apologize for."

"Yes, I have," she said firmly. "For years." She paused, her hands working. "What Farley pointed out—what I didn't want to hear—is how I've been using those spells of mine to manipulate you."

"Farley Phelps has no business—"

"Just let me talk, please. This is hard enough. Farley noticed that I was having spells whenever you were about to do something that would take you off by yourself or put you in a situation I perceived as dangerous."

"There's nothing wrong with wanting to protect me," said Reade.

"Maybe not, if I was actually protecting you, but we're not talking about real danger here. You weren't swimming with sharks with raw meat in your hand—you were paddling off with Jackie in a kayak. Or going biking by yourself."

"I did split my chin," he pointed out ruefully, touching the scab with the tip of his finger. "Anyway, you weren't sick either time, so—"

"Actually, I was," she said. "I would have called you back to stay with me both times if Farley hadn't stepped in. And then there was the headache I just coincidentally got when you wanted to go parasailing, not to mention the last six years' worth of incidents I came up with. I was about to send someone to stop you from racing last night when I realized that I was doing it again."

"You've had three attacks that you haven't told me about?"

"They're not attacks, Reade. Not really. They never have been."

"One was," he reminded her.

She sighed. "You're right. One was. And one of your father's was, too, which I have a feeling is even more relevant to this discussion."

The image of his father's face, ashen gray as he lay dying at the side of a mountain trail, floated up from the place Reade kept it buried. They had gone out that day, just the two of them, to say good-bye. One last hike before Reade was to take off for Venezuela.

"You never made it to Venezuela," said his mother, as if she were seeing exactly the same vision.

He nodded, then pushed the image back down so he could speak. "Kit went back to Europe, and Ash was tied up on that tour with . . . who was it? Elton John, I think."

"And you, being the eldest, and the most responsible of my irresponsible lot, postponed your trip."

"You were so lost without him, Mom. You needed someone there."

"I would have been fine," she said. "Eventually. But it was easier to have you around for another month or two.

Except then, right before you were finally supposed to leave, I conveniently had a heart attack."

"You can't convince me you did that on purpose."

"I might as well have, as neatly as it worked to keep you home."

"I had to withdraw, Mom. They needed someone in the field, and I wasn't about to leave, not with you sick."

"That was just an excuse for both of us. Dr. Huddleston knew right away that there hadn't been any permanent damage. You could have gone. But I let you stay—encouraged you to stay—because I was selfish and scared, and I didn't want you out there in the jungle where there was no help if you got hurt or sick."

"Like there was no help up on that mountain for Dad," said Reade, suddenly understanding something about them both.

"That wasn't your fault," she said.

"If I hadn't asked him to go with me, he wouldn't have been up there. And if I hadn't run ahead, he would have had help thirty minutes earlier."

"Then he would have died washing the car or mowing the lawn or, God forbid, shopping with me. Imagine him keeling over in a dress shop. Wouldn't that have just ticked him off?"

Reade had to smile, despite the pain. Dad had hated shopping with a passion exceeded only by his love for his wife.

"We have both done him a disservice: you by feeling guilty, and me by taking advantage of your guilt." His mother sighed deeply, an exhalation that sounded as if it came from the same pain-filled place where Reade kept his memories of his father. "Do you remember the first time I had one of my spells?"

He considered for a moment, then shook his head. "Not exactly."

"I didn't either, until Farley asked me what I got out of being sick. And when I answered the question, I remembered. Exactly. It was about six months after my heart attack. You were going to go backpacking with Terry Kryznokowski."

"Oh, yeah."

"Looking back now, I think I realized you were getting stir-crazy, and that your trip was a kind of test. If I did okay on my own, you might eventually sign up for another expedition. I panicked—actually panicked—and that's when you found me hyperventilating in the middle of the kitchen floor. Voilà. No trip. And a pattern was set for both of us. I swear, I didn't do it consciously."

"I know, Mom. It's not all your fault. I knew you weren't as sick as you thought you were."

"Then why the hell did you let me get away with it?" she demanded.

"I chose to stay home. I never knew when the next spell would be another real heart attack. And what if I went skipping off and you keeled over like Dad did?"

"That's what I thought." Her lip curled with disgust. "God, we're a mess, aren't we? The only possible mitigating factor in all this is that I didn't realize what I was doing. But now I do, and it's going to stop. Right here. Right now. I am not having any more of my so-called spells."

"Mom, I appreciate the sentiment, but you can't just stop getting sick because you decide to."

"Maybe not. But I can stop telling you every time I feel a twinge or have a little palpitation. I can get some counseling. And I can certainly stop insisting you do something when there's nothing to be done anyway. You're going to have to help, too, though. You're going to have to get over this idea that sticking close to me is going to keep me from dying. It won't."

"It worked before," he said. "If I hadn't been there. . . ."

"Then you would have been in Venezuela—maybe fishing around in that witch doctor's pot, and Ash or Kit might have been around, since they wouldn't have been relying on big brother to take care of everything. Or I might have hired myself a maid who would have called

911. Or you're right, I might have died. Who knows?

"That's how life works, Reade; it's a series of uncertainties ending in one certainty—death." She reached over and finger-combed his bangs off his forehead, just the way she had when he was a kid. "I am going to die one day, and so are you. But in the meantime, we both have to start dealing with life a little better. Beginning now."

She stood up. "I'm going to give you some time to process all this. Farley is taking me back up to Redoubt Colony to buy that carving I liked—sort of a commemoration of my new life—and then we may head to Port Meredith for that dinner we skipped the other night. I'll see you later this evening, and we can talk some more then."

Reade stared at her. Seven years of his life had just shifted like a tectonic plate, and she was going gallery-hopping. "What the hell am I supposed to do while you buy art?"

"Just try—" She stopped herself, then smiled sadly. "I don't know, darling. That's *your* job to figure out. I've screwed you up enough for one lifetime."

She brushed his hair back one more time, pressed a kiss to his forehead, then headed off toward the lobby, leaving Reade alone with his newspaper, his thoughts, and the bottom half of her iced tea. And she hadn't even been considerate enough to make it booze.

"How did it go?" asked Farley as Lenore joined him at the front entrance.

"He's guilty and confused. I'm guilty and confused. We're a merry pair." She glanced back toward where Reade sat, even though she knew she couldn't possibly see him from here. "I hope I haven't made a huge mistake."

"Everything will work out fine." Farley put his arm around her shoulder and gave her a comforting hug. "If it will make you feel any better, I bumped into Jackie

down by the pool and put a bug in her ear that Reade
might need a little extra attention today."

"I'm not sure she's the one to give it. You do realize
they're competing over your grant money."

"No. Really?" Farley's eyes sparkled with amusement,
and suddenly Lenore felt very much better. Things *would*
work out fine. "Do you have everything you need?" he
asked. "Money? Pills?"

She touched her purse. "Yes."

"Then let's go. We have an appointment to keep."

As dim and artificially air-conditioned as any sub-
urban fern bar, the Pirates Cave was the only lounge
at the resort. It was perfect for those who wanted to preserve their northern pallor and an excellent spot for people
who wanted to hide out.

Except, apparently, from Jackie. Reade saw her in the
mirror, scanning the bar from the doorway. She spotted
him, walked over, and slid onto the stool next to him.
"Drinking our lunch, are we?"

He pulled the pickled bean out of his drink and
chomped off the end without so much as glancing her
way.

"At least you're getting your veggies. What he's
having," she told the bartender. He moved away to mix
her drink. "Pretty gloomy place."

"It's quiet," said Reade. "At least, it *was*."

"Do you want me to leave so you and the other cirrho-
sis candidates can be alone?"

He shrugged. When the bartender brought her drink,
she thanked him and stood up to go. As she reached for
her glass, though, he changed his mind. He shot a hand
out to cover the glass, holding it to the counter.

"Okay." She sat back down. "Although what I'm supposed to do with a guy who doesn't want me around but
doesn't want me to leave, either, I have no idea." She
took a sip of her drink, then waved the bartender back.

"Excuse me. You forgot to put the liquor in this Bloody Mary."

He held out his hands apologetically. "You said you wanted what the gentleman is having."

She picked up Reade's drink and tasted it. Her eyes narrowed. "You faker. You're not getting drunk."

"I never said I was."

"I'm sorry," she told the bartender. "I assumed he was on a bender."

"I can add some vodka or some white rum for you," he offered.

"No. This will be fine." She turned back to Reade. "What the heck is going on?"

"I make it a policy not to drink when I feel like I really need to."

"Sensible, but it does beg the question of why you're playing lounge lizard if you don't intend to get drunk."

"The environment suits my mood."

"Ah. That's one lousy mood."

"Yeah. My turn to ask a question," he said when she took a sip of her Virgin Mary. "Did my mother sic you on me?"

"Nope. Farley," she said. "Frankly, I resisted, but when I saw you were in here, I knew it was a desperate situation."

For the first time, a smile touched the corners of his mouth. "So you came to rescue me."

"Just call it payback for not letting me drown the other day."

She *was* rescuing him, and it was amazing how good that felt. He'd never thought of himself as the kind who needed rescuing. After all, he was the one who had pulled his brothers out of ponds and bailed them out when they'd blown their rent money on skis or flight lessons. But he needed it today, and what made it work was that Jackie didn't act like she was rescuing him. None of that touchy-feely, *tell me how you really feel* crap that most women would dish out. Just the usual smart-ass comments. Perfect.

"Thanks." He took her hand and pulled it to his mouth to press a kiss to her knuckles. Jackie laced her fingers with his, and they just sat there. It was strange. He'd slept with her, he'd done things with her that would make a whore blush, but that simple act of holding hands seemed like the most intimate act he'd shared with a woman in years.

After a few minutes, she cleared her throat. "Did your mom give you bad news about her health or something?"

The irony of her question made Reade snort. The snort turned into a chuckle and then swelled into a belly laugh before it dissolved back into a chuckle.

"I'll take that as a no," said Jackie.

He got himself back under control and swiped at the corner of his eyes. "Take it as an 'or something.' My mother is fine. Perhaps finer than she has been in years."

"Perhaps?"

"The jury is still out."

"So why are we sitting here having this pity party?"

"Good question." He stood up abruptly, still keeping his grip on her hand. "Come on. I know the perfect place to not get drunk together."

"Hold your horses, Bucko. I told you, I'm not going to—"

"Not *there*," he said. "This is a place the bartender told me about. You'll love it. I'll pour out my tale of woe over a glass of pineapple juice, and you can tell me how pathetic I am, and then when we're both thoroughly depressed, we can throw ourselves off a cliff."

"Sounds fun," said Jackie, and she let him lead her out of the bar.

fifteen

Jackie had assumed Reade was kidding about throwing themselves off a cliff. Now she wasn't so sure.

The Potted Palm, the bar to which he'd dragged her via one of the island's colorful jitney buses, was a ratty, tin-roofed building, barely more substantial than the watering holes in some of the smaller villages they had passed along the way. But if location is everything, the little bar had what was arguably the best location on the island for watching the sunset—nothing but clear, blue Caribbean all the way to the western horizon.

The thing was, that view was so gorgeous because the Potted Palm sat at the edge of a cliff, some eighty or ninety feet above the ocean. Considering Reade's current emotional state, Jackie hoped they were both still alive to see that evening's sunset.

They found a table next to the thick stone wall that surrounded the patio and ordered two of the biggest, fruitiest, nonalcoholic drinks the place offered. Then Reade proceeded to recount his conversation with his mother. Jackie was stunned.

"Do you think she meant it?" she asked softly. "That she's going to get better? That she can?"

Reade stared at the ocean as though he could find the answer somewhere out there along the horizon. "I hope so. I would love to see Mom get back to her old self."

"What was she like?"

"Remember Auntie Mame, in the movie? Mom was like that—full of piss and vinegar, always encouraging us to grab life with both hands. She even had the Rosalind Russell black hair, right up until Dad died. Then she went gray in a matter of months."

Probably because she stopped dyeing it, suspected Jackie, but she wasn't about to suggest such a thing to Reade. He had more important things to come to grips with than his mother's hair color.

"What about you? I have a feeling there's an old Reade that you need to get back to."

"Possibly. I'm not sure I remember who he was."

"Oh, he's in there someplace. If you're like the men in my family, you have an amazing ability to stuff things down where you don't have to look at them—and then forget where you stashed them."

"That's a guy thing. They teach it to us during gym class in seventh grade."

"They should teach you to dance."

Laughing, he signaled the waiter for another round. "I read a study that said we men have trouble verbalizing our feelings because the two halves of our brain don't communicate well, which makes it hard to connect words to emotions. Whereas women's brains chatter back and forth twenty-four/seven, so you're ready to talk to anyone, anytime, about anything, from someone else's divorce to how you feel about your favorite brand of panty hose."

Jackie rolled her eyes. "Why don't you say what you really think?"

Grinning, Reade took her hand again. He'd been doing

that a lot since she'd found him in the bar—nothing sexual, just a warm, natural grip that sent a pleasant glow through her system.

"Were you really planning to go to Venezuela?" she asked, trying to get back on topic.

"I was way beyond planning," he said. "I had the visa and all the shots and permits, my gear was packed, the tickets were purchased, and my contact information was posted on the folks' refrigerator. I had put in years getting ready before that, too. Did you know I can hit a monkey-sized target with a blowgun at fifty paces?"

"Now there's a skill that must be useful in downtown Pittsburgh. I'm curious—by any chance was your childhood hero Tarzan?"

"Yep. Him and Carlos Finlay."

It took Jackie a few seconds to recall the name: Carlos Finlay was the Cuban doctor who tested his hypothesis about the transmission of yellow fever by letting an infected mosquito bite him. She shook her head. "This should not surprise me."

"I bet your heroes were the Dewey who invented the decimal system and Jonas Salk."

"Wrong-o. They were Rosalind Franklin and. . . ." She hesitated, embarrassed. It seemed so stupid, naming one of the discoverers of the DNA double helix and—

"Who?" he prodded.

"The Professor on *Gilligan's Island*."

He hooted. "And you ragged on me about *Flipper* reruns. I love it."

"The Professor taught me that the proper name for aspirin is acetylsalicylic acid," she said defensively. "And he was proof that brains are important and can even be sexy. He had just one flaw, and that. . . . What on earth are those people doing?"

A small group of men had left the bar grounds and were picking their way around the cliffs that formed the narrow, hourglass-shaped inlet that abutted the Potted Palm.

"They're going to throw themselves off," said Reade.

"Although I believe around here they refer to it as cliff diving."

"Oh, God. You weren't kidding."

"Nope. Don't worry, we'll just watch for now. What was the Professor's big flaw?"

"Huh? Oh. That he wasn't a woman. The Professor should have been female, and the movie star should have been a self-centered boy toy, to balance things out better. Those old shows from the Sixties were incredibly sexist."

"And to think you made it to graduate school despite their evil influence."

She barely noted his sarcasm because she was busy watching the first divers jump from a ledge on the cliff opposite. These were the pros, she could tell from the way they dived cleanly, no screwing around. The next pair to take a turn weren't quite as smooth. As they stood on the ledge, the breeze carried back voices rising with fear and testosterone, and sprinkled with phrases like "dare you" and "chicken shit." Eventually they jumped in tandem, windmilling and bellowing like the beer-soaked college boys they probably were. They hit the water like rocks, but quickly popped up. The people on the patio cheered.

Despite their lack of style, their survival set off a buzz of interest. Reade and Jackie returned to their conversation, but as the afternoon wore on toward sunset and the rum flowed, a trickle of copycats, mostly young and male, headed off to the cliffs, one and two at a time.

From her seat, Jackie had a perfect view of the action. She could watch them walk the path around the inlet to clamber down onto the diving ledge. She could watch them work up courage and take the leap. She could hear them screaming, all the way down.

"You're not paying attention," said Reade.

She realized he'd been talking, but wasn't sure what he'd said. "Sorry. I just can't believe you want to do that."

"Drunk tourists manage it every day. How dangerous can it be? It'll make a great first jump."

"But why?"

"Because there's nothing quite like a free fall to clarify your life for you, and I could stand a little clarification about now. And because it's a blast."

Now she got it. "You've done this before."

"Not exactly, but I used to skydive. And I've made a few bungee jumps. Now those are a kick—you get to fall over and over and over." His head bobbed up and down as though he was watching someone on the end of a bungee cord.

"So when you said it'd make a great first jump, you were talking about . . . ?"

"You," he said.

"Oh." Jackie's head whirled just thinking about it. Across the way, another person made the dive. She pointed, as casually as she could. "Have you noticed that every single person who goes off that cliff screams in terror?"

"That's exhilaration," he countered. "Show me one person who jumped this afternoon who wasn't stoked when they came back."

She looked around the patio, searching for signs of residual fear in the scattering of damp patrons. Damn, if they weren't all glowing triumphantly—even the ones who had screamed like little girls. "All that proves is that they suffered brain damage when they hit the water."

"Weren't you on the swim team in high school?" Reade asked. "It's no worse than the ten-meter platform."

"In case you haven't noticed, the swim team *swims*. Diving is an entirely different sport, one in which I do not participate." She remembered using the same argument on Coach Lehmkuhl during her junior year. "Besides, that's the equivalent of two ten-meter platforms, plus a little."

"I thought you told me you didn't have a problem with heights."

"At the time, we were discussing standing on something, not jumping off it."

"You're scared."

"I'm sensible. It's at least eighty feet down, and salt water is harder than fresh. Plus the last time we even talked about going off cliffs, you ended up with Harrison Ford's chin." She traced a line on her chin that matched his future scar. "It's a nice look on you, but I don't think I'd like it."

"That was just an accident."

"Precisely."

"It had nothing to do with cliffs." His eyes filled with mischief. "If you don't go, I'm going to ask Guillaume to name a new dish after you: Chicken Barnett."

"*Bawk ba-bawk bawk.* Farley's not around, Hunter. I don't have to prove anything."

"Not even to yourself?"

Her denial stuck near the back of her throat. That was a legitimate question: Did she need to prove something to herself? That seemed to be the theme of this whole trip, after all, even though she hadn't started out with that intent.

The tuna tower, the kayaking, the gambling—she'd proved something to herself with each of those activities. She suspected that her wild night with Hunter had proved something, too, although she hadn't worked that one out yet and wasn't sure she'd like her conclusion when she did.

At any rate, she was now pretty sure she wasn't boring, that she was willing to take risks, but this cliff thing would cement it. People who jumped off cliffs could never be called boring.

She stared across at the ledge and traced the flight path down to the water. Her stomach knotted at the thought of jumping. But it had knotted just as hard the first time Coach had forced her up the tower, and she'd managed to jump. She hadn't been happy about it, and it certainly hadn't been pretty, but she'd managed. She might be able to manage this, too.

When she came back to herself, Reade was watching her closely. For the first time that day, his eyes held a hint of the edgy, sexual Hunter she'd come to know and lo—... appreciate. Her heart rate ratcheted up a notch.

"What about you? What are *you* out to prove?" she challenged.

"That I still have it. That the Reade Hunter who was ready to go up the Orinoco didn't die a sedentary death in the industrial Northeast." The familiar smirk quirked his lips, this time softened by the humor in his voice. "That I'm not as boring as you are."

"Didn't you get the memo? I'm no longer boring. It became official last night when I whipped your ass on the pushcarts." *Oh, God.* She stood up before she could change her mind.

"So you're going to jump?"

"You're the one still sitting there with your feet up."

"That can be fixed," he said, fixing it. He flagged the waiter and asked him to hold their table. "Let's do it."

The bar provided a simple check station for jumpers—it was easier to notify the next of kin if the driver's license wasn't wet, she imagined—so they stopped by to leave their valuables before they headed around the inlet. Jackie's hands started to shake the instant they stepped off the patio.

By the time they reached the rough stairway that led down to the dive ledge, her heart was pounding in her ears and her stomach was twisting like she'd swallowed poison. Using skills she'd perfected under Coach Lemkuhl's sadistic tutelage, she reached down deep for the willpower to walk down those hand-carved steps. So long as she kept one hand on the rocks and her eyes away from the drop, she was fine.

An older man stood on the ledge, waiting to help the jumpers. "You okay, lady?"

"Sure. I'm fine." She sidled over to make room for Reade.

"Are you jumping together or one at a time?" the man asked.

Reade gave Jackie a questioning look.

"You first," she said. "I want to listen to you scream, and decide whether it's exhilaration or not."

"A'right," said the man. "First thing, put your shoes in the basket. They'll be here when you climb back up." He waited for them to kick off their sandals. "Now I want you to take a look down to see how far it is. Both of you."

Jackie sucked in a deep breath, held it, and edged out next to Reade. Okay. Not so bad. She braced herself securely and stretched forward just enough to see the men in the water below. That was okay, too—no vertigo today. She could do this.

"The water is near sixty feet deep, but you'll want to take a good step out so you don't bump the cliff," the man said. "Nothing fancy. Just stay straight up and down and keep your toes pointed. You don't want to hit flat-footed, and you sure don't want to belly flop."

"Gotcha. See you at the bottom." Reade gave Jackie a peck on the cheek, then took his position. As he stood for a moment to compose himself, Jackie stepped back. She didn't really want to watch this.

"Nice big step," said their coach. "One, two, three."

"Aa-a-aaa-aa-a—" Reade's Tarzan yell ended abruptly with a far-off splash. The crowd opposite cheered wildly. He must've done something flashy on the way down.

"Your turn, miss. He's waiting for you down there."

Jackie crept back to the edge and peeked over. There was Reade, treading water and waving, a smile on his face so big she could see his teeth from here. He'd loved it.

He'd loved all of it, she realized suddenly—even crashing his bike. He adored it. The man was a natural risk taker, not a weenie from Cedar Falls who needed a dare and a big grant to motivate her. He might have let his concern for his mother shackle him for a few years, but now that Lenore was off his back, Reade would be back out there surf running and skydiving and charging ahead full bore—whether she and Farley were around to egg him on or not.

She, on the other hand, would head home with her tales

of glory and no intention whatever of repeating the adventure. For all her mouthing off, she was about as exciting as potato salad at a potluck. Worse, she was a complete and total phony.

"Are you ready, miss?"

Ready? Far below, the ocean surged and receded and kept receding, getting farther and farther away. She'd stood there too long; the vertigo had caught up to her. Reade and his smile grew dim, and she swayed out into space as though trying to catch a glimpse.

"Whoa, there." The man caught her and pulled her back with callused hands. Across the way, the barflies catcalled and booed. "You're not going, that's for certain." He pushed her against the cliff and held her there until the mass of rock grounded her.

She blinked and took a deep breath, then clutched at his arms. "Thank you. Thank you so much."

"You shouldn't let that fellow of yours talk you into things you're not suited for. You go on back now, and he'll be along shortly—it takes a few minutes to climb up." The man returned her sandals and made sure she got up the stairs safely. He called up to her from the bottom. "Don't you mind those fools at the bar. Most of them sit over there talkin' brave but they never walk over and look down. And the ones who do are mostly so drunk they can't find their thing to piss with. At least you were willin' to face it down sober."

She appreciated his efforts to make her feel better, but her sense of embarrassment was deep. Not because of what the drunks across the way thought, or even what Reade thought. It wasn't her failure at the cliff, per se, that ate at her. She was disgusted with herself all the way around. What a phony. She wanted to crawl into a hole and hide.

As she plodded back toward the bar, dejected, she spotted her escape when a taxi pulled up to let out a couple. She hustled over to speak to the driver.

Two minutes later, she'd collected her purse and watch

from the check girl, scrawled a message for Reade on a
bar napkin, and was on her way back to Fair Winds alone.

"*Shit.*"
    Reade stood at the bar, shirt and shorts clinging
soggily to his body, reading the note Jackie had left for
him. She'd run out on him again, right when he most
wanted to be able to wrap his arms around her. This was
getting to be a habit.

She'd left a note this time, although it didn't make
much sense—something about outing her, and he was
pretty damned sure she didn't mean as a lesbian. At least
she'd left a note, though. It was progress.

Now he just had to get her to stop regretting the other
night, a mission he wasn't going to accomplish stuck at
the Potted Palm. He got his wallet back from the check
girl and headed for the bus stop out front.

Jackie hid out in the one place she hoped Reade
wouldn't think to look in the dark, Farley's hammock. She would have ducked into the spa, but it was
closed, and her room would be the first place he'd check,
so it was the hammock. Fortunately, the same security
guard was on duty, and she was able to convince him that
it was still okay for her to be there.

The hammock was also the ideal spot to mull over her
life—perhaps not as immediately clarifying as a fall
through space could be, but safer.

So she mulled and she analyzed and in two hours she
figured out precisely nothing that she hadn't known standing on the edge of the cliff. She hadn't been so confused
about so many issues at once since she was twelve and
her hormones had kicked in.

That was probably the key—hormones. Heaven knew
she was under the influence. She'd realized they were
making her stupid sexually, but maybe they were making

her just plain stupid. She certainly was having trouble focusing. And she was doing things she wouldn't ordinarily do, just because a man wanted her to—or in some cases, didn't want her to—something she thought she'd outgrown in high school. Of course, there were three men involved, but as pushy as Walt could be, and as manipulative as Farley was, she knew darn well she was doing all this because of Reade.

Reade. Aggravating. Sexy in the extreme. Funny. Cynical. Unexpectedly tender. Mercenary. Damnably attractive. An all-around pain in the butt. The feelings he stirred up were as full of contradictions as the man himself, and she was soon lost in trying to sort them out.

"Miss?"

Startled, Jackie jerked so hard she almost flipped the hammock. She clung to the sides as it swayed. "What?"

The security man stood on the beach. Moonlight and the terrace lights bounced off his silver buttons and badge. "The man who bothered you the other day is here. He says he'd like to talk to you."

She looked toward the terrace. There stood Reade, one hand raised in a half-wave. She sighed.

"Shall I run him off?" the guard asked.

"No. Let him come down here. Just stay close by, please." There. If she couldn't trust herself, she'd at least get a chaperone.

"As you wish, miss." He waved Reade on down. As they passed, he said, "Mind your manners this time."

"Yes, sir." Reade nodded and came to stand at the foot of the hammock. "You're a difficult woman to keep track of."

"You might consider the possibility that I want it that way."

"I know. You're embarrassed. But you shouldn't be. You gave it a shot."

"But I didn't jump. *You* did. Speaking of which, how was your moment of personal enlightenment?"

"Enlightening," he said. "And personal. Scootch over."
He swung a leg up on the hammock.

"Wait a minute," she protested, but a hammock doesn't
make a good place from which to repel an invasion unless
you want to end up on the ground. With much swaying
and shifting and adjusting, he installed himself with his
head at the opposite end, facing her.

"Ever sleep in one of these things?" he asked.

Her mind leaped from sleep in a hammock to sex in a
hammock in a single bound. "Only naps."

"I've used them a few times. It takes some adjustment
when you're a stomach sleeper like I am."

She remembered. He'd been sprawled facedown when
she'd left, and she'd stopped to pull a sheet up over him
before she opened the door. And though she'd never admit it to anyone—particularly not him—she'd also taken
a moment to run a hand over his butt. He had great
cheeks, rock hard, with just enough roundness to fill out
his jeans. She hadn't been able to resist.

"A penny for whatever thought is putting that moonlit
smile on your lips."

Hoping the dark hid her blush, if not her smile, she
shook her head. "Very poetic, but if you don't have to
share your epiphany, I don't have to share my thoughts."

"Fair enough," he said. He reached into his shirt pocket
and pulled out a bar napkin, which he held out between
two fingers. "So I suppose that means you won't translate
this?"

"Bright boy." She snagged the note, blotted her mouth,
and reached over to drop it on the table next to her glass.
The hammock rocked violently as she leaned out, then
settled back into its gentle sway.

Neither of them said anything for a long time, but eventually they felt their way into a wandering conversation
about nothing in particular. Every once in a while, when
the hammock had been still for too long, one of them
would dangle a foot over the side and give a push.

It should have been an altogether pleasant way to spend

an evening, and it was, on one level. But despite Reade's continued good behavior, there was an underlying tension, a certain anticipation. Jackie couldn't decide whether it was mutual or purely her hormonal imagination, but either way, it slowly built until it was like a third party hanging out behind the tree, watching to see what would happen, urging her to do something.

The hammock slowed again. "My turn," she said. She dropped a foot over the side and stretched to reach the ground. Pain shot through her instep. Tears filled her eyes as her second and third toes tried to swap positions. "Ow, ow, ow, ow, ow."

Desperate, she jumped up. The abrupt change of balance whipped the hammock upside down, dumping Reade face first into the sand.

"What the hell?" He sat up, spitting grit.

"Major foot cramp," she said between pained laughter and groans. "Ooo, ow. I'm sorry. Ouch. Geez Louise, that hurts." She hobbled down to the beach and back, every step agony, flexing her toes to try to stretch the cramping muscles so they would relax.

"Oh, hell." Reade touched his chin. "I'm bleeding."

Jackie grabbed the bar napkin off the table and tossed it at him as she passed. Reade refolded it clean side out and pressed it against his chin, then crawled out from under the hammock and stood up. "Fine thing. Dumps me on the ground and won't even take a minute to check my wounds."

"I said I was sorry. If I stop, the cramp will come back."

"Is everything all right down there?" called the security guard.

"Great," muttered Reade. "Now he's going to be certain I'm a mugger."

"We're fine," said Jackie, snorting as she tried to hold back the laughter. "Dr. Hunter fell out of the hammock, that's all."

"A klutzy mugger," added Reade under his breath.

"I appreciate your being so conscientious," said Jackie, still talking to the guard. "We'll be leaving in a few minutes. Thank you."

"Leaving?" asked Reade.

"I haven't had supper yet. Ouch." She rocked up onto her toes again as another twinge hit.

"I haven't either, come to think of it." Reade blotted at his chin one last time, then stuffed the napkin in his back pocket. "Sit down and let me massage that foot for a minute."

Jackie had immediate images of where that path would lead, and as tempting as it was to follow it, she shook her head. "It's better to walk it out. Besides, the grill will close soon. It's already after ten." She scooped up her sandals, grabbed her glass from the table, and started off slowly. Reade followed.

When they reached Grumby's, the chef was already scraping the grill.

"I thought you were open until eleven," said Jackie.

"Every night but Sunday," he said. "You'll have to order from room service."

"Thanks." She turned to Reade, who was wearing a wide grin. "Don't even think it, Romeo."

His grin turned to a pout. "Great date you are. You ditch me at the bar, shove me out of your hammock—"

"I did not!"

"And now you won't even share dinner with me."

"There are reasons for that, and you know very well— Ow. Oh, shoot. There it goes again." She limped over to the nearest chair.

"Now will you let me massage it? You've got fifty people around to make sure you're safe from big bad me."

Biting her lip, she nodded. He pulled another chair directly in front of hers, sat down, and picked up her foot. Pressing his fingertips into the arch, he worked the muscle, carefully bending her toes up while she winced and moaned.

"Relax," he murmured. "Just let me do it." She groaned again and he started chuckling.

"What?" she asked.

"I was thinking that we sound an awful lot like Charlie and his girlfriend. Maybe he was just giving her a foot rub."

"He was *not* rubbing her feet." She started to sit up, but the cramp promptly returned, stronger than ever. She yowled and pushed her foot back at Reade. "More. Harder."

"Mmm, baby."

Jackie swung schizophrenically between giggles and groans. As Reade rubbed, he speculated about the identity of the mystery lovers. The cramp slowly faded, and so did the conversation as Jackie relaxed into the rhythm of his hands. After a time, she noticed something had changed.

"Technically speaking, ankles are not part of the foot."

"I know." He slid his hands up as far as her knee and slowly massaged his way back down. "But if your calf is tense, you'll just cramp up again."

Okay. That sounded reasonable, even though she knew it was largely an excuse for him to fondle her leg. A long while later, he put that foot down and switched to the other one.

"That one's fine," she said.

"If I don't do it, you'll be out of balance."

Out of balance. Off balance. Unbalanced. Around Hunter, it all amounted to the same thing. But it felt so good, she let him continue—until she realized that her fifty chaperones had dwindled to four, none of them nearby.

She slowly pulled her foot away. "Thanks. That was very helpful, but if I don't get some food, I'm going to keel over." She felt around for her sandals and slipped her feet in, then stood up. "I'll see you in the morning."

He rose, too. "I'll walk you back to your room."

"No, thank you." She walked off.

"I insist," he said, following. "What if you get another

cramp and you need someone to carry you to bed?"

"I'll call for volunteers."

"Ah, but I would help you undress."

"I bet you would," she said.

"Sure. And you wouldn't even have to be embarrassed, because I've already seen you naked."

Her cheeks heated up, but she kept walking. "We are not going to have this conversation."

"Yes, we are—no. You know what? You're right."

"I am?" she asked, wary.

"Yes. I want to make love to you, Jackie. I want to seduce you. Sweep you off your feet. But I'm not going to. Not right now. I have too much on my mind to get it right."

"Out of ideas, huh?" she asked, knowing full well he was talking about the situation with his mother, but succumbing to a reckless demon he had stirred up with his teasing.

He stopped dead in the middle of the path. "I don't know, Jackie. You tell me. We'll start with that hammock."

Oh, God. Now she'd done it. "Let's not. Good night."

She stalked off, but he came after her. "Do you have any concept of how difficult it was to just lie there and talk to you when what I really wanted to do was curl up against you and take you slowly from behind?" His voice was low, barely audible, but she felt like he was shouting to the world. "Or we might have just sort of slid together in the middle, facing each other, and I could have watched your face as we swayed back and forth. Did you know your eyes go all soft and cloudy just before you come?"

"Stop it." Desire raced through her like an arson fire. "For God's sake, we're in public."

"You won't let me in your room to talk to you in private," he pointed out. "Or there was the lagoon. I'd have loved to lead you out into that warm water. Imagine floating on your back while I—"

"Damn it, Hunter."

"Now there's another thing," he said. "My name is Reade. Not Hunter. Not Dr. Hunter. Just Reade. You haven't called me Reade since you took off on me the other night. There are moments when I want to push you down on whatever's convenient and kiss you until the only thing you *can* say is my name."

"God, you make things difficult."

"Good. I want things to be difficult. I want them to be fucking impossible."

"Why?" she demanded. "Why can't you just accept the fact that I don't want to sleep with you again?"

"Because I don't believe you. You may think we shouldn't sleep together, but you do want to. Sometimes when you're thinking about it, you get this look that. . . ." His voice grew husky. "It's this damned mess with Farley hanging between us. And the craziness with my mom."

"It's more than that."

"Maybe. But nothing that can't be overcome with a well-negotiated cease-fire," he said. "That's why I want to make things impossible for you, so that when I come knocking on your door tomorrow and ask if I can come in and make love to you, you will say yes."

"Tomorrow?" she repeated before she could stop herself.

"Or the next day. Whenever it's right. The next time we make love, I do *not* intend to wake up alone afterward. That's why I'm going to ask you in the cold, clear light of day—so that you can't claim it was the moonlight or that you were swept away. And here is your cabana, so I'll say good night."

He pulled her around to kiss her, just a sweet, little goodnight kiss, but it was like pouring gasoline on a fire. Everything inside of Jackie went incandescent, and she moaned and curled her fingers into his hair.

"Damn." He mustered some of the willpower that she was rapidly losing and firmly set her away, although his fingers stayed curled around her shoulders. "Go on. Get out of here before I change what's left of my mind."

He said it, but he still didn't release her. His eyes burned into hers, silently asking the question he had said he wouldn't ask until tomorrow. And even though she tried to hold back the answer, she knew it was there in her eyes, and they both knew that whenever he got around to asking, she would say yes.

A soft smile touched the corners of his mouth, and he slowly uncurled his fingers and dropped his hands to his sides. "Good night. Sweet dreams."

Dreams. They would be of nothing but him. He would be in her bed all night, keeping her awake anyway. Besides, it was just a vacation fling. . . .

"Cease-fire," she whispered.

"Jackie . . ."

She turned and walked toward her door, fumbling with her key card because her fingers, her whole body, felt hot and thick and clumsy with wanting him. She slid it into the slot, and the little green light flashed. Go.

She pushed the door open and stood there, unwilling to turn around, for fear she'd see him walking away. And then a soft scuff on the patio and told her he was there, right behind her, full of heat and flame and everything she wanted.

She went inside and flipped on every light, until the room blazed like the Vegas Strip. When she went back to stand in front of him, he was still in the open doorway.

"It's not the cold, clear light of day," she said, "but it will have to do."

He nodded. "Yeah, because I can't stand it anymore, either. Jackie, may I come inside and make love to you?"

"Yes."

There was a hesitation, a moment of stillness, and then the soft sound of them exhaling in unison as he touched her.

She laughed and kissed him, and in the next breath, they were ripping each other's clothes off and pushing each other down on the bed. As he started to pull her on top of him, her brain reengaged just long enough to re-member the condoms in the other room.

"Hold that thought," she said. She wrestled free and dashed to the bathroom.

The mirror threw her reflection back at her—she looked wild, wanton, and so totally out of control she barely recognized herself. She was crazy, letting herself get this way about a man so totally different from herself. But it was just a fling, after all, just a few days of delicious craziness, and then back to normal. She smiled and grabbed the box.

When she stepped back around the corner, Reade was lying in the center of the bed, his erection pointing sky-ward. She stood there for a minute, enjoying the sight.

"Are you going to make me come after you?" he asked.

"After me. Before me. With me." She tossed the box of condoms on the bed beside him and headed for his crotch, a smile on her lips. "Every which way I can. Merry Christmas, Soldier."

She was making love with Reade. They were in the hammock in the backyard at her folks' house, with the summer stars above them and the sounds of traffic far away on the highway. She had carried a light blanket out from the house, and they had it over them, more for cover than for warmth. He'd pulled her skirt up in back and slipped her panties down, and she'd taken him inside her, moving languidly because they had the whole night and all of time ahead of them.

Not the backyard. Here. Now. Jackie drifted awake as Reade slipped his hand down her belly. A moment later, still half asleep, she came, a slow pulse that arched her back against him.

"Good morning."

"Mmm." She seemed to have lost the power of speech, so she showed her appreciation in the most instinctive way, moving her hips in the slow circles that she'd al-ready figured out drove him wild. He moaned and pushed into her more deeply, his hand on her belly, and although neither of them were rushing, it didn't take any longer for him than it had for her.

Afterward, they lay tangled for a long, lazy hour, watching the light brighten around the edge of the curtains. Eventually, Reade slipped out of bed and started pulling on his clothes.

"Where are you going?"

"To my room to shower and change."

She stretched and yawned. "You can shower here. With me."

"We would never get clean." He leaned over and kissed her. "Shower by yourself and I will be back in a little while."

"Okay." She heard the door click shut and rolled over. She was so sleepy. Just a couple of minutes more. . . .

There were woodpeckers in the backyard, and a huge one was pounding the tree just above their heads. Jackie heaved a pillow in the general direction of the disturbance. The woodpecker pounded again, this time calling her name.

"Jackie. Come on. Wake up."

Dreaming again. Not Cedar Falls. St. Sebastian. Not woodpeckers. "Reade?"

"Let me in."

Fighting a tangled sheet, she rolled off the bed and stumbled to the door. She kicked the pillow out of the way and cracked open the door. In the bright light, deep lines etched his face.

"Don't tell me you're horny again already," she teased. "It hasn't been that long."

"Jackie, listen. Mom never came back last night."

sixteen

It took Jackie's groggy brain a moment to shift gears. "How do you know?"

"I stopped at her room to tell her we'd talk later, and the drapes were open. Her bed was never slept in. Neither was Farley's."

She gaped at Reade. "You checked his bed?"

"It's not like I had to work at it. His drapes are standing wide open, too."

"Good grief. You can't run around spying on people in their bedrooms, even your own mother." She opened the door wider and pulled him inside before anyone could hear him and report him to security. "You're going to get yourself arrested, poking around Farley's cabana."

"I tried to call first," he said, like that made it okay. "It's pretty clear they haven't been there all night."

"They probably decided to enjoy a little romantic interlude somewhere else for privacy's sake. The sound of you cheering outside the window could get a little embarrassing."

He was not amused. "She would have called."

"God, you sound like her father, not her son. Didn't you two just have a long talk about this? She doesn't have to report every move to you. You don't have to report to her."

He shook his head. "This is not the same. And it's not like her."

"Maybe it's like the new her."

"She specifically said she'd be back last night so we could talk. Granted, I wasn't available, but she didn't know that. She should be here."

"Okay. Let's think this through." She tugged him over to sit on the armchair while she got her robe. "Tell me exactly what she said."

His heels drummed the floor in agitation. "She said they were going up to Redoubt and then maybe to dinner in Port Meredith. And that we would talk more when she got back later."

"Oh." He might be right. Her gut told her Lenore wouldn't stay out when she'd promised to talk to Reade, but saying so wasn't going to help. "See if this makes sense to you. Their dinner turned romantic and they lost track of the time. They didn't want to drive home because they'd had a little too much to drink, and they didn't want to call because it was so late. So they checked into one of those nice old colonial hotels in Port M., and they're still asleep. Like we should be."

"Maybe," he conceded.

"You just don't want to admit your mother might be shacked up with someone she met a week ago," she said. "Not that I blame you—I have trouble with the idea that my folks lock the door every Saturday night. But guess what? Moms have sex, too. Eight to one they'll turn up by lunchtime, blushing." Something she was familiar with. "Now go away so I can take that shower."

"Do you want to have some breakfast afterward?"

"You're kidding, right? I never did have supper last night."

"Okay. I'll meet you in half an hour."

"Then afterward, we can park ourselves by the front door and stare at them when they come in, the way my parents used to when I blew my curfew."

That got a glimmer of a smile. "Okay. But you never blew a curfew in your life."

She stuck out her tongue and blew a raspberry. "Get out of here."

With him safely on the other side of a locked door, she went in to brush her teeth. Under the harsh light over the vanity, she realized her robe was nearly transparent. Reade hadn't even batted an eye; he was worried, big time.

Thirty minutes later, they were in line at the breakfast buffet. They spent the morning sipping iced tea, checking the front desk for messages, and taking turns walking back and forth between Farley's cottage and Lenore's room, just to be sure the two lovebirds hadn't sneaked in by another entrance. The more time passed, the deeper the lines around Reade's eyes and mouth got, and the more Jackie worried on his behalf.

He waited with her through lunch, but when the resort staff started clearing the last of the buffet, Reade stood up.

"You lose."

"*Mr. Phelps often disappears for several days at a time*," said the manager of the resort. His tone was matter-of-fact and pleasant, and probably soothing to a person not on the edge of mayhem.

That person was not Reade. They'd been passed through three people to get here. He wanted to punch Mr. Samuels in his matter-of-fact mouth.

"Does he usually take other guests with him when he does this disappearing?" asked Jackie, somewhat more calmly than Reade could have.

"It has happened. He's a very free spirit for a man of his age and accomplishments."

"Yes," said Reade, tightly. "But my mother isn't."

"People tend to get swept away by him and his enthusiasms."

"Swept away or not, she would have called."

The manager's mouth opened as though he might debate that, but Reade glared him down.

"Well, we can at least ensure there hasn't been an accident." He hit a button on his speakerphone. "Miss Battersby, please bring me the license number and description of the Jeep Mr. Phelps is using, and then ring up the constable."

A few minutes later, an efficient-looking black woman breezed in with a folder. "Constable Sergeant Evans is on line three."

He lifted the handset and punched a button. "Sergeant. Luther Samuels at Fair Winds, here. We have a little situation." He explained briefly, gave out the license number of the vehicle, and asked about accidents. "No? Good. How about any trouble in Port Meredith?"

He looked at Reade and shook his head. "Fine, fine. I'm sure they just went off on one of Mr. Phelps's adventures. You know how he is."

Reade signaled that he wanted to talk.

"I understand. The lady's son wishes to speak with you." He handed over the phone, but gave Jackie a shrug to indicate the pointlessness of it all.

Reade introduced himself to the voice on the phone, then got straight to the point. "I would like to file a missing person report on my mother."

"I'm sorry, sir, but that's not possible. A competent adult must be missing seventy-two hours before we take a report. Unless there are indications of foul play, of course."

"My mother felt that Mr. Phelps was being stalked," he said, reaching for anything that would get the officer's attention. "And resort security ran a man off the grounds of his cottage a few nights ago."

"Really? That could change the complexion of things. Let me speak to Mr. Samuels again, please."

Feeling a small victory, Reade handed back the phone.

"It was a minor incident," said Mr. Samuels after a moment. "A local boy trying to break into the cottage. We didn't call you because there was no harm done. . . . Yes. I'm afraid Mr. Hunter is grasping at thin straws here. . . . All right. We will let you know the moment they return. . . . Thank you, Constable." He hung up.

"That's it?" asked Reade.

"Of course not. They will keep an ear to the ground, and of course they'll contact the stations at Redoubt Colony and Port Meredith and ask them to watch out. I'm sorry, Mr. Hunter, but there's really nothing official that can be done right now."

"Damn it, my mother is out there someplace."

"I'm sure Mr. Phelps will take excellent care of her, Mr. Hunter."

"If he's able to," said Jackie. "Look, they're probably having the time of their lives and we'll all laugh about it later. But you must understand *Doctor* Hunter's concern. His mother is on medication—which she may or may not have with her."

"I didn't realize. . . ."

"I know. However, now that you do, I'm sure you'll understand that we're going to check things out on our own."

"Of course."

"We'll need Farley's license number and a car to get to Redoubt to start looking," said Reade.

"Certainly." Mr. Samuels reopened the file and copied the number onto a pad, then picked up the phone again. "Arrange a car for Mr.—excuse me, *Doctors* Hunter and Barnett. . . . Oh, yes. I momentarily forgot. Thank you." He laid the phone down slowly. "I'm afraid this is a bad day for cars. There's a large wedding at six o'clock, and every car we have is reserved for the afternoon and evening."

"Where's the nearest rental company?" asked Reade.

"At the airport." Samuels checked his watch. "And I'm afraid you just missed the shuttle. There will be another in two hours."

"I'm not waiting two hours to start looking for them."

"I can ask one of the maintenance people to give you a lift up to Redoubt Colony. He'll have to come back directly, but he can at least get you there, and you can either take a bus or hire a taxi to get back."

Reade felt his blood pressure climb.

"That will help a lot," said Jackie quickly. "Could you ask him to meet us in front in fifteen minutes or so?"

"Of course. Here's my direct line," Samuels said, scribbling a telephone number beneath the license number. "Please check in from time to time. I will direct my staff to report to me the instant they see either one of them, and I will relay the news to you."

"You do that," said Reade.

"Come on." Jackie dragged him out of the office. The door barely shut before he exploded.

"That's it? Two people are missing, and we get a license number, a one-way ride, and access to his private line?" He batted viciously at a dangling branch, sending leaves flying. "Son of a bitch!"

"Take it easy. Punching out a fig tree won't help. And at least we know where to start looking."

"I just wish we had more to go on."

"Maybe we do." She hesitated. "You're not going to like this one, but what you said about the stalker reminded me. Didn't your mom say she had a picture of that man, from that day at Mystery Falls?"

"Let's find out." They headed straight to his mother's room. Everything was in place, as if she'd stepped out for a walk. They found the camera bag on the closet shelf. Reade quickly went through the memory cards.

"Here's the first one." He slipped it in and turned the

camera on. They scrolled through the pictures: a roadside vendor with stacks of straw hats, a taxi traffic jam, the tour guide at the falls, Farley at the falls, the ocean, Jackie with her first sip of Ting.

"Wait a second," she said. "Go back a couple."

Reade pressed the minus button to back up.

"Oh, God. Zoom in." She pointed to a face that showed just over Farley's shoulder, a man with heavy dreadlocks and eyes so intense they gleamed even in the tiny view screen. Reade zoomed in. She took the camera out of his hands, and her face went pale under her sunburn. "It's him, Reade. This is one of the men I saw talking to Farley up at Redoubt. Your mom was right. Someone was after him."

Grim-faced, Reade picked up the phone and punched zero. "Do you have some kind of business center with computers? Put me through."

Thanks to the high-speed printer in the computer center, they soon had two prints each of the original photo, the enlargement of their mystery man, and a picture of Lenore on the bamboo raft that Farley had apparently snapped. Reade handed one of each to Jackie to hold and got an envelope from the receptionist for the others. He quickly scratched out a note, slipped it in with the pictures, wrote "Mr. Samuels" on the outside of the envelope, and tossed it in the Out box.

"Why don't you just hand it to him?" Jackie asked.

"He'd toss it on a pile and forget about it in five seconds. This way, he'll receive it later today or maybe even tomorrow, and either we'll be back by then or he'll realize he now has three missing people."

"Four," she said. "You've been saying 'we' all along."

"Things have changed."

"Well, if you think I'm going to let you go off and rescue Farley and get all the glory for yourself, then you're not as bright as you think you are."

"This isn't about the grant, and it's not a game. This man—these men—may be very dangerous."

"If they are, you'll need someone to watch your back. I'm going. It's not your decision."

He stood there, shaking his head. "You are the most . . . All right. Come on, the car's waiting."

"I need better shoes," she said. "And so do you. We can't traipse around the island in flip-flops."

"Three minutes, out front." He reached for the pictures.

"Nope." She held them behind her back. "These are my insurance you won't leave without me." She ducked out the door before he could grab her and dashed for her room.

Okay, so maybe it wasn't about the grant. Or maybe it was. It was all very convenient, his mother making up with Farley just in time to disappear with him. Now that Jackie had had a few minutes to think about it, she wasn't convinced that the man in the photo had anything to do with Farley. She was going to have to think about it some more, but she didn't have time right now. She had to stick with Reade.

She hit her cabana at a dead run. Her sneakers were next to the dresser. She slipped them on without untying them, hit the bathroom for the world's fastest pit stop, then paused by the sink to wash up and collect a few things they'd need. Sunscreen. Insect repellant. A first aid kit might come in handy. . . .

Oh, heck. She scraped the whole mess off the counter into her purse—who knew where they'd end up and what they'd need? And Reade, being Reade, wouldn't carry anything more than his wallet. She could always toss some of it later, when she had a chance to go through things.

On the way out, she grabbed a sun hat and her one long-sleeved shirt, and picked up the photos. The door slammed behind her as she dashed for the front entrance.

Reade, now wearing running shoes and a baseball cap, was standing with his foot on the running board of a lemon-yellow resort van, staring at his watch. "That was four minutes and twelve seconds."

"Bite me."

When they were in and on their way, Reade pulled some papers out of his shirt pocket and tossed them at Jackie. She unfolded them just far enough to see they were copies of the photos. "Oh."

"You left me in a room with a color copier and the originals," he said.

In other words, if he'd wanted to leave without her, he could have. He hadn't.

Of course, maybe he would have, if she hadn't bothered to tell him she figured he would. It was sort of like Heisenberg's Uncertainty Principle, as applied to humans. By telling a person what you expected them to do, you sometimes changed what they actually did. The problem was, not only did you not know if they would change their minds, you didn't even know for sure when they *had*. You just had to take their word about what they would have done before your comments. Someday she was going to get together with a psychologist and write a paper for the *Journal of Irreproducible Results*.

However, for the time being, neither her paranoia nor her theories of human behavior mattered. He hadn't left, and they were going to Redoubt together. What's more, he seemed glad to have her along—as the car turned onto the highway, he took her hand, and he held it all the way up the mountain.

The woman at their first stop, Cho-Cho, was cooperative but not very helpful. Certainly she remembered Farley and Lenore; they'd been back yesterday afternoon. The lady had bought a wood carving, an obeah woman with a basket of herbs. She and the gentleman had been in good spirits. They'd left at about two o'clock. No, she hadn't seen anyone with them, and she hadn't seen them since.

Reade thanked her, and they went outside to reconnoiter.

Jackie pointed across the street. "That's the doorway where I saw those two men."

"Did they go inside?"

"I don't think so." She closed her eyes as she tried to recall. "They backed into the shadows when I hollered to Farley, but I don't think the door ever opened."

"Let's go see whether they know anything."

They cut across the road between cars and entered the little store. It turned out to be a tobacco store with a few herbs, over-the-counter drugs, candy, and a few paperback books for good measure.

The elderly man behind the counter was initially as co-operative as the lady at the gallery. He listened to their questions and studied the pictures of Lenore and Farley before shaking his head no. But when Jackie held up the enlargement of the man with the dreadlocks, his manner suddenly chilled.

"Never seen him," he said bluntly, barely glancing at the photo. "Are you going to buy anything or not? I have things to do in back."

"Just this." Reade grabbed a package of gum from a box on the counter and threw enough change on the counter to pay for it. "Thanks for your help." He took Jackie by the elbow and steered her outside, not turning loose until they were well away from the door. "Well, that was interesting. He knows who our mystery man is, and he's covering up for him."

"Gee, do you think?"

"Okay, so I'm stating the obvious. Shoot me." He stood there, eyes narrowed under the brim of his cap, looking up and down the road. "Want some gum?"

"Thanks." Jackie took a piece of gum and slowly unwrapped it. "Know what bothers me? Those two men were supposedly bumming cigarettes off Farley, but they were right outside a tobacco shop."

"They were probably broke, that's all. I wonder if Mom and Farley decided to get something to eat up here before they headed to Port Meredith."

"Something to drink, at least." She pointed at a restaurant down the road. "Let's try over there."

There were exactly two sit-down restaurants, three bars, and one inn in town. Reade and Jackie visited all of the them in quick order and the only facts they established were that Farley and Lenore had not eaten anywhere or checked into the inn, and that no one was going to admit to knowing the man with the dreads. Three times, they saw a flicker of recognition in the person they were interviewing, but it quickly vanished behind suspicion or fear or the general reticence small-town people everywhere had when dealing with strangers.

"Let's try the constable," said Jackie. "Maybe we can get more action up here, without that ass Samuels around to minimize everything you say."

They found the constable's office, but a sign on the door informed them that *The Constable Is Out*. A handwritten note below said he had business in Port Meredith and would be back in the office the next morning.

" 'Emergencies should contact the constabulary in Runaway Bay.' Like they're going to help. Damn it." Reade growled and smacked his open palm against the side of the building. "This entire goddamned town is conspiring against us."

"Don't blow a gasket yet. There has to be someone who will talk to us."

They started hitting the other galleries and the few stores they had missed. Their luck finally changed at the grocery, where they discovered none other than Ginger behind the cash register. She came around the counter wearing a broad smile and gave them each a hug. "What are you doin' up here? I never imagined I'd see you again, too."

"Too?" Reade grasped at the word. "Have you seen my Mom?"

"Oh, yes. She and that Mr. Phelps came in yesterday."

"When?" asked Reade and Jackie in chorus.

"About three o'clock, I think it was. Is something wrong?"

"We're not sure," said Reade. "We're hoping you can help us."

As he explained, Ginger's face grew grave. Oddly, her concern was a relief to Jackie. At least someone on this island cared that Lenore and Farley were missing.

When Reade finished, Ginger stood for a moment, scratching the corner of her eye. "Maybe they went off with their friend."

Reade froze. "What friend?"

"Some fellow with dreadlocks. They were all three talkin', over there by the canned vegetables."

Feeling slightly sick, Jackie pulled the photos out of her purse and shuffled the mystery man to the top. "Is this the same man?"

Ginger took the print from her. "That's him all right. Even if you shaved his hair off, I'd recognize those eyes. Ooh." She shuddered. "Your mama didn't seem to like him much at first, but Mr. Phelps had a good talk with him, and by the time they left, she seemed to be feelin' a little friendlier."

"They left together?" asked Reade.

"Well, now, they left at the same time, but I can't say they left together, if you be understandin' me."

Jackie and Reade stared at each other, blinking as they tried to absorb this new information.

"Do you know who he is?" Reade asked.

Ginger stared down at the photograph. "No. I've seen him around town a time or two, though. It shouldn't be too hard to find out."

"You'd be surprised," said Jackie. "We've been asking all over town. Several people have seemed to recognize him, but no one would tell us anything."

"That's because you're outsiders," said Ginger. "We can get around that." She walked to the screened back door and gave a holler. "Children, tell your papa I want him."

A moment later, the door screeched open, and Newton and all three kids poured into the store, bouncing and hollering and slapping hands with Reade in greeting.

"Settle down, you lot." Ginger herded the children back outside. "Newton, these people need our help today. They're trying to find Miz Lenore."

Newton shook Reade's hand again. "Whatever I can do, mon."

Reade quickly explained and showed him the pictures. Newton nodded thoughtfully. "I've seen the man, but I don't know who he is."

"Well, go and find out," said Ginger.

Newton nodded and folded Reade's copy of the enlarged photograph to stick it in the back pocket of his shorts. "Be patient. I may have to lubricate a few throats."

"Here." Reade pulled out his wallet and handed Newton a couple of bills. "Let me buy, at least."

Newton dipped his head in thanks, and the bills disappeared into a front pocket.

"Now, don't drink so much you forget what you're supposed to be doin'," said Ginger.

"No, ma'am. Won't get drunk, ma'am." He gave her a smart Limey salute and a wink, and took off. They could hear him whistling as he headed up the road.

Ginger shook her and chuckled. "You may as well settle in for a wait. There's a shady spot out back. Make yourselves comfortable, and I'll bring you something to drink."

The tiny yard behind the store was a rainbow of bougainvillea dotted with white jasmine clouds, and as they pushed open the door, the fragrance washed over them. It was like stumbling into a perfume factory. A big catalpa tree shaded a cluster of chairs and the ubiquitous upturned bucket. A scrawny but amiable-looking dog trotted up and sniffed at Jackie's ankle, then moseyed back over to lie down in the cool dirt at the base of the tree.

Chattering about the races and the popsicles and everything that had happened in their lives since Saturday, the kids dragged Reade and Jackie over and dusted off the best-looking chairs with their hands. A few minutes later, Ginger came out with two glasses of lemonade.

"I'd sit out here with you, but I have to watch the store," she said.

"We'll sit with them, Mama," volunteered the girl.

"That would be fine," said Ginger. "But who will I feed all those biscuits to?"

"Biscuits?" Three pairs of eyes went wide in excitement.

"A box fell off the shelf. I can't very well sell them when they might be broken," she said. As the kids scrambled for the door, she grinned at Reade and Jackie. "That should give you a few minutes without them jabbering at you." She vanished inside after her children, the screen door slamming shut behind her.

The hummingbirds and bees flitting through the bougainvillea made a pleasant drone in the oppressive, late afternoon air. Jackie picked up her glass and held it against her forehead. "What the hell is going on?"

"I have no idea," said Reade. "None of this makes any sense." He slugged down half of his lemonade, then stood up and started pacing the yard. "If Farley knows this guy well enough to go off with him, why wouldn't he have said something when Mom claimed the man was stalking him? And if he didn't know him, why would he and Mom go off with him?"

"Maybe they didn't. I know I'm the one who said your mom was right, but maybe she wasn't. Maybe it's just coincidence that he keeps turning up—Redoubt and Mystery Falls are both tourist areas. You and I showed up at both places, so why not him? Anyway, I'm still clinging to the theory that they're shacked up in Port Meredith and simply enjoying themselves so much that they lost track of what day it was."

"God, I hope so." Reade stopped pacing. "And do you have any idea how bizarre it feels to say that? I'm going to find a phone and call Mr. Samuels, on the off chance you're right and they finally crawled out of bed." He winced at the thought.

There was a pay phone in one corner of the grocery. Jackie stayed in the back yard, but stood where she could see Reade while he talked. He didn't look happy, but he didn't look like the news was terrible, either, so she turned away to give him some privacy. A few minutes later, he emerged, frowning.

"No word, huh?"

"None. The constable in Runaway Bay apparently did take things seriously enough to check all the hospitals and clinics on the island, and neither of them turned sick or injured."

"That's good."

"Yeah." He walked over and plunked down on a chair. "But that's just another place they aren't. We still don't know where they *are*. Or why they're there."

The cookies didn't hold the children for long, and they were soon back, begging Reade to pull coins out of their ears, the way he had Saturday evening. He cooperated, though his heart didn't seem to be in it.

Newton came back about the time the smell of food from neighboring houses began to overwhelm the jasmine. He was dripping with sweat and had clearly run the last bit of the way.

"His name is Mateo Delatour," he said excitedly, between long, thirsty draws on a glass of lemonade his wife handed him. "He's definitely into some kind of funny business, maybe drugs. Some folks say he has a big ganja patch somewhere in the mountains above Rumdog."

"What would a drug dealer want with Farley?" asked Jackie.

"There are a couple of possibilities, neither of which makes me very happy," said Reade. "A, they kidnapped him as a way of picking up some extra cash. Or B, he and this Mateo are partners."

"Farley? You can't possibly think. . . ."

"It would explain a lot," said Reade, his face grim.

"Now wait a minute," said Newton. "All I got was gossip. We're not even sure that he is involved with drugs. Nobby had a completely different idea."

"Who's Nobby?"

"That nasty rass at the tobacco shop," said Ginger.

"Who happens to be my second cousin, woman, if you don't mind." Newton turned back to Reade. "He's a scratchity old thing, but he's got a good heart. And you were right, he's frightened of this Mateo fellow. He says he lives over by Blackwater someplace. He also said he's a houngan." Newton made a finger sign like he was warding off a hex. "A voodoo priest."

"Voodoo?" repeated Jackie doubtfully.

"A lot of people on the island still believe in the old ways," said Ginger a bit defensively. "Obeah and voodoo, both. Not so many practice anymore, but they believe."

"I'm sorry," said Jackie, embarrassed. "I didn't mean any disrespect. Voodoo's just not something we hear a lot about in Minnesota. About the only thing I know is that it's not like we see in the movies."

"Some ways, it makes more sense that a houngan would take them than that a drug dealer would," mused Newton. The baby crawled up on his lap, and he cupped his hands over the child's ears before he said, "I don't know if it's true, but Nobby claims they kidnap people to turn them into zombies. He says Mateo has a pen over by Blackwater."

Reade got up and paced to the fence and back. "Did anyone besides your wife see Mateo yesterday?"

"Nobby may have. He saw him sometime on the weekend, but with so many strangers up for the races, he's confused about who he saw when. Two other men told me they saw someone hanging about that old shack of Bull Madras's, up past the old warehouse. They didn't see whoever it was up close, but they said he had dreads. And they were sure it was yesterday. It might have been your man."

"Well, then, I think we should go poke around that old

shack," said Reade. "See what was so fascinating to whomever it was."

"That was my idea, too," said Newton.

Old shacks made Jackie think of thick spiderwebs and their slim, fast occupants lurking in corners, but she bucked up and went along, as did Ginger and the children and the dog. They traipsed up the road through town, looking more like they were on a picnic than a manhunt. The walk and the good company, particularly the high spirits of the children, took the tension right out of Jackie's shoulders.

Even Reade relaxed a bit—right up until they turned up the lane to the warehouse and saw, sitting there in the weeds at the side of the road, Farley's white Jeep.

seventeen

"*Son of a—*" *Reade ran to the Jeep and yanked the driver's side door open.* It was Farley's, all right. His mother's jacket lay on the backseat. Relief that it wasn't her body warred with increasing concern over where she was.

Jackie came up behind him, comforting him with a hand on his shoulder. "We'll find her."

Newton peered in the rear window. "There's something back here, mon. Pop the latch."

Reade did so, then stepped around to the back to check Newton's find—a small wooden crate with a Cho-Cho stamp and an invoice attached. "This must be the statue Mom bought."

She wouldn't have gone off and left it in an unlocked car, not by choice.

"Reade." Jackie motioned for him to join her at the passenger side door. When he did, she pointed at the ignition, where the broken end of the key jammed the switch.

His scrap of relief turned to dust and blew away. "Shit. That explains why the Jeep's still here."

Maybe, but it left a thousand other questions open. Did they decide to get a ride after the key broke off, or did someone break it so they'd need a ride? Did they get that ride with the mysterious Mateo? Was he—or whoever had them, if anyone—holding them against their will? If so, where?

And if not, what was the Sebastiani government's official position on matricide? Because if his mother was jerking him around, he was going to kill her himself.

"I hope they're not with that Mateo man," said Ginger earnestly. The children had gathered around her, wide-eyed and, for once, silent. "His eyes gave me the shivers."

"Amen," said Jackie.

"What are you going to do, mon?" asked Newton.

Now there was the one question Reade could answer, so he did.

"That's easy. I'm going to go find them."

Easier said than done.

Armed with a map that she produced from her purse, Jackie and Reade sat at Ginger's kitchen table finishing a quick tea and planning their next step. The problem was, Rumdog, the supposed location of the drug-dealing Mateo's marijuana patch, sat on one side of the island, and Blackwater, the supposed location of the voodoo priest Mateo's compound, sat at the other.

"It would help if we had some idea which one is right," said Jackie.

"Assuming either one is," added Reade.

"I wish I could be more help," said Newton. "Everybody talks like they know, but they don't really. It's all just gossip with some supposing thrown in."

Reade traced the routes between Redoubt and each location. Rumdog was slightly closer as the crow flies, but considerably farther away by the island's meandering roads. "I have to go with logic. Pot growers are a lot more common than voodoo priests, even down here. We should check out Rumdog first."

"If he's a drug runner, we should leave him to the police," said Jackie. "We'll get ourselves killed."

"You're right about that," said Ginger. "Those bwoys protect their plots with shotguns and machetes."

"Maybe so, but the police aren't interested, remember?"

"Circumstances changed the minute we found the car," Jackie argued. *Shotguns and machetes? No way.* "The constable will be back in the morning and we can try—"

"I'm not waiting another twelve hours to start looking for my mother. If you don't want to come, that's fine. I already told you that. But I'm going after them."

"Then let's start in Blackwater. It's closer, and if we leave right now, maybe we can be there before dark."

"Things get dark early in Blackwater," said Newton. "It's on the wrong side of the mountain. And if you wind up staying overnight, there's no hotel."

"We'll be stuck no matter where we go," said Jackie. "Unless the buses run late."

"Don't you have a car with you?" asked Ginger.

Reade shook his head. "We couldn't pry one loose at the resort."

"I could hot-wire the Jeep," said Newton.

Reade shook his head. "We'd better leave it where it is. The police may need to look at it. Does anyone in town have a car we could rent?"

Ginger and Newton looked at each other, shrugged, and shook their heads.

"I'd let you use ours, but the fuel pump went out last month, and I'm still waiting for the new one to come." Newton pondered for a moment. "I know. My cousin Albert can drive you to Rumdog. It's his night to visit his girlfriend at Jackass Creek. I'll ring him." He went to the phone and dialed.

"Is everyone in town a cousin of Newton's?" Jackie asked Ginger as she helped clear the table.

"He's one of fifteen, and his father was one of nineteen, mostly bwoys. Everyone on the whole island is either a cousin or a nephew," said Ginger, chuckling. She dropped her voice a little. "I told him after Maurice that I wasn't like his mama and that three were plenty. Can you picture me with twelve more? I made him go to the doctor." She snipped at the air with two fingers, like scissors, then gestured at Reade. "You do the same thing with this fella when the time comes."

Reade's eyes went wide.

"I'll take it under advisement," said Jackie, keeping a straight face only with great effort.

"You can just as well go by way of Rumdog," shouted Newton into the phone. "You do most weeks, anyway. . . . All right, then. They'll be there." Newton hung up and clapped his hands together to get attention. "You must come along. He doesn't want to drive up here, so we're going to have to get to him. It's a bit of hike."

"Hold the goat."

"Say what?"

"The goat. Hold him." Albert shoved a scrawny kid through the window toward Jackie and Reade. "He's going to Rumdog, too. You may as well make friends."

This was turning into the ride from hell. In between maniacal bursts of speed accompanied by lots of horn honking and a total disregard for basic traffic laws, Albert had stopped at several hamlets along the way to pick up and drop off items for friends and family. Apparently he and his trips to his girlfriend's house functioned as a makeshift, intra-island delivery service. The back of the truck was completely full, with the overage spilling into the cab. The three of them were now squeezed in around several gallon jugs with unknown contents, a case of kumquat marmalade, and a large bag of ugli fruit he'd picked up in Twelve Mile—plus Jackie's purse, which seemed to have grown. She suspected Ginger had stuffed something in just before they'd left the house, but she hadn't been able to look so far, because, in addition to everything else, she was stuck in the middle, and her long legs simply wouldn't fit around the stick shift. She was forced to sit sideways, her legs thrown over Reade's, in order to give Albert room to change gears. Even so, more often than not his hand ended up against her backside when he shifted into fourth. She hadn't decided yet whether the contact was accidental or his way of having a little fun.

"I don't like goats. Can't you put him in the back?" Jackie eyed the kid, calculating how much less maneuvering room she'd have with it on her lap. She suspected that was part of Albert's plan.

"No crate, and no room for one if there was," said Albert. "You have to hold him."

"Come on, he's just a little thing," said Reade. "I'll hang onto him."

"Hey, it's still my lap on top, and it's me he'll hit if he isn't housebroken. Have you ever smelled goat urine?"

"Uh, no."

"I have. My best friend raised the little garbage disposals for 4-H. There are reasons I don't like them."

Albert settled things by simply dropping the goat on Jackie's lap and leaving her and Reade to deal with it while he came around and got behind the wheel. Their efforts to control the kid set off a round of bawling that stopped only when the animal smelled the gum in Reade's shirt pocket and started nibbling.

"Hey, that's a good shirt." Reade transferred the gum to a pocket in his shorts, but that just changed the target to something more valuable than a shirt. He flinched. "Ow. Stop it, you little assassin."

"It's just a little thing," cooed Jackie.

Reade made a face at her, retrieved the gum, and pulled out a piece for a bribe. Billy lunged for it, then settled across Jackie's thighs with his prize.

"Gum can't be good for a goat," she said. "Especially with the wrapper still on."

"You peel it," suggested Reade.

"It won't hurt him," said Albert.

While the kid happily chomped, Reade started groping around under the tangle of legs and goat.

"What are you doing now?" demanded Jackie.

"Trying to put the gum in the glove compartment so he'll stop looking for it."

"That's *not* the glove compartment."

"I know." Grinning, he gave her a friendly pat before moving on.

With the rest of the gum inaccessible, Billy succumbed to the swaying of the truck and fell asleep with Jackie scratching him behind his ear.

"See?" said Reade.

As Albert passed on a yellow line yet again, she saw, all right. She saw that she was going to die smelling like a goat, with two men feeling her up, and someone was going to have to explain it to her parents.

Fortunately, Albert's reflexes were as quick as his foot was heavy, and they arrived in Rumdog intact shortly after sunset. He pulled up in front of the only lighted business in town, a bar called Sistah B's, got out and immediately went inside with two of the gallon jugs, leaving Reade and Jackie to fend for themselves. By that point, Reade was wedged so tightly against the door that when he opened it, he rolled out on the ground like an armadillo.

"*Oof.* I may never stand up straight again."

"I'm going to need some help, here, too." The kid had awakened and was struggling to jump out of the truck and vanish into the night. Jackie gripped it by its ankles, two in each hand, until Reade could relieve her.

"That's a good goat." He tucked it under one arm and helped Jackie unfold with the other hand. Her feet tingled as the blood rushed back.

Reade looked over the bar. "You may not want to hear this, but bars are male territory down here. I need to look like I'm . . . in charge, for lack of a better term, even if you and I both know better. If I don't, we could wind up in serious trouble."

"In other words, don't get uppity in front of the men." She reached back in the truck for her purse, grunting as she boosted it. "Shall I walk three paces behind, too?"

He laughed and gave her a kiss on the cheek. "Just two."

Albert came back for a couple more jugs. "I told Sistah that you're friends of Newton's."

"Is she another cousin of his?" asked Reade.

"Of course she's a cousin. She's my sistah, isn't she? You come on inside and she'll take care of you."

"What do we do with the goat?"

"Bring it along. It's probably thirsty, too."

Skeptical, they followed him inside, past faces full of suspicion. At the bar, he introduced them to a female version of himself. Sistah, as she insisted they call her, took the jugs and set them behind the counter, then frowned at the goat. "Who does that puny thing belong to?"

"The old lady with the cabins," said Albert. "Rosalie. These two will want to meet her anyway. They can take her the goat when they go to get a room for the night."

"Wait a minute," said Jackie, but he was out the door again. A moment later he returned with one of the boxes out of the back of the pickup, and she continued, "We don't want to hang out with a goat all evening."

"No different than hanging out with Albert," said Sistah.

"Ha," said Albert as the other men in the bar laughed. "All right, I'll take the goat in a minute and tell Rosalie you'll be coming along. Meantime, give the poor billy a drink, girl. And open a couple of beers for my friends."

He made another trip out while Sistah opened two ice-cold Caribs and drew a mug of water. Reade held the mug while the kid drank, then fed it a couple of peanuts from a bowl on the bar.

"You'll want to put that thing outside now," warned Jackie.

"Where? We can't tie it up, it'll eat the string."

"I'm just telling you."

Albert carted in another box. "This is the last of it."

Sistah handed him a small package. "For Margaret's birthday. Give her my love."

"I always do. Anyone else want me to carry something?" No one raised a voice, so he tucked the package under one arm, took the goat under the other, and headed for the door. "You all take care of my cousin's friends. They're good people."

The screen slammed behind him, and in that instant Jackie felt more isolated than at any moment in her life. Here they stood in a room full of smoke and strangers, with only Albert's quick assurances between them and the outright hostility she'd seen when they first walked in. Lenore and Farley were missing, possibly kidnapped. They knew no one within twenty miles. She just wanted to get their questions answered, get out of the bar, and find a hotel room with a sturdy lock on the door and a warm shower.

Reade had other ideas. He settled in for some serious chitchat with Sistah and the man to his left. Jackie kept her mouth shut and watched with a mixture of anxiety and growing respect. By the time he bought a second round and pulled out the picture of Mateo, he was no longer a total stranger, and Albert's endorsement carried more weight. His new friends were happy to look at the photo.

Until they saw who it was. Then their faces went flat and the man turned away, clearly disturbed.

"What would you be wantin' with the likes of that?" asked Sistah.

"A friend is . . . visiting, and I have to get a message to him. To this man." He showed them Farley's picture, then Lenore's. "And this lady is with him, I think. Have they come through town in the last day or so?"

Sistah laughed sourly. "Once daylight comes, you'll see

there's not much of a town to come through. Why is it you think they'd be in Rumdog?"

Reade glanced around, then dropped his voice. "I heard Mateo has a place up the mountain from here."

Her eyes narrowed, and then she slowly nodded. "He did, but not for two, maybe three years. He and all his crew moved over by Blackwater."

Jackie glanced at Reade, but kept her mouth shut.

"Then I guess we go to Blackwater tomorrow."

"You couldn't pay me to go 'round that bastard again," said the man next to Reade.

"Don't concern yourself," said Sistah. "Nobody's paid you for anything in years. They're not likely to start now."

Her wisecrack released the tension in the room. Reade took advantage of the moment to buy a round. When everyone had been served, he quietly asked about the rooms at Rosalie's.

"I'll show you." Carrying a glass, Sistah walked them to the door and pointed to a lane that cut into the forest a few yards from the bar. "About a chain up that way. She keeps a light on."

"Three questions," said Reade. "Where can we get a meal in the morning?"

"Rosalie will feed you. Eggs and bammy, most likely."

"Sounds great. How do we get to Blackwater from here?"

"There's a bus early, about seven. You make a transfer at Twelve Mile." She polished the glass in her hand. "What's the last question?"

"Mateo." He lowered his voice so it wouldn't carry back into the bar. "I need to know what I'm getting into before I walk in there. Is he involved with drugs somehow?"

Sistah glanced back over her shoulder. "No. Not the way you mean, anyway. Now you get out of here. That must be an important message, to go through all this."

"It is," said Reade. "Thank you."

The moon was bright enough for them to pick their way

down the lane, but the bare bulb on Rosalie's porch was a welcome beacon against the incredible blackness of the forest. She answered on their third knock.

Reade took off his hat and held it in his hands. "Albert and Sistah said we should talk to you."

"Aah. You're the folks brought the kid goat from Zelia. You'll want a room."

"Yes, ma'am."

"I have one cabin free. It's twenty pounds for the night."

Reade handed over the cash, and she called her daughter to take them to their cabin. "I put breakfast on the table at six. Be out by ten."

A pretty girl of about eighteen appeared in the doorway and led them down a path to their cabin, a tiny wooden cottage that looked like it would fall over in a stiff breeze. It was furnished sparsely with a high double bed on a white metal frame, a sink, and a single wooden chair. Two doors led to a closet and a toilet. There was no shower, and the lock could have been picked by a two-year-old.

"Perfect," said Reade.

The girl smiled shyly. "Albert said you helped with the kid goat. I wanted to thank you."

"No problem," said Reade.

"He's just a little thing," added Jackie, unable to resist one last dig.

"We'll fatten him up soon enough," said the girl. "I'm getting married next month. He's for the wedding feast."

"Oh." The smile froze on Jackie's face.

Reade cleared his throat. "Congratulations."

"Thank you. Anyway, good night." She backed out the door and pulled it shut behind her.

"They're going to eat Billy," said Jackie.

"Sounds like." Reade crossed the room and opened the only window. The floorboards squeaked with every step. "We're spoiled in the States. Most of us never have to deal with the reality of where our food comes from."

"I've eaten chickens I've known personally, but they

didn't sleep on my lap first. He was pretty sweet. For a goat."

"Just think of it as carrying a very precious wedding present for that young woman."

"Maybe. But I still feel like a Judas."

"I know. Me, too." He flipped back the covers. The sheets sparkled under the bare bulb that lit the room. "Good. They're clean and nothing moved."

"Geez, Hunter, thanks. Like I needed to think about bugs right before bed." She scanned the room for six-or-more-legged occupants. The only thing she spotted was a moth, bashing suicidally at the light bulb. Moths, she could handle.

"Sorry. I figure it's better to know who you're sleeping with." He stripped off his T-shirt and hung it over the headboard, then went over and jammed the rubber stopper into the drain so he could fill the sink. He looked around, opened the door to the toilet, and checked the shelf in the closet. "There's no soap."

"Hang on a second. Let me see if I have some." Jackie pulled her poor, wadded-up, long-sleeved shirt out of her purse and hung it on a nail with her hat, then carried her purse to the foot of the bed and dumped its contents onto the blanket. There was a paper bag she didn't recognize. She opened it and discovered two toothbrushes, a small tube of toothpaste, a bar of soap, and a package of hard candies.

"Aha. I knew Ginger had put something in here. Bless her heart, she sneaked us a CARE package. Try this." She sniffed the soap before she tossed it his direction. "You'll smell like a perfume counter, but you'll be clean."

He peeled the bar, lathered up, and started washing, and it was all Jackie could do not to volunteer to help. Trying to ignore the flex of his muscles as he scrubbed, she started sorting.

"What *is* all that?" he asked.

"I grabbed a few things I thought we might need."

"A few?"

"Three minutes didn't give me much time to make decisions." She separated the useless from the potentially useful, packing the keepers back in her purse and putting discards like eye makeup remover and cuticle cream and the stupid damn static spray in the paper bag. "I hate to throw all this out. Maybe that girl would like it."

"Good idea," said Reade, toweling off. "Give her as much as you can. You don't want to be carting all that junk through the jungle tomorrow."

"What's left is not junk."

"It's still heavy. And noisy."

"And may come in handy," she argued. "Are you done yet? I stink, too, thanks to you and your goat."

"I would have shared the sink, you know." He stripped down to his briefs and crawled into bed, pulling the sheet up to his waist. "Go for it."

While he watched? "You realize we don't have any condoms."

"There aren't any in that drugstore-in-a-bag of yours?"

"No. So I don't think a striptease is wise. Roll over."

"You don't trust me?"

"I'm trusting you with my life," she said. "But that doesn't mean you get any without a condom."

"Okay, okay. I'm going to sleep now. You can get naked with no threat." He closed his eyes.

She stood there, arms folded, watching him for a long time, until his breathing slowed and grew regular, and then she watched a while longer. Convinced he really was asleep, or nearly so, she quickly stripped and washed, then pulled on the long-sleeved shirt as a nightgown. It took her just a few minutes to rinse out her undies in the sink and hang them to dry, and then she slipped into bed beside him.

As she lay down, he slid his arm around her and pulled her close.

"You louse. You were awake the whole time," she said.

"So shoot me. I very much need you tonight. Not sex. Just this."

He smelled of soap and water and nothing more, and she still went all soft and moist with desire. Any pheromones at play were all Reade's. She sighed and gently brushed a curl off his forehead, then wrapped her arms around him. "We'll find them tomorrow."

"I know." He kissed her, a long, comfortable kiss that demanded nothing more than that she be there. And since she had no desire to be anywhere else, there she stayed, in his arms, all night long.

The nine o'clock bus to Blackwater was running late, so they took advantage of the wait and the fact that Twelve Mile had a well-stocked grocery to round up some food for later. While Jackie shopped, Reade checked in with Mr. Samuels. Afterward, seething from the phone call, he waited outside on the front porch, one end of which was occupied by an old-fashioned soda cooler, the kind where you have to slide the bottles along metal racks to get the one you want into position. Dents pocked the machine's surface, and the original Coca-Cola red lay at least three coats of paint beneath the current sky blue, but it seemed to be in working order. He dropped in the necessary coins and pulled an orange soda through the maze and up through the release. The opener on the side was damaged beyond usefulness, so he popped the cap off on the edge of the porch rail, then leaned against the machine to watch for the bus and try to calm himself.

Jackie wandered out a few minutes later, a plastic bag in her hand. "We now have a couple of meals and some bottled water."

"Good."

"Is that pop cold? I want something really cold. I have a feeling it's going to be a while before we see ice again."

"You may be right." He stood up, fished a handful of coins out of his pocket and started feeding the machine. "Would you like orange, orange, or orange?"

"Orange."

He yanked a bottle out, then repeated the railing trick.

"Ever try one of these?" she asked, holding up a bottle opener that dangled from a string by the window.

"That makes it too easy. Puts my masculinity at risk."

She laughed and let the opener drop back against the window frame, where it rang like a bell. "I take it they still haven't turned up."

"Nope. And Samuels is still being a butt, even though they've been gone forty-eight hours. When we get this settled, I'm going to find out who owns Fair Winds and get that jackass fired."

"I'll help," she said. She took a sip of pop. "Did Newton report the Jeep?"

"I couldn't get through to the store. I assume so."

"Then the constables should be looking for them by now. Maybe someone will meet us in Blackwater."

"Don't count on it. I've been thinking about what we're going to do when we get there. We had an in at Rumdog because of Albert, but we'll be walking into Blackwater cold. Things won't be half so friendly."

"Maybe we should take a goat."

"I'm not joking, Jackie. It's going to take some work to get anyone to talk to us, and then if we do manage to convince someone to tell us where Mateo's camp is, we'll probably wind up out in the forest overnight. And if we don't, Newton said there's no place to stay in the village. I think you should take the bus back to Runaway Bay and stay on top of the police so—"

"No."

"Jackie, it doesn't make sense for both of us to risk our necks. And what are you going to do when we have to sleep outside with the spiders and snakes?"

She couldn't control her shudder, but she wouldn't back down. "I'll probably freak and you'll have to pump me full of Valium."

"I don't have any Valium, so unless you happen to have some in your purse. . . . You don't, do you?"

"No. But I have bug repellant. And I bought some medicinal rum. I'm going. I have to."

"Why? Because of the grant?"

"Partly. And partly because I'm still trying to prove something to myself. But mostly I have to go because you need me."

The simple truth in her statement took Reade's breath away. He did need her. He wondered if she had any idea how much. He was just starting to grasp it, himself.

"I think I see the bus," she said. She stared down the road. "I can handle this, Reade. Your mother's out there, God knows where, dealing with God knows what. I can handle a few piddly-ass bugs to help you get her back."

There was determination in her face and in the set of her shoulders, and Reade had had enough experience with Barnett the Bulldozer to know just how far that determination could carry her. He nodded, just as the green and purple jitney pulled up.

"Okay, Doctor. Let's go see what Blackwater looks like."

eighteen

"You don't want off here." The bus driver curled his hand over the door lever and held it there.

"This is Blackwater, right?" said Reade.

"Right."

"Then this is where we want off."

"But foreigners never come out here," said one of the other passengers. "Especially women."

"I'm adventurous," said Jackie.

"She is also stubborn," said Reade.

"But there's no place to stay," said the driver. "And there won't be another bus until tomorrow."

"We know," said Jackie. Her inclination was to throw herself at the driver's feet and thank him for stopping her, and if she could have figured out a way to keep Reade on the bus with her, she would have. But the only clues they had pointed to Mateo and Blackwater, so he was going to get off, and that meant she had to get off. "It really is where we need to go. Thank you, but we'll be fine."

Reluctantly, the driver pulled the handle. A moment later, they were standing in the dust as the bus rolled away.

Jackie took one look around and very nearly ran after it. Rumdog had been tiny; Blackwater was nearly non-existent. The whole village consisted of a dozen houses clustered around a single store. Period. No bar. No restaurant. Not even a school. The only gathering place seemed to be an ancient, splintery table with benches on the shady side of the store, where three men sat eating and playing dominoes.

"Looks like lunchtime," Reade said. "Shall we see what the store has to offer and join them?" He held up the bag of food they'd bought in Twelve Mile. "We can hang on to this stuff for later."

"Sure." Her voice sounded artificially bright, even to her.

Reade eyed her carefully. "Maybe you should stay inside while I talk to these guys."

"I'll be fine," she protested. "Really. I was just thinking about all the money I forked out for an all-inclusive resort package, and they didn't include this on any of the tours."

Chuckling, he gave her hand a quick squeeze. "Okay. Just don't let the nerves show too much. Oh, and by the way, if anyone asks, we're married."

"All right. Nice proposal."

"I'm a romantic."

Under the watchful eye of the grocer, they picked out two sodas, a melon, a can of Spam, and a box of soda crackers, which they carried outside.

"Is it okay if we sit at this end?" Reade asked the domino players.

They grunted their assent, so Reade and Jackie sat down and stated laying out their feast. They flattened the cracker box to use as a carving board, and Jackie dug her trusty Swiss Army knife out of the bottom of her bag.

There was clearly too much food for two, so after a

few minutes, Reade offered the extras to the men. Two of them declined, but the third, an ancient-looking fellow with stone gray hair and a face as wrinkled as a sharpei's, allowed as how he'd like some ham. And maybe some crackers.

Reade cut several slices and, using the lid off the can as a platter, passed him the meat and a stack of crackers. "Do you mind if I watch your game? My grandfather and I used to play Five-Up when I visited him during the summer."

The old man cocked an eyebrow. "And where was that?"

"Boston. He was Italian. Hell of a domino player."

And it was as simple as that. Jackie watched in awe as Reade turned a couple of slices of meat and a game into an opening that led to an afternoon of conversation and play. After a while, she cut the remaining melon into thin slices and put it on the table where the men could reach it, but she otherwise stayed out of it and tried not to show how nervous she was.

By and by, after Reade had demonstrated that he did actually know how to play dominoes and wasn't just jerking them around, one of the men got curious and asked what brought him and the lady to Blackwater.

"A couple of friends are visiting Mateo Delatour," said Reade, sticking to the same story he'd told in Rumdog. "I have an urgent message to get to them. I'm hoping someone can point us toward his pen."

Three faces shuttered over like a storm was brewing.

Reade didn't push it. He laid a double six on the end of a run and play continued. A little while later, the old man said, "Is Mateo even up there these days?"

"Think so," said another.

Jackie would have immediately asked for directions, but Reade continued to play, apparently unconcerned. After a bit, the old man spoke again. "How far would that be?"

"Three, four hours, if you walk fast."

"It's not easy to move fast in the jungle," said Reade. "Especially if you don't know the trail. Of course, a man could hire a guide, if he knew one."

"Maybe," said the third man. He'd been the quietest all afternoon. "Or maybe no one would take him."

"That'd be a shame." Reade didn't have a match, and he pulled another domino—or bone, as Jackie had learned they were called. "But I bet he could find someone who would." He put a subtle emphasis on the word *bet*.

Another long spell passed in which the only sound was the click of the bones as they were flipped and placed. "You're a wagering man?"

Reade nodded.

"Okay, then. We'll play for it. You win, I'll take you myself—for a hundred pounds. You lose, you pay me double and we go nowhere."

"Whooo." The other two chuckled over the exorbitant demand.

Read laughed too, shaking his head. "It's an important message, but not that important. Twenty-five to take us."

Jackie bit her tongue, certain he was blowing it.

"Seventy-five," said the man.

"Fifty," said Reade. "And we leave right away."

"Done." He cleared the current game and started flipping the bones facedown. "But only because I'm going to have an easy hundred when I beat you."

"That's a risk I'll have to take. By the way, my name's Reade Hunter. This is my wife, Jackie."

"Dermott Jones," said the man.

Reade put out his hand. "Nice to meet you, Dermott. It will be good having you to guide us."

An hour later, doing some good-natured grumbling about "white bwoys who won by twenty damn points," Dermott led them into the forest. The change in the atmosphere was immediate and oppressive. The breeze died, the humidity shot sky high, and the buzz of insects grew so loud it sounded like the big amps warming up at a Rolling Stones concert.

They moved quickly, partly to get where they were going and partly to stay ahead of the mosquitoes and black-flies. As long as they kept moving, the bugs were tolerable, but as soon as they took a break, the little blighters zeroed in. Even liberal applications of Jackie's bug juice only kept them down, not off, advertising claims notwithstanding. She expended much of her energy fanning to keep them away from her face until Reade suggested she spray the brim of her hat.

Not all was misery, however. Along the path, trailing stems of heliconia, delicate orchids, bright spikes of ginger, and an almost infinite variety of bromeliads made a display as bright and exotic as any florist could hope for. Overhead, green and orange parrots and parakeets squawked, finches sang, and hummingbirds flitted. Geckos perched on the wide leaves of banana or streaked under the multitude of ferns, hunting. Every time Jackie spotted one with a creepy-crawly in its mouth, she gave it a thumbs-up.

"You're switching that purse back and forth a lot," said Reade after a mile or so. "If it hurts your shoulder, get rid of some of that crap."

"Like what? The insect repellant, or the pocketknife?" she asked. "Or the sunscreen, or the first aid kit? Or maybe the toothbrushes and soap? You travel light, but I notice you use what I have."

"Only because it's there. If you didn't have it, I'd get along without."

"Well, I don't want to get along without, thank you." *Men.*

Shortly after that, they arrived at their first stream. It was fast and had cut into the soft limestone, making a narrow gully—not too deep, but definitely not a wader. Someone had strung a rope bridge across, one of those V-shaped things where you walk one rope while holding onto two others. Dermott scooted across like it was nothing, but Jackie stalled on the near end. It wasn't that high—she could make it, but her purse was so heavy it pulled her to one side. She backed off the ropes.

"Get rid of it," said Reade.

"I've got it." She looped the strap over her head so it crossed her breasts bandolier style and shifted the bag until its weight was balanced. She gritted her teeth and stepped out again. The first steps weren't bad, but as she got out toward the center, the flimsy bridge began to jiggle and sway. Jackie froze.

"Keep moving," Reade called. "Look ahead, not down. Straight ahead. There you go."

One step at a time.

"I've got you," said Dermott. He leaned out to grab her. "Just a little more."

One, two, three. She reached out and met his extended hand, and then she was off the bridge and breathing again. Reade strolled across. As he hit the end, he smacked a mosquito that had discovered the side of his neck.

"Want some more bug spray?" she asked as he stepped onto the trail beside her. "Or should I throw it out?"

"We'll see what you say later."

Three hours later, her shoulders ached and they were losing the race with the sun. As it settled lower, bats came out to scoop up the extra bounty of bugs that emerged at dusk. Jackie was watching the aerial show when she walked into Dermott's back.

"Sorry."

"We must stop for the night," he said. "You two don't walk as fast as I do, and it's taking longer than I thought."

"I have a flashlight," said Jackie. She turned and stuck out her tongue at Reade.

"Will the batt'ry last two hours?" asked Dermott.

"No," said Reade. "But the moon is still nearly full."

"This isn't the beach. The trees eat all the light. And you don't want to come up on Mateo's pen in the dark. The duppies guard it. They'll snatch your heart right out of your chest and eat it." He pointed to a narrow track that led off the main trail. "There's a old shack just up the way. We'll stay there. It's a good place—used to belong to a Rastaman friend of mine."

"Good" was relative, Jackie discovered. Sitting in the middle of a clearing that was rapidly returning to jungle, the shack was tiny, with barely enough room for the three of them inside. It was definitely not someplace she'd stay under normal circumstances, but it was way better than the open ground, and she would have to agree with Dermott. It was good.

He quickly cleared the fire pit and started a fire, then disappeared into the forest with his machete. Meanwhile, Reade broke off some fern fronds, made a crude broom, and swept out the shack. Jackie heard the occasional stomp and a couple of swear words, but when he emerged, he declared the space to be spider free.

She thanked him, touched. "You know, you make a pretty good husband, for someone who's just a vacation fling."

"Thanks." Something odd flickered through his eyes. Jackie searched for a clue to what it was, but he just covered with a sappy smile and gave her a kiss on the cheek. "You're not half bad as a wife, either."

"There you go getting romantic again." She glanced around to make sure their guide wasn't nearby. "What do you make of what Dermott said about Mateo's place? Duppies eating your heart, all that. Duppies are ghosts, right?"

"Yeah. Sounds like a great rumor to cultivate if you want to be left alone, for whatever reason. A duppie here, a zombie there, and the country people stay away. A person could get away with just about anything up here with a phantom army like that around him."

Even kidnapping, thought Jackie, though she wouldn't say it aloud. Poor Lenore. The only thing she'd done was to date the wrong guy at the wrong time.

Dermott came back a few minutes later carrying a hand of bananas, a pineapple, and a lumpy green breadfruit as big as his head. When the fire died down, he raked a spot in the coals and tossed the breadfruit in, then disappeared back into the forest. By the time the breadfruit finished roasting an hour later, he had gathered enough moss and leaves to make them each a loose nest in the shack.

Reade contributed a can of their beans and some bottled water to the feast, and they ate their dinner in the dark, off banana leaf plates. Dermott tossed enough green material on the fire to keep it smoky, so the bugs stayed down.

When they were full and the sky was pitch black, he walked them away from the fire just far enough to see a glow high on the next hill.

"That's Mateo's pen," he said. "Listen."

Over the insect drone and the rustling of whatever lived in the underbrush, they could hear distant music, wild and full of drums and chanting. Trance music. Voodoo music. A high-pitched ululation sent a shiver up Jackie's spine, and she reached for Reade's hand in the dark.

"Duppies," said Dermott firmly, and led them back to the fire.

Conversation seemed pointless after that. They tossed a last batch of green leaves on the fire and left it smoldering while they went to bed. Working by the glow of the tiny flashlight she used to find keyholes in Minneapolis, Jackie pulled her nest closer to Reade's, keeping him between her and Dermott. They cuddled up together, silent, and strained to hear the distant music until they finally fell asleep.

For about half a second after she came awake, Jackie was convinced that duppies were eating her feet.

Then she realized it was a pig. A boar. A wild boar, nibbling on the toe of her shoe. She screamed and shot to her feet. Squealing, the boar scrabbled backward, bumped the wall, and bolted forward, toward her.

She screamed again, leaped over its back, and streaked

out the door, smack into Reade. They tumbled together, landing in the cold coals of last night's fire. Ash billowed around them like smoke.

"What the hell?"

"In there." She pointed, hand shaking, at the shack. "A big old nasty wild boar, and it was trying to eat my foot."

Reade jumped to his feet and looked around for a weapon. He found the stick Dermott had used to stir the fire and, like a gray caveman with a club, peeked in the door of the shack.

He froze. His shoulders began to shake.

"What?"

He backed up a step, chuckling. "Here, pig-pig-pig. Sooooey."

A cute little pink porker trotted out with the handle of Jackie's purse in its mouth. It saw her and cut sideways, dragging the purse and dumping bottles and Band-Aids all over the ground.

"Get it," she shouted.

Reade dove for the pig and barely managed to snag the purse. There was a momentary tug-of-war, and then the pig decided that the purse wasn't worth the fight, turned it loose, and trotted off into the jungle, grunting his displeasure all the way.

"I know a wedding feast that wants you," Jackie shouted after it. She glared at Reade, who was clutching her purse and laughing. "Give me that." She snatched it away and started picking up her things.

"Wild boar?"

"It woke me up from a sound sleep. And it *was* chewing on me." She held out her foot, where teeth marks and pig slobber were still visible on the toe of her running shoe. "Where were you, anyway?"

"Out back." He glanced down, then turned his back and zipped up. "Excuse me. I got here as fast as I could."

"Humph. And I suppose Dermott was out back, too? Here I have two men along and neither one of them is around when I'm attacked by wild animals."

"That pig was not wild."

"It was taste-testing my body parts. That's wild enough for me." She finished picking up outside and moved inside to gather the rest of her things. "Where's my camera?"

"It must be in there somewhere."

"It's not." She started poking through the bedding with her foot. "Could a pig swallow a camera?

Reade came in, and together they tossed the whole place, then searched outside again. Jackie sat down and went through her purse item by item. "Shit. My Swiss Army knife and my wallet are gone, too. Where, exactly, is Dermott?"

Reade's eyes widened and he quickly patted his own wallet, then blew sigh of relief. "He was gone when I woke up. I figured he was rounding up breakfast. Apparently not."

"Apparently. So, let me get this straight. We're out here, halfway between nowhere and some guy who may be a criminal, a voodoo priest, or both, with various sized animals eating me one bite at a time, and our guide just robbed and abandoned us." Her voice cracked as she fought back a sob. She wasn't usually the crying kind, but really, this was too much.

Reade wrapped his arms around her as the first tears dripped. "That's about it."

"Well, then I guess it's a good thing I didn't have anything in my wallet except a little cash."

"You didn't? Where's the rest?"

"Here." She patted her cleavage. "I stuffed everything in my bra last night when I ducked out back before bed. It's the one advantage of being overendowed. Lots of storage space."

Laughing, Reade kissed her forehead. "I keep saying this, but you really are amazing."

"Yeah. A lot of good travelers checks and credit cards are going to do out here. I want my knife. My grandpa gave me that knife." She sniffled again, indulging for one more minute before she pulled herself together. "So what are we going to do?"

He leaned his forehead against hers. "I don't think we have much choice. We keep going."

What had looked like a generally flat route to the base of the hill where Mateo's compound sat turned out to be an optical illusion. Between the shack and the pen lay a series of gullies that had to be climbed into, crossed, and climbed back out of.

Reade kept a close eye on Jackie. Her momentary lapse into tears had really thrown him, it was so unexpected and so unlike the Jackie he knew. Obstinate, sharp-tongued, sexy woman with control issues, yes. Teary female, no. For the first time, she seemed vulnerable.

As he watched her haul her silly duffel bag of a purse down into the third gully, he kicked himself for bringing her along. Not because she couldn't handle it—she clearly could, wild boar attacks aside. He was the one having trouble with the whole thing. If she got hurt. . . .

But she made it down, crossed the stepping-stone path across the stream at the bottom, and scrambled back up the other side in fine style, just as she had managed every other obstacle. Now if he could somehow guarantee the same outcome when they met Mateo. All he wanted was to get Jackie and his mother out of this safely. Farley would be a bonus, but was barely on his radar at this point. Priorities.

By midafternoon, they were close enough to the pen that they could make out the individual stakes of the stockade between the tree trunks. Reade moved off the trail and they ducked down behind a clump of ferns.

"You're not planning some sort of Rambo assault, are you?" asked Jackie.

"Maybe. Okay, no," he admitted when her eyes widened with shock. "But I do want to size things up before we walk up to the front gate and knock. Let's see if we can get a little closer without being seen."

The necessity of staying out of sight, combined with the jungle, played havoc with their rate of progress, but when Reade spotted the first guards, he was glad he'd taken the precaution. They carried automatic weapons—lightweight, lethal-looking things designed to kill people. He put a finger to his lips and led Jackie into the grotto under the buttress roots of a tall tree.

She hesitated, then ducked in next to him, barely in time. Moments later, the guards walked by less than a dozen yards away as Reade and Jackie held their breaths. Sweat poured off Reade, pooling in the center of his back.

When the coast was clear again, Reade shifted so his mouth was next to Jackie's ear. "I'm going in by myself."

"No." Her mouth formed the word silently.

"You stay here. If I'm not out by morning, hike out of here and get help."

"No," she repeated. Her voice barely carried. "We'll look less threatening as a couple. A single man could be an assassin or a thief. Together, we're just lost researchers whose guide ran off. With all our gear."

Reade's every instinct said to make her stay here, hidden away from those men and their guns, but she had a point, damn it all. "Okay. We'll go back to the trail and brazen this out. Wait until we see the guards pass again, so we know where they are. And if you have any good luck charms in that purse, this would be the time to haul them out."

"Ready?"

Jackie nodded. Well after the guards passed, it still took a conscious effort for her to breathe, much less speak, but she'd never been so anxious to move in her life. Between the guys with guns and the feeling that *things* were crawling in her hair, she was about to lose it.

Getting out from under this tree would at least solve one problem.

Reade stuck his head out and looked around, then nodded and crept out between the long, arched roots. Jackie followed. The guards had passed, headed away from the trail. She turned the other direction and took a few steps before she realized Reade wasn't with her. She backtracked.

He was still crouched there, just outside the grotto, frozen. His face was white with the strain. She stepped back, ducking to make herself less obvious. "What?"

He motioned her closer with his eyes, still not moving. His voice was a bare whisper. "There is something on my neck. Look and tell me what it is."

The something moved, and Jackie jerked and fell backward. The leaf litter made a soft rustle as she landed, then crabbed back another foot or two.

"Spider?" asked Reade.

She nodded. "Big. And agitated. Don't move."

"I have no intention of moving." He was in an awkward position, though, and there was no way he could stay that way for long. "You're going to have to get it off for me."

She scrunched her eyes shut for a second, working up the courage to look closely.

Oh, God. It was right at the edge of his hair, and it was big enough to take out a hummingbird. It had huge fangs that looked as though they could inject quantities of venom, and as she shifted slightly closer—just slightly—it tapped its front legs in warning. Reade flinched involuntarily, like a horse shaking off a fly. The spider took a step toward his collar. If it went down his shirt, he could be in major trouble.

"Any time now."

I can't. The words were ready on her tongue, but she nodded. "Hang on."

She looked around for something that would keep her far enough away from that monster to maybe deal with it. A fern frond. She quickly broke one off and held it in front of the spider. It took a tentative step onto the tip of the frond, and she freaked and jerked away. The spider squatted back, angry.

"Reade, I can't even get rid of a tiny little spider in my bathroom."

"But you can do this," said Reade. "I need you to do this."

"Okay." She tried again. She laid the frond down again, this time so it covered the edge of Reade's collar. Then she blew a puff of air, very gently, at the spider's hind end. It stepped forward. One leg. Two. Three.

She waited until the spider had all legs but one on the frond, then took a huge breath to steel herself and slowly lifted. Up, up. As the frond came away from Reade, it swayed, and the startled spider rushed toward Jackie's hand. With a shriek, she tossed the whole mess away. Fern and spider went sailing off into the forest.

"Ohgod, ohgod, ohgod."

"Shh." Reade threw his arms around her and she clutched at him. "Come on, we have to get out of here."

"Too late," said a thick voice. "Look what we have here, J. C. A party."

Still clinging to each other, they looked up into the muzzle of an automatic rifle. The man on the other end smiled the kind of smile that makes small children break into tears.

"Party's over."

nineteen

It was like a scene from a movie. The intrepid ar-
chaeologist/spy/explorer and his female counterpart,
captured by hostile forces, are marched into a hilltop jungle camp to face the wrath of the local warlord.

Except he and Jackie had no high-tech spy gear, bull-
whip, or faithful bearer lurking in the bush to get them out
of this. Just their wits, and Reade wasn't so sure his were
working anymore. If one of these pigs so much as looked
cross-eyed at Jackie, he was going to come unglued.

"At least we're going in through the front gate," said
Jackie under her breath.

"Quiet." The guard touched her shoulder with the muzzle of his rifle.

"Does your mother know you do this for a living?" she
asked.

The guard growled, the snarl of a mad dog ready to
bite, and Reade warned Jackie with his eyes. She clamped
her mouth shut.

The drumming started again, the same pounding rhythm

that had throbbed over the jungle most of the night. Up close, it vibrated through the soles of his shoes and into his gut, but the overlying sounds were less threatening. In fact, it sounded less like a voodoo ceremony than a party with laughter, singing, and general merriment.

Jackie must have picked up on the same thing, because she was wearing a look of consternation.

They passed through the gate and into a compound of tidy thatched buildings. It was much larger than Reade would have thought. In fact, it appeared to be an entire village, complete with children who ran up to check out the prisoners. There was no hostility or fear in their faces; in fact, most of the people looked downright cheerful as they passed.

The chasm between expectation and reality made Reade's brain hurt. Jackie frowned at him and mouthed a question, "What is going on?"

He shook his head, confounded. There was nothing to do but keep walking toward the sound of those drums.

They emerged into what could only be called a village square of neatly packed dirt trimmed out with . . . roses?

"What the hell?"

"This is creeping me out," said Jackie.

"Keep going," ordered the guards behind them. "Straight ahead. The pavilion."

Pavilion? What kind of hideout had a pavilion? What kind of jungle army *called* it a pavilion?

They were marched into an open air structure as big as the dance floor at Saul's. After the brightness of the square, the shade seemed as deep as that in the jungle, and it took Reade's eyes a moment to adjust. The area was packed with people, some dancing, some sitting, A man with dreadlocks and the eyes of a wild animal sat on a low stool in the corner, amid the musicians and drummers.

Mateo. Reade braced himself for whatever came next.

But no amount of bracing could have prepared him for the sight of his mother, sitting cross-legged on a grass mat next to Mateo, a drum in her lap, happily pounding away.

Next to her, Farley raised a hand in greeting.

"About time, you two. I figured you'd track us down eventually, but I thought you were going to miss all the fun."

"Reade!" His mother noticed him and struggled to her feet, using Farley's head for support. She rushed over to give Reade a hug. "Oh, sweetheart, you found us. And you, too, Jackie. Good for you."

This does not compute. The cliché line ran through Reade's head on a loop. He snagged onto the one important fact in the whole mess.

"Mom. You're okay." He wrapped his arms around her, just to make sure he wasn't hallucinating. Maybe that spider had bitten him after all, and this was part of the aftereffects. The sullen guards who had marched them in seemed to have morphed into smiling daddies, tickling their kids.

"I'm fine, sweetie. I'm sorry if we worried you."

"If?"

"You had us running all over the island looking for you," said Jackie. "We thought you'd been kidnapped."

"Oh, no. We simply came up here to visit, and I'm afraid we got a little distracted." She sounded like she was explaining that she'd decided to go to a movie instead of shopping, and that's why she was twenty minutes late.

"For three days?" Reade was quickly moving from confused to furious.

"Has it been that long? Oh, my. I'm sorry."

"It is my fault," said their captor, host, whatever he was, rising to his feet. He came forward, hand out in greeting. "I am Matthieu. Your *maman* and Farley had trouble with their Jeep, so I gave them a ride. We began to talk, and I invited them to come see my home. We intended to return the next day, but we have partied too much."

"For three days?" repeated Reade.

Matthieu Mateo shrugged apologetically.

"Didn't anyone think of using a telephone someplace along the line?" demanded Jackie.

"Cell phones won't work up here," said Farley. "And then your mom got a touch of dysentery, so we couldn't hike out."

Reade's anger vanished in a flash of concern. "Are you okay, Mom?"

"I'm fine," she said. "Matthieu gave me some kind of milky water and the runs cleared right up."

"Diluted breadfruit latex," said Farley. "Worked like a charm. Matthieu tells me breadfruit has at least eleven legitimate medical uses."

"Really?" Reade's interest was piqued. "Are you some sort of folk doctor?"

"I study the old ways," said Matthieu. "There is much truth in the so-called folk tales, n'est-ce pas?"

"Do you know if all those medicinal uses for breadfruit have been properly investigated? Lab work, chemical analysis?"

"Double blind tests?" asked Jackie.

"Some have. All? I am not certain. Perhaps we can talk while we eat. Come, we have a pig roasting."

Reade was really into this. Jackie sat to one side, scribbling notes as fast as she could while he probed Matthieu's brain for more details about a folk treatment for dermatitis. Their after-dinner conversation about breadfruit had evolved into a marathon discussion of local plants and animals and their uses in treating disease, with Matthieu producing leaves and bits of root and bark and the occasional dead beetle to show what he meant—all accompanied by lubricating doses of rum and lime. Jackie had been completely sucked in by Reade's enthusiasm, and by his total inability to keep up with the voluble Matthieu's encyclopedic knowledge. She had filled her own little purse notebook, then quietly scrounged a pad of lined paper from one of the children. Asking questions to fill in the blanks Reade missed in his excitement, she had accumulated enough notes to keep both of them busy for several years.

Even Reade and Matthieu had limits, though, and near dawn they began to run out of steam. Matthieu ordered everyone off to bed—"We cannot cure the world's ills in one night, *hehn*?"—pointing her and Reade toward a vacant shanty.

"That was amazing." Reade was still buzzing, even though he looked like he was about to fall over. "Let's see your notes." He riffled through her sheaf of papers, eyes wide, as though he could absorb even more information on the spot. "I didn't get nearly this much. Damn, we make a good team."

He picked her up and spun her, kissing her dizzy. "Did I ever have a chance to say thank you for getting that spider off me? I know that was hard for you, but you came through. You always seem to come through."

"I try," she said. She did feel pretty proud of herself, even though just the thought of that spider made her want to throw up. "Can you come down off your cloud enough to lie down with me, or do I need to tether you to the floor?"

"Ropes? Ooh, you *are* a kinky girl."

"That's not what I meant."

"I know." He nuzzled her neck. "But consider the possibilities."

"Right now, there's a strong possibility I'm going to find somewhere else to sleep."

"Not a chance," he said, pulling her hard against his chest. "I'll behave. I'm too tired to do anything worthwhile, anyway."

He kissed her once more, then released her, and they made basic preparations for bed. Remarkably, once he settled down beside her on the narrow bed in the corner, he was asleep in minutes. It was Jackie who lay there awake, her mind churning. She had so many new ideas, she could hardly wait to get back to the lab, but underneath the

excitement lay the knowledge that Reade would be headed
back to his own lab. By himself.

Her throat tightened at the prospect of walking away
from him. Somewhere along the line, things had changed.
She wanted more than a vacation fling. Maybe all her
concerns about not being his match in the risk-taking department were just so much wasted angst. Nobody really
lived the kind of life they'd had for the past two weeks.
It was all like some big Outward Bound expedition, intense while it lasted but finite, thank God. Reade would
settle back into his life, she'd settle into hers, and maybe,
just maybe, they would find some way to meld them.
Maybe she could even convince him to move to Minneapolis. Walt would hire him.

As she was drifting off to this fantasy, a movement by
the door jerked her bolt upright. A big black banana spider, three times the size of Reade's friend, sat there staring
at her with beady eyes.

"Reade." She poked him, but he was so lost to the
world that he didn't even flinch. She shook him hard and
got a slight grunt.

Okay, she could be Jungle Jane one last time. Cautiously, she reached down for her sandal, took careful aim,
and heaved it across the room. It hit the wall and bounced
down in front of the spider, which quickly scuttled back
under the door. She waited long enough to make sure it
was really gone, then collapsed in a sweaty heap next to
Reade. Wrung out, she curled against his side for security.
She was asleep in seconds.

"Do you have everything?" asked Matthieu as they
gathered during the afternoon to eat a meal before
they said good-bye.

Reade touched the canvas bag he'd bought from one of
the villagers. It held treasure—the samples he'd collected
and his scraps of notes. Jackie had her notes in her purse,
folded neatly. They would be hitting the copy machine at

Fair Winds as soon as they got back, so they could each have both sets. They would divide the samples, too. And in a little less than two days, they'd divide their lives.

Vacation fling, hell.

When they were ready, Matthieu walked them partway down the hill.

"Farley, you remember from here, eh? Always to your left."

"Bear left. Gotcha."

They shook hands all around, and Matthieu waved them on their way.

Fifteen minutes later they hit the road. Farley pointed across, to a slight pullout. "We can flag down the bus right over there. It should be along in a few minutes. Maybe."

Jackie gaped. "This is it? We could have strolled up the hill instead of doing that death march through the jungle?"

"Isn't this how you came?" asked Lenore.

"No," said Jackie weakly. "I can't believe this."

"We got off in Blackwater," explained Reade. "That's where people kept telling us."

"And you made it here in one day?"

"Not hardly," said Jackie. She and Reade told the tale from beginning to end, from their flatfoot investigation in Redoubt to Rosalie's goat to Dermott and the pig and Reade's Little Miss Muffet adventure with the spider. While they were talking, the bus rolled up and they all got aboard.

Farley laughed at their tale until tears ran down his cheeks. "I'm sorry you had to have quite such an adventure. I hope you at least got something worthwhile out of it."

"I did," said Reade. "This bag. It represents a lot more than a bunch of bark to be analyzed. I haven't felt so good about my work in years. In fact. . . ." He took a deep breath. Everything was on the line here. "In fact, it reminded me that I have never been completely happy in the lab."

"I knew it," said his mother. Her eyes glittered as they filled with tears. "Go for it, son."

"I have to go for it, Mom. I'm thirty-two years old. If I don't get out there soon, it will never happen." He turned to Farley. "I intend to resign my position in Pittsburgh and find someone who's mounting a field expedition to the Amazon Basin, even if all they need is a junior assistant. Therefore, I'd like to withdraw my application for the Phelps Foundation grant in favor of Dr. Jacqueline Barnett."

"Reade!" Jackie's nails cut into his forearm. He flashed her a smile and patted her hand and prayed she wouldn't take it. He didn't want to leave her in a lab in Minneapolis.

"What makes you think the grant is yours to give up?" asked Farley abruptly. "Or that if you do give it up, Jackie will get it?"

"I, uh. . . ." Reade stuttered and stumbled. "I assumed, since we're both finalists."

"You and three other people," reminded Farley. "Remember the old saw about if you assume, you make an ass out of you and me? Well, I hate to burst your little bubble, but I selected Greg Kawasaki three weeks ago."

"You what?"

"All the paperwork is on my desk. Press releases, the whole shebang. We're just waiting for the announcement date to send it out."

Reade and Jackie stared at each other, then dissolved in laughter.

"All that for nothing."

"Walt's going to die."

They clung to each other, tears streaming down their cheeks, laughing so hard that Lenore and Farley had to laugh with them, and then the driver and the other passengers caught the giggles, too, even though they had no idea what was going on.

"Are you done?" asked Farley. "Because I have a little more to say."

They each snorted a few more times. Jackie dug into

her magic purse and produced one last tissue that they shared to dry eyes and blot noses.

"Okay." Farley laced his fingers, pushed his hands out, and stretched. "Here's the deal. The lab grant is gone, but the foundation has lots of other money to spend. We're launching an ethnopharmacology center in southern Surinam, and we need a director. Codirectors, really, because I feel the two of you have complementary skills that will make the center a success. I'm pleased to say that you have already started to mesh into one hell of a team. In fact, this whole week has more than exceeded my expectations."

"Expectations?" Reade's mind leaped from comment to conclusion. "You arranged this whole thing."

"What?" Jackie was half a step behind, but right on track. She nailed Farley with eyes turned to icicles. "You . . . son of a bitch."

"Now, calm down, both of you. I spend a lot of time looking at those files, and occasionally I see something that intrigues me. In your case, it was strengths and weaknesses that correlated almost one for one." He fitted his fingers together like the teeth on a gear to demonstrate, "Combined with a competitive streak that has kept you from even troubling to meet each other for years. So I decided to pull a few strings and maneuver you both down here."

"You didn't maneuver me," said Jackie. "Ben and I were coming anyway."

"Well. . . . Do you remember when you two first decided to come to St. Sebastian?"

"I don't know. I think we were out at dinner with Walt and Marilyn and. . . . Shit! You got to Walt. No wonder he kept dropping brochures on my desk." Her eyes widened, then narrowed. "Did you make Ben blow me off, too?"

"No. But it worked out well, didn't it? I figured that given the opportunity, you and Reade would discover you make better partners than enemies. And I was right—

although I didn't figure you'd actually fall in love."

"Who says we did?" demanded Jackie.

"Your faces," said Lenore. "Don't tell me you haven't gotten around to telling each other yet."

"Mother," Reade warned.

"Oh. Well, you will."

Jackie stared at the floor of the bus, her face blazing, but she obviously wasn't going to discuss it here and now. "How did you manage all this? The logistics of subverting an entire island to your . . . whims are mind-boggling."

"It's not as hard as you might think," said Farley. "First off, I own Fair Winds—through a couple of subsidiaries, of course—so everyone there pretty much does what I ask."

"Samuels," said Reade. "No wonder he didn't want to get the police involved."

"Matthieu, or Mateo, as the locals call him, is Haitian, and he is an obeah man, but he was also my roommate at Princeton. His wife happens to be Newton's older sister. And all those other people—"

"Are cousins," said Reade, smacking himself in the forehead. "Dermott the thief, too?"

"Dermott, too. I want to apologize for him, by the way. He's a bit of a klepto. However, he always returns what he takes. Lenore?"

Reade then experienced the mixed pleasure of watching his mother pull Jackie's stolen wallet, camera, and pocket knife out of her purse. Jackie's fingers curled around the knife with joy.

"Damn it, Mom, I can't believe you're in on this, too."

"Just since Saturday. When I realized what I'd done to you all these years, it dawned on me that I needed to find a way to help you find your way back to what you love. Farley suggested that I join him, and it seemed like a good way for both of us to break a few bad patterns."

"It would have been a lot harder to get both of you to come along without her," explained Farley. "Although I had a little something set up."

"I bet," growled Reade.

"If it will make you feel any better, you're not the first."

"You mean you've screwed with other people like this?" asked Reade. "You know, I'm surprised you're not dead, because I swear, I'm about this far from killing you myself."

"I know, I know. But that will pass. It always does. So." Farley clapped his hands together and rubbed them enthusiastically. "How about those jobs in Surinam?"

Jackie yanked on the bus signal cord. "Go to hell."

"Ditto," said Reade. He yanked the cord again.

The driver hollered back, "There's no stop here, mon."

"There is now," said Jackie, standing up. She strode to the front of the bus. "Pull over, or I swear, I'll jump off anyway."

The driver pulled over. "There's no other bus until tomorrow."

"I'm adventurous," said Jackie.

"And stubborn," said Reade coming up behind her.

"Oh, no." The driver glanced over his shoulder, and immediately hit the brakes. "I should have known it was you two, again. I won't even argue. Get off—and please quit ridin' my bus."

They got off and watched the bus pull away, Farley's shocked face framed in the side window next to Lenore's more concerned one.

"Good-bye and good riddance," said Jackie.

"My mom's right, you know," said Reade, without looking at her. "I am crazy in love with you. Shocked the hell out of me when it came to me about halfway down that cliff at the Potted Palm, but there it is."

She turned slowly to face him, wonder in her eyes. "That was your epiphany?"

"Yep," he said, grinning at her. "Pretty good one, huh?"

"Yeah. Pretty good." She reached out and laid her hand against his cheek and kissed him, and he didn't have to hear her say the words because he could feel it in every molecule of her skin against his. He sighed, satisfaction deep in his soul. "How long do you think we should yank Farley around before we accept his offer?"

"I . . . I don't know." Deep creases formed between her brows, and the corners of her eyes pinched up as though the sight of him hurt her eyes.

"What's wrong?"

"I can't . . ." she began, and then shook her head. "I can't believe what we just did. How are we going to get back?"

"I don't know. I figured you had a plan." He wrapped his arms around her. "You always have a plan."

"I don't this time."

"It's okay. You have your purse. We'll be fine."

"What are they going to do?" asked Lenore, craning to watch their shrinking figures through the rear window of the bus.

"Hitchhike," said Farley. "Or walk. It'll only take them a couple of hours to get to a phone."

"Reade is furious at both of us."

"I know. They always are. They get over it when they realize that I've set up an opportunity for them to do exactly what they've always wanted to do. I've only had one failure in ten years."

Lenore felt a little better, hearing that. "I understand about Reade. He's wanted to go exploring since he was a boy, but Jackie hardly seems the type."

"A minor in cultural anthropology and extra units of botany tell me differently. So does the fact that she does a lot of her work with samples she begs, borrows, and steals from people who do go out on expeditions, just like Reade does. That's why they're at odds so often, because they're always working on the same thing. She's got the interest, all right."

"Interest is one thing, going into those extreme field conditions is another. I didn't get the impression that Jackie had very much fun out there in the jungle."

"Not the way Reade did, no. But she got something out of the experience, I can almost guarantee." His face grew pensive. "The question is, will she grab it with both hands? There was something in her face. . . . I'll be honest with you, Lenore. I'm concerned that Jackie may be my second failure."

"Oh, I hope not. Reade has fallen awfully hard."

Farley smiled down at her, and reached out a finger to touch the tip of her nose. "So have I, kiddo. We'll just have to see how both of us make out. Pun intended."

A *beer truck picked up Jackie and Reade an hour* later. The driver apologized for having to make so many stops, but eventually he took them all the way to Runaway Bay, dropping them on the road in front of the resort shortly before midnight. The bellmen and front desk crew looked askance as they came in—undoubtedly something to do with how they looked and smelled.

"That's one adventure down, a lifetime to go," said Reade as they strolled down the promenade.

A lifetime. *Oh, God.* Jackie shook her head. "No more adventures. Not until I get a long bath and twelve hours of sleep."

"Sounds good. Your room or mine?"

"Neither. I mean, both," she said. "I'm so exhausted I can barely think. I need a little time to sort myself out and clip my toenails and sleep. Can we just meet for breakfast? Late."

"Sure. I could probably stand a little serious personal rehab, too. I don't think I've had a full night's sleep in a week." He brushed a strand of hair off her cheek, and the rough tenderness of his fingers against her skin made her chest squeeze so tightly it hurt. "Tell you what. Let's just skip breakfast entirely and go straight to lunch."

"Sounds good. And we'll say good-bye here so we won't be tempted." She kissed him hard, desperately needing that one last moment of contact.

"Whoa," he said. "You keep that up, you won't sleep for another week." He kissed her much more gently, showing her how sweet it could be—should be—between them. "Good night."

She couldn't bear to watch him walk away, so she turned and ran to her cabana.

There. She'd made it. And she'd never had to admit out loud how much she loved him.

She'd been fighting it for days, even as she'd given into and reveled in the physical relationship. Reade was smart and sexy and outrageous. He made her want to be something that she wasn't. And that was the problem.

How ironic was it that Reade had realized he was in love with her at the Potted Palm, almost at the same instant she had realized she wasn't the woman he thought she was? His Jackie was the phony, temporary one, the one who raced pushcarts and thought she could jump off cliffs and wore sexy swimsuits. His Jackie went charging into the jungle after missing relatives and threw sandals at spiders and was brave and bold. His Jackie was smoke and mirrors. Make-believe.

She, on the other hand, was boring, plain vanilla Jackie from Cedar Falls, Iowa. She was Barnett. She was the stick-in-the-mud he'd loathed for years. She was a wuss and phony, and she could no more go with him to Surinam than she could fly to the moon unassisted.

It had hit her when he'd asked how long to jerk Farley around before they accepted. For him, accepting was a given. For her, it was outrageous—as absurd as last night's fantasy of getting Reade to move to Minnesota. He had mistaken her stubbornness for a sense of adventure and had fallen in love with the woman he thought possessed it. But that woman was a chimera, an unrealizable dream.

"You shouldn't let that fellow of yours talk you into things you're not suited for," the man at the cliff had said. That's exactly what she'd been doing, and what she'd be doing for a whole lifetime if she followed Reade to Surinam.

Oh, she could force herself to keep up with him for a while, just as she had here, but eventually she would revert to type. Either she'd end up resentful of him for making her be something she wasn't, or worse, he'd wind up hating her for holding him back. She loved him too much to replace Lenore's stranglehold with her own.

That's why she had to run away one more time.

She showered quickly, scrubbing off three days' worth of dirt, washing all that it represented down the drain.

It took her ten minutes to pack, and two hours to write the letter to Reade. She arranged for its delivery at ten the next morning.

The taxi took her straight to the airport, and the ticket agent was very understanding about her personal emergency, waiving the fifty-dollar service fee. She would be on the first plane in the morning, leaving at 7:03 A.M. from Gate D.

She found a seat at the gate and sat there, awake, the rest of the night. There would be plenty of time for sleep later, after she was home. After things were normal again. After she'd had a chance to cry.

A persistent knock woke Reade just after ten o'clock the next morning. Expecting that it was Jackie, he pulled on a pair of shorts and opened the door with a cheery "Good morning."

It wasn't Jackie.

"Message for you, sir," said the bellman, holding out an envelope and a clipboard. "Please sign right here."

Reade scribbled his initials on the line and the man took his leave. He stared at the envelope, fuzzy-headed from the combination of too much sleep on top of too little sleep.

Who would be writing him on hotel stationery? Maybe Farley was feeling the pressure and wanted to apologize. He ripped the envelope and pulled the letter out.

Dear Reade, By the time you get this, I'll be halfway back to Minneapolis.

The world stopped.

He had to be reading that wrong. He squeezed his eyes shut, opened them, and tried again.

Please know that I never intended to hurt you.

He finished the letter. Two minutes later, he was in a cab on the way to Port Meredith.

He was too late by several hours. She was gone.

He rode back on the public bus, bouncing along for hours while he read and reread the letter and tried to get his mind around what had happened.

He disagreed with everything she said about herself. She wasn't a phony—she stretched herself. And she wasn't a wuss—she had courage in the deepest sense of the word, doing what needed to be done no matter how afraid she was. She'd rescued him at least twice, once physically, once emotionally, by being nothing more than she already was.

A part of him wanted to get on a plane and fly after her. To beat down the door of her apartment and convince her with words and touch that she didn't belong anywhere but at his side.

But if she couldn't see that on her own, he knew he couldn't force it on her. She would have to come to it by herself, figure out for herself who she was, what she wanted, and who she loved. All he could do was hope that when she got to the end of the equation, he was the answer.

When he got to the hotel, he hunted down Farley, finding him at the side of the pool.

"I'll take your offer of the position in Surinam, but only if you'll take me alone. Jackie won't be going." His voice sounded stark, even to him, It matched the way he felt inside. Hollow. Void.

Farley's face fell. He slowly shook his head. "I'm sorry, Reade. I guessed wrong about her."

"No, sir. You didn't. She guessed wrong about herself. And about me."

twenty

One year later.

Around, over, and tuck in, and the final lashing was finished. Reade stood back and admired his crew's handiwork.

Melutepu Station was starting to take shape. A huge step toward getting the center up and running had been the arrival two weeks ago of what Reade referred to as his "lab in a box." It was Farley's idea: a half-size shipping container outfitted to Reade's specifications as a fully functional lab, self-contained, solar-powered, and portable—if you happened to have a flying crane sitting around. It was already proving its usefulness, both as a lab and as a makeshift medical clinic for the few people who lived along this stretch of the river.

But while a shipping container looked perfectly reasonable sitting on a dock in Paramaribo, it was butt-ugly when dropped at the edge of a remote jungle village, not to mention hotter than blazes, so Reade and his crew of villagers had covered it with a loosely thatched roof and

woven mat side walls. That necessitated remounting the
solar panels and satellite dish, but they had just finished
that project, and he now had the first all-electronic grass
shack in Surinam—just in time for Farley's first visit.

In fact, he was due any time, now, accompanying a load
of supplies coming upriver by dugout. They should have
left Apetina four days ago, and Ryk usually took four or
five days to get here, but there was no use watching the
river—travel schedules were flexible to the point of non-
existence. They'd get here when they got here, and meanwhile, there was plenty to do. Reade went back to work.

It was nearly noon when the sound of the forty-horse
engines Ryk used on his canoes rattled the jungle. Reade
took a minute to hang a can of water over his cook fire
and then walked down to the river to join the waiting
crowd.

The first of the boats cleared the bend and cruised up
to the bank. Ryk jumped out and tossed Reade a beer and
a rubber-banded stack of mail, just as he had each of the
three times he'd come upriver since Reade had arrived.
"You have a visitor in the last canoe. Very impressive.
Here is your bill of lading. Start checking me off."

A thirty-foot canoe could hold an amazing amount of
gear, and being full of his Dutch ancestors' Protestant
work ethic, Ryk always got straight to the point: work
first, party later. As Ryk called out the numbers on various
crates and boxes and passed them to the men waiting to
carry them up to the lab, Reade popped the top on the
beer and took a sip, savoring the sharp hops flavor. He'd
grown to appreciate warm beer, if not love it. Anything
tasted good after boiled river water, but beer especially
so. "Watch that one, it's fragile. Take it straight to the
lab."

The second boat pulled in next to the first, and Reade
shifted a couple of feet over so he could check off goods
from both boats. He was pleased to see the cases of sam-
ple envelopes. He could do without almost anything else,

but there was no point being out here if he couldn't bag and tag.

"A ghost woman!" He heard the exclamation behind him, and then the clamor of others taking up the cry, half afraid, half excited. Farley was going to love this. That's what he got for wearing a ponytail.

Reade turned with a greeting on his lips. It froze there as the third canoe glided up to the bank and its passenger stood up. Blonde hair, blue eyes, fair skin. Ghost woman.

"Jackie?" The world restarted.

In the space between heartbeats, he had her in his arms, swinging her off the boat as he kissed her, confirming what his eyes told him. She was here. He wasn't crazy. Around them, voices murmured in understanding. "Ah. His woman."

Not his woman. Reality smacked him up against the side of the head like a baseball bat.

He *was* crazy. She wasn't here for him—she couldn't be, not after a year. She was delivering supplies, that's all. She was playing tourist, passing through and slowing down just long enough to stare in curiosity at the traffic accident that was his soul. He set her down and backed off, quickly stuffing his heart back into his chest where he could protect it.

"Sorry," he muttered. He took a draw off the beer still in his hand in an effort to wash the taste of her away before he fell in love with her all over again. *Too late.*

"Don't be," she said. She smiled, but her voice was as tight as the lines around her eyes. "Bet you're surprised to see me."

She was thinner. A little tougher-looking. Sexier, if that was possible. He swallowed hard, trying to remember how to speak, and when he did, his voice came out sounding harsh. "Yeah. I thought Farley was coming."

Her smile wavered and faded. "He is. He took a couple of extra days in Paramaribo, but he'll be along. I, uh, decided to come ahead with the supplies."

A pack of children crowded in around Reade to stare.

He understood. He wanted to stare, too, to absorb the sight of her before she vanished back downriver with Ryk. She squatted down to child level and crooked a finger at them. One of the bolder boys stepped forward and said something. Jackie looked up at Reade, questioning.

"He asked if you're a ghost."

She looked at the boy and solemnly shook her head, then held out her hand. Suspicious, he poked her palm with a dirty finger, found it substantial, and laid his hand in hers. She gave it a little squeeze, then lifted it to her cheek. The other children instantly crowded forward, surrounding her, freely touching her arms and cheeks and running fingers through her hair. Envy racked Reade's soul.

"Hey," called Ryk, "shall we take a break and unload later?"

"No. Hang on." Reade motioned to his assistant. "Manu, this is Dr. Barnett. Please see that she gets whatever she needs." He added, to Jackie, "Feel free to look around. I need to finish up here, and then I'll give you the fifty-cent tour."

He returned to his work, grateful for anything that required him to stop looking at her. Behind him, he could hear the group of children, still chattering, move away with Jackie.

Ryk stood with his foot on the bow of the canoe, watching her and studying Reade. After a moment, he took a final drag on his cigarette, threw the butt in the river, and picked up a box. "It looks like this trip will be more interesting than I thought. Maybe we will stay an extra day. 31685-Isopropyl alcohol."

"31685. Check. Go to hell."

Ryk laughed.

 "He is avoiding you," said Ryk, blowing cigarette smoke toward a swarm of gnats circling over his head.

"No kidding," said Jackie. She watched Reade consult with Manu and the village headman about yet another non-situation. He'd been coming up with excuses to step away every time she got within ten feet. She'd finally resigned herself to watching him from the shade of an open-sided hut, where the smoke from a tiny fire and Ryk's incessant cigarettes kept the insects to a minimum. "Not that I blame him."

"What did you do to him?" asked Ryk.

"What I thought was right."

Reade and Manu picked up a crate and carried it into the lab. The chief came over to Ryk and pointed at his cigarette. Ryk pulled out a pack of a local brand and handed him one, then pulled a stick off the fire and lit it for the old man. He smoked only American brands himself, but kept the cheaper ones in his pocket to pass around to the villagers.

"What are you going to do now?" he asked when the chief was puffing happily.

"What I think is right."

Ryk grinned. "I'm a nosy bastard, eh?"

"You are," she said. "But in a nice way."

"That's me. A nice bastard. And a romantic one, too." Ryk tipped his head toward the lab. Manu had come out, carrying a broom. "Here is your chance. *Veel geluk.* Good luck." Ryk stood up and strolled toward Manu, steering him away from the lab as he pulled yet another cigarette out of his pocket. American, this time.

He was giving her a shot at Reade. Jackie scrambled to her feet, grabbed her bag, and made a beeline for the lab. At the doorway, she hesitated.

Reade was inside, fiddling with the leveling knobs on a brand new scale, his back to her. As she stepped into the doorway, the light changed, and he turned toward her. His expression went flat. "Do you need something?"

"No. Yes. I need to talk to you."

"I'm busy right now." He returned to his knobs, his back a wall of resistance.

At least he didn't walk out. After a moment, Jackie
drifted in and began to look around the lab.

"This is amazing," she said, pulling the cover off a
phase-contrast microscope that sat on the counter. "Farley
showed me plans, but the reality of walking through a
village that's barely out of the Stone Age and then stepping into a complete lab is ... amazing." She colored
slightly. "I seem to be running short on words."

"I can empathize." He took the dustcover away from
her and dropped it back over the microscope. "Why are
you here?"

"To apologize."

"You already did. In writing."

"The letter is part of what I want to apologize for. That
was a cowardly way to tell you." The ache that had sat
in the back of her throat for the past few hours boiled up
into tears that stung her eyes. She swallowed them back.
"I just couldn't face you. I couldn't face a lot of things.
I guess that was the point. But I'm here now, and I'd like
to explain."

"It's been a year. Don't you think it's a little late?"

His words were like a slap, but she held her ground.
"Probably. But you're going to get one anyway. In fact,
you're going to get the illustrated version." She hooked a
lab stool with her toe and pushed it toward him. "You
may as well sit down."

"No, thank you."

"Fine." She lifted her purse onto the counter, and
Reade's eyes narrowed. The bag was identical to the one
the pig had hijacked, just newer. This time, however, instead of bulging with assorted bottles and tubes, it held
one large item. She pulled it out and laid it on the counter
in front of him.

"A photo album?"

"And a story," she said. "We can call it Jackie's Excellent Adventure."

"I don't want to look at your travel pictures."

"Yes, you do." She opened the album to the first page,

where there was a picture of her on cross-country skis. "It took me about a month to figure out that immersing myself in work was not going to get you out of my mind."

"It took me less time than that."

She clung to that scrap of revelation. "You weren't starting out as stupid as I was. Anyway, I decided to get away from things."

"Skiing?"

"I saw an ad. There was a special on a nice little trip up by the Canadian border. I signed up. We were supposed to ski between two inns. A nice, relaxing trip." She flipped the page to a picture of whiteout conditions. "We had a sudden, freak blizzard and ended up camped in a snow cave for two nights before the search parties found us. This was not the peaceful escape I had envisioned, so I decided make it up to myself by visiting a friend in Cincinnati. The weather was beautiful, so we went to Six Flags. The Ferris wheel jammed." She flipped the page and showed him a newspaper clipping, complete with a photo of the fire department rescuing people with a cherry picker. "That one's me. Seventy feet up."

He peered at the picture. "You're smiling."

"Yeah. I was having an epiphany. It turns out you don't have to jump off something to have one."

"Really?" The corner of his mouth twitched, and for the first time, she felt a little hope. She needed hope. Her whole life was on the line here.

"Really. There I was, doing two supposedly safe things and nearly getting killed anyway. I decided the universe was trying to teach me something, and I figured if I was going to have to learn the lesson anyway, I'd better take charge of the course plan. So I tried a few things." She flipped to a picture of her kayaking in a lake. "Starting small. And working my way up." The next photo was of her doing an Eskimo roll, and the one after showed her diving into white water on a river in Kentucky. "And then this amazing thing happened. There I go, using *amazing* again. I've really got to expand my vocabulary."

"Not right this minute," he said. "What was the amazing thing?"

"I started enjoying myself."

"Imagine that."

"Anyway, I decided that maybe, just maybe, I could go a little further with this idea." She flipped through the next series of pictures. Her on a climbing wall. Her roped to a rock face. Her dangling from a parasail over Lake of the Woods. Her skydiving. And finally, her jumping off a cliff into the sea.

"That's the Potted Palm," he said, his voice husky.

"It is. And I jumped three times, too, because somewhere in there, I finally figured out what you get out of all this. I actually got hooked on the rush. So then I went to work on the really big one." She slowly flipped through a couple of pages: her with a crab, her smashing a spider, her with a black widow in a jar. "Now that creeped me out. But I persisted. It took me two months to work up to this." The next photo was her, holding a big, hairy tarantula on her hand.

Reade touched the picture, his fingers tracing over it as though he was touching her. "You did all this for me?"

"No. I did it for me," she said, trying to ignore the shiver that ran up her spine in response. "So that I could work my way up to this." She crossed her fingers and turned the page.

The final photo in the album was her with the tarantula sitting on her head. But the really scary part was the hand-lettered sign she held in her hands: *Will you marry me?*

"Will you?" she asked, her voice barely audible. "I do love you. I haven't been very good at showing it, but I do."

Reade was staring at the picture, so absolutely still that he looked like a wax statue. The only sign of life was the flutter of pulse in his temple.

Finally, he took a breath. "I'm not going home, Jackie. Not for a very long time."

"Neither am I."

He looked up sharply.

"I'm your new lab assistant. Farley hired me, contingent on your approval."

He shook his head and she thought her heart was going to break. "I don't need an assistant."

"Oh." She turned away, her hand over her mouth to hold back the wail of despair that welled up in her chest. She could walk out of there with dignity, if she could just make her feet work.

"I need a codirector." Reade's fingers closed over her shoulder. "And a wife."

She turned and looked up into his eyes and saw that he meant it. "Oh."

"One who won't run out on me," he warned.

"Never." Tears streamed down her cheeks. "I only left because I thought you were in love with that phony Jackie that was running around St. Sebastian. But she's not a phony anymore. I'm actually the person you fell in love with."

He cupped her face with both hands, wiping away her tears with his thumbs. "Don't you know, Jackie? You always were."

His mouth came down on hers in a kiss that melted away a whole year of pain and left nothing but love and desire and the knowledge of how close she'd come to losing this remarkable man who understood her better than she understood herself. They stood there a long, long time, absorbed in each other, until someone cleared his throat.

Ryk stood in the door, wearing a sappy expression. "Excuse me. There is a float plane coming in."

Reluctantly, they released each other and walked outside just as a small plane passed over with a whine.

"The river is low," said Ryk. "I hope they have a good pilot."

"Farley hires the best," said Reade. "I just hope he brought a priest."

"He did," said Jackie, as Ryk exclaimed and thumped

them both on the back. The one that married Farley and Lenore, but she'd let them tell him that. "Your mom's on board, too."

"She what? Manu." His assistant came running over, and Reade switched to the local language, firing off several orders. The man asked a question, and Reade answered, then sent him off.

"What was that all about?"

"I told him we are having more visitors and that they will stay in my hut while you and I sleep in a smaller one. He reminded me there is no bed in the small one. But I told him it was okay, we'd sleep in a hammock."

She went crazy hot in a heartbeat, and he grinned down at her, his eyes telling her he knew precisely what he'd done. "A whole lifetime of adventure, Jackie. Let's go meet the plane."

Dear Reader,

They say, whoever "they" are, that writers must suffer for their art. But have you ever wondered just what that suffering entails, what we writers actually go through in order to bring you a book?

Well, I'll tell you—and it isn't pretty. During the course of this book, I ran up a frozen food bill that could have funded last fall's tax rebates, consumed enough chocolate and coffee to kill every dog in the continental United States, abandoned my children for days at a time (okay, I left them in the loving care of their father, but my soul says I abandoned them), and gained twelve pounds. Yep, for you, I got a fat ass. And we won't even discuss the hotel bills I ran up trying to get enough peace and quiet to concentrate . . .

So, now I want to know if it was worth it, and since I like my news direct from the source, I'd like to call you and talk about it. (Yes, really!) Here's the deal: I will make a phone call to any organized readers' group that reads *Runaway Bay* during March, April, or May of 2002. On my dime, for up to one hour, you can ask questions, talk about the book or about writing in general, or just chitchat about the weather if you like. Simply have the bookstore owner or group leader arrange things through my website (www.lisahendrix.com). Then read the book and find a good speakerphone so everyone can talk. I'll take care of the rest.

If you're not in a readers' group, you can still let me know what you think. Post a review online someplace, drop me a note, or visit me at my website and tell me how much you loved *Runaway Bay*. I have contests, a Reader/Reviewer program under way for my next book, and who knows what else going on—after all, publication is months from when I'm writing this, and I may have thought of something really terrific by then.

Meantime, I'm working hard on my next book and the chocolate's close at hand. I hope my arteries—and my jeans—can take it.

Love, Lisa

Lisa Hendrix
c/o Berkley Publicity Department
Penguin Putnam Inc.
375 Hudson Street
New York, NY 10014

E-mail me at: lisa@lisahendrix.com
Visit me online: http://www.lisahendrix.com
(Readers' group questions available at site)